ook !

Bob

My Girlfriend
The Vampire

Robert Northam

This is a work of fiction. Names, characters, places, and incidents are products of the author's imagination or are used fictitiously and are not to be construed as real. Any resemblance to actual events, locations, organizations, or persons, living or dead, is entirely coincidental.

World Castle Publishing, LLC
Pensacola, Florida
Copyright © Robert Northam 2019
Paperback ISBN: 9781950890286
eBook ISBN: 9781950890293
First Edition World Castle Publishing, LLC, July 22, 2019
http://www.worldcastlepublishing.com

Licensing Notes

Cover: Karen Fuller
Editor: Maxine Bringenberg

Chapter One

My story with Lyria began on a foggy night, as one might expect.

Not that a foggy night in Boston is anything unusual—far from it. I actually came to enjoy the fog when it presented itself on my evening strolls. This despite the fact that I really began walking as a way to admire the architecture in the Beacon Hill area, which I could barely see on this occasion. Frankly, my lack of a social life or interest in anything that was on television might have been factors in my newfound exercise routine. Normally, I regarded exercise of any kind as just a way to ensure that you die healthy. Okay, so I didn't really have any alternatives for evening activities, but once I did start walking, I thought the architecture of the brownstones, apartment buildings, and expensive condo complexes was boffo. Anyway, I was really okay with the fog. It might be an extension of my philosophy on nightclubs; the darker it is, the better I look.

My name is Conner, Conner David, and please spare me the jokes about guys with two first names. I'm a financial analyst with a well-known Boston investment banking firm called Beacon Hill Associates. The founders must have stayed up all night thinking up that name, since the offices are located on...Beacon Hill. If I have to be honest, my job could be described as entry level, which was fitting since I joined the company right out of college. And yes, I live among the social elite on Beacon Hill. You're probably wondering who I was in good with to set up that arrangement, and again, being up front here, the answer is my parents. I'm in pretty good with them—at least from time to time. My looks? Truth be told, I look...well, like a financial analyst. I'm tall and thin, with moppish brown hair and glasses—rather nerd-like, if I have to be completely honest. Rating my overall appearance, I'd say that I didn't take a full ride on the looks truck. Someone must have pushed me off about halfway to a completely handsome finish.

My decision to become a financial analyst was an easy one. My father made a not-so-small fortune as an investment banker, and made it known to me at a very young age that he would very much like for me to follow in his gigantic footsteps. I wasn't so sure that was what I wanted, at least until I got to college and started hearing horror stories about graduating students being unable to find employment. Once I got my degree, dear old Dad pulled some strings and got me on with BHA. He also pulled some of my own strings and convinced me to accept his offer to buy me a place on Beacon Hill.

"This is where you need to live to be a player," he said in his booming voice that shook the walls in our home, not to mention all four chambers of my heart.

I wasn't really sure what "being a player" meant, but hey, who was I to turn down certain employment and fully paid housing within walking distance of my new job? Suddenly, being a financial analyst didn't seem so bad.

Most people know that financial analysts put in a lot of hours and face a vice grip of pressure to perform. Both of these premises are true, so when I got home at a decent time, which was rare, I took up walking for three fundamental reasons: I found that it helped to relieve my stress, it kept me from going insane with boredom sitting around my condo, and it fed my ever-present disbelief that I was actually living and working on Beacon Hill.

These factors, combined with my not-so-active social life, caused me to be up and around The Hill area on a fairly regular basis. The streets are winding and narrow, and the magnificent residential buildings seem to be sprouting from the ground. I once had a thought that if you didn't know your way around, or were somehow cognitively-challenged, Beacon Hill would be an easy place to get lost. This thought came back to me with a roar as I realized that I didn't exactly know where I was. The dense fog had succeeded in obscuring all my visual reference points and, I guess like most men, I never really paid much attention to street names.

I remember taking long drives with Dad and the rest of my family when I was young. Dad would be tooling along and would never let on when he wasn't sure how to get where he was going. Mom, ever the organizer in the relationship, would have a map spread out in her lap.

"What street are you looking for?" she would ask.

My siblings and I would just cringe in the back seat, knowing that we would never have the fortitude (read: guts) to confront Dad the tyrant in such a blatant fashion. But as we aged, we came to learn that Mom could get away with a lot with Dad that was unthinkable for us.

Dad didn't look at her when he answered. "Not really sure," he grumbled.

There would be an uncomfortable pause, and we were wondering if this was going to be a major conflagration or just a little spark.

"Do you know how you're going to go?" asked Mom.

Another pause, then Dad said, "No, but we'll find out when I get there."

And that was the end of that.

The results of these exchanges would not incent me to pay more attention to street names as I grew up, because Dad always got us where we were going. Of course, he could never give directions worth a hoot. He'd say, "Well, I don't know how I went, I just got there."

So here I was, wandering around the fancy streets of an upscale part of Boston, blinded by the fog and getting no help whatsoever from coming across familiar sights. Yes, I had to face the fact that I was virtually in my own backyard, and also, lost. There wasn't much I could do, except to keep on roaming and hoping that I would come across something I recognized.

I was so focused on getting a better look at the surrounding real estate that, somehow, I didn't see her coming.

She emerged from the fog as if she had just materialized right in front of me. She was tall, slim, and wearing a print dress with colors that truly "popped." My immediate thought was that she must be cold, as the dress didn't have much material and there was a definite chill in the air. She had brown hair that curled around her shoulders. Oh, and yes, I noticed right away that her figure would be classified in the "knockout" category. Hey, I'm still a guy, right? Her face was nothing short of stunning, with high cheekbones, an angular chin, and flawless skin.

When I was hitting the singles scene with my friends, we would bestow names on girls we were scoping out based on a celebrity we thought they resembled. This would come in particularly handy if, as was often the case, we never found out their real names because we all chickened out from introducing ourselves. The next day we would be like, "I was this close, this close, to introducing myself to Carrie Underwood last night." Then you would have to ignore the snorts of derision from your buddies.

The girl I encountered that evening, this vision, put me in mind of a young Megan Fox, but more...perfect. She was, I daresay, exactly the type of woman I was attracted to. She was physically close to me, walking steadily, almost gliding. It was weird, but she didn't seem to displace any air as she moved.

We made eye contact, and I thought I detected the hint of a very slight smile. I knew from the singles-hookup business that this was like gold. But I was so unprepared for the encounter that the best I could come up with was a croaked-out, "Hi." She floated on past me, but not before turning her shoulders slightly and flashing a little more of a smile that was enough to make my heart skip a beat.

She disappeared into the fog without actually saying anything, and I was left standing there like a complete numbskull looking in her direction. Suddenly, I felt stress in my chest and realized that I wasn't breathing. It took a moment to collect myself, gasping to make up the oxygen deficiency.

I remember thinking, Geez, Conner. Get a grip on yourself, boy. Is this like the first time you've encountered a female of the species, or what? Despite the self-rebuke, I was still rooted to the same spot. I started walking on my original course; that is, away from the girl of my dreams.

Then I thought, Hey. Maybe Megan knows where we are. I should go ask. Brilliant! But I wondered whether asking for directions was the kind of first impression I wanted to make. Maybe not so brilliant.

I didn't really have an alternative, though. I definitely wanted to see her again. Besides, I'd probably already blown the first impression with my inability to speak clearly in my weak attempt at a greeting.

It was settled. I'd go after Megan and see if we could help each other find our way out of the fog. We can talk about the weather! Hey, if that doesn't scare her off, probably nothing will.

I turned around abruptly and almost ran headfirst into a person. Now, as I said, I'm on the tall side. This guy was about my height, but wiry and scraggly looking. But what really stood out was his "ink."

He had tats over pretty much his entire body, at least the part that I could see. This included his hairless scalp, which made him look like he was wearing some kind of helmet. He was wearing tattered jeans and a ratty looking denim jacket. He had a desperate look in his eyes that sent shivers down my spine. I hadn't lived in the city that long and was used to preppy, suburban types. This guy looked like he had just escaped from rehab.

I stammered out a "sorry" and tried to move past, but he shifted his position to stay in my way. I almost bumped into him and got a whiff of body odor which disrupted the perfect Boston night air.

"Stay right where you are, asshole," he said, and I noticed with a start that he was holding a pistol in a shuddering hand.

Not exactly being the heroic type, my first instinct was to hightail it out of there. But when I turned, there was another tattooed dude, this one short and broad, but also wearing what I would think of as "hobo chic," and with a look of hungry despair. I looked down into his bloodshot eyes and noticed he had pupils the size of pinheads. Much to my chagrin, "Short and shaky" was holding what appeared to be a switchblade knife in his quivering right hand. The weapon didn't look that big, but waving around in this drugged-out dude's mitt, it might has well have been one of those gigantic swords the gladiators used to haul around.

The guys closed in on me and I started to panic.

"Where do you think you're goin', man?" the second guy spit out in a raspy voice. "My boy said to stay put—you deaf or somethin'?"

***

Thoughts of Megan Fox drained out of my brain as I froze in place. I tried to sound brave, although my heart was about ready to pop out of my chest—I absurdly thought of seeing it still beating on the sidewalk. I was trying to think of something to say that could get me out of this pickle, but all I could come up with was, "Wh...what do you guys want?"

"Oh, we were just out for a little stroll," said the first guy — Helmet head. He sniffled after about every other word, and I wondered what he was putting up his nose. "You know, we like to get out and meet new people sometimes. Gets kinda boring just hanging around the joint all day."

The second guy snorted. I found myself looking back and forth between them, like I was watching a tennis match.

"Okay, asshole," said the second guy. "Let's see whatcha got." Then he stuck the knife up close enough to my neck that with one spasm of his already unsteady hand, it could have gone right into my windpipe.

Valuing my breathing apparatus, I stammered out, "Huh? What I got? What do you mean exactly?"

They both guffawed a little. "Geez," said Helmet head. "Your mommy let you walk out here on the streets all alone? On a foggy night like this? Well, all the better for us, I guess. C'mon, asshole. Out with it."

I stood there, still not comprehending. "I...I'm not sure what you want...."

Helmet head moved closer and stuck his gun up under my chin. Despite his shivering and constant sniffling, his voice was chillingly controlled. "We want to see if you can give us a little advance on our take home pay. Okay, asshole? See, we're a little short this week, and ain't had a raise in a while."

The other guy, Short and shaky, laughed out loud this time. It just then registered that I was being robbed, at gunpoint, by two guys who looked like they'd filet their own "mommy" for their next fix. Hey, it didn't take a whole lot of street smarts to do the job that I did. And I always naïvely thought an upscale neighborhood like Beacon Hill would be safe. I reflected on the guy's comment about my mother, and answered to myself, Well, no. Mom would not, in fact, be very happy with me walking out here by myself.

Helmet head must have been getting impatient. He grabbed my arm hard, keeping the pistol held firmly under my jawbone. Amazing what one thinks about under these circumstances. I was wondering about the trajectory a bullet would take if he fired. Might not be fatal, but sure would lead to a heck of a dentist's bill.

"Check his pockets, Vape," he barked to Short and shaky.

I squirmed a little as reality started to settle in. Helmet head's grip tightened like a vise. I was amazed at his strength because of his wiry build.

"I wouldn't advise that, fuckhead," he said.

Definitely not a Harvard man.

"We can still hang out when this is over as long as you behave yourself."

Vape reached for my front pocket. These guys are good, I thought. That's right where I keep my cash. They must have done this before.

But before he reached the contents of my pocket, Vape stopped suddenly when Helmet head uttered a "Wha?", let go of my arm, and disappeared into the fog with a whoosh. I actually felt a slight brush of air as he left our presence. I heard him give out a wail, more of a noise than any formed word. Then there was silence.

I stared stupidly at the spot where the druggy had been just a second ago. Vape backed away from me, his eyes suddenly wide open and wild. His head was on a swivel looking for an answer to come out of the fog. He waved his knife from side to side, but without a target. I came out of my trance and moved to book it out of there, but Vape, now in a total panic, jabbed the blade at me and yelled, "STAY WHERE YOU ARE." I froze again as Vape looked like he was ready to go into convulsions. I wondered if he thought the whole thing was a drug-induced hallucination. He called out, "Spider? SPIDER? You there?"

It seemed that the air pressure around us changed. We both sensed it and actually looked at each other, seeking understanding. It was suddenly difficult to get a breath of air. If anything, Vape's terror got more intense as whatever this change in air density meant, it clearly couldn't portend well for him. We both froze; it was as if time had stopped.

Sure enough, Vape made an "unh" sound and was pulled upward into the fog as well, as if someone had sucked him into a giant vacuum cleaner. The last sound I heard from him was an "ooooh," and then nothing. Now, I know I hadn't done any drugs, but it was as if I had imagined the whole sequence. The street, the fog, everything was just the same as before I encountered the druggy-robbers.

I started wondering if whoever, or whatever, had taken the two homeboys intended for me to be next. And I started running.

CHAPTER TWO

I managed to find my way home that night, although I couldn't describe how if my life depended on it. Later, I realized that it never occurred to me to call the police and report the attempted robbery. What would I do, tell them that the guys didn't get anything from me because they were sucked up into the fog before the theft could be consummated? Something told me they would fit me for a temporary residence in a rubber room, and I couldn't afford to miss work.

Living on Beacon Hill felt surreal, especially for an entry-level financial analyst. If one was magically transported there and didn't know where they were, they'd probably take a stab at early 20th Century London. The streets were narrow, some actually still paved with cobblestones and lit by gaslights. I learned that this section of Boston was so named because it was once the home of a beacon, which was the highest peak in the city. Of course, the beacon wasn't there anymore, but, hey, who was I to quibble? I lived in a section called the South Slope, the most exclusive part of an extremely exclusive area.

The original inhabitants were the Boston Brahmins, a name that in many parts of the city could get you punched out just because of the way it sounded. At some point, the Brahmins figured the suburbs were a better deal and made hay in that direction, leaving developers drooling over this expensive and suddenly uninhabited real estate. Many of the buildings were converted to apartments and condominiums, a fact that no doubt had the original Brahmins doing backflips in their graves. The architecture was still stunning, with brass doorknobs, decorative ironwork, tall narrow windows with purple glass, and fancy window boxes housing plants whose names I couldn't pronounce. Even though I'd lived there for a little over a year now, I still pinched myself every time I walked into my building. Thank you, Dad!

While I was still in my own personal fog, I somehow made it up to my second-floor bedroom. I laid in bed that whole night, sleeping only in fits. In one of my brief doze-offs, I must have achieved REM. I dreamed that I was on a small deserted island with my newfound buddies Spider and Vape. The situation was desperate. There was nothing to eat, and the two druggies were approaching me with their gun and knife. Hey, nobody actually thinks they'd commit cannibalism until there's really nothing else to eat. It seemed that the end of my life was imminent. I wondered if anyone would water my plants after I died, and the thought occurred to me that I really needed to get out more.

Just as Spider and Vape were about to close the deal, a giant shark sprang out of the ocean and swallowed Spider whole. Vape looked just like he had earlier that evening, waving his knife around, a paralyzing dread in his eyes. Then, sure enough, the shark popped up behind him, on the opposite side of the island from where Spider had been, and gobbled up the chubby druggy. I was standing on the island by myself, astonished at what had just happened, when Megan Fox, the mystery girl, came out from behind the only tree on the tiny patch of land. She moved forward as if floating on air, her brightly-colored print dress sashaying in the wind. I stood mesmerized by her beauty, and kept telling myself, "Don't say anything stupid. Don't say anything stupid." Since that seriously limited my choices, I stayed still, not saying anything. She had slid over next to me.

"Well Conner," she said, her voice sounding like Megan Fox's. "Looks like it's just you and me now...."

I woke up, my heart pounding, and my first thought was that my subconscious mind wanted to keep me from blowing it with the girl.

Ah, what a wondrous thing, self-confidence.

I realized that with all the excitement I wasn't sure what day it was, and actually had to look at my phone. Blast it. It was Friday, and I had to get up for work in about an hour. Since there was virtually no chance of getting back to sleep, I got up and slugged down a cup of coffee. If working the Keurig were an Olympic sport, I'd be a gold medalist. I sat in my TV room and flipped on the tube in a sad and frequently repeated attempt at providing myself with some company. Thoughts of the events from the previous evening swirled in my head. The fog, the robbers, the girl.

Mostly the girl.

Her looks were pretty close to my ideal for the perfect female. I had been alone and unattached for so long that I had just about written off any chance of encountering the mate of my dreams. I pictured myself settling, going the married-with-kids-move-to-the-suburbs route, and putting an advance deposit down for my fully expected membership in AA. As I thought about Megan, I started wondering what she was like, what she was doing wandering around by herself in the fog. It wouldn't be a total surprise for a classy woman like that to live on Beacon Hill, a thought that I was sure wasn't reciprocal on her part when she saw me. I pondered her personal details. Is she married? Does she work? Does she have children? My conclusion was that a woman who looked like that was surely not single and unattached. She was probably married to some megabucks dude who flew her to Paris for lunch on his own private jet. So, what was she doing out last night? And did she really smile back at me, or was that a figment of my currently oversexed imagination? Did she have a fight with Mr. Megabucks? If so, how bad a fight?

I realized that I had been thinking (obsessing?) for so long that it was almost time to leave for work. Drat. Now, one thing you should know about financial analysts—they don't like loose ends. Their purpose in life is to bring issues to a conclusion, all neatly tied up with a pretty little bow on top. As I hurdled upstairs to hit the shower, I came to a conclusion from all the effort I had been putting into reflecting on the girl I had encountered on that crazy night. My conclusion was that whoever she was, she was definitely out of my league.

CHAPTER THREE

Fortunately, I wasn't late for work. The office I worked in was within walking distance from home, which really came in handy when there was inclement weather, when I needed extra time to recover from activities of the previous evening, or when I'd rather jump off a cliff than have to deal with Boston traffic. When I first started at BHA, I really tried hard to keep the fact that I lived on Beacon Hill under wraps. People seeing an entry-level analyst living in this section of town would instantly assume that I was a spoiled child of privilege, whose every need was taken care of by Mommy and Daddy. All of that was essentially true, but I didn't want my coworkers knowing it.

The fact of the matter was that it was near impossible to keep such an intimate part of my life a secret from the folks I worked with. BHA, like most office settings, was a fertile nest of rumormongering. One of the things they don't teach you in college is that you will spend more time with the people in your office than you will with your family and your friends. And, people being people, they will all want to know every little juicy tidbit of information that can be mustered about your personal life. It doesn't even have to be factual as long as it's titillating.

I worked with a bunch of single guys, and we often scoped out the local social scene together, looking for the next celebrity look-alike female who we could fantasize about after she shot down our feeble attempt to connect. Naturally, my living situation eventually became public knowledge, and was a source of frequent teasing and ridicule among my buddies. I felt like I had to work extra hard to prove that I was just one of the guys, and gain acceptance among the populace. Most people came into town from somewhere in the 'burbs, and often had to deal with torturous commutes. There were days when almost everyone was late because of a huge traffic tie-up or a blizzard. When everyone else straggled in, I would be in my cube, working away at my desk and fighting the urge to unleash a "neener neener" to the group in general. My restraint in such instances had not historically been very good, but it was all part of my effort to fit in.

Entry-level analysts at most investment firms work long hours and don't make a whole lot of money. They do it for the potential big payoffs down the line. BHA was an independent investment banking company. We dealt in such exhilarating efforts as underwriting securities and acting as a broker and/or financial adviser for other companies. As I said, it was not exactly downhill ski racing. Along with a handful of other analysts, I worked in the mergers and acquisitions department. As the name implies, we did scads of analysis on potential acquisitions for firms that simply didn't have the analytical resources to do the work themselves. It was a pretty sweet setup for the client. They signed with us for a flat fee, and got to abuse us low-level peons to do countless scenarios and analyze a potential deal seven ways to Sunday without causing their own employees to quit or threaten to unionize because they were treating them so badly. As with most professions, there was a lingo associated with M&A work, and it involved such electrifying terms as conglomerate mergers, horizontal and vertical integration, spin-outs, stock swaps, and reverse, dilutive, and accretive mergers.

Take me now, Lord.

Along with the marathon-like hours, there was a significant

amount of stress associated with our jobs. We were not just expected to crunch a bunch of numbers, but also make firm, "yes or no" recommendations on potential deals. And it was made abundantly clear from the outset that with an incorrect reco, maybe two if you were lucky, your ass was the veritable grass.

Sometimes I wondered whether Dad had pushed me in this direction because of the income potential, or whether he was getting even for something I did wrong as a child.

Anyway, I got to work and immediately started banging away at the latest effort to make someone else rich. I had to force myself to concentrate, as my mind kept wandering to the night before. I found it very interesting that despite the fact that I was almost the victim of an armed robbery by two pretty desperate-looking dudes, I wasn't traumatized or pondering how lucky I was that Spider didn't pull his trigger or Vape provide me with a new bodily orifice by mistake. All I could think about was her. I kept telling myself, "Refocus, Conner!" I was practically hip-deep in data, poring over income statements, balance sheets, cash flow tables, and ratios, to the point where I wanted to poke myself in both eyes so I didn't have to look at any more numbers.

I looked up and suddenly realized that half the morning was gone already. It was almost time for our usual coffee break.

"Drop your cock and grab your socks, Conner!"

After working in silence for a couple of hours, I jumped a little at the intrusion into my cube.

"Don't you ever knock, Boof?"

"News flash for you, buddy. We don't have doors."

Our cubes were arranged in rows. The wall adjacent to our little boxes housed our boss's office. He had a door.

I just shook my head, and knew immediately that castigating Boof would do absolutely no good. Boof Parsons worked in the next cube over from mine and, I'm a little ashamed to say, was probably the associate with whom I was closest in the office.

Despite his personal shortcomings, which were numerous, Boof was a highly regarded analyst. He lived for two things—crunching numbers and sex. And, I was pretty sure, not in that order. He was a little guy, maybe five-four or so, and on the portly side. He had barely-controlled brown hair and Coke bottle thick glasses. Not exactly every woman's dreamboat, but you could never fault him for lack of effort. Boof's real name was Edwin, but nobody ever called him that. I learned from some of the guys who had been there longer than me that when Boof first started with BHA and had a successful "conquest," he would saunter in the next day with a big shit-eating grin, and his first word would be—you guessed it—"Boof!" So everyone started calling him Boof, and the name stuck.

"Ready for coffee? Hey, you look like hell. Did you get action last night?"

I shook my head and muttered, "Not the kind that you mean."

"Oh yeah? Hey, what happened? C'mon, you can tell me. Lemme guess...her husband came home while you were mid-tango, right? You had to haul it out a window or bail down a laundry chute? Something like that? Ahh, but what a way to go—"

"No, Boof, nothing like that. Let's just go get coffee. The other guys ready?"

"What do I look like, the social director? Razor! Stillwell! Berman! Hop to, boys, we're losing daylight here. Hey...," Boof sauntered up close and got quiet. "You think we should invite Vicky?"

"Only if you can roll up your tongue and stop drooling."

"Whaddaya mean?"

"Whenever you even mention Vicky's name, you start looking like a hungry dog in a meat locker."

"Ah, that's all your imagination. I treat Vicky with the same amount of respect as you doorknobs."

21

"That's what worries me. Look, is there even a remote possibility that you can behave yourself if Vicky comes along?"

Boof raised three fingers on his left hand. "Scout's honor. Besides, I gotta have something to look at other than you guys' ugly mugs. The glare gets in my eyes from all the glasses at the table. It looks like a bookkeeper's convention."

Being a financial analyst was not the most exciting way to make a living. In fact, if we all pondered how boring it actually was, we'd all be nose-diving out the nearest window—or in our case, since the windows in our office didn't open, off the roof of the building. If you said we all lived in a state of denial, you wouldn't be far from being correct. The guys in my group got by with sarcasm, busting chops, and fantasizing about unattainable women. I had no idea how Vicky got by.

Vicky Temerlin was the only female member of the M&A Analysis group. Vicky was single, but was somewhat mysterious about her relationship status. She was, as we forlorn men would say, easy on the eyes. She was about five-two with long, dark-blonde hair and a slim, but shapely figure. Vicky dressed conservatively and kept her hair up in a bun. She was very good at her job, and was probably the only one of us who didn't complain about the long hours and low pay. She got along pretty well with the rest of the group, although there were times when she gave us all a look that said she thought we were just a bunch of sophomoric, overgrown teenagers in adult male bodies. She efficiently put Boof in his place when he would be all but slobbering in her presence.

"Well, okay," I said. "Why don't you politely see if Vicky wants to join us?"

Boof's eyes lit up as he put on a formal air and walked over to her cube. I was rolling my eyes as he stood at attention in her doorway.

I heard Vicky say, "What do you want, Boof?" and pictured

her continuing to work on her current project.

"Mademoiselle Temerlin," he said. "Your associates request the honor of your presence as we attempt to stave off the inherent sleep-inducing nature of our occupations by ingesting a large quantity of stimulants in the bistro downstairs."

Just then Razor Rojas moseyed by. "Translated? We're hitting the coffee shop. Wanna go?"

CHAPTER FOUR

We got to the shop just in time to beat the mad, midmorning rush for supplemental caffeine. The investment banking business could probably keep the coffee industry afloat all by itself. BHA was okay with us indulging multiple times a day. The brass probably figured it was better than hearing everyone's head hitting their desktop in unison during the workday. The analyst group's philosophy was, they could work us all hours of the night, starve us, deprive us of all external stimulation, but couldn't deny us our coffee. Otherwise, their staff would consist of a bunch of four-eyed zombies with caffeine withdrawal symptoms. The M&A group was lucky to stave off the other desperate java junkies from BHA, and get a table where we settled in with our various forms of brew.

"Crazy in here today," said Fernando "Razor" Rojas. "Must be a lot of money in the marketplace. Sure hope we're getting our share."

Razor got his nickname because he always looked like he needed a shave. Rumor had it that when he first started at BHA, a senior member of the firm had stopped him in the hallway early in the day and asked why he hadn't shaved that morning. "I did shave, sir," was Razor's response. As the story goes, the guy stammered something like, "Uh...well, very good. Carry on."

Razor had earned his way through college and into the firm despite growing up in a rough part of Boston that might as well have been on another planet as far as most of the other associates were concerned. He had an eidetic memory for numbers. It wasn't unusual to hear someone shout over their cube, "Yo, Razor. What was the interest rate assumption we used in the so-and-so deal three years ago?" Razor wouldn't even look up from what he was doing. "Eight and a quarter." We also considered Razor our enforcer. He was the only one in the group who looked tough enough to fend off any trouble seekers looking to bother us when we hit the bar scene.

"Yeah, I hear underwriting is involved in some high-tech IPO," said Vicky.

There was not a lot of intergroup information passed around BHA. It was almost like we were working in separate companies from our counterparts in other groups. Our firm was involved in underwriting and acting as an advisor in large and complex financial transactions. We had heard that analysts in that area made bigger bucks than we did, not that that was saying much. Petty jealousy was never far from the forefront of our feelings towards our intercompany partners.

"Sure," said Boof with a sneer. "There's Perkins from underwriting. He gets a latte with a donut. He might just as well be a girl. Hey, Perkins," he yelled across the cafe. "They giving out shots of testosterone with that order?"

Perkins glanced over at our table like he was looking at a pen full of piglets at the petting zoo, but continued on his way without a response to Boof's barb.

"See that?" said Boof. "We're so far beneath them you can't even goad them into a pissing contest." Razor snorted, but Vicky looked a little disgusted.

We were joined by the other two analysts in our section, Chauncy Stillwell and Larry Berman. We called them the twins, primarily because we rarely saw one without the other, but also because they really looked like twins. They both could have fallen off the bookshelf of the typical financial analyst—average height, slight of build, business-short hair, and yes, the ever-present thick glasses. Both were on the intellectual side, but would become easily lost if the conversation veered away from anything having to do with financial analysis. If someone brought up any such pedestrian subjects as, oh say, sports, the latest movies, or even current events, the twins' eyes would glaze over. But if the discussion turned toward the latest mind-numbing analysis techniques—arbitrage, neural networks, bootstrapping, Martingale pricing, risk modeling, historical simulation, etc.—the boys' eyes would light up. They were in their element. Leave it to Boof to put it so succinctly, but he once suggested that Berman, the only member of our little team who was married, probably pulled out a Forbes instead of a Playboy to get himself primed before getting in bed with the wife.

"Oh, don't worry too much," said Stillwell. "IPO activity tends to ebb and flow with market activity. Whereas M&A's are a steadier business."

"Hey, speaking of steadier business," said Boof. "We should hit the Good Life tonight. I hear the clientele might be more to our liking than The Hill."

There was no doubt in anyone's mind that Boof meant there were probably more women there. The single guys in the group— myself, Boof, Razor, and Stillwell—made a regular Friday night foray to The Hill, a local lounge within walking distance of BHA. Berman occasionally joined us when he got permission from his wife. And yes, even Vicky, when she was feeling brave enough, made a rare appearance.

"Don't get yourself in a lather, Boof," I said. "The Good Life is a dance place, remember?"

"Yeah, but they let the babes...er, that is...uh, women...get in free."

Vicky just shook her head, staring down into her coffee.

"The sight of you dancing would scare any reasonable woman away anyway," said Razor.

"Who says she has to be reasonable?" asked Boof.

"Razor's right," I said. "When you attempt to dance, you look like someone undergoing electric shock therapy under his clothes."

"Yes, I believe it was April 17th of last year when you broke that woman's nose," said Stillwell. "You were, in fact, dancing with her at the time, were you not?"

Vicky got a laugh out of that.

"You remember the date?" said Boof. Stillwell just shrugged.

We all laughed. Then I said, "I think it would probably be safer...uh...better if we just stuck to The Hill."

Boof looked disappointed. "You guys were a lot more fun before Shrek took over."

The mention of our boss brought everyone's mood down. Darren Dobson had taken charge of the M&A group about six months earlier. Our previous boss, John Bauer, was a true mentor. He was a gentleman, sympathetic to our needs, understanding, willing to teach, and always trying to help us along our difficult career paths. He judged his own personal success on the advancement of his charges.

In other words, he was the polar opposite of our current boss in every way.

We called Mr. Dobson Shrek because — well, that was the only ogre we knew. And it may have been our collective imagination, but once we bestowed him with that nickname, he actually started to resemble Shrek. He was a burly man, and always wore suits that looked too small. He had thinning reddish hair, a ruddy face, and a bulbous, veiny nose — very Shrek-like. He had what my college buddies referred to as a "drinker's face." He always seemed like he was in a foul mood, and we theorized that he was trapped in some semi-permanent state of being hung over. He treated us like chattel, and made it abundantly clear that we were all eminently replaceable.

"Has anybody seen Shrek today?" asked Razor. "I haven't heard him chewing anybody out all morning."

"He's with the executive committee," said Berman and Stillwell at the same time. We all just looked at them.

"C'mon now, admit it," said Boof. "You guys rehearsed that, right?"

We all laughed, but our mirth was short-lived as we realized that our quiet morning wasn't the beginning of any kind of new trend for Shrek to start treating us like human beings. In fact, if the executive committee meeting, comprised of BHA's most senior VIP's, wasn't going well, we could probably expect a brutal afternoon and evening, as our boss would have a plentiful supply of anger and frustration to take out on us.

"So," said Vicky in a forced cheerfulness, "anybody do anything interesting last night?"

I was aware of everybody kind of shaking their heads, giving a "No, not really" kind of response. But Vicky's innocent question brought back thoughts of "her." This girl, this woman I couldn't stop thinking about.

My tablemates must have noticed my change of mood. "How about you, Conner?" asked Vicky with a thoughtful smile.

"Yeah," shouted Boof. "Out with it, dude. I thought you had that 'partied 'til I was beaten down' look about you this morning. Who is she, and what does she look like?"

Vicky gave Boof a "Tsk," but his question took me by surprise.

"Hey, I was only busting you. Look at that face. Did you really get a woman last night? I knew it. See? It's not fair. Chicks always go for the tall guys. Conner looks every bit the geek that I do, but add a few inches — okay, maybe more like a foot — in height, and babes are throwing themselves at him."

"Trust me, Boof. Nobody is throwing themselves at me. Far

from it. No, I...went for a walk in the fog last night, and...got a little lost is all."

"Lost? On Beacon Hill? I don't know, guys, but that sounds like bullshit to me," said Boof.

"That's enough, Edwin," said Vicky. Whenever anyone used Boof's real name, he got pissed off enough to temporarily put a clamp on his banter.

It was time to head back to the office, so we reluctantly got up. I was a little surprised when Vicky moved over toward me and said quietly, "You did look a little upset there, Conner. Is everything really all right?"

I stammered, "Uh, yes. I'm just a little tired, I guess." Then I instantly realized how lame that sounded, and started kicking myself inside.

"Well, if you ever need to talk, just let me know." I was a bit stunned as Vicky then caught up to the group heading for the elevator.

Boof fell back from the pack. Now he was up close and talking confidentially.

"Your new girlfriend," he whispered. "It isn't Vicky...is it?"

CHAPTER FIVE

Our post coffee-break morning continued on the quiet side, as Shrek's executive committee meeting kept him out of our hair for a while longer. Lunch was uneventful. Razor and the twins got caught up in a conversation about the asset types eligible for accelerated depreciation; Boof droned on about needing to refine his methodology for approaching women in a bar; Vicky took on the challenge of figuring out how she could sit at a table with a bunch of guys and pretend not to know them.

As we were headed back to our desks, Boof said to me, "We're still good for The Hill tonight, right?" I had actually been pondering the possibility of retracing my steps from last night to see if I would encounter her again, but then I realized that I really didn't know where I was at the time. "Yeah, Boof. Yeah, we're good."

"Okay, excellent. I'll see if Razor and the twins want to come too. Strength in numbers, y'know?"

I tried not to get caught up in the fact that my Friday night outings to The Hill essentially made up my entire social life. Too depressing to consider. Besides, it beat sitting at home alone.

I didn't have a chance to continue my internal debate. As soon as we got back to the cube farm, we were greeted by the imposing figure of Darren Dobson, a.k.a. Shrek, standing in front of our doorways. He wasn't wearing a uniform, but he looked like one of those burly Russian soldiers guarding the Kremlin.

He didn't waste time with any kind of greeting. "The executive committee thinks we're taking too long with the analysis on our current deals," he bellowed. "I want to see status reports from all of you first thing Monday morning. But I have some good news." He sported an evil grin that made us hold our collective breath. "I got the building engineers to promise to keep the lights on for the entire weekend." He looked at me, and I knew what was coming. "Coming in shouldn't be a big problem for you, David. You can practically fall out of bed and you're here." Then he stormed off to his office. It seemed to stick in Dobson's craw that I lived on Beacon Hill, when he, my superior, couldn't afford to do so.

"Boy, whatever his problem is, I bet it's hard to pronounce," said Boof.

We all guffawed a little, but also realized that we would probably have to work late tonight and a good part of the weekend. None of us wanted to turn in an unsatisfactory status report to Shrek. The consequences were too painful to consider.

We all took on a very glum air as we sulked into our cubes and started banging away on our keyboards. A while later, Boof stuck his head in my doorway. "I think Shrek is full of shit. The executive committee probably didn't say anything about our projects. He was just using their name because he knows we don't have any respect for him." And then off he went, back to his cube to keep working. I just loved being Boof's sounding board. In fairness, we probably all had the same thought, but nobody wanted to risk that Shrek might actually be telling the truth about the executive committee.

Any way we cut it, this was going to be a long weekend.

***

The time had reached "Dark O'Clock," which was how we referred to it when afternoon had somehow slipped into late evening, and everyone lost track of what time it actually was. It was amazing how a group could get in sync once it worked

31

together for a while. We stood up in our cubes at just about the same time, and everyone agreed that we had had enough. There was no getting around the fact that we were all going to be in the office for at least part of the weekend, but we had reached the point where working any longer tonight would lead to sloppy results. The unspoken factor was that we all wanted a drink.

"Last one to The Hill is a horse's ass," yelled Boof, and he made a beeline for the exit. The remaining troops all laughed—even Vicky, who, under normal circumstances, barely acknowledged Boof's sophomoric, emotionally-stunted behavior.

"Sure you don't want to join us?" I asked her. "Maybe just for a little while?"

"No thanks, you guys go have fun. You deserve it. I'm going to go sink into a bubble bath and try to resist the urge to drown myself when I think about coming back here tomorrow." Then she did something she had never done before. She put her hand on my forearm. "You sure you're okay, Conner? You did look pretty upset earlier."

I was my usual suave self, reacting to the unexpected touch stimulus. "Huh? Oh...yeah...sure...yeah, I'm fine. Thanks, Vicky. It was really nothing. I just...thought about something...no big deal. Thanks again."

She just laughed. "Well, remember, if you need to talk my offer's still good. G'night."

I found myself watching as she walked away. My lack of social interaction had led me to conclude something about myself, and that was that when it came to reading subtle signals about whether a girl might have some interest in me, I was a complete pinhead. I stood there wondering if Vicky was trying to get some signals through to my thick skull, or whether it was a hopeful manifestation of an overactive imagination.

Then I was like, Nah. Girls who look like Vicky just don't go for guys like me. She was just being a caring coworker, is all.

"Conner?"

I nearly jumped out of my skin. I looked around and realized that Razor and Stillwell were standing there watching me. Had they seen my interaction with Vicky?

"You about ready to go?" asked Razor.

"Yeah. Yeah, sure. I'm ready. Where's Berman? Not joining us tonight?"

"Nope, headed home to marital bliss. Sometimes I wonder who's luckier, him or us," said Razor.

"Considering he's the only one with a regular female partner," said Stillwell, "I'd wager to say that he's getting lucky a lot more frequently than we are."

Razor and I stopped in our tracks and stared. Stillwell kept walking at first, then looked back at us when he realized we had stopped. Razor and I started cracking up. Stillwell blushed.

Razor went over and put his arm around Stillwell's shoulder. "A little off-color humor from one of the twins? I guess anything really is possible. Chauncy, my friend, there is definitely hope for you yet."

Chapter Six

The bar was not exactly hopping when we got there. The Hill was a classy place where people like us went to decompress after work. It had soft earth tone colors, mood lighting, and a mahogany bar. But, a pick up joint? Not so much. The place had an upscale decor and a dazzling array of liquor in front of a mirrored wall behind the bar. It was a wonder there was anybody sober left in this world. There was a dance floor, but nobody on it. Soft jazz was playing at a low volume in the background. The few other patrons, mostly couples, were nestled at tables around the perimeter talking quietly amongst themselves

"Toldja we should've gone to The Good Life," said Boof. "The only way to get laid in here is if one of these rich guys decides to share his wife. This place should be labeled, 'BYOB.' As in, Bring Your Own Broad."

"Hey, let's just have a couple of drinks and go home," I said. "We're all going to have to work most of the weekend. It doesn't always have to be a 'trim hunt,' as you call it."

"Sure, that's easy for a rich kid like you to say. You can always just flash some of Daddy's money around. The rest of us have to get by on our looks and natural charm."

I let the barb pass. Razor, Stillwell, and I looked at each other with slight smiles. We were probably all thinking the same thing. If Boof was getting by on his looks and natural charm, he was in big trouble.

We ordered our drinks. I went for a scotch on the rocks, figuring it was a classy enough drink for this classy bar. Razor ordered a draft. When the waitress turned to Boof, he said to bring him a bottled beer because he didn't want "any of that watered down crap." Stillwell asked for a vodka tonic.

"Conner, have you thought about pursuing Vicky Temerlin?" asked Chauncy Stillwell. "She seems to like you."

"Yeah. How about that, guys? She's never offered to be my sounding board," said Boof. He adopted a high voice, apparently imitating Vicky. "'If you ever need to talk, Conner dear, just let me know.' Seriously, man, I think Vicky is looking for a beef injection."

Razor and Stillwell snorted.

"Gee, Boof, I wonder why Vicky never wants to hear your problems," I said. "Maybe it's because she'd have to wash her ears out with soap afterward."

The other guys laughed, but then I caught something out of the corner of my eye. I looked over at the bar and my jaw just about hit the floor.

It was her.

The girl from last night, "Megan Fox," was sitting by herself at the bar with some red-colored cocktail. She looked just as breathtaking as the first time I'd seen her. She was wearing a white dress this time, which contrasted with her flowing brown hair to perfection. With her sitting, the hem rested mid-thigh, and her legs were toned and perfect. There was nobody else at the bar and she was looking idly into her drink, circling it slowly with her stirrer.

Had she been there the whole time? It wasn't possible that I missed her when we came in. Then again, if she had entered the bar after us, I was sure I would have seen her.

"CD? What's up, you look like you've seen a ghost?" asked Boof. He only called me CD when he was drinking. Then Boof saw her too. "Hey, things are looking up. Razor, lemme borrow your glass." Before Razor could protest, Boof swiped his beer mug and used it as a makeshift mirror, making a feeble attempt to mat down his unruly hair while he held the glass up in front of him.

I said, "Boof, get yourself under control, man," and got up from the table.

"Hey, since when are you the lead dog? What're you gonna pull, some shit like 'I saw her first?' What is this, kindergarten? Maybe I would like first shot." Then Boof swiped his hand around the table. "Or maybe Razor. Or...even Stillwell here. Why don't we draw straws or something?"

I nearly panicked when I thought about the possibility of Boof scaring Megan off with his hypersexuality. "Wait," I said, putting my hand on Boof's shoulder. "I...I know this girl. I've seen her before. Just let me talk to her, huh? If there's nothing there, then she's fair game. Okay?"

Razor and Stillwell were watching for Boof's reaction. They didn't really have an inkling about putting the moves on themselves. Boof looked resigned, and I walked off quickly before he changed his mind. I heard him grumble something like, "Typical. Rich kids get all the good twist."

As I was walking over to the bar, my mouth felt like the Gobi Desert and I kept repeating to myself, Don't come off like a fool. Don't come off like a fool.

"Ah...hi...I mean...excuse me...hello...." I thought, Way to not look like a fool, Conner boy.

She turned to me and smiled slightly. I felt my knees start to buckle.

"Hello," she said. Her voice sounded like she was singing. With the same expression, she turned her attention back to her drink.

"I, uh...I don't mean to bother you, but by any chance did I see you out walking last night? I'm sorry to say I don't know exactly where I was. I got a little lost because of the fog." As soon as the words were out of my mouth, I regretted it. He-men weren't ever supposed to get lost, right? Or at least not admit that they were lost. I started repeating to myself, You're a turd, Conner. A total turd.

Still sporting an expression of slight bemusement, she looked at me curiously, as if she was checking out a new species of tadpoles at the aquarium.

"The reason I ask," I continued—now it was if I was verbally falling down the stairs and just couldn't stop myself— "I, uh, ran into a couple of guys. They, uh, looked like they were up to no good. But, then they just like...disappeared. They were there one second and the next they were gone. It was really strange. And—well, I thought I had just seen you...walked by you. It was somewhere in the South Slope area."

She looked at me fully and flashed me a smile with dazzling white teeth. It felt like my heart had stopped beating.

"I did go for a walk last night," she said. "I quite enjoy the fog." I knew she didn't enjoy it for the same reason I did. The darker it is, the better I look. "But as far as seeing two guys disappear into the night? No, I'm afraid I can't help you there." Her smile got wider. "And what, pray tell, were you doing out last night? Just getting some exercise? Or did you get lost on the way to a romantic interlude somewhere?"

I laughed a little, but thought I shouldn't let on that the idea of me out for a nighttime rendezvous was as absurd as it really was. "Uh, no, nothing like that. I...well, I work as a financial analyst, and we put in some long hours. Sometimes I just like to get out to clear my head."

"Ah, so it was a de-stress walk. I see. Did it work?"

"It was working okay," I almost added, "until I realized that I was lost," but stopped myself, thinking, there's hope for you yet, Conner. "But those guys. Frankly, they tried to rob me. One of them had a gun."

"Oh my. Seems like you're not safe anywhere in the city anymore. You weren't hurt, were you?"

"No. I mean, just my wits, as in, scared out of them."

I was mentally kicking myself again, but she just laughed, and her laugh sounded like musical tones.

"And you say those men just disappeared? Did they run away? Maybe you scared them off?" The brilliant smile again, as if acknowledging what we both knew—that I would have trouble scaring off a fly.

"No, they didn't exactly run away...." I stopped myself. Let's see, I thought. I've already positioned myself as a wimp and a coward. If I describe how it seemed like those dudes were just swept up into the sky, I could add complete whack to my list of undesirables.

I couldn't immediately think of anything else to say, so I blurted out, "By the way, my name's Conner."

"Well, hello Conner. I'm Lyria."

"Lyria...," I said. The name fit her. It was a beautiful name for this stunning vision. Normally, I got all fumble-mouthed when I tried to talk to someone this amazing looking. But Lyria's relaxed countenance, her easy smile, and her singsong voice were putting me at ease.

"Did you want to say something else, Conner?" she asked, still smiling, and I realized that I was just standing there like an idiot after hearing her name.

"Oh, uh, so...Lyria." I just loved the way her name sounded. "Do, uh...do you...come here often?"

The lamest pickup line in the history of mankind. I should be locked away and prevented from having any contact with the outside world.

But Lyria laughed. "I come here every once in a while. How

about you? Are those your friends?"

I glanced over at the table. Boof, Razor, and Stillwell were trying to look nonchalant and make like they were talking to each other, but I knew they were watching, fully expecting me to crash and burn. Boof was probably chomping at the bit, awaiting his turn.

"Yes. I mean, we work together. We're all financial analysts." I wondered why I cringed every time I said that.

"That's great. Your office must be nearby. Nice place to come hang out."

"We work at Beacon Hill Associates. It's right up the street."

"Oh, BHA, huh? I read about you underwriting the Stevenson IPO. Were you involved with that?"

I was almost to stunned to answer. "You...you know about BHA? You know about the Stevenson deal?"

She laughed. "Does it surprise you that I might read the newspaper?"

"Yes...I mean...no. I mean...I don't know. I'm just...surprised. A girl like you...uh...how shall I put this? Isn't usually interested in the type of business that I'm in."

"I was surprised their board approved going public," she said. "Leaves the company pretty highly leveraged."

I was completely speechless. This vision of beauty knew about corporate financial structure.

She laughed again and hit me with the full megawatt smile. "Conner, why don't you pick your jaw up off the floor and sit down." She nodded to the seat right next to her.

"Oh, thank you," I said. I was staring at her. In awe. Like most guys, I had an image of what the perfect woman for me would be like. And all of a sudden, seemingly out of nowhere, here she was, sitting next to me at The Hill. I had an awful feeling that this was a dream and I was going to be jarred awake by my alarm clock, and I would realize that none of it was real. And I would have to drudge off to my boring job and continue with my boring life.

But so far, I wasn't waking up. And it occurred to me that this could actually be the real deal.

Lyria was looking at me, still smiling. "Is there something you want to ask me, Conner?"

"What?"

"You look like you would like to ask me something."

"Oh, yeah, I'm sorry, I didn't mean to stare."

"Well, what is it you want to ask me?"

I just kept looking into her eyes. I wanted to ask her what her story was. Where she was from. What she did for a living. A woman like this must have guys swarming around her like vultures. Was she married? Engaged? In a committed relationship? What were her hobbies? Where did she go in her spare time?

I realized with a jolt that I had zero experience with this—meeting a woman at a bar. Especially a woman like this, a perfect woman. Should I ask her these things? Or was that too forward? Would it scare her off? My biggest fear right now was that she would see me as a total dweeb, come to her senses, and go running out of the bar. An even worse thought came to me. That she would be right, and I wouldn't blame her if she bolted and left me in her wake.

Then I heard myself say, "I was wondering if you would like to dance?"

She looked out at the empty dance floor. "Why, yes. I would like that very much."

She took my hand, and much to my amazement, I was headed to the dance floor with the woman of my dreams.

***

"I'm actually not a very good dancer," I said, and suddenly I was aware of my surroundings, especially the guys at the table. They had dropped any pretense of not paying attention to me,

40

and were outright gawking at us. Razor and Stillwell were slack-jawed, but Boof looked pissed off. I was sure he was cursing my existence for scooping him with this beauty.

Lyria said, "Oh, don't be silly. These days, you don't have to have any dancing ability at all. You just go with the music and do what feels right."

"At this moment, sitting back down would feel about right."

She tossed her head back and laughed. Suddenly, we were moving to the music. As she said, we were doing whatever came naturally.

"Hmm. You dance pretty good for a financial analyst," she said with her beaming smile. We were about a foot away from each other. I was concentrating on maintaining eye contact, because first, I was basically shy and had a habit of looking away, and second, I was doing everything I could to cover up my nerdiness. But, I admit that I was also very aware of her knockout figure, and my eyes were wanting to wander in that direction in the worst way. Again, I was inexperienced, but I knew that ogling someone who was still a relative stranger would scare her off. Besides, I could tell without looking over that Boof would be doing enough ogling for both of us.

"Thanks," I said with a laugh. "You dance pretty well too, for a.... I'm sorry, we haven't really talked about what you do."

"No we haven't, have we?" She was still smiling, and after a moment's pause, it was clear that she wasn't going to shed any light on her background, and I certainly wasn't going to push it.

The piped-in music had been playing a soft-rock number, but that song ended, and I assumed we would head back to the bar. The next selection was a slower song.

"Oooh," she said. "I love this. Can we stay out?"

"Oh, uh...sure. Sure thing."

I stood there like a moron, not knowing what to do. Lyria sensed my discomfort and laughed. She slowly walked over, took my left hand, and put her arm over my right shoulder. I was still not sure what to do, and wondered again why she hadn't gone running from the building. She took her left hand off my shoulder and gently guided my right hand to her waist. "It's okay to touch me," she said. "I promise I won't break." Then her hand went back to my shoulder and we were moving on the floor—an actual slow dance, with a stunning beauty. This night was full of firsts.

She was tall for a woman, but I still had a head on her, and I was looking down into her eyes. It didn't seem to bother Lyria that she was pretty much leading our dance. I knew the guy was supposed to do that, but I was pretty sure that rule didn't apply to nerds.

"What are you thinking about, Conner?"

I hesitated. "Oh, I don't really want to say."

"Aw, come on," she said with her brilliant smile. "If you tell me, I'll tell you what I'm thinking...."

I couldn't help but smile back. "Okay," I said. I was still leery of saying what I was truly thinking, but then I thought, Oh what the heck, it's probably obvious to her anyway. "I'm thinking that you're...about the most beautiful woman on the planet, and I can't honestly believe that I'm actually dancing with you." I didn't know whether to expect gratitude for the compliment or a slap across the face.

"What a nice thing to say," she beamed. She let go of my hand, put both hands around my neck, and moved even closer. My empty hand somehow ended up on her waist, and she put her head on my left shoulder. Our feet were still moving, albeit slowly. I was sure she would hear my heartbeat, as it was pounding so hard, it felt like it would erupt at any moment.

The music stopped, and I was mentally swearing at the songwriter for not making the tune longer. Lyria looked up at me, and we stood there for what seemed like forever, looking into each other's eyes. Finally, she took my hand and we headed back to the bar. I was worried that my letting her lead, first on the dance floor and now off of it, would cause her to conclude that I was as much of a tool as I actually was.

But we sat back down, and it didn't look like her mood had changed at all. "There now," she said. "That wasn't so bad, was it?"

"So bad? No, that wasn't so bad at all," I laughed, and then she laughed too. "Hey, wait a minute," I said. "You were supposed to tell me what you were thinking about." Her embrace had temporarily chased that out of my head.

She laughed again. "Well, I was thinking that you never really know when you're going to meet someone who could be special to you, and how funny life is sometimes."

That response staggered me to silence.

"So, tell me a little bit more about your job," she said.

"Seriously? You really want to hear about financial analysis?"

She laughed again, and I thought I would never get tired of hearing that sound. "Absolutely," she said. "Have you worked on any exciting deals lately?"

Well, I thought, she must be somewhat interested in the subject. She knew about the Stevenson IPO. It wasn't even major news. Probably only merited a paragraph in the business section. She even knew that the company ended up with a lot of debt on their books.

So, I started yammering about our office, and the members of the analysis team. I told her about Shrek, although I left out the part about him being jealous of where I lived. I talked about some of the analyses we were doing, keeping company names out of it where necessary. I had a fleeting thought that Lyria was some sort of corporate spy, and that she was feigning interest in me to pump me for some inside scoop, but I pushed that thought back to the recesses of my mind where it belonged. Overall, I was hitting on some pretty boring stuff, but Lyria's interest never waned, and she even interrupted with questions along the way.

Much to my dismay, it was nearing closing time for the bar, and Razor had appeared next to us. "Hello, miss," he said. I introduced him to Lyria.

"Very nice to meet you," she said. "What's your real first name?" she asked with a smile.

"Uh, Fernando, miss," said Razor, and he was smiling too. She has that effect on everyone, I thought to myself. "Conner, can we talk to you for a second before we all go home?"

"Yeah...uh...yeah, sure. Uh, Lyria, I'll be right back."

"Of course."

Razor and I walked over to the table. He and Stillwell were smiling like Cheshire Cats, and I wondered how many drinks they had put away.

"You're a dog, CD," said Razor.

Stillwell said, "You're also kind of my hero right now."

The three of us laughed, but Boof remained serious. We were all looking at him. Finally he smiled a little. "Next time, I get to go first, got it?"

I thought about saying, Sure, the next time I encounter the most beautiful woman in the world, you get first shot. But I said, "Sure thing, Boof. Sure thing." And we all laughed this time.

"Well, I guess we're taking off," said Razor. "You gonna be okay?"

"Sure...I mean...I hope so." More laughs.

"You still going to make it in tomorrow?" asked Stillwell. "Not sure Shrek's going to accept 'meeting the prettiest girl in the world' as an acceptable reason to be late with his status report." Now I knew the alcohol had flowed pretty freely. I wasn't sure I had ever heard Chauncy refer to Dobson as "Shrek" before.

"Oh yeah. I'll be there."

The guys got up to leave and I turned back toward the bar. I stopped short in my tracks.

The bar was empty. Lyria was gone.

CHAPTER SEVEN

When I got home, my mind was churning with frustration. I had stayed at the bar for a while in case Lyria came back. The other guys all left, passing along muttered condolences as they went by. I asked the bartender if he had seen her leave and he said that he hadn't.

"Maybe she's just in the ladies' room," he said, but his eyes told me something different. This guy had probably seen his share of weaselly looking guys like me getting ditched. After a couple of minutes, he apparently took pity on me and said he'd send the waitress into the ladies' room to check. As she walked by shaking her head, she gave me the same pathetic look, and I wondered how a night that started out so magical had turned so disastrous so quickly. The humiliation was complete, so I slinked out of the bar.

Cool air hit me when I got outside, and I looked around. My clueless, ever-hopeful brain pinged in with, Well...maybe she's just being playful and is waiting to spring out from behind a car. 'Hah hah, gotcha,' she'll say. 'Thought I left you high and dry, huh?' Hey, Lyria seemed like the playful type. But, of course, no such thing happened and I headed on home, my head slung low. I actually hoped that Spider and Vape might magically reappear and finish off their heist. That's how bad I felt. Getting robbed would be the perfect way to end this evening.

It was so bad, I couldn't even get robbed.

The thought of going into work in the morning made me curse Shrek, his mother, and his whole family. I felt like I'd rather jump off a cliff than hump into the office just so that douchebag could get his jollies busting on the rich kid and his friends.

Big surprise, I couldn't sleep worth a damn, so I actually headed to the office early and, to put it mildly, I was in a foul mood. Fortunately, there was nobody else there yet, so I buried myself in my work.

I wasn't even conscious of the other people arriving until I became aware of a lot of rat-a-tatting on computers in the other cubes. Normally, we'd all pow-wow in the common area before beginning work, but this was no normal morning. The guys who were at the bar the previous night were probably avoiding me, and Berman and Vicky were going with the flow. They would hear what had happened in due time, if they didn't know already. Stillwell had probably called Berman as soon as he got home. There were no secrets between twins. And Boof was always looking for excuses to go talk to Vicky, so it was only a matter of time before she was let in on the dope. I had to face the fact that it was pretty close to impossible to keep secrets in this office, especially with this tight-knit group. I kept banging away on my keyboard, but I was also fantasizing about owning an invisibility cloak from the Harry Potter books.

After a while, I heard a rustling from my doorway. I looked up and Boof was standing there. Normally, Boof was about as subtle as a charging rhino. He usually barged into my little cube, plopped down in my only guest chair, and immediately started blabbing about his latest failed conquest. This time he was just standing in my doorway. For once in his life, he looked like he didn't know what to say.

As I said, not a normal morning.

"Hey, Boof." I decided to break the ice, still facing my computer.

"Hey, buddy, how you hanging in there?"

"Oh, great Boof. Just great," I barked. Then a realization came to me and I turned quickly in his direction, causing him to back up a few steps.

"Hey, let me ask you something."

"Yeah? What?"

"I was facing away from her last night, so there's no way I could have seen her leave. But I was talking to you guys, so you were facing in her direction."

"Hey, man...what are you getting at here?"

"Real simple question, Boof. Did you see her leave?"

"Heck no. You think I would have seen her splitting and not said anything to you?"

"That's exactly what I'm thinking. Unless she disappeared into thin air, somebody must have seen her leave."

"Geez. I'm hurt that you would think that about me. What do you think, Razor and Stillwell were in on the conspiracy too?"

I had to admit to myself that it didn't seem very plausible.

Boof softened his tone a bit. "Buddy, I would never do that to a fellow cruiser. Okay, so my underwear got in a bunch for a while there, you hitting on that sensational cupcake when it rightfully should have been me...."

I thought to ask him how on earth he figured that, but I let him go on.

"But, I know better than anybody how it feels to get stiff and then get stiffed. I've had babes crawl out bathroom windows in my time. I would never pull that on a pal. After a while, we were all rooting for you."

I almost felt bad about going after Boof. It was easy to forget that he was an actual human being with feelings.

"All right. Hey, I'm sorry, okay? Just a little frustrated is all."

Boof came over and sat in my guest chair, and I felt like things were getting back to normal.

"Been there. Hey, it could have been worse. It really sucks when they bail after you've already got your clothes off."

I truly didn't want any more details, so I quickly changed the subject. "How's your status report coming?"

"Ah. It's getting there. I'm gonna try to finish tonight so I don't have to haul my carcass in here tomorrow. So, hey, if we're both here late...."

"No, Boof."

"No what? I didn't even ask anything yet."

"I know what you're going to ask. And no. I don't want to hit The Good Life tonight."

"Aw, c'mon. You gotta get back on the horse, buddy. Besides, every Saturday is ladies' night. Free admission, half-price drinks, the whole nine yards. The girls get good and juiced for practically nothing, and all their inhibitions and good judgment fall by the wayside."

"Forget it, Boof."

"Hey, you gotta strike while the irons are hot, Conner."

"In what universe are my irons hot?"

"Okay, so last night didn't work out. But look at it this way. You almost got lucky in The Hill. That's like scoring in a mausoleum. And that babe was off the charts. At least you got some face time. And a couple of dances. Hey, let me ask you, during that slow dance—"

"Stop."

"Okay, okay. But what do you have to do tonight that's better? I know you don't have any plans."

"My plan is to go bury myself under my covers to keep from jumping off my balcony, or calling my doctor and begging for a double prescription of Xanax."

"Ah, keep your chin up, man. You got a lot going for you. You're good-looking...in a bookwormy, geeky sorta way. And more important, you got the buckeroos...and the fancy digs. Your place is like a pussy palace. Let's be honest, taking a babe back to my closet-sized apartment in Winthrop doesn't exactly make 'em want to drop their draws on sight, you know."

I laughed a little. First time all day, and I had to admit, it didn't feel bad.

"There you go," said Boof. "You're getting back in the swing now. So, how about it? Should we alert the women in Boston to look out for the deadly duo tonight?"

"No, seriously, I'm just not up for it tonight. My male ego is lower than whale shit, and I gotta give it some time to recover. We'll hit The Good Life some other Saturday night, okay? I'm sure there'll still be some booze left, and hopefully girls' judgments won't get any better by then."

Boof got up to head back to his cube. "All right. But let me know if you change your mind, okay?"

"You'll be the first. Oh, and Boof?"

"Yeah?"

"Thanks, buddy."

Boof just smiled. "No worries. Just wait. You'll be back in the saddle before you know it."

***

As hard as it may be to believe, talking to Boof did make me feel a little better. I only saw the other team members in passing, as everyone seemed intent on finishing their reports that day so we wouldn't have to come in again on Sunday.

It was late and I had just about wrapped up my report. The petty part of me wanted to email it to Shrek so he would see that it came in on Saturday night, and that he had only screwed up half my weekend, not the whole thing. Hey, we must take little victories where we can get them.

I hit "send" with a certain amount of satisfaction and felt a little guilty for having such juvenile feelings. But I got over that pretty quickly. I was ready to slink out. I couldn't tell whether anyone else was still there, but I wasn't going to say anything anyway. I figured I could heal my bruised ego all day Sunday and come in Monday morning all peppy and act as if nothing had ever happened. I quietly put everything away, locked my desk, and had turned to leave when I saw Vicky standing in my doorway. I remember thinking, I was inches from a clean getaway.

Vicky was dressed casually, it being Saturday and all, but I have to say, she looked sensational. She was wearing some tight designer jeans that I thought must have cost about as much as my entire wardrobe, and a tight, thin-fabric pink sweater that did a fairly remarkable job of accentuating her figure. I was more than a little ashamed of thinking that way, but I figured that wouldn't change as long as I was a male of the species.

"Hi, Conner. You heading out?"

"Uh, yeah Vick. How'd you do? Did you get your status report done?"

"Pretty much. I'm taking the rest home with me. I just couldn't face coming back in here tomorrow."

I had my jacket and was still moving toward the door, hoping to avoid a prolonged conversation about what had happened the previous night.

"Yeah. I hear you. Well, g'night."

"Conner, I won't keep you. I...I just wanted to say...that I'm sorry about what happened at The Hill."

"Ah, no big deal. See you...."

"...and I don't think you should feel bad about yourself. Anyone you meet in a bar is probably not going to work out in the long term anyway. Whoever she was, I'm sure you can do better. Will do better."

Vicky looked so sincere that I had to at least appreciate the effort she put in to come over. I sat back down resignedly and Vicky sat in my guest chair.

51

"Thanks, Vick. I...it's just that...."

"What? You can tell me. Unlike Boof and...well, basically all the other guys on the team, you can be sure that I won't say a word to anyone else about what we talk about."

I couldn't help but smile. "No, I'm sure that's true. I was just shocked that she left. I felt like we had clicked, you know? I realized when I was talking to her that I had no idea what I was doing. I've never picked up...or, I mean, really met a girl I liked in a bar before."

Vicky laughed a little. "It's okay. You can say 'picked up' if you want to. I've been around long enough to understand."

I laughed a little too. "I know it probably won't come as a huge surprise to you, but I.... Well, honestly, my experience with girls...er...women, is pretty limited. But she reacted so naturally. Like I didn't know if I was sharing too much, not sharing enough...but she seemed really interested in what I was saying. She even knew about financial analysis, can you believe it? She knew about the Stevenson deal, and thought it left the company with too much debt."

"Really?"

"Yes, but one thing did keep nagging at me a bit, and maybe it was a precursor of her splitting on me."

Vicky leaned forward. "And what was that?"

"Well, she wasn't sharing much about herself. I mean personal details. Maybe she was a bored housewife or something. She had to have someone in her life — I mean, this girl — this woman — was really beautiful. And I couldn't help but think later that if I had more — you know — experience, maybe I would have picked up on her not talking about herself as a sign of trouble. I don't know, I guess I shouldn't get all tied up in knots over it. Boof says it happens to him all the time."

She laughed again. "Now that's very believable. Listen, Conner, as I said, don't feel bad about yourself. You're not Boof.

I'm sure you'll meet someone wonderful in time. But I can almost guarantee you that it won't happen in a bar."

I laughed and said, "I guess you're right. Hey, thanks Vicky."

"No charge, my friend. Well, guess I'd better get going too. I've got a hot late-night date with a glass of Chablis and this new thousand-thread pillow sham that I bought online the other day."

We walked out together, and before we went our separate ways, I said "G'night, Vick."

I was more than a little surprised when she walked over, gave me a quick peck on the cheek, patted my face gently, and said "Good night, Conner," then walked away.

I was standing there a bit stunned, watching her walk away with, shall we say, a high degree of admiration. I said to myself, Dad never told me there were financial analysts that looked like that. Then I headed toward home with a bit more spring in my step than I would have thought possible a little while earlier.

***

A few minutes later, I became aware of the fact that I hadn't taken my usual, more direct route home. I was actually a little surprised, as if I hadn't come this way of my own free will. But when I came to my senses and looked up, it all made sense. Sure enough, I had walked over to the entrance of The Hill.

"Conner, you are truly out of your mind," I said to myself out loud, then looked around to see if anyone else had heard. I started to go in the other direction several times, but I couldn't make myself proceed. I recognized that some impulse in the deep recesses of my brain wanted to be sure that Lyria wouldn't be there again tonight. I did everything short of slap myself in the face to break out of this insane line of thinking, but I was surprised again when I found myself walking in.

I stood at the entrance for a while before making my way to the bar area. Rather than wondering why I seemed to have a penchant for self-abuse, I was hoping beyond hope that there were different people working. I didn't want to face the barkeep and waitress who'd watched this hopeless sap slither out of there last night. I really wanted to forget this crazy scheme and go home, but I walked to the bar anyway.

The lights were dim, and I was once again impressed with how classy the place looked. There was a smattering of people sitting at tables around the dance floor, quietly talking amongst themselves and paying me no never-mind. The barstools and dance floor were completely vacant and, much to my relief, there was a different bartender and two unfamiliar waitresses. More importantly, there was no sign of Lyria.

Part of me was disappointed, another part relieved. I sat down at the bar and started to order a beer, then changed my mind. "Scotch please. Neat." After the past twenty-four hours I needed my libation to be on the strong side. I sat there sipping my drink and contemplating life. Then I became remotely aware that the same slow song that Lyria and I had danced to the previous night was playing again. My immediate thought was that the background music must be piped in, and I wondered what kind of fee the bar paid to keep it going.

Hey, what can I say? Once a finance geek...well, you know the rest.

The scotch was warming my stomach and succeeded in calming my nerves, but I thought I'd better wrap it up and get out of there before the night turned into a college-level bender.

"Excuse me. May I have this dance?"

The voice sounded almost musical and was eerily familiar, causing my stomach to lurch anew. I turned around slowly and, sure enough, it was Lyria.

To say she looked stunning would be like calling Bernie Madoff a petty thief. She was wearing a yellow print dress that contrasted her long brown hair flowing over her shoulders. Her beautiful face was flawless, with those angular features and high cheekbones. She did look like a young Megan Fox, only better. She was smiling with perfect white teeth that made my knees weak. And that body — don't get me going on that body. Sorry, but I'm a guy, and I notice these things.

"Have...have you been here long...?" was all I could manage, and with such a smooth way of relating to the opposite sex, I hoped my parents didn't have their heart set on grandchildren.

She hesitated. "I got here a few minutes ago. I...was hoping you'd come back."

"What happened last night? Where did you go?"

She sidled onto the barstool next to mine. "Conner...I was very taken with you last night. But I didn't want you to think that I was normally available for a quick bar pickup. Plus, your friends were here. And I know that office workplaces can be gossipy. Is yours like that?"

"Well...yes. Ours is probably worse than most, but only because the size of the team is so small. We work in a large conglomerate, but it seems like everyone knows everybody else's business. Or they think they do. Sometimes the biggest excitement of the day is when we hear something about a BHA associate in another division."

She laughed, and I thought, I would pay good money to hear that laugh on a regular basis.

"That's what I was worried about," she said. "I didn't want to start any hot rumors about Conner David's great bar conquest."

Then I was laughing too, but I was also searching my mind to think about whether I had told her my last name. Because I normally didn't, usually trying to avoid those "two first name" jokes.

"So, how about it?" she asked, interrupting my pondering.

"Huh? Uh...how about what?"

The exquisite laugh again. "I asked you to dance, remember? Are you going to keep a lady waiting? Or just playing hard-to-get?"

"Hard-to-get? Me? Uh, no, that would never occur to me. No. I mean...yes...yes I would love to dance." That voice in the back of my head reappeared. Smooth, Conner. Real smooth.

***

We were slow dancing again, and my mind strayed to what kind of odds I would have given that the two of us would be back on this floor, dancing to the same song as the previous night less than twenty-four hours later.

"Penny for your thoughts," said Lyria.

"I just can't believe this is happening."

"What? That we're dancing? Not that unusual, Conner. We were here last night. Remember?"

"Oh, do I remember. No, not necessarily that we're dancing, although that's fairly unbelievable in its own right. That you're here again. And that you're dancing with me. That you would even talk to me, for that matter."

"And why wouldn't I talk to you? And why is it so unbelievable that I'm here? And that we're dancing?"

Maybe it was that she had actually come back and my confidence was unusually high. Or maybe it was Captain Dewars providing a "liquid courage" boost of self-assurance. During the previous night, I had been very careful with what I said, leery of saying anything that might scare her off. But, after fretting all day over what had happened, I really wanted some answers.

"Lyria, don't get me wrong—it's hard for me to imagine myself being happier than I am right now. But, girls—that is, women who look like you—don't usually pay any attention to me. I picture you with some international playboy who drives around in a Ferrari and buys you diamonds."

She beamed, "Hey! Do you know a guy like that?"

I stood slack-jawed until I realized that she was busting on me. We both started laughing. Then she suddenly looked serious.

56

"You shouldn't put yourself down like that, Conner. Or carry around these pre-conceived notions of how a 'woman like me' would act. I'm just a person who happened to meet someone she likes. Now, I'll grant you, that doesn't usually happen in a bar, but...well, okay, I do have a bit of a confession to make...."

I remember thinking, Here it comes. She's married. Or has a heavily-armed Navy Seal boyfriend.

"I do remember seeing you the other night in the fog," she said.

About the last thing I was expecting out of her was a confession. When she saw my stunned look, she laughed a little.

"Don't look so surprised. I...well, I liked the way you looked. Like someone I might want to meet. When I saw you here last night, it was like fate had brought us together. Do you think that's silly?"

"Silly? No. No, not silly at all." I thought of asking her again whether she had seen Spider and Vape, but I let it go.

"And after getting to know you, I found out that I did really like you. So I came back, hoping that you'd be here again. Is that so unbelievable?"

I thought that it was, but said, "No. Of course not." I smiled. "By the way, how did you manage to leave last night without anyone seeing you?" asked Captain Dewars before I could manage to shut him up.

"Nobody saw me?"

"No. My friends, the bar staff...."

She hit me with the megawatt smile again. "What can I say? Over time I've found it useful to be stealthy when I needed to be."

I thought, Now that is totally believable. She's probably spent a good part of her existence skirting total losers who were panting like thirsty dogs at the sight of her.

The song ended and we stood in place. "So, did I pass?" she

asked.

"What?"

"You know. The inquisition. Were my answers good enough that I might join you?" She nodded toward the bar.

I smiled. "Yes. You passed. And, I'm sorry. I didn't want it to seem like an inquisition. I just...had a couple of thousand doubts running through my head last night. And some of them came bursting out. Almost like it was against my will."

She laughed that laugh that made my stomach do cartwheels. She said, "It's okay. I deserve it for running out on you. I'm just glad you're not angry."

We headed to the bar as I shook my head in wonder that this woman could possibly be worried about me being angry with her.

"Can I get you a drink?" I asked, but she declined. We sat close, facing each other. She reached over and took my hand. We were looking into each other's eyes, and I was pretty sure I'd never before had the feelings that were coursing through my body. The desire to know more about her came surging forward, but before the torrent of questions started, I managed to quell the flood. I was afraid if I continued the "inquisition" she would think I was the total drag that I was worried about being, and she would figure it wasn't worth it and take off.

Again.

And at that very moment I feared her leaving worse than death itself, or so it seemed.

"So, did you work on anything exciting today?" she asked.

"How did you know I was at work?"

"Oh, you mentioned it last night. All your friends were going to have to go in, right? Working on your status reports for Monday?"

I had no recollection of talking to her about our bleeding status reports, but I must have, right? Otherwise, how would she have known?

I was remotely aware of a commotion in another part of the bar, but I was sporting a laser-like focus on Lyria, so I didn't even turn to check it out.

"Yes, that's right," I said, shaking my head again. "And no. It was nothing exciting. In fact, it couldn't very well be any less exciting. It's like doing work twice—working on a project and then writing a report about the work you did. Very repetitive. And not very productive."

"So why did you do it? Especially on a Saturday?"

"Our boss, Darren Dobson—we call him Shrek. That's the only ogre any of us knew. He goes on these power trips. To him, a financial analyst is totally replaceable. Kind of like a doorstop. He has no qualms about abusing us as much as he feels like. Some days are worse than others. We all wonder whether...ah, never mind."

"No, what? Tell me." She beamed again, and I thought I would do anything she asked if the request was accompanied by that smile.

"Well, we wonder if the bad days are because he didn't get any from Mrs. Dobson the night before."

She threw her head back and laughed heartily. I felt another charge down my spine all the way to my toes.

"We even plot ways we might get her in the mood during our lunch. We were going to order a catered dinner for them and say it was from the BHA CEO. Every part of it was going to be loaded with aphrodisiacs. Oysters for him. Salmon would be the main course—you know, lots of omega 3 fatty acids? Pomegranates and chocolate for dessert."

"Chocolate?"

"Oh yeah. Chocolate's supposed to be packed with phenyl ethylamine. Kind of a natural stimulant."

She was still laughing. "And when were you going to carry

59

out this caper?"

"Oh, we might still do it. We're trying to think strategically. Like when do we want to keep Shrek out of our business? The company shuts down the week between Christmas and New Year's, so we thought about sending it the night before our last day in the office. You know, to keep him from cooking up some insane way to make us come in during the holidays."

Her laugh was infectious, and soon we were both going at it and holding onto each other. She reached up and touched the side of my face. "Oh, Conner, you are so funny. Maybe...maybe we could have that dinner some time." We were still close, and suddenly we were both serious, getting closer. It felt so natural and our lips were about to meet.

"Well, isn't this a cozy little scene?"

I looked up and the cause of the commotion I had heard became clear. Some guy who looked like a polar bear in a suit came staggering towards us, and he'd clearly had a dozen or so too many. It looked like he had gotten up from a table at the back of the bar and proceeded to knock over every chair in his path. Some of the people who had been sitting nearby looked very wary as they watched the guy move.

Our new friend had a ruddy face and a business haircut. His clothes looked expensive but unkempt—the top of his shirt was unbuttoned and his tie loosened. It looked like he had spilled something down the front of him. He still had a drink in his hand as he approached us. To say his gait was unsteady was a serious understatement. It looked like he was searching out a soft place to fall down. But his eyes? There was no question about his focus—he was making laser beams directly at Lyria. I suddenly felt the effects of Captain Dewar fade away to nothingness as my heart started doing double time.

Watching his hulking form stagger forward, I knew just the kind of guy he was. Definitely a corporate type, more than likely fairly high up in the chain of command. And he was a bully, no doubt about it. I'd dealt with a number of these guys in my time. He was kind of like our own Shrek Dobson on steroids. He no doubt used his physical stature as an intimidator. One would think such things didn't matter in the corporate world but, trust me, when it came to interpersonal communication and the way power was bandied about in a business, size definitely mattered.

My eyes were fixed on the behemoth, but I glanced over at Lyria. There was no fear in her eyes. She was looking at him as if he were a stranger passing by on the street. Her expression, if I dare be so bold to decipher it, was a combination of boredom and irritation. The thought came to me that a woman who looked like Lyria had probably dealt with her share of bar louts.

As he got closer, he said, "I'm likin' the way you move out there on the dance floor, baby. Only problem being that you have the wrong partner. Now, why don't you send your little brother here home to play with his toys? Then you can move up the man scale to someone better suited to your needs."

With that charming introduction, King Kong shoved his way between Lyria and me and stood with his elbow on the bar, positioning himself right up in Lyria's face. All I could see was the massive back of his suit jacket. He nudged me backward in the process, and almost knocked me over onto the floor.

I said, "Hey, c'mon mister."

Lyria got out of her chair, took a trek around Mount Obnoxious, calmly reached for my hand, and said, "Come on, Conner. Let's go someplace else."

Gigantor turned around. "Conner? A babe like you bein' with a scrawny little worm is bad enough. But Conner? Hah. Something definitely wrong with that picture." We started to walk away, but the guy grabbed Lyria around the waist. "Hey! I like this song. This'll be perfect for our first dance, don't you think?"

61

Without thinking through what I was doing, I grabbed his left hand. "Let go of her," I yelled.

He looked at me as if he'd forgotten I was there. The drunken glaze in his eyes was suddenly burning with a building fury. He easily reversed my grip, and was now holding my right hand so hard that I almost instantly lost feeling in my fingers. He pulled me close. Even though I was tall, he was towering over me, and was so wide he blocked my view of the rest of the bar. In a quiet voice, he said, "Now look cutesy, or whatever your name is. I'm only gonna say this once. The lady and I would like some privacy. So, I'm expecting you'll be excusing us. Now do what's good for you and go home and play with your toys, or play with yourself, whatever. Just beat it." He pushed me back using my arm as leverage, and I went tumbling out onto the dance floor.

Now that he'd brushed the gnat (me) away, he turned back toward Lyria. From my prone position, she came into view, looking at me, still showing no fear. I guess I had that territory covered for both of us. If anything, her expression of annoyance had gotten more intense.

"It's all right, Conner," she said. Then she addressed the gorilla. "If I have one dance with you, will you promise to leave us alone?"

He yelled, "Atta girl! Protecting your little brother, I like that. C'mon...."

He took her waist again and maneuvered her toward the open floor. A rage came over me that I honestly didn't know I was capable of. Before I knew it, I was charging at the guy without the slightest clue of what I was going to do when I got there. "LET GO OF HER!"

He turned with agility belying his size and grabbed me by my shirt, picking me up off the floor and pulling me to his face. I could feel his hot, boozy-smelling breath as he said, "I told you to FUCK OFF."

With that, he effortlessly hurled me backwards. My butt hit the hard floor first, then my head whipsawed with a sickening thud and I saw stars swimming in front of my eyes. For an indeterminate amount of time, I thought I was at home waking up from a deep sleep to get up and get ready for work.

I shook my head and my reality came into focus. I was dizzy, the room was swirling. I looked up and saw King Kong with a firm grip on Lyria's waist. He was leading her toward the exit, and I heard him say, "Come on, baby. This place is a drag. Let's go someplace where we can be alone."

Lyria was looking back at me. She still didn't look afraid, but she was eyeing me with concern and a visual message that might have been self-generated by my head injury. The message was, "Don't follow."

***

Someone was holding my arm—it was the bartender. He and the waitress were looking at me with concern. "Hey, buddy. You okay? Want me to call an ambulance?"

I sat up and felt like I was going to be sick. But all I could think about was Lyria. I started to get to my feet.

"Easy now, cowboy," said the bartender. "Maybe you'd better just lie still for a bit. Amy?" he called to the waitress. "Get a glass of water. Or do you want another scotch instead?"

"No, no," I slurred. "Help me up. Did you see where they went?"

"Your friend and the big guy? Take some advice, buddy. Let that one go. You're fighting out of your weight class. Or, above your pay grade. Isn't that how you business types put it? There'll be other girls, let that one go."

I managed to stand up and head for the door without hurling all over the shiny little dance floor. I got outside and the fresh air felt good at first, but then I felt dizzy and nauseated again. I looked around for Lyria, but I saw no signs of her or my assailant.

Still apparently not in my right head, I yelled out, "LYRIA" into the night, causing other passersby to eye me warily. I knew something wasn't right, because, hey, I was a financial analyst. We don't yell out loud. Our idea of a rash show of emotion was pounding on the Clear key on our calculators.

I started running, not sure in which direction. The dizziness and nausea were taking on a life of their own. I stopped, leaned down on a beautifully arranged rock garden, and threw up all over it. I was still hunched over when I saw the garden had been set up by a company in Winthrop, and I wondered if Boof was familiar with them.

The mind takes you on strange journeys at times like this.

I thought about getting up and starting to run again, but my new friend Mr. Dizzy Spell had other ideas. I slumped down to the pavement with my back leaning against the wall of the rock garden, and felt myself falling sideways. My last conscious thought was that I probably looked like a homeless guy sleeping one off on the sidewalk. Then everything went black.

CHAPTER EIGHT

I was in the middle of an amazing dream. I was at home, lying on my downstairs sofa. Lyria was sitting on the edge of the couch, her face hovering closely over mine. The dream was remarkably realistic. I could see my sparsely furnished living room in the background. I thought, Geez, at least I could dream up some nice wall hangings, or a decent easy chair. My upscale townhouse had only the minimum amount of fixings to get by.

For some reason, Lyria looked especially beautiful, but her expression was one I hadn't seen before. It looked like concern, and I remember thinking she probably regretted getting involved with a wimpy financial analyst who couldn't protect her from bar bullies. I realized that I had a headache, and it was a doozy. I tried to sit up and got dizzy, with stars swimming in front of my eyes.

"Hey now," said Lyria. Her voice sounded like angels singing. "You just stay where you are, mister. You can fight the world's battles another time."

She put something cold on my forehead and the feeling made me realize that I wasn't dreaming. I was awake. I was home, and Lyria was there with me.

She held the ice-cold compress against my forehead. It felt incredible, and had the effect of numbing some of the pain shooting through my noggin. I thought the relief had something to do with constricting the blood vessels in my head, and I wondered why I was worrying about a diagnosis.

Once a geek, always a geek, I guess.

"Lyria? Are you really here? Tell me I'm not imagining all this."

She smiled. "No, it's real. You have a nasty bump on your head. You need to take it easy for a while. And no more playing tackling dummy for a guy twice your size. Understand?"

"A guy...holy shit...! Uh, sorry. That guy. The bully. What happened? He dragged you out of the bar. I came out looking for you but I couldn't find you. Are you...are you okay?"

"I'm fine. Stop worrying about me. You're the one who's hurt. You probably have a concussion."

"But what happened to King Kong? He didn't...hurt you?"

"No. Like most bullies, he was all talk. I only left with him to get him out of the bar. And away from you. I was afraid he would hurt you even more."

"How did you...how did we get here?"

"I came back and found you out on the ground. You didn't look too good, so I figured I'd better get you home."

"But how? How did you even know where I live? How did you...get me home?"

"Hey, calm. You're not in any shape to be getting up. Just rest. And you're limited to one inquisition per day, and you've already had your chance. We're here and you're safe. Just hold this." She took my hand and put it against the compress on my forehead. Her hand was warm, almost hot to the touch. "I'll make you some tea."

Lyria headed for the kitchen, wearing the same yellow dress. This was the first time I had seen her outside of The Hill since that first night when I saw her in the fog, and I noticed again how she glided when she walked. I thought there couldn't possibly be a more graceful creature on God's green earth.

After a few minutes of pondering life's imponderables, she was at my side with a steaming cup of black tea. I was something of an amateur tea collector and had a wide assortment in my kitchen, but black tea was definitely my favorite. I took a sip and it tasted wonderful.

"Ah. Black tea is my favorite. It's pretty remarkable that you chose this out of all the others."

She beamed again. "I can get lucky at times."

I took another big sip. "I think I'm the lucky one here. It's hard to believe that someone so beautiful could be so...."

"What?"

"So...caring, I guess. And that you could care about me, above everything else."

She reached over and touched her palm against my face. I noticed again how warm her hand was.

"Sweet Conner," she said. "You're worth caring about. You were so brave. Going up against that monster. For me."

I put the teacup down on the floor and reached for her other hand. She was still close, and we were gazing into each other's eyes.

"I've never met anyone like you," I said. "A little while ago... when I first saw you here...I thought I must be dreaming. In a way, the last few days all seem like a dream. I'm having trouble thinking back to the time before I knew you. It's like...none of that even matters anymore."

"See? I told you I felt a connection. And I promise this is not a dream. It's real, and I'll be around as long as you still want me."

She leaned down closer and we were kissing. She sat back up, smiling. "Now, now," she said. "Let's not get all worked up again. There'll be plenty of time for that. Right now, you just need to rest."

I felt groggy and excited all at the same time. Normally I was extremely self-conscious in my dealings with women, like knowing in the back of my mind that it was only a matter of time before I said or did something stupid and scared the girl away. I didn't feel that way around Lyria. It was as if I could be completely natural with her and it would still be okay.

I heard myself ask her, "Could you lie down with me for a while?" I shifted over toward the back of the couch.

"Of course," she said. I heard her drop her shoes to the floor and she swung her legs up. I put my arm around her as she snuggled up next to me. She had her hand on my chest and put her leg up over mine. Her body felt warm and amazing. "Now sleep, sweet Conner," she purred, and before I knew it, I was out.

***

The man watching Conner David's apartment was odd looking, to the point where people moved away from him when passing on the street. He was short but stout, bald, and had huge buck teeth. Glasses with thick frames covered his eyes, which bulged out of his skull and seemed to go off in different directions. In all, if his likeness were drawn up in a cartoon, viewers would have said that his appearance was unrealistic. But this was how he looked, and his biggest problem was staying inconspicuous, as his looks almost invariably drew unwanted attention. He wore dark clothing on this warm October evening, including a black knit hat pulled as far down over his big bald head as it would go.

His name was Mikolaj Babka. He stood a couple of blocks away from Conner's front door, positioning himself downwind, knowing that that scent was an issue. He stood in the shadows of the streetlight at the mouth of an alley, watching the townhouse, occasionally glancing through a small set of binoculars. This certainly wasn't the worst setting he had been in when carrying out these surveillances. She tended to stick to urban areas, and the worst times were in the middle of the summer when city smells became more pungent and he sometimes found himself ankle deep in trash. At least this was an upscale neighborhood.

He leaned up against the building wall to his right and settled in for a long night. Mikolaj knew he would probably be there until shortly before dawn.

CHAPTER NINE

I woke with a start, not knowing what day it was. Then I realized it was Sunday, and I remembered finishing my infernal status report the day before and that I didn't have to go in to the office. The sun was streaming through my living room window behind my couch, and I was surprised. Falling asleep on the sofa was unusual, not to mention that with the strong sun, it must be late morning at least. I sat up and pain skyrocketed through my brain, and the entire prior evening came back in a rush.

"Lyria?" I called out. I remembered falling asleep with her and wondered again whether the whole thing was a dream. I managed to sit up and knocked over my teacup. It had to be real, but Lyria was nowhere to be found. I wondered if she had gotten up and made herself some coffee or tea. I went into the kitchen. "Lyria?" I said again, but there was no sign of her. I checked the bathroom. Nada.

I thought, Geez, she really can be stealthy, and my habitual self doubts came pouring back into my consciousness. Why does she keep disappearing? If she's trying to prove how good she is at it, she's succeeded with flying colors.

With nothing else on my agenda, I laid back down on the couch, this time with the comforting presence of an icepack. I must have dozed off again, because the next thing I knew, the sound of someone knocking on my door brought me around. I looked up and it was after noon, and a thrill ran through me thinking Lyria might have come back.

My living room abutted a short hallway that led to the front of my palace. But when I opened the door, it was a different, but still familiar voice and face that greeted me.

"Hey, big bro. Whoa, you don't look so good. Don't tell me... you were chasing after some blonde and you tripped over your own feet."

"Nice to see you too, Carly. And you should know that I prefer brunettes. Come on in."

Carly David, my little sister, was a frequent visitor. We had always been close, and took great joy in chiding each other the way brothers and sisters could, without causing any harm or hurt feelings. I had plenty of ammunition on my side, because Carly was the youngest in our family, a slender and pretty blonde (hence my crack about brunettes, although it was also true), and spoiled rotten, as I understand happens often with the youngest child. My brother Caden and I used to call her "Barbie" because she looked like the doll. But, we found out the hard way that anyone calling her "Barbie" had better be ready to duck a left hook. Carly saw my living in Boston as an excuse to come to town more often. But she also knew that Mom would want a report on my well being when she got back home.

She spied the icepack in my hand. "Hey, are you really injured? Or just sleeping off a bender? I told you not to hang out with that guy Boof as much. He's enough to make anyone want to drink themselves into a stupor."

"It's nothing serious," I said as we made our way over to the couch. "But your crack about tripping over my own feet was not far from the truth."

I thought this was a way to avoid talking about the whole scene with Lyria and the bully without outright lying to Carly. My clumsiness was well known amongst my siblings and parents, and a frequent subject of familial barbs. But I wondered to myself why I was hesitant to tell my sister about Lyria. Maybe it was because I knew so little about her myself. I could almost hear Carly's line of questioning. "You mean this woman spent the night on your couch and you don't know where she lives? What she does? Or even her last name??" I thought I'd spare myself the discomfort of having to listen to queries for which I clearly had no answers.

"Your place always looks the same," she said as we plopped down on the couch. "Are you sure you even live here? It's always so neat and put together. And you didn't exactly go broke furnishing the place, did you?"

"Well, I'm not here that often. Been working a lot of hours, as usual."

"Yeah? How's the job going, anyway?"

She had raised eyebrows, and I knew where she was headed with this. Carly had always felt — and not without justification — that Dad had pushed me into investment banking, and that it was not a field that I ever would have chosen on my own. After my recent dealings with Shrek, I had to admit to myself that I had my doubts. But I wasn't about to admit that to my little sister.

"It's going okay," I said with as much certainty as I could muster. "Hey, you can't really argue with living on Beacon Hill, right?"

"Oh sure. Anyone can see how you've really taken to the place." She looked around again, and for the first time, I became self-conscious about how few personal touches there were in my townhouse. Oh, it had the perfunctory furniture and all, but there were no pictures, memento's, bowling trophies, or anything else that would indicate that Conner David lived here. If Spider and Vape broke in, they'd probably think it was some corporate owned property where a top executive could sneak off for a quickie with his secretary at lunchtime.

"How are Mom and Dad doing?" I asked, trying desperately

to change the subject.

"Oh, they never change," said Carly. "Dad plays golf like six times a week now. He'd probably go for seven, but Mom still guilts him into church on Sunday. Mom stays busy with her knitting, lunch crew, and book club. She's always off to some function or another. God, I hope I never end up like them."

"Why? It seems like they've reached that comfort zone where they're doing what they like to do. They live in suburban heaven, they both have hobbies. They're not hanging around the house driving each other crazy. Sounds like a decent setup to me."

"Ahh. Guys just don't get it. Mom and Dad have no relationship. It's like their worse fear would be if they ever had to spend time with each other. They'd probably just sit there with nothing to talk about, counting the minutes until cocktail hour. I'd like to think that when I get married and we get old, we'll want to grow old together, you know? Do stuff together. Mom and Dad are like strangers living in the same house."

"Speaking of you," I said, and she looked at me, knowing what was coming. "How's the current love of your life doing? What's this one's name? Brett?"

"Brent. With an 'N.' And he's not the love of my life. We've only gone out a few times."

Carly became somewhat tense, which I had rarely seen before. She was wearing an expensive-looking pair of jeans and a long-sleeved sweater. She always looked perfect, never a hair out of place. But now, she was definitely frazzled.

"Sorry. It just seems like every guy you go out with falls in love with you. But, all kidding aside, is everything okay with this guy?"

"Yes. Well...okay...not really. I don't know. I've seen some red flags recently. I read this article about control freaks in Cosmo. You know, what to look for to see if your guy is one? That type of article. And it's like they must have interviewed Brent to write the piece. He has like every symptom."

"Cosmo, huh? Well, at least you're getting your information from a reputable source."

"Very funny."

"Sorry, just trying to keep things light. What's this guy doing that's got you worried?"

"He...like...always wants to know my business. Wants to know where I've been every minute of the day. He doesn't like it when I go out with my friends. Last week, I was going to a concert at TD Gardens with Beth and Amy. It wasn't starting 'til late, so he asked if we could have dinner first. I didn't really want to, but I agreed. So we drove downtown. He was going to drop me off at the Garden afterwards. We're having dinner and he's eating very slowly. It was like watching a film in super slow motion. I was already done and ready to go, and he's like a third of the way through his steak. So the time's ticking away and I kept checking the time, hoping he'd get the hint to speed it up, but he kept raising a piece up and chewing and savoring, and then sitting back and taking deep breaths as if he hadn't eaten in a month. It was almost time for the concert to start and the act was still going on. It took every ounce of strength I had to keep from crowning this idiot with my dinner plate. Or grabbing his steak knife and plunging it into his chest.

"I was trying to be polite, but I finally burst and said, y'know, something like, 'Brent it's getting late. Is there something wrong? Like, why are you eating so goddamn slow?' He just smirks and says that he's trying to lose weight, and he read somewhere that if you eat real slow, it keeps your metabolism from speeding up to digest the food. That sounded like bullshit to me, so then it dawned on me that this was just a plot to keep me from going to the concert with my friends, which he didn't want me to do anyway. He figured I'd be too polite to leave him sitting there chewing away and go grab a cab to the concert. And, sure enough, it worked. By the time he finished, it felt like another ice age had passed and it was too late to go. Of course, I'd shut off my phone for dinner, but when I turned it on, there were like a thousand texts from Beth and Amy asking where the fuck I was. Long story short, I missed the concert. When he got to our house, I stormed out of the car without saying a word. Later that night he was calling my phone, leaving messages saying how sorry he was and that he really cared about me, blah blah blah."

"Geez. Why don't you just break it off with the guy?"

"I'm going to. It's just hard for me. You know how I don't like hurting people. And we've had some good times before. I keep telling myself that this is just a phase and that he'll get more used to me and figure that he can trust me, and everything will get better. But...the other thing is...."

"What?"

"No, never mind, it's probably nothing."

"Come on, Carly. I'm invoking the big brother clause. Tell me what you were going to say."

"Well, I think he's...stalking me."

Now she really had my attention. "Stalking you? You mean online?"

"No. In person. The other day, I got out of work at the boutique and I thought I saw his car. But I looked back and it was gone. I stopped over at Beth's on the way home. We were upstairs at her house and she went to go to the bathroom, and I just casually looked out the window and saw what looked like his car at the end of Beth's road. I ran downstairs—I was going to run out and confront the jerk—but when I went crashing out the front door, he drove off. Beth came running down after me, looking at me like my glue had come completely undone. I told her what happened and she went white. She insisted on driving behind me when I went home. I know he'd never try anything at home, not with Dad around. He's enough to scare the feathers off a bird. But now I find myself looking over my shoulder wherever I go. It took me twice as long as normal to get here today. I kept taking quick turns to see if anyone was following me. That's what they do in spy movies, right? Almost caused a few accidents, but I was pretty sure I was alone."

"I don't like it, Carl. Maybe you should call the police."

"They won't do anything until after I've been kidnapped, raped, and murdered. Wonderful system we've got here, isn't it? No, don't worry, I'm sure he won't try anything. I can handle Brent. Knowing him, he'll just call for a date and act as if nothing has happened. He'll get an earful from me for sure. So, you got any prospects you're working on? Any hot brunettes waiting in the wings?"

I laughed and my mind immediately went to Lyria. "No. Nothing really."

"Just exactly who do you think you're talking to? Your eyes just lit up like Times Square on New Year's Eve. Spill it, Conner. Who is she?"

I laughed again. "Okay, well, I met a woman at The Hill. But I know nothing about her. Probably won't come to anything."

"Okay, the first thing you need to do is get out of The Hill. A chance meeting in a bar is one thing, but it does nothing for a continuing relationship. Call her and take her someplace else. Anyplace else. Bar relationships are just...boozy. And they never last."

I sat looking at my hands.

Carly asked, "You do have her number, don't you?"

I just looked at her. She rolled her eyes.

"I love you dearly, bro. But you are truly hopeless. What are you going to do, keep showing up at The Hill, hoping you'll meet her again?"

I didn't answer, but I thought I didn't really have any alternatives. So that was exactly what I was going to do.

Carly moved over next to me and took my hand. "Conner, the look on your face just now tells me this girl is something special to you. If that's the case, you have to build a relationship with her. Take her out to dinner. Go to the movies. Go for a drive up the coast. Anything but having a nightly contest to see who can get pickled the fastest."

"You're right. I've...I've only seen her there twice. But you are right. I'll ask her to do something else the next time I see her."

Carly's eyes lit up and I instinctively knew what was coming next.

"Hey," she said. "Why don't we double?"

"Take me now, Lord."

"I'm serious. It would help both of us. I do see some good qualities in Brent, but he always ends up acting like a Neanderthal. But he couldn't possibly misbehave with my brother there. It'll be a chance for me to see if there's any hope or whether I should just give him the boot. And you could get your girl out of that beer joint. Find out if she's still such a goddess when you're sober. What do you think?"

"I think I should move and not leave a forwarding address."

"Come on. You know I'm right. I'm always right. Make it for this Friday."

I sat thinking for a minute, Carly looking at me with great expectations. I had to admit, her plan made sense.

"Okay. I'll see what I can do and let you know."

"That's my big bro. What would you do without me around to point out all your faults and deficiencies?"

I laughed. Carly always had that effect on me. She could make me laugh no matter what kind of mood I was in.

We hugged briefly on the couch and she got up to head home. We said our goodbyes and she stopped at the door.

"Don't forget. Friday night. Let me know," she said.

"I'm sure you wouldn't let me forget, but don't worry. I

77

promise I'll ask the next time I see her."

Then I opened the door, half expecting to see Lyria out on the sidewalk. She wasn't.

"Whenever that might be," I said.

**

After Carly left, I still had a headache that could kill an elephant, so I laid back down on the sofa. I was worried about this nutcase boyfriend of Carly's. I'd heard about these control freak psychos who would go to any length to ensure that their women stayed with them and nobody else. I didn't think it could hurt to meet this guy, although with my appearance, I don't think there would be much of an intimidation factor.

I also thought about Lyria. I know, big surprise there, right? I wondered where she was right at that moment. What was she doing? Who was she with? Where in holy hell was she?

I got a fresh icepack and laid back down. Next thing I knew, it was Monday morning and time to go to work. Oh joy! My internal alarm clock woke me up and I was still very groggy, but my shower and coffee made me feel like a viable human being again, so it was a pop of Advil and I was off. Shrek didn't allow people to call in sick. Whenever the subject came up, his familiar refrain was along the lines of, "I've never called in sick once in my entire career, so if you don't feel good, suck it up and get your butt in here." Being at the low end of the totem pole in an investment banking company, we were regularly subjected to this kind of abuse, and there wasn't a blessed thing we could do about it—except get our jollies among our peers by making up insane ways to do in our boss, none of which, of course, would ever come to fruition.

Thankfully, the office was quiet at the onset of the day. Any loud noises probably would have caused me to try to close my head in my top desk drawer. I actually thought it was unusually quiet. My group normally took some time to debrief on what everybody did for the weekend. Then it hit me. Shrek was no doubt reviewing all our status reports, also known as his attempt to ruin our days off. My compadres were all nervously awaiting his verdict. I would have been too, but my brain was not yet fully functional.

I tried not to think about Shrek as I plugged away on one of my current projects. All of our work was intended to be of equal importance, but we all knew differently. One of the many factors we would be evaluated on was our ability to prioritize our workload, and although we got little to no direction on which jobs were the most important, it was well known that we should knock out the ones that could potentially make the most money for the company. And how were we to know that, one might ask? Well, we were financial analysts, right? The first task we undertook when given a new assignment was to evaluate its earnings potential so we would know how much time to spend on it.

Likewise, our most important jobs would always be listed first on our status reports. Failure to do so would bring about a Shrek tirade in front of your peers and friends, a little slice of heaven we could all do without.

I was working pretty steadily, the pain in my head subsiding, when I had a sudden urge to talk to Vicky. With all the craziness over the weekend, I had forgotten about our conversation on Saturday — and the kiss on my cheek. I thought, Lyria must be having some impact on me if that slipped my mind. There was a time, not very long ago, where that kiss would have represented a seminal moment in my life.

I tiptoed over to the opening in my cube and checked to see if the coast was clear. I felt like a teenager sneaking out of his house after curfew. I figured everybody else was still cowering in their offices, as the little hallway between our cubes was empty. I grabbed a document off my desk. It had absolutely nothing to do with Vicky, but I wanted it to look like I was visiting to discuss a business issue.

I crept over and had to remind myself to breathe. I whispered, "Hey Vi—"

I stopped short when Vicky looked up. I was shocked by her appearance. She looked extremely pale, her hair was disheveled, and she had bags under her eyes that almost extended to her nose. Now, understand, it was a shock because Vicky Temerlin always looked totally put-together. She didn't come off as a person who slaved endlessly on her looks, but she had this natural look of beauty that never wavered. Even dressed casually on weekends, she always looked sensational.

"Vicky?" I said in a regular voice, no longer conscious of being busted by Shrek. "How...how are you feeling? Is everything okay?"

She seemed mildly perturbed by the questions. "Yes. Fine." Then it appeared that she became aware of sounding short. "Sorry, Conner. I'm okay. How are you? How was your weekend?"

"It was good," I said, thinking, aside from the assault and concussion.

"Is there something you need?"

"Oh, um, no, nothing specific. I just stopped in to say hi. Seems like everyone's waiting for the shoe to drop on our status reports."

She managed a weak smile. "Yes. I didn't even hear the twins compare notes on their weekends. That's very rare."

I laughed a little harder than I should have. "Yeah. Then again, they talk on the phone about a dozen times between Saturday and Sunday anyway. So there are probably no surprises."

She chuckled, which was good to see. She said, "Heck, even Boof didn't come in to check out what I was wearing today. Talk about rare."

We both had a laugh. "Well, guess I'd better get back. Sure

you're all right?"

"Yes. Do I look that bad?"

"Oh...no, of course not. You just look...tired, is all."

She thought for a few seconds. "Yeah. I guess I am a little tired. I don't know from what though. I didn't do much since Saturday evening. Felt pretty weak yesterday, and spent most of the day in bed watching reruns on TV. How's that for a hot social life? Hope I'm not coming down with something. I'd hate to be the first person in history to use a sick day in the Financial Analysis Department."

"Nah. Probably just the Monday morning blues. Personally, I think Monday should be outlawed."

"I agree," she laughed. "Thanks, Conner. See you at lunch?"

"You bet." I felt better after seeing Vicky cheer up a bit, turned to make a beeline back to my cube, and walked right into Shrek. Since he was about twice as wide as me, the impact sent me stumbling back a few steps. Shrek didn't budge an inch.

He held up some paper that I realized with dismay was my status report.

"Huh," he said. "Judging from this report, I'm surprised you have time to socialize, David. My office. Five minutes."

***

When I first started at BHA, there were a number of stories floating around about what made Darren Dobson, aka Shrek, ascend to the heights of asshole-ness that he had achieved. Most of the reasons bandied about were clearly just mean-spirited, the result of ire, frustration, and an ever-dangerous habit of alcohol-fueled mutual consolation at The Hill after a long week of work. Some of the more outrageous possibilities, which I discounted right away for lack of conceivable proof, were that he had been dropped on his head as a child, that he was really a plant from a competing investment banking firm determined to drive away all the local talent, and that he was frustrated because his desired sexual proclivity of inter-species intercourse (with dogs) was generally frowned upon by society.

I had discussed the subject with Larry Berman, the married member of our analysis group who had the most tenure with the company. Larry was always the contemplative type. Before speaking, he sat back and carefully thought through the issue. All that was missing was a pipe. I remember thinking that he even looked like Chauncy Stillwell, his twin with whom he hung around incessantly.

He told me a much more believable story. He said that Shrek was the product of an ultra-competitive environment when BHA first started up.

"You think we have it bad now," Larry had said. "When these companies first start up, there are no ongoing jobs to support a regular revenue stream. All the clients are new, and there are inevitably some spans of weeks and even months where there is no money coming in. And, of course, there are still bills to be paid. So you have these mega-ambitious guys heading up the fledgling firm banging on your door every morning wanting to know how much money you brought in that day."

"So, Shrek was started out doing what we're doing?" I asked. "He was a financial analyst?"

"Sure. Everybody has to start somewhere."

"I know. But it's just so hard to imagine."

"I understand that he actually wasn't that great of an analyst. The brass just looked at him as an ass-kicker, someone who could whip the troops into shape. Dobson looks at it like he paid his dues to move up the ladder. And he'll be damned if he'll allow any one else to do so before they pass muster with him," said Larry.

"You might think that someone who worked under such brutal conditions would try to make it easier for his charges. Especially now that the company is so well established, and stable financially. You know, kind of like a father who is raised poor and wants his kids to have everything that he didn't have growing up."

"Yeah." Larry thought about that for a minute. "Then again, maybe there's something to that sex with dogs theory...."

All of these thoughts were running rampant in my mind as I waited in my cube to go see The Man. As I left Vicky's cube, she had given me a "You poor schmuck" look, and I went back to check over my status report to try and anticipate Shrek's assault. I knew his wanting five minutes to start the meeting was just a ploy to build up my anticipation of the beating I was about to take, and I had to admit, it was effective. As I mentioned before, Shrek took particular pleasure in coming down on me. He looked at me as a child of privilege who got his plum job with such a great company because of his daddy pulling some strings. This was essentially true. I had immediately felt his anger as soon as I joined the firm. And I knew for sure that I wasn't imagining matters getting worse when he found out I had a big-bucks townhouse within walking distance of the office.

The time came, and I walked slowly over to his office and knocked on the doorframe. He lifted his chin up quickly, indicating the chair in front of his desk. I thought, this is gonna be bad. I didn't even get a "Come in."

Dobson's office was a little like my home. It was an enclosed square about twelve by twelve. It was neat as a pin, but there was very little personalization. No diplomas, unnecessary tchotchke, or pictures of Mrs. Shrek. There was a small conference table in the corner, and two chairs directly in the line of fire in front of his desk. Among my coworkers, these chairs were known as "the place where analysts go to die."

I sat down as Shrek continued feigning interest in an unrelated document. He was going for maximum impact, extending my discomfort for as long as possible. He eventually put the paper down in a pile and looked up at me as if just realizing that I was there.

"Ah yes. David," he said, picking up my status report. All his underlings were on a last-name basis except Vicky. He called her "Ms. Temerlin." "I can't rate this report as 'bad.' I can't even say, 'poor.' How about 'piss-poor?'"

He let that hang in the air for a while, and since he didn't ask me a question, I just sat silently.

"Do you understand the importance of the Simmons-Haverstein merger to Beacon Hill Associates?" he asked.

"Yes, I believe so."

"You believe so? You mean you're not sure?"

"No. I mean.... No sir. I'm sure. It's a very important deal to the company. I know that."

"So, you're not intentionally trying to kill it, right?"

"Intentionally trying to kill it? No." I almost said, "Why do you ask?" But that's like asking to get whipped with barbed wire instead of a belt.

"Well then, I'm wondering why your projected revenue of the conglomerate is lower than that of the two discrete companies combined."

"Oh. Well, they do have some overlapping businesses. And each firm is so large that I assumed some would have to be sold off to keep the FTC from killing the merger for anti-trust reasons."

Shrek just sat there glaring at me. We both knew that it was a valid assumption. And I was sure he hadn't expected me to come up with it.

After what seemed like an eternity, he asked, "Why are your projected operating costs so low? You expect me to bring an unrealistic profitability projection to senior management? If this deal goes forward based on this piece of shit and the income comes in at half what's shown here, you and your little friends will all be out working at McDonald's. Which is probably where you belong."

I came close to asking, "Really? Hey, do you think they have an employee discount on Quarter Pounders?" But I managed to keep that to myself.

I said, "I projected some operating cost benefits from synergies between the two raw material buying organizations. If they can make one big purchase instead of two mid-sized buys, they should be eligible for a discount from the suppliers."

More staring. Shrek's face was taking on the tint of the wild cherry Nerds that I liked to snack on.

"Why didn't you do a 'worst-case' scenario?"

I was getting a little bold now that I realized he didn't have much ammunition. "I did. But you've always only wanted our 'most-likely' scenarios in our status reports. Just following your directions, sir." That sounded a little more smarmy than I intended.

At that point, Shrek looked about ready to leap up over his desk and lunge for my throat. When he spoke again, his words were virtually hissed through clenched teeth. "You really think you're smart, huh? How about you never mind what I've asked for in the past and get what I want now?" He threw my report across his desk. "Now take this piece of shit back and add a table of summary results for your 'best-case,' 'most-likely,' and 'worst-case' scenarios. Get going."

Shrek then plunged back into his pile of paper and I got up to leave. I almost said, "You have a nice day now," on my way out of his office, but I thought that would have been pushing my luck.

And it was clear that when it came to my dealings with Mr. Darren Dobson, I was going to need all the luck I could get.

**

Turned out, my meeting with Shrek was only a precursor to what turned out to be an extremely long and very bad day.

Apparently, after I left, Dobson called Boof in to review his status report. For all of his, shall we say, "interpersonal issues," Boof's financial projections were usually spot on, and it was rare that Shrek could find much fault. But I heard the boss's door close and a bit later, it opened and Shrek went storming away, grumbling loudly. I caught something about him needing to hang a "Slow, Children" sign at the end of our hallway.

Boof appeared in my doorway and his face was ashen.

"Thanks a lot, Conner," he said.

"What? What happened?"

"You tell me. Whatever went on with you and Shrek really got him tuned up for the rest of us. What'd you do, pee in his Cheerios?"

"Hey, there wasn't much I could do. You know he's always had a hair across his ass for me. He started picking apart my status report, and got pissed off when I actually had answers for his stupid questions. What did he say to you?"

"Just think of every swear word insult you can and it probably came up at one point. I think my favorite was 'incompetent oversexed dwarf.' That one hit home. He didn't really bring up any business issues. I just think whoever follows you into Shrek's office should be prepared to get their ass eaten out."

"I heard him stomp off. I wonder where he went."

"Maybe he went down to the gym to work his frustrations off. Or home to take it out on Mrs. Dobson. Or maybe he has a place where he can go throw darts at a picture of you."

I snorted. "Yeah. Maybe."

"So, now down to more important business," said Boof. "What's your strategy in seeking out that hotty from the other night? You got any plans?"

I really didn't want to discuss Lyria with Boof. Couldn't possibly see what good could come of that. "No, Boof. No plans. I'm not an expert in non-verbal signals, but it occurs to me that ditching me at the bar seems like a loud and clear expression of disinterest."

"Hey, I know what you're going through, man. But, that was a Grade A prime babe you had there. You're probably wondering why this complete babeaholic would be interested in a skinny, bookwormy nerd loser like you in the first place, am I right?"

"Well, I didn't exactly think in those terms, Boof, but thanks for crystallizing it for me."

"No problem." Boof was definitely sarcasm-challenged. "But, you shouldn't just give it up. I'm telling you, man, there's a time-honored reason why you two might match up despite being on opposite ends of the looks and coolness scales. You want me to tell you what it is?"

"If I say no, is there any chance you won't tell me anyway?"

"No. I think you need to hear this."

"That's what I thought. Okay, go ahead. Hit me with it."

"The answer is, who knows why?"

"That's the answer? Sounded more like a question."

"No, what I mean is, some gorgeous babes will only go for the GQ types, right? She's clearly not one of them." I just hung my head as Boof went on. "Some will actually go for little fat guys with big glasses. Not enough of those kinds of girls around in my personal opinion, but they're out there. And others just want their own skinny little doofus. The Lord works in mysterious ways, Conner. And when we come across a gorgeous doll who, for whatever weird reason, goes against type and seems to have an achin' for our bacon, we shouldn't tie ourselves up in knots wondering why, or how it possibly could have happened. We should just go with it and take full advantage before she comes to her senses."

"I don't know if I should feel better or go lay across a railroad track somewhere."

"Think about it. You'll realize that I'm right."

"You think about this a lot, don't you, Boof?"

"Sure. What else am I gonna think about? Depreciation rates and discounted cash flow projections? That's some boring shit, man. Well, guess I better get back. According to Shrek, I 'wouldn't know a good financial projection if it came up and bit me in the ass.' So looks like I still have to spiff up my current projects some."

After Boof left, I spent some time spiffing up my current projects as well. We all took lunch back to our desks. Around mid-afternoon, I still didn't hear Shrek, and figured he was out partaking of whatever stress relief he had devised as a result of our meeting. I moseyed back over to Vicky's cube to see how she was doing, but she wasn't in. At first I thought maybe she had just gone to the ladies' room, but it looked like her desk had been cleaned off. Had she actually left work early? That was almost as unheard of as calling in sick. Stillwell walked by on his way to the copier.

"Hey Chauncy, have you seen Vicky this afternoon?"

"She headed out a while ago. She didn't look very good. Think she probably just called it a day."

I nodded and went back to my cubbyhole, thinking, Geez. I meet this incredible woman who keeps pulling disappearing acts on me. Vicky gives me a peck on the cheek, and comes in the next Monday looking like death warmed over.

One thing Boof had said definitely made sense. The Lord truly does work in mysterious ways.

Chapter Ten

It was a little past seven when I wrapped up and headed on out. I was dog-tired, but at least my headache had finally subsided. It was unseasonably warm for an October evening in Boston, and I again realized how lucky I was to be able to walk home and not have to deal with the nightly traffic nightmares of people who commuted from the burbs.

I came to a cross street where taking a right would take me home and a left would head me toward The Hill. I hesitated. I surely didn't want a drink tonight, but I wondered if The Hill was the only place I was going to see Lyria again. I knew my sister was right. If the relationship was only based on meeting in a bar, then there wasn't much substance to it. On the other hand, what was my alternative? I didn't have her phone number. I didn't even know her last name, so I couldn't look it up. I shook my head, turned right, and headed home, my mind whirling, not knowing how to proceed. Here I was, a young, urbane professional, a college graduate with a good job, a well-to-do family, and an awesome place to live. But I felt like a hapless teenager with a crush on the head cheerleader.

My mental state didn't get any better once I got home. I heated up a tasteless frozen dinner, then restlessly went in search of something to help pass the time before I could finally go to bed and pray for unconsciousness. Tried reading a book. No good. My eyes were just scanning the pages, not taking in the words.

Turned on the TV. Mindlessly flipped through the channels, but nothing was striking my fancy. How could there be so many damn stations and nothing to watch? I had some work I had brought home, but the thought of looking at that about made me want to stick one of my mechanical pencils into my eye and hope that it hit my brain.

"A walk," I said to myself. "I definitely need a walk."

I quickly laced up my walking shoes, threw on a windbreaker, and headed out. I realized it was my first walk since I'd encountered Lyria and the druggies. It made sense to retrace my steps. Maybe Lyria walked the same route every night. Then I realized that I had been completely lost that night because of the fog. So I roamed the hilly streets of Beacon Hill without a specific destination in mind. After seemingly walking for an eternity, I thought I had covered the entire Beacon Hill area, and even wandered into downtown Boston for a bit. On the upside, I didn't get robbed. But on the downside, there was no sign of Lyria. By the time I headed home, I was just as frustrated as when I had left.

I got into my townhouse and my feelings came to a boil, and I let out a wail. It was so unlike me that I felt self-conscious and didn't end up yelling with all my might.

"I can't even get that right," I said to the walls.

I flopped down face first onto my couch, grabbed a couple of throw pillows, and held them against the sides of my head.

I laid there for a while and must have dozed off, pillows still in place. I was walking down the aisle in a church, my bride holding onto my arm. I looked over at her and her veil was covering her face, so I kept walking. The aisle seemed to stretch on forever. We were almost to the front. Reverend O'Malley, my pastor when I was a child, was waiting for us. I looked at my bride again and realized I didn't know who she was—her face was still covered. The reverend was looking at me expectantly, as if there was something I was supposed to be doing. I thought, Well, what I really want to do is find out whom I'm marrying. I looked back at my mother, father, sister Carly, and my brother Caden. They were looking up from the front pews. I sensed they wanted to know the bride's identity as well. I turned back and reached for her veil, but I hesitated. "Go ahead, Conner," said Reverend O'Malley. So, I started lifting the veil, but stopped when the church bells started ringing loudly. Everybody in the church looked up, as if the bells were coming from the heavens. I rose slowly to consciousness, and was confused because the bells were still ringing. It took me a moment to realize that it was my front doorbell. Someone was ringing my doorbell.

I had no concept of time as I got up off the couch and headed for the door. My mind had cobwebs that could stop a semi in its tracks, and without thinking, I opened the door. Then my eyes were wide open and I was suddenly awake and alert as I was face-to-face with the late-night visitor on my front walk.

"Hello, Conner," said Lyria.

***

My mind might have been activated, but my mouth still wouldn't quite function.

"Lyria! Holy...I mean, wow. I, uh, didn't come you were knowing...I mean—"

"Ah, still my silver tongued little smooth talker, I see."

"Hah, yeah. Some things never change. I had just dozed off and.... Anyway, I'm really glad to see you."

"Conner, honey?"

"Yes?"

"Do you think I might be able to come in?"

"Come in? Oh! Yes, of course. What a great idea. Sorry. Please."

I moved aside and Lyria glided in. I thought at some point I'd have to ask her how she moved so smoothly. It was as if she didn't even displace air. Her presence had its typical impact on me. She was wearing a dress as usual. It had bright floral colors and fit her perfectly, accentuating her killer figure. Her long brown hair was flowing around her shoulders, and she smelled like heaven on earth. I had to remind myself not to stare.

"Hope I'm not stopping by too late," she said. "I didn't want to come over last night—I figured you needed time to rest from Saturday."

"Saturday? Oh yeah. Lyria...I'm really sorry...."

"Sorry? About what?"

"Well, I didn't do much to...keep that guy away from you. I wish I had been able to...I don't know...do more."

Lyria smiled and came over, putting her arms around my neck. I'm tall and gangly, so I still had a slight height advantage.

"Conner," she said. "I thought you were very brave." I put my hands gently on her waist and my heart about stopped in its tracks. "You stepped right in. That guy was nothing but a big oaf. And he hurt you. But you still came out looking for me. Not saying it was the smartest move, but you shouldn't feel like you could have done more. There was nothing more you could have done."

We were close, looking into each other's eyes. I moved forward and we kissed. It felt so natural. Usually, I tied myself up in knots worrying about whether the girl wanted me to kiss her. Sometimes it took so long, the girl would lose interest and walk away, saying something like, "Sorry, but I have to go graduate from college." But with Lyria, it just happened. And happened again. She was smiling.

"Here," she said, taking my hand and walking over to the couch. "I woke you up. You sit back down and I'll go fix you a cup of tea."

I just smiled back. "That sounds great."

"I know black tea is your favorite, but do you want to try

something different? How about regular, herbal, or chai latte?"

"Those are my other favorites. How did you know?"

"I took it upon myself to peruse your kitchen the other night. Typical single man. If we got stuck here for any length of time, all I can say is we'd both better like Cocoa Puffs."

I laughed and said, "A chai latte would be great."

As she headed off to the kitchen, my head lolled back on the couch. I felt that any second, I was going to wake up and discover that this whole thing had been a dream. My subconscious had conjured up the perfect female, and she actually liked me. It was the only logical conclusion—I was dreaming. I thought back to what Boof had said, and was instantly worried that I was harking back to anything that Boof had said. Essentially, the Lord works in mysterious ways and there's no accounting for taste. It seemed that Lyria was into tall, skinny, bookwormy types, and that I had been in the right place at the right time.

Then I thought, Well, what the heck. If it is a dream, I'm going to soak it for all it's worth.

Lyria floated on back over with a steaming cup of tea. I noticed she was holding the round body of the cup, extending the handle to me. I took it and the cup felt burning hot. "Wow," I said, taking her hand. "Didn't you get burned?" Her hand felt normally warm.

She sat next to me. "No, it's not very far from the kitchen. So, I know you went to work today, even though you probably have a concussion. How did you feel? Tell me everything that happened."

I forgot about the cup looking at her amazing face. Normally, I would think this was pure lip service. How could anyone want to hear about a financial analyst's day? But she seemed genuinely interested.

"Well, okay. Do you want to get some tea for yourself? Might help keep you awake hearing about my day."

"No thank you. I'm good."

"How about coffee? I have coffee too."

"Oh, I know. We'll have a choice of coffee or tea to wash down our Cocoa Puffs."

Unbelievably, it seemed that Lyria had yet another quality that I really liked. She was sarcastic.

"So, did you feel all right this morning?" she asked.

"Yes. Overall I felt like a viable human being. Plus, I'm not really allowed to call in sick."

"What? Why not?"

"Well, my boss is kind of a mix between Mussolini and Attila the Hun. I told you a little about him before. Remember? We were going to trick him into an amorous evening to put him in a better mood?"

"Ah, yes. Shrek, right?"

I laughed. "Yeah. Shrek. Anyway, his philosophy on work attendance is that unless you're on your deathbed or you've lost a limb, you'd better get your butt into work. Actually, make that two limbs. If you only lost one leg, you could learn to hop. And if I lost my right arm, he'd call me 'Lefty' and expect me to work my computer one-handed."

"So, if you get the flu, he just wants you to come in and spread the germs around? Won't that just lead to others getting sick and calling in?"

"No. From his perspective, he doesn't care if we're all sick, he still expects us to be there. And not miss any deadlines."

"Goodness. That environment can't be much fun. I hope they pay you handsomely to make up for it."

I laughed. "Not really. We're just analysts. It's an entry-level tier on the org chart. We make our work lives tolerable by ragging on each other and making up sick plots about Shrek." I hesitated. I thought that I shouldn't have admitted to Lyria that I didn't make that much money. Suppose Boof was right? There

I go again, referencing Boof in my mind. I have to start hanging out with the other guys more. He told me that my abode alone would make women think I was better off than I really was. What if Lyria's inexplicable interest in me disappeared now that I'd admitted that if I were on my own, I couldn't afford the closet of a basement apartment on Beacon Hill?

She said, "I admire you for getting along like you do." She was right up next to me on my left. She crossed her left leg over her right and leaned in close, putting a hand on my left shoulder. "So you went to work," she continued. "You must have had a whopper of a headache."

"I did. Plus Shrek sought me out to bust me on my status report. I had turned it in on Saturday evening, before—"

"Yes, I know before what. So why did he harass you about your report? I'm sure it was very good."

I laughed a little and shook my head, thinking, Please don't wake up. This is too good to be true.

"I thought the report was good. But Shrek seems to have a particular dislike for me."

I thought I was imagining it at the time, but Lyria's eyes seemed to darken and her vivacious smile went away.

"Why would that be?" she asked.

"Don't get me wrong. He mistreats everyone. But my team all agrees that when it comes to abusing analysts, I'm the apple of his eye. I think he sees me as a child of privilege, and that bothers him. See, my father helped get me my job with BHA."

I half expected her to clap her hands, say "Okay, I'm done here," and bail out the door. But she stayed where she was, so I went on.

"And Shrek knows that I live in this townhouse on Beacon Hill, which no analyst could ever afford on their own. Heck, even he couldn't afford it on his salary. So he has a strong degree of resentment towards me. He feels that I haven't paid my dues and didn't earn my way there, like he had to. I have to be honest, I agree with him to a certain extent, but I don't think it warrants the way he treats me. My first boss at BHA was a saint, and he knew all these things too. But it means I have to work harder than everyone else, and...."

"What? Tell me."

"It seems like no matter what I do it isn't good enough. And frankly, he isn't the brightest guy ever. Today, he wanted to bust my chops about my report and he picked on a couple of assumptions that are pretty fundamental. When I told him my reasons, he didn't even have a comeback. I think he gets his jollies rousting me, and when I prove him wrong, it about sends him into orbit."

Lyria looked like she was thinking deeply, and I wondered whether she was having doubts about taking up with such a crybaby.

"Anyway, I really shouldn't complain," I said, hoping to break that train of thought. "I have a great job and a great place to live. I can put up with a myopic boss. Plus, now...."

The brilliant smile was back. "That's right Conner. Now you have me."

I reached over and took her left hand.

"And don't ever make apologies for your place in life," she said. "All someone can do is be the best person they can with what they've got. And I think you turned out pretty good."

Even being the numbnut that I was, I knew the timing was right. I put the tea down and leaned over and we kissed.

And kissed again. And again. I had like zero make out experience, so I didn't know if tongue was appropriate. I had the horrible thought that I might have to ask Boof for more advice.

As if reading my mind, during our next kiss, she probed my mouth lightly with her tongue. Then we were full out. My high school French teacher would have been proud.

What Lyria did next will stay with me forever. She got up, hiked up the skirt of her dress, and straddled my legs, facing me, resting on my lap. "I want to get a little closer," she said.

And the kissing got even hotter. My heart was pounding in my chest, and I said a little prayer to myself. I was like, "Please Lord, if you're going to let my heart burst, just wait a little while longer."

My hands were on her waist and I slowly moved them up. In addition to being off-the-scale excited, I was also terrified that I was doing too much. That I wasn't doing enough. That I didn't know what I was doing. I knew the last part was definitely true.

Lyria certainly didn't stop me as my mitts headed north. If anything, the kissing got hotter. I lightly brushed her amazing breast with my left hand and she moaned. So encouraged, I squeezed a little tighter, hoping that I wouldn't pass out. Lyria sat back, running her fingers through the side of my hair.

"Just like a real girl, huh?" she said. I assumed that meant that she was aware of the godly pedestal on which I already had her firmly perched.

I said, "I'm sorry, Lyria. I hope I'm not being.... I mean, I don't really have a lot of experience...."

I dropped my hand, but she quickly took it and put it back where it had been. "No apologies," she said.

I had completely lost any sense of time, so I can't say whether it was a few minutes or a few hours later, but she broke our embrace again.

"You know, Mr. Conner David, you haven't been a very good host."

"What? Why? Do you need something? Want something? Anything...I'll do anything."

She laughed. "No, I only meant that you haven't showed me the rest of your place. Isn't your bedroom upstairs?"

I gasped and felt like I inhaled enough air to fill up the

Goodyear Blimp. "My bedroom? Upstairs? Yes, I think so. I mean, yes...I know so. Yes, it's definitely upstairs."

She laughed again, stood up, and took my hand. "Well, I think we should go check it out. Come on."

At that very moment she could have walked off a cliff and I would have gladly followed. But there were no cliffs in sight. Lyria and I were headed upstairs.

***

Most men's perception of the perfect female body is probably from the surreal images of Victoria's Secret models. Or maybe the Sports Illustrated Swimsuit Issue. Of course, these women all have the built-in advantages of thousand-dollar-an-hour makeup artists, top-of-the-line glossy photography, and professional air brushers. I'm here to tell you that Lyria had them all beat. And she was there, with me. This was no dream, it was real.

She masterfully guided me through our first time, for which I was eternally grateful.

"Sorry," I said. "That was really quick."

"No apologies," she said. "We'll get better with practice. Trust me. Oh, and Conner?"

"Yes?"

"The next practice session will start in a few minutes."

Chapter Eleven

Detective Grace Garvey had advanced in the Boston Police Department where so many other women before her had not, and she knew she had one personal quality to thank.

Grace had exceptionally thick skin.

She had to laugh when she would read about PDs around the country, and the world for that matter, who had welcomed women into their ranks in the interest of diversification. That was so not Boston, she thought. The BPD had been dragged into the world of broadening their line of officers, kicking and screaming the whole way.

Grace had ten years in, and when she joined, she really had no idea she would be intruding on one of the more firmly established "Good Old Boy Networks" in the entire U.S. of A. She also had no idea that she would be subjected to every form of harassment, aggravation, provocation, and debauchery imaginable from her male counterparts. She had seen many women wilt under the pressure—women who she considered good cops, and who she thought were tough. Whenever one such woman would leave the PD, her self-doubts would come charging back to the forefront of her psyche. As in, if they couldn't make it, what makes me think I can?

But, so far at least, she had survived.

Grace hadn't grown up wanting to be a police officer. She had a relatively normal childhood in a middle-class home in the

Roslindale section of Boston. Many times during her tenure at the BPD, one of the louts she worked with would ask if she was a cop because she didn't get enough of Daddy's attention growing up. Nothing could have been further from the truth. She was a total Daddy's girl. Her family didn't have any boy progenies, just Grace and her sister. Jennifer was two years younger, and was what Grace considered a "girly girl." Grace was the tomboy of the two, and her father devoted himself to all of her athletic endeavors. Was he making up for not having a boy? Maybe, but Grace didn't waste any brain cell energy worrying about it. She just enjoyed the growing relationship with her father while Jenn and her mother stayed home busying themselves with the latest baking or sewing project. Grace's favorite sports were soccer and field hockey. She was always on the slim and petite side, so it behooved her to gravitate toward sports that relied on foot speed and agility. Dad had emphasized the need to be tough. Grace's slight stature would impel competitors to try to dominate her physically. It caused Grace to develop a fierce competitive spirit that she was certain benefitted her career in law enforcement.

In one of their many conversations, her father had admitted having an ulterior motive in encouraging Grace's behavior, which could have been viewed as very "unladylike" by traditional standards.

She remembered him saying, "It's a tough world out there, Grace. I hate to say it, but especially for girls. People will look for every opportunity to take advantage of you."

"That's why you're so into my athletics?" she asked.

"It's not the only reason. But I want you to be able to protect yourself when...."

"When what Dad?"

"When I'm not around to do it anymore."

Grace breezed through college, continuing to participate in team sports. After graduating, she was at a crossroads of deciding what to do with her life. She hadn't really had any serious relationships. She dated, sure, and with her blonde hair, pretty face, and slender figure, there was never a shortage of suitors. When she self-analyzed, she decided that none of the guys she was with measured up to her father, thinking a psychologist would have a field day with that one.

She took the test to become a police officer almost on a whim. She always admired the way her father had been protective of both her and her sister, and thought being a cop would be a good way to extend that kind of protection to others. She would think, You didn't hear the phrase Daddy Issues from me!

She aced the written exam and was invited to take physical and psychological tests. Grace found the physical part so easy that it made her worry about the people out chasing after robbers and other criminals. Were they really in any condition to do that? The psych exam didn't worry her. Well, other than the potential Daddy Issues popping up along the way. Her background check came back squeaky clean, and she worried that perhaps she hadn't lived it up enough in her formative years. She also breezed through the academy and the civil Service exam and, low and behold, she was a member of Boston's finest.

Little did she know that the testing, as it were, was only beginning. In a very short time, it became abundantly clear that women BPD officers faced a multitude of psychological pressures, not to mention a generally icy reception from their male colleagues. It seemed that the men wanted to assess which, if any, of the crop of rookie women officers could hack it in the traditionally male dominated field.

But these guys didn't know who they were dealing with. Grace prided herself on having skin as tough as an elephant's hide.

It wasn't long before a tirade of practical jokes began. Most of them were pretty harmless. The first time she took a car out on patrol, someone had put glitter in the AC vents and turned the fan up to high. When she started the car, she got coated with sparkles, but she calmly got out, brushed herself off, and went on her way. She didn't even object when one of the boys put Saran Wrap over the toilet, although that took a little more time to clean up.

She even had to laugh a little (privately to herself, of course) when a bunch of the guys were mulling around grumbling something about random drug testing being unfair. She asked one what it was all about, and he told her they all had to provide a urine sample to the lieutenant as part of a new unannounced cadence of drug tests for officers. They thought it was out-of-line, but everyone had to do it. One officer pointed to a stack of little cups, and told her she'd better hurry as the deadline was approaching. So she generated her sample and hustled into the lieutenant's office with her cup. But, of course, there was no such test, and she was left trying to explain to the LT why she was presenting him with a cup full of her pee. When she walked back out, the guys were about busting a gut. She laughed a little, saying, "Good one, guys," and moved on.

Some of the ruses, however, tended toward the nasty side. One time, she got into her squad car and immediately was hit with an overpowering foul odor. She searched the vehicle and found an open can of sardines with a piece of paper attached. The note said, "Smells fishy, huh? Now you know how we feel." Another time, she opened her locker and someone had rigged a gas canister to be triggered when she opened the door. The tube from the canister was attached to a condom hanging at face level, and before she knew what was going on, a gigantic inflated penis was staring her in the face.

Grace was able to brush these crude instances aside. She was determined not to let these infantile chowderheads get to her. She had heard stories of women who complained to the brass about their treatment. Their careers were essentially shot at that point. And the retaliation had gone as far as delaying calls for backup when out on patrol. Grace thought that conditions had improved a little since then, but she didn't want a blemish on her career, because...well, it was because she had to admit that she liked being a cop and honestly thought she was pretty good at it.

Once she was more established, Grace even took a little revenge on her jokesters. She found out who had put the glitter in her squad car. When the opportunity presented itself, she smeared his steering wheel and inside door handle with Vaseline. Grace was in the break room when he came howling through the halls running for the men's room to get cleaned up. She had a glint in her eye that not many of her associates noticed.

Grace actually felt that women officers had an advantage over men in certain circumstances. One of the most dangerous kinds of calls for a patrol cop was a domestic dispute. After several such cases with the same partner, a decent guy named Don Halberton, he began to notice that Grace had an inherent ability to diffuse tense situations, especially those involving men. Grace tried not to think about the fact that some of these perps had Mommy Issues, and that could be the reason why they almost instantly calmed down in her presence. She preferred to credit her above average verbal acuity. Truth be told, it wasn't at all unusual for a male suspect to hit on her, so sexual attraction was also a factor in play. She also became an above average interrogator, probably for many of the same reasons. Suspects who were about as responsive as a block of granite suddenly wanted to open up to Grace Garvey. She not only obtained some confessions, but heard a significant chunk of the perp's life story, not much of which was relevant to the case, but which gave her further confidence in her talent.

Whatever the reasons, Don was impressed. He had always treated Grace with respect. He was happily married with young children, so he set himself apart from many other cops by not spending all his waking hours and a not-insignificant amount of energy trying to get into her pants. Their positive relationship took on additional meaning when Don got promoted to detective sergeant and was moved to the downtown precinct, an area of responsibility which included Beacon Hill. When a detective's position opened up in missing persons, Don Halberton pulled some strings and got Grace promoted. Halberton recognized that most MP cases were solved through information gathered in conversations with family and friends of the victim, and he felt Grace would excel in that role. Of course, she leap-frogged a slew of street cops with seniority over her, some of whom had been chomping at the bit for a detective's gold shield. The resentment towards her manifested itself in some nasty rumors that had her banging half the department brass to get her coveted position. But Grace was now a seasoned pro at working through the harassment and barbs, and she knew that, given time, she would prove herself worthy.

It was a beautiful October morning, and Grace was contentedly working away at her pile of paperwork and intending to catch up on some phone calls when Don came moseying over.

"How's my favorite missing persons detective doing today?" he asked.

"Uh oh. You must want something."

"Now that's a mighty callous attitude there, GG." He had taken to calling her GG while they were still patrolling together. "Is that any way to talk to the guy who rescued you from the animals down at Southy? At least up here on Sudbury Street you're dealing with a better class of animals."

"Sorry, Don. I'm doing just fine. It's a great morning, and I'm going to spend the day getting caught up. That is, unless there is something that will cause me to drop everything and mess up my day's plan."

She gave Don a knowing smile and he tried hard, but ended up laughing.

"I never could put anything over on you," he said.

"Of course not. Whatdya got?"

"I got a senior executive from a big insurance company over on State Street. Guy named Arnold Shaw. Hasn't been seen or heard from since this past Saturday. Apparently spent the day in the office, but never made it home. Here's the touchy part...."

"How come I always get the ones with a touchy part? You know I don't like touching. Total germaphobe."

"I wish it were that simple. No, the touchy part is that Mr. Shaw was a big contributor to the campaign of our wonderful mayor this past election cycle. In fact, when he didn't come home on Saturday night, his missus didn't call the local precinct, she called her good buddy, hizzoner."

Grace raised her eyebrows. "Huh. Impressive. Well, let's see, today is...Tuesday, so if the guy was just shacking up with his GF, he'd probably at least be coming home to dry out by now."

"Right. The missus admits that he often hits his favorite watering holes after work. Especially on Saturday. But she says no matter where he goes, or...she even said this...who he's with, he always comes home. Sometimes in the wee, wee hours, but always home. Plus, he didn't show up at work yesterday, and that never happens."

"Does she have any idea which watering holes?" asked Grace.

"Yes, she gave us a few names, but can't promise that she knows every one. Guess the guy lives hard and parties hard. And Mrs. Shaw admits that he can be a nasty drunk. And he's a big guy, so the occasional brawl is not out of the question."

"Sweet."

"Yeah. Anyway, here's the file." Don handed her a manila folder. "It has some pictures and the list of bars. All bullshit aside, Grace, there are going to be a lot of people watching on this one.

At the same time, we want to keep it as low key as possible."

"Okay, but I have to ask around. How else am I going to put my formidable talents to use? You put me here because I'm not good at wrestling gorillas to the ground, but I can get them to ask me to dance within five minutes. Remember?"

Halberton laughed. "No. I know. I want you to put your talents to use. But if Mr. Shaw was, in fact, off getting his ashes hauled somewhere, and was having such a good time that he decided to take an extended vacation, we don't want that leading the Metro section in the Globe."

"Ah. I understand, boss. Anything else?"

"Nope. That's it for you. I got another new case, but I'm giving it to Gebelein. It's small potatoes compared to this one."

"What's that one about?" asked Grace.

"I told you, it's not for you. You've got enough to worry about."

"I know, I'm just curious. I get off on MP cases, okay? Do I give you shit about your hobbies?"

Don again made an effort, but ended up laughing. "I keep saying I did this to myself. No, it's nothing really. Guy's a meth-head. Name's Dylan Cavey. Nickname Spider. Pastimes are drug dealing and armed robbery. Mother reported him missing this weekend too. She says he strays occasionally, but that he's really a 'nice boy.' She lives in the Back Bay, but she says Dylan hangs out downtown. Been to rehab a few times. We'll probably dredge his body up from the harbor at some point. I'm putting Parker Gebelein on it. He'll ask around the tombs a little bit, then tell his mom that Dylan probably went to L.A. to be a movie star. You just worry about Mr. Shaw. That's where our bread is getting buttered."

"Gothcha boss." Halberton started to walk away. "Oh and hey, Don?"

"Yeah?"

"Thank you for the faith you've shown in me," said Grace with a sweet smile.

Don Halberton laughed, shook his head, and continued on his way. "I did this to myself," he said.

CHAPTER TWELVE

This time, I was not the least bit surprised when I woke up and Lyria was gone. Okay, so she liked to sneak out after I fell asleep. Was I going to complain after the greatest night of sex in my life? Okay, the only night of sex in my life. Oh, I wasn't a virgin before last night, don't get that impression. But compared to the night's gymnastics with Lyria, my previous sexual encounters were eminently forgettable. And this was truly the first time a woman had stayed with me, at least through most of the night. Although honestly, I hadn't a clue what time she departed the premises.

The fact that we had essentially taken our budding relationship to the next level and I still knew no more about her than I did the day before, or the day before that, probably should have bothered me, but it didn't. I wouldn't allow my mind to stray back to the mind-piercing notion that she was having a fling on an inattentive husband or boyfriend, hence her continued secrecy. Nope, not going there, at least not today. This morning, I'm just going to revel in last night. I'll store away the onset of the suspicion/obsession/paranoia for another time. I left for the office with extra pep in my step.

When I reached the end of my street, I saw a weird looking little guy and thought he was staring me down. He was short and pudgy, wearing an overcoat and a stocking cap. He had wicked buck teeth that looked like they could gnaw your arm off without much trouble, and he wore thick glasses covering large bulbous eyes that seemed to dart off in different directions. My impression was that he had been standing around that corner for a long time, although I couldn't say what gave me that idea. He seemed to be sizing me up, and after the previous week's encounter with Spider and Vape, I was hoping my good mood wouldn't be disrupted by another robbery attempt. I kept on walking, and when I looked back, the strange little man was gone. I had an odd thought that if that was Lyria's boyfriend, I actually measured up pretty well. But no, probably just another of the good Lord's unique beings, which one tended to come across with greater frequency living in a city.

I got to the office thinking that even Shrek couldn't upset my rare post-coital upbeat outlook. As I started hammering away on my computer, working on my latest mind-numbing analysis project, my brainwaves took a sidebar with none other than my compatriot, Mr. Larry Berman, taking center stage. Berman was the only married member of our group. He also seemed to be best able to roll with the flow when the pressure on our team was ratcheted up a notch, whether because of a newly installed deadline by upper management or an unexplained tirade by Shrek. Even his "twin," Chauncey Stillwell, tended to freak out in his own quiet way. Chauncey wouldn't verbalize his stress, but he would be so tightly wound at his terminal that if you snuck up and tapped him on the shoulder, we were all pretty sure that what was left of Chauncey would have to be carted off on a gurney. Or in a box.

Razor Rojas wasn't the loud, panicky type either, but if you interrupted Razor while he was facing down a deadline, he looked like he wanted to gut you like a freshly caught cod on a Boston Harbor fishing tour.

But Berman? He was cool, calm, and collected even in the tensest of times. And I thought I understood why. As a married man, it reasoned to follow that Larry had a more active, regular sex life than the rest of us. Boof would probably put up an argument on that point, but I'd then have to assert that a pay-per-view video chat with a girl in Sweden didn't count. So Berman almost assuredly "got it" more often than the other guys in the group. None of us knew about Vicky. And I felt virtually invulnerable to anxiety after last night's tryst. So I had it. A definite casual relationship, the type that we financial analysts always went in search of but rarely found. A healthy, regular sex life made the rigors of the office more bearable. How about that?

My reverie was disrupted by a shrill yell that sliced through the white-noise-enhanced quiet that was the norm for the financial analysis group. About the only one who ever raised his voice around there was Shrek, but this wasn't his voice. I stood up and could see that Shrek's office was dark. He was probably stuck in traffic as usual. No, it was definitely a female voice. I thought, is that Vicky?? I stopped and listened.

"Get your sorry ass out of my office right now, Edwin."

Edwin? This must be bad. Vicky's yelling at Boof and calling him by his real name.

I rushed over to her cube, hoping to prevent a homicide.

Boof was standing in her doorway with his hands out in front of him. "Easy Vicky...uh...Ms. Temerlin. I didn't mean anything by...it."

"Oh, calling me Ms. Temerlin now? You think that's going to solve everything, huh? The way you talk to me...the way you ogle me like a piece of meat. I'm tired of it, and I'm tired of you, Edwin. I'M TIRED OF ALL OF YOU!"

I rounded the corner of her cube and was startled when I saw Vicky. She was more pale and drawn than the previous day. She had huge bags under her eyes, and her normally perfect hair was sticking out at all angles. She was wearing a print dress that I knew usually hugged her curves, but it looked like it was two sizes too big. She was honed in on Boof with bloody murder in her eyes.

"Hey, you two," I said, trying to calm the situation. "You know yelling is against the house rules in FA. What's going on?"

"Hey, all I did was say 'Good morning.' I didn't think that was worth dying over," said Boof.

Vicky spoke more quietly, but the intensity was still there. "Good morning? You said 'Good morning?' Get him out of here, Conner. Take him back to your office, and maybe you'll get the little shit to admit what he really said to me. And as for you, Edwin...." She spoke his given name with such vehemence that Boof took a step back. "You ever come in here again, you'd better have a good reason. And checking out what I'm wearing doesn't qualify. You'd better have business to discuss, or else...." Boof and I just stood there. It was like waiting for a train wreck. We couldn't move without hearing the end of her threat. "Never mind. Just go away."

"C'mon, Boof." I took him by the arm and we got out of the danger zone, and went back to my cube. "What was that all about?" I asked. "I've never seen Vicky like that before."

"I have no idea. Like I said, I just told her good morning and she came unglued."

"Good morning? Is that really what you said?"

"Well...I might have said something more —"

"Out with it, Boof. What did you say to her?"

"I don't even remember. Could have been something along the lines of 'You're looking particularly saucy today.' Nothing unusual."

"Oh, good God."

"What? What, are we all gonna turn PC around here all of a sudden? Have to watch every word? We gonna turn the office into some kind of monastery or something? I didn't mean any harm. Frankly, I thought I was doing her a favor, you know?

111

Let's be honest, she's been looking a little ratty the last couple of days. I thought I might boost her spirits some. Hey, that's it!"

I just sat staring at him.

"It's that time of the month for her. Must get worse as a girl gets older. I gotta go mark my calendar for twenty-eight days from now. We'll just make like a nuclear zone around Vicky's office on those days. That should solve the problem. Pretty good how I figured that out, huh?"

"Oh yeah. Who says chivalry is dead?"

"Right. See you later, Conner."

"Uh, Boof, you might want to leave Vicky alone for a while."

"Yeah. At least for the next five to seven days."

With that bit of Zen, Boof went back to his office. I waited a while for things to cool down, then walked cautiously over to Vicky's cube and stuck my head around the opening. But Vicky wasn't there, so I thought maybe that she had gone down to the coffee shop to clear her head.

I had to be honest and admit that I was worried about her. And that my good mood from earlier in the day was now a thing of the past.

***

That evening, Lyria was lying next to me in bed. If the previous night was any indicator, I had about ten minutes or so before the action began anew.

"What's your last name?" I asked her.

She had a droll look in her eyes as she raised up on one elbow. "Smith," she said.

I was staring into her beautiful eyes, and a part of me wanted to just leave it at that. I still had a residual fear of saying or doing something stupid and causing her to run screaming from the building. But my curiosity and frustration at the lack of details about her got the better of me.

"Is that really your last name? Lyria Smith? Doesn't have

112

much of a ring to it."

"Well, I'm not much of a poet, but I could make something up that sounds better if you want."

I laughed. "No, that's all right. Lyria Smith. Okay. Maybe it will grow on me."

"Unless I'm mistaken, I think something's growing on me right now. Now, do we want to deal with that? Or would you like to discuss my last name some more?"

I answered a little too quickly. "The growing thing," I said. "Definitely the growing thing."

After that session, and...oh, okay, the next one, I was completely spent. But I was dog determined to stay awake and watch Lyria if and when she decided to make her clandestine exit. We were bunched up close together, and I was stroking her hair while she made soft cooing sounds. I couldn't honestly remember ever being so comfortable and content. And the next thing I knew, my alarm clock was going off.

And, of course, Lyria was gone.

"Damn," I said out loud.

***

For Vicky Temerlin, living alone had been a panacea. She grew up with well intentioned, but domineering parents who wanted a say in her every move. Even now that she was an adult.

Vicky knew that the guys at work had a rabid curiosity about details of her social life, and she got along pretty well with everyone considering the odd dynamics involved with a group consisting of five males and one female. But financial analysis and investment banking were still largely male dominated businesses, so her situation was not unusual. Even so, Vicky managed to keep her coworkers at arm's length in terms of sharing personal details. She wanted to fit in with the boys, yes. But she wanted to advance in her career and at least make a dent in the glass ceiling for women even more.

The men would be interested to know that Vicky had been in two long-term, committed relationships in her time. Both guys had everything that her girlfriends growing up had put forth as qualities of an ideal mate — they had looks, outgoing personalities, and families with money. They were both, in the eyes of many, great catches. They also both saw Vicky as a potential trophy wife, over whom they wanted to exert an undue amount of influence. But her personality development with her ever-watchful mother and father had caused her to sport a fierce streak of independence. She wanted no part of the "living through your husband" world that had engulfed so many of her friends. When she made it known that she was going to college to major in business, her father and her then-current beau had objected loudly.

"You don't have to study business," her boyfriend had said. "Heck, you don't have to study anything at all. I'll make enough to support us. And our kids, when we have kids."

Her father was beaming nearby.

"Oh, okay," she said. "Maybe I'll just switch my major to 'Home Economics.' Would that suit you better?"

Her father then looked glum.

She knew at that very moment that this guy was going to hit the streets. Her boyfriend in college wasn't much better.

Vicky remembered comparing notes with her best girlfriend Gloria at a college bar on a night when the boyfriend had actually let her out of his sight.

"I sure can pick 'em," Vicky said.

"I know," said Gloria. "Your guy's a dream."

"More like a nightmare."

"What?"

"What is it about me that makes guys want to own me? Lock me up behind a white picket fence, so I spend my life staying home taking care of our house full of kids."

"Doesn't sound that bad to me. If I had your looks, I'd be in line to be a trophy wife too."

"Gloria, I want to make my own way in this world. I need to find someone who would look at me as an equal. As a partner. Who wouldn't only want me around to cook and clean and look good at company parties. I had my mother and father making every decision for me growing up. I don't want a husband doing that too. I want to be the next Sheryl Sandberg. How come I always end up with guys wanting me to be the next June Cleaver?"

"Well, if that's what you want, you have to have that filter in place up front. Let the guy know how you feel, and if he doesn't like it, there's the door. You could certainly have the pick of the litter."

"That's just it. Guys are so phony when you first start going out. They'll all say and do just about anything. But they start changing right after you go to bed with them. Then their real personality comes out. And if you're not careful, they get you knocked up, and before you know it you're wearing June Cleaver dresses and aprons hanging out in the kitchen."

There had been nobody serious since Vicky gave Mr. College his sneakers. When she first started at BHA she'd tried living at home, but got tired of the disapproving looks from Mom and Dad. They didn't as much as say it, but she felt they were thinking along the lines of, "You can start spitting out grandchildren ANY TIME NOW." It was clear she needed her own place. And she wanted to live in Boston. Prices in the city were outrageous, but she managed to find a cubbyhole studio apartment in the Back Bay. It was easy trolley ride from work.

Being a woman in this type of work environment was definitely taxing, and she always looked forward to going to her apartment and holing up by herself for a while. Her place didn't have much in size, but in terms of warmth and comfort, it became home very quickly.

That is, until the nightmares started.

She felt childish thinking that way. How could a strong, independent woman be brought down by a couple of bad dreams? But these were so vivid, so lifelike, that Vicky actually felt like they had affected her physically.

They had started on Saturday night, after she left the office with Conner. She got home in an upbeat mood. She liked Conner — he was cute, in a bookwormy sort of way. And he was shy, so getting him to open up felt like a major accomplishment. If you got past the incessant "ball busting" that took place between him and the other guys, she felt like he had a nice personality. Besides her pleasant talk with Conner, she had finished her status report and didn't have to go back to the office on Sunday. She celebrated with a glass of wine and fell asleep on her sleeper sofa, watching some old movie on cable.

The dream started in total darkness, as if someone had dropped a thick black velvet blanket over her. She felt paralyzed and was having trouble breathing. Suddenly a beautiful woman's face came into view. Vicky could only see her face. The woman was a classic beauty, a perfectly shaped visage with prominent cheekbones. She had a pleasant expression, and Vicky felt like she knew her, like this woman was her friend.

The face slowly contorted. Her eyes were now angry with black, dilated pupils. The woman was enraged, and Vicky stopped even trying to breathe. The face conveyed uncontrolled fury. Vicky tried to scream, but nothing came out. The last thing she remembered seeing was the woman's mouth. Her lips were pulled back in a snarl. Her canine teeth were two or three times their normal size, and she was coming closer. Vicky tried to move, to run, but she couldn't. Vicky could no longer see the face, but she felt pain. Pain everywhere, in every fiber of her being. And then everything went black.

Vicky didn't dream anymore that night. In fact, it felt like she had been more unconscious than sleeping. She woke up feeling weak, drawn, and alone, as if the terrifying dream had gone on all night. She remembered thanking her lucky stars that it was Sunday and she didn't have to go into the office. When she looked in her bathroom mirror, she gave a start. Her normally healthy complexion looked pale and waxy. She had massive bags under her eyes. If she had to cover those over, she'd go broke on makeup.

"I must be coming down with something," she said to herself.

She hit the hay and pretty much stayed there the entire day. She tried eating a little, but didn't really have much of an appetite. She hoped that perhaps a day of bed rest would help her through whatever this was.

Now, it was a couple of days later. The terrifying dream had recurred each and every night. The pretty face becoming the horrible face, the fangs, being unable to scream, barely able to breathe. Vicky kept feeling worse each day. She barely made it to work on Monday, remembering Shrek's rules against calling in sick. She noticed the way the guys were looking at her, probably wondering, as she was, what had happened to her looks. Even Conner looked at her that way. Then today, this morning, she had bitten Boof's head off. Granted, he was a little pig and had it coming, but she always figured him to be essentially harmless. After that incident, she called it quits and headed on home. She called and left a message on Shrek's phone, thanking God in heaven when he didn't pick up.

Now, she was sitting on her bed, feeling as bad as she could ever remember feeling. Two startling realities came to the fore of her consciousness.

One was that she was afraid to go to sleep.

And the other was that she no longer thought living by herself was such a great idea.

CHAPTER THIRTEEN

For the second straight day, I had an extra bounce in my step as I headed out the door. Okay, so Lyria was a little different. She was secretive, but I didn't think she was being deceitful. She just held close to her privacy. Nothing wrong with that. Maybe that was just how it worked. With time, she'd start to trust me with more personal details. I could wait.

Besides, she was a knock-down, drag-out, beautiful, amazingly sexy babe. And she was with me.

Like I said. Different.

I was headed to the office, lost in these extremely rare thoughts, when a strange voice called my name.

"Mr. David?"

My instant analysis was some kind of European accent. And since I didn't know anyone with a European accent, I turned around with a not-so-small amount of trepidation.

I instantly recognized the weird little chubby guy I had seen the day before. I thought he had been looking at me, but I had passed it off to Lyria-induced paranoia. Aside from his size, this guy would stand out in a crowd. He was about as odd looking a creature as I had come across. He was short and round, with thick glasses covering eyes that were indeed going off in different directions. And he had buckteeth that would make a beaver proud. The guy looked like a cross between Bob the Minion and Danny Devito playing The Penguin.

I couldn't imagine what this little man wanted, but in the back of my mind, I knew it had something to do with Lyria.

I sputtered out an, "Uh, sorry. Headed to work."

He said, "I know. But I must see you during daylight, you see? And you come home late. Usually after dark. This is the only chance I have. You see?"

"Uh, no. I don't see. Look, if you're looking for a handout, you're hitting up the wrong guy. I know I live in an expensive townhouse, but I'm really not well off. I'm sure a couple of my neighbors would be better targets."

"Handout? Oh...no, Mr. David." Then he emitted what I could only interpret as a laugh, although it sounded more like he was clearing his nostrils without a tissue. "Nothing like that," he continued. "Must speak with you about her. About Lyria."

That stopped me in my tracks. I turned and looked at the strange little man. My first thought was, he couldn't be an ex of hers. That gorgeous woman and this guy? He looked like a bowling ball with clothes. Then the nagging voice in my subconscious mind jumped in, saying, Well, she's with you, isn't she? Maybe she got tired of short and fat and decided to go with tall and skinny. Besides, as weird as this guy looked, he was apparently someone who knew Lyria. In some way. And my burning curiosity to know more about her got the better of me.

"Okay. I'm listening," I said, as I started walking again. "But I'm also in a hurry, so please get to your point. You're not...her husband or anything, are you?"

"Husband? No...not her husband." More sniffling, laughing. "But must warn you. She is not what she seems."

"How's that again?"

"You think she is simply a beautiful woman, yes?"

"Well, yes. What are you trying to say? She's not a beautiful woman? What was she...born as a man? Cause if that's what you're telling me, I don't believe you. Look, if you have some sort

119

of crush on her and you're trying to scare me off, you're going to have to do better than that...uh...what did you say your name was?"

"Did not say."

I stopped in front of the guy. Fortunately, he stopped too. If he kept going, he would have steamed over me like one of those paving trucks with the big rollers. "What exactly are you telling me about Lyria? I'm almost at my office, and I don't have time for games. So, out with it, mister. Cause I'm out of patience."

"Is impossible to explain in so short a time. I know you are in a hurry. Here."

He handed me a slip of paper with a phone number on it.

"At some point, you will see that you need my help. Keep this number. Please. I am always available. But must meet during the day. Must go now, Mr. David. Be careful."

With that, the little man walked away with deceptive speed, turned a corner, and was gone.

I stood in place for a moment, looked up at the sky. "Can't one of my good moods last until at least noon?" I said to nobody.

***

I got to my cube without any more interruptions, and started working. The office sounded quieter than usual. First thing in the morning, the group normally went through a brief catch-up on the prior night's activities. At a minimum, the twins would do some debriefing. But this morning, there was nothing breaking through the white noise.

I was digging in on one of my ongoing projects when I sensed a presence in my doorway. I looked up and saw it was Razor. But I was speechless for a moment because I had never seen this expression on Razor's face before. He looked...scared.

"Razor," I said. "You look like you've seen a ghost. What... what's wrong?"

"It's Vicky."

120

I waited, but he didn't say anything else.

"Vicky? What about her? Is she okay?"

"I don't know. She must not be."

"Why? Razor...talk to me."

"She called in."

"She—"

"Yeah. This morning. We heard Shrek swear and slam his phone down. Yelled something about how he knew he should never have kept an effing woman on his staff. How his group's perfect attendance record was now shit, and it was probably because his bitch analyst was on the rag."

"You mean Vicky actually—"

"Yes. She did it. She called in sick."

***

I tried Vicky's cell phone several times that morning, but she didn't answer. Only at BHA, in the financial analysis group under Darren Shrek freakin' Dobson, could a person calling in sick be treated like an act-of-God disaster on the scale of a hurricane, flood, or nuclear bomb strike. It had been pretty clear on both Monday and Tuesday that Vicky wasn't feeling well. And, from what I could see, whatever was affecting her went way beyond her menstrual cycle. So she had the unmitigated gall to try to take a day's rest and get better and, in the process, not get anyone else sick in case she was contagious. We should call for help.

Call the Center for Disease Control. Call the FBI. Why not call in the marines while we're at it?

Unbelievable.

I, for one, wasn't the least bit worried about Shrek's precious attendance record. We all knew he had a borderline obsession with breaking the damned record. It stood at 1,157 straight days under the prior head of FA, John Bauer, who was a saint of a man. John probably had developed such loyalty with his analysts that they were coming in with all kinds of injuries and illnesses

121

just to keep the streak going. Whereas, with Shrek at the helm, we had secretly plotted to draw straws to see who would call in sick when the department was within one day of the record to see if that would finally send Shrek over the edge and make him drive off the Zakim Bridge on his way home.

Shrek had an obsession, not only with the attendance record, but with Bauer himself. Not only had all the analysts loved their former boss, but he was well regarded within the company, and, indeed, within the always-cutthroat investment banking industry. After John retired, Dobson went crazy gathering data on the department's productivity and personnel records from Bauer's reign. And Shrek was determined to better them all, to prove that the company did right by showing faith in giving him this promotion. That if they thought Bauer was good, with his touchy-feely approach to inspiring his workers, Shrek would show them what could be done by ruling with an iron fist. And the analysts themselves? They were totally expendable. What? Someone died at their desk because of all the pressure? Well, goddamn it, wheel 'em out and get someone else in there. Preferably someone with a pair, someone who could take it. Don't send me any more of these lily-livered, chickenshit college kids or I'll just keep killing them off.

That was our beloved Shrek.

I was worried about Vicky, though. After we got back from lunch, I tried her phone again, and this time after ringing several times, I heard it click. But there was still silence on the other end.

"Hello? Vicky?" I said.

"Y...yes? Conner?" It barely sounded like Vicky's voice.

"Yeah, it's me. Hey, how you feeling? I...I was worried."

"Oh. Oh...thank you. No need to worry. I didn't feel up to coming in this morning. Honestly, I had trouble even getting out of bed. I slept all morning. I feel a little better. I'm hoping that with rest this afternoon I'll be back in tomorrow."

"Oh, that's great. What do you think, you got a virus or something? Maybe the flu?"

"That's the thing. I really don't think so. I don't have any other flu symptoms. I'm just so tired...so weak. I can barely lift my head up off the pillow. And I haven't eaten much."

"Do you have a doctor you can call? If not, I could call my family doc and get him to squeeze you in. The guy usually has like a twenty-four-month wait for new patients. But my family practically paid for his vacation home over the years, so I could get him to see you if you want."

Vicky uttered a weak laugh. "Thank you, that's the first time I've laughed in a while. I think I'm going to give it another day or two and try to get my strength back. I'll let you know though. Maybe if I'm not feeling any better tomorrow...."

"Sure. Sure. Of course, just let me know."

"How're the other guys doing?"

"Okay, I guess. Although your calling in almost gave both Shrek and Razor the big one."

Another weak laugh. "Shrek I get. He's probably pissed about his attendance record, huh?"

"I think that's a fair assumption."

"Razor? Was Razor upset?"

"Oh, I think his was just shock. Nobody had called in for so long. It had kind of a traumatic effect. He'll survive, though."

She laughed again, sounding a little stronger this time. "Thank you for calling, Conner. That was very sweet."

"Oh sure. No problem at all. You...you take as much time as you need. Shrek's record is shot anyway. And, really, if you need me to bring you anything, just let me know, okay?"

"Okay. I will. If I can't come in tomorrow, I'll...call you to let you know how I'm doing."

"That would be great. Okay, Vick. Get some rest, and I'll talk to you tomorrow."

"Okay...bye."

We hung up and I was feeling better after talking to her. But, once again, my euphoria was short-lived. I looked up and Mr. Darren "Shrek" Dobson's boxy body was blotting out the light in my doorway. To say he didn't look pleased would have been the understatement of the century.

"I hope I'm not interrupting anything," he said through clenched teeth.

"Uh...no sir. What can I do for you?"

"What you can do for me, David, is get your butt into my office so we can talk about personal phone calls during office hours. Oh, and if it's not too much trouble, you can do it NOW."

***

I was stroking Lyria's arm that night.

"Your skin feels cool," I said. "Are you feeling all right?"

"Didn't I feel all right to you?" she asked with a smile.

I laughed. She still had a real talent for throwing me off my train of thought.

"No. I mean...yes. You felt fine. You felt great. You felt unbelievable."

She laughed. No matter how intimate we had been, I still occasionally slipped back into dweeb mode.

"It's just that Vicky...a friend of mine from work...she got real sick this week. Whatever it is, it drained her strength. Must be real bad. I was hoping that something wasn't going around. You know...hoping you didn't have the same thing."

"I don't think you have to worry about me. So this Vicky... she's a friend of yours?"

"Yeah. Poor thing. She's the only female in the financial analysis group. And one of the few in the company. Investment banking as an industry is a little behind the times on integrating its ranks. It's still pretty much a male dominated industry. Vicky does great work, but she must be really tough to have lasted this long."

"I can imagine. Did you two ever date?"

"Date?"

"Yes. You know. When a boy and girl have mutual interests and they decide to follow through on them together? And maybe one of their mutual interests is each other. That sort of thing."

I laughed again, but I wondered where this question was coming from. Was it even remotely possible that Lyria, this incredible creature, was actually jealous? Then I thought, Nah. Can't be. I could see me getting jealous, but her? What on earth would she have to be jealous about? It wasn't like I had women beating down my door, was it?

"Yeah, I know the concept of a date. But no. Vicky and I have never dated. Never will date. I think dating someone in such a close-knit work group would be a mistake. Besides, none of the guys know Vicky's relationship status. For all we know, she could be going steady with a Navy Seal. Or a martial arts instructor. Somebody like that."

"So, how do you know how serious it is? This illness she has?"

"I called her this afternoon. You know...to see if she was okay. Besides, it had to be serious. She called in sick."

"Ah, yes. Your boss doesn't allow people to call in sick. I remember."

"Right. Our boss, Darren Dobson? We call him Shrek?"

"Um hmm."

"Well, he does have this unofficial rule about calling in. If you break your leg, he expects you to crawl. He was hung up on breaking the group's record for perfect attendance. It was set under our previous boss. The record was over three years. Vicky hosed up the current streak, so it'll be a while before we get close again. And, I'm not sure I'll be around long enough to know if we'll ever do it."

Lyria snuggled up close. "Why not? Why wouldn't you be around? I'm sure you're an excellent financial analyst. You'll probably be running the place by the time his record comes around."

It was impossible to keep the smile off my face. "Well...I am good at what I do. But it's Shrek. He mistreats everybody, but he really seems to have it in for me."

"Is he still behaving badly toward you?"

"Yeah. After I got off the phone with Vicky, he took me into his office and chewed me out for ten minutes straight about having a personal call during business hours. I mean, the call was maybe five minutes, you know? And you'd think where it was a member of his staff who was sick, there might be some concern? Not a chance. I told him I was checking on Vicky, but it made no difference."

Lyria seemed to be thinking, staring off into space.

"Anyway, it's my problem." I didn't want to come off as a crybaby. Again. I had enough working against me in the personality department. "How was your day today? Did you do anything special?"

"Other than tonight? Here with you? No. Nothing even close to that special."

The involuntary smile was back, but so were the niggling doubts about her secrecy and how little I knew about her. She was very good at dodging the issue. I had to find a way to break the ice without sounding needy and whiny. No small task, because the potential dialog running through my head sounded very needy and whiny. Then, a light bulb went on.

"Oh, I've been meaning to ask you," I said.

"Yes...." She sounded leery, as if she was expecting me to ask another of my annoying personal questions.

"My sister wanted to know if we would double with her on Friday."

"Double?"

"Yeah. You know. Double date. She's going out with some guy who she suspects is a closet control freak. She likes him, but she's afraid he might be a serial abuser or something. She wants to give him another chance, and thought it would be better if she wasn't by herself. Like, the guy's not going to go postal with her big brother sitting right there. That type of thing." The statement sounded a little absurd considering my physical stature, and I was afraid Lyria might start laughing hysterically. But she looked like she was actually thinking it through.

Then my self-conscious nerd self came roaring back to the fore. Damn, you idiot. You just messed up the best thing you've ever had going. Lyria shows up at your place every night, you spend a little time canoodling, and you end up in bed. With this goddess. Now you want to scare her off by taking it to another level. Dipshit. Why didn't you leave well-enough alone?

"Of course, if you don't want to, I'll understand completely. I'm sure my sister will be fine. Hah. What an idiot, suggesting such a thing. I'm sorry. I'm really sorry. Can I get you anything? Do anything for you?"

Lyria reached over and stroked my face. "My sweet Conner. No, that sounds lovely. I'd very much enjoy meeting your sister. Where does she want to go?"

"She didn't say. Out to dinner someplace. I know she likes Grotto, over on Bowdoin Street? It's an Italian place. But we can go anywhere if you don't like Italian. We can do Mexican, Chinese, Indian...you name it. Whatever your favorite food is, we'll go to one of those restaurants. Or we can go to a movie... whatever you prefer..."

She laughed. "Conner, relax. Grotto sounds fine. It's just that—"

"What? Oh, I knew it. It was a stupid idea. I'm sorry. Let's just forget the whole thing."

She laughed again. "No. It's just that I have a prior commitment for early Friday evening. But I could meet you and your sister there for a drink after dinner. How would that be?"

"A drink? After dinner? Sure. Yeah, a drink would be fine. That would be great. You're sure I'm not disrupting your plans? You're sure it would be okay? To meet us, I mean."

"Yes, sweet Conner. It will be fine. It's a date. I'll get there as soon as I can on Friday night. I can't wait to see if your sister is as special as you are."

I let out a huge breath. "Yes. Carly, that's my sister. She's great. And she'll be excited to meet you too."

"Speaking of getting excited," she said, reaching down for me.

The "previous commitment" was bothering me. Another man? And, I had a notion about asking her about the weird little guy from this morning, but suddenly, she squeezed, and all those thoughts evaporated.

***

Vicky was out again on Thursday. I wanted to call her, but I had to wait until Shrek wasn't around. It was funny how we could sense when the boss was in his office. Barring a traffic delay, he usually got in early and kept his door closed, but we somehow knew when he was there. We called this sixth sense the "Shrekoscope." And I was relying on my Shrekoscope to advise me when it was safe to check on Vicky.

Before I knew it, it was lunchtime, and Shrek had been holed up all morning. I met the other guys downstairs. When I approached the table, I could see Boof was carrying on about something.

"...all I'm saying is, we can put a man on the moon, but we can't come up with an implant that feels like a real breast."

Razor was working on his lunch and looking bemused. The twins were making an attempt to talk quietly amongst themselves,

128

hoping nobody they knew would see them.

"I'm serious. The babes think guys don't care as long as they...you know...stand out. But, I'm telling you, you get a girl with those silicon jobs and you let them get on top, those puppies can knock you out cold."

"Geez, you can tell that Vicky's not around," I said. "It didn't take long for our conversation to go downhill." Razor snorted.

Boof said, "Oh, what are you, mister sweet and innocent all of a sudden? What, just cause you're Vicky's favorite, you don't want to talk about real world issues any more?"

"That's the best real world issue you could come up with?" I asked. "The excessive density of artificial breast tissue? What happened to war? Or politics? Or world famine?"

Boof made a psshhh sound and went back to his lunch, as if those matters were beneath his notice. Suddenly, Chauncy and Berman emerged from their mini conclave.

"Ms. Temerlin...er, that is Vicky," said Stillwell. "She does seem to favor you, Conner. The only time she comes to see me is if she has a question about discount rates, or some other such dry subject matter."

Then his partner perked up. "No doubt about it, Conner," said Berman with a big smile. "In this group, you're her sugar daddy."

That brought Boof back around. "Yeah. That's right. For whatever strange reason that certainly none of us can understand, Vicky's chosen you as her sugar daddy."

Even Razor had a laugh.

"Sugar daddy?" I said. "I don't even know what that means. I've never given Vicky any money. Isn't a sugar daddy supposed to be someone who gives a person money?"

"Not necessarily," said Boof. "It just means that when she... you know...needs some sugar, she comes to see you."

The other three guys nodded in agreement.

"Sugar?" I asked. "What exactly do you mean by sugar?"

"You know," said Boof. "Some sweet talk. A shoulder to cry on." Then Boof affected a high-pitched feminine voice. "Oh, Conner. It so sucks being a hot girl in this world. And being the only female in our group. With five other guys who all want my body. I knew I could tell you all about it. I knew you'd understand...."

Now even the twins were cracking up, although they didn't normally cater to such pedestrian bantering.

"You guys got it all wrong. I don't know Vicky better than any of you," I said, not so convincingly.

"Oh yeah? Have you talked to her since she's been out?" asked Boof.

"Well...yes. Only once. I called her to see how she was feeling. And got chewed out by Shrek for making a personal call, by the way."

"Aw gee. That's too bad. So you called her...what? At home? On her cell?"

I knew where this was going, but the damage was done.

"On her cell," I muttered.

"Huh. On her cell. Funny, but let me check." Boof took his phone out of his shirt pocket and made a show of scrolling through. "Yeah, seems Ms. Temerlin neglected to give me her personal number. How 'bout you, Razor? Do you have Vicky's cell phone number?"

"Nope," said Razor with a rare smile.

"Chauncy? Larry?"

The twins shook their heads in unison.

"How about that? Looks like you're the only one with her number, you lucky dog."

I decided to quit while I was behind, and focused on finishing my lunch as quickly as possible without bringing on a bout of indigestion.

"All kidding aside though, Conner, how is Vicky doing? I'd imagine that whatever she has, it has to be bad to call in," said Razor.

"She was feeling more weak than anything," I said. "She didn't really have any flu symptoms. She was just tired. Needed some rest."

"What'd I tell you?" asked Boof.

"I know I'm gonna regret this, but what are you talking about?" I asked.

"She's on the schmatta."

"The what?"

"You know. The rag. I had a Jewish roommate in college. Remember the other day? Her coming unglued at me? Had to be it. I recognized it immediately. I have two sisters, I know all about these things. My one sister, we about wanted to have her caged when that time came around. My father went around removing all the sharp objects from the house. I'm serious, we all feared for our lives."

"With all due respect to your vast medical knowledge, I think whatever's affecting Vicky is more serious than her being on the...what did you call it?"

"Schmatta."

"Right. Schmatta. Anyway, I told her if she wasn't any better, I'd hook her up with our family doctor."

"Of course," said Boof. "Cause that's just what a sugar daddy does."

I exhaled and prayed for someone to change the subject.

"You know, come to think of it," said Berman. "Shrek didn't look so good either today, did he Chaunc?"

Stillwell always thought before he spoke. "No. He didn't. He was quite pale, actually."

"Hey, wouldn't that be something?" asked Berman. "If Shrek got so sick that he had to call in? That would be...outright historic."

"Yeah," said Boof. "Especially if he got what Vicky has. It'd be the first guy in history to miss work because of his menses."

Razor blew some air out his nose, but the twins looked like they were thinking it through.

I said, "Forget it guys. The man is a psycho. If he lost both legs in a car accident, he'd have somebody wheel him in the next day."

"If he lost his right arm," said Boof, "He'd learn to type left-handed. Hey, do you guys know what you call a guy with no arms and legs who lays in front of your door?"

Nobody wanted to answer so we just sat looking at him.

"Matt," he said. "Get it? Matt?"

"And on that note," I said. "It's time to get back to the office."

***

My work effort that afternoon was half-hearted. I was waiting for Vicky to call, as she said she would, to give me a status update. I didn't want to call her for the second straight day. And, truth be told, I was still stinging some from the sugar daddy conversation at lunch.

Around mid-afternoon, I noticed my Shrekoscope was indicating that the boss wasn't in his office. It made me curious, so I grabbed a piece of paper and headed over to the copier. Sure enough, I glanced through Shrek's door window. His lights were out and his office was vacant. I thought, No way. There was no way the indestructible Dobson left because he was sick. He must be in a meeting with senior management or a client. Although usually, prior to such meetings, he raged through the analysis department like a wildfire out of control, making sure he was completely up to speed on all current issues. The guy may not be good at much, but he was an ace at anticipating questions that he wouldn't be able to answer on his own. That's why we were around, and it gave us the only sense of job security that would ever be available to us while Shrek was around.

With no boss, it wasn't necessary to continue my charade about making a copy. As I was heading back to my cube, a thought occurred to me. I stopped in Larry Berman's doorway.

"Hey Larry." I was speaking quietly because I didn't want Chauncy Stillwell to hear. "By any chance, you got time for coffee? Downstairs?"

"Sure. My Shrekoscope is off. I assume...." He nodded towards Stilwell's cube.

"Right. Just us. If that's okay."

"Sure thing."

So we slunk around the corner without raising Chauncy's suspicion or fear of abandonment, and headed down to the coffee shop.

"I'm guessing that since you didn't want Chancy along, this has something to do with a woman," said the ever-perceptive Berman. "Just one question, Conner. Is it Vicky?"

I exhaled a little laugh. "No. Despite what Boof thinks, I'm not much closer to her than any of you guys. In fact, last Saturday night on the way out of here, we had the first, what I'd call personal talk ever. I was actually a little surprised. But, I was guessing that it was because we were the only human beings left in the building, and I had had something of a...traumatic event the night before. She figured I needed to talk to a woman. And, honestly, it did help some."

"I heard about your traumatic event. But I'm glad it's not Vicky you wanted to talk about, 'cause I'm not sure I'd be completely comfortable with that."

"I totally understand, Larry. No, it's actually the girl...the woman from the traumatic event."

"Really? From what I heard, she was a real looker. In fact, the guys described her as being...."

"What? Totally out of my league?"

"Well, honestly, yes."

"I agree. She was. And is."

"So, you're still seeing her?"

"Every night this week. And it got...serious. Real fast."

"Serious. As in...."

"Yep."

"Wow. Good for you. So, what's the problem? Maybe she just has a thing for tall, skinny, accounting type guys. It's rare, but it does happen."

"That's what I've always told myself, but I never really believed it. The thing that's been bothering me is that she's still really secretive. I don't know a whole lot more about her today than I did when we first met."

"Huh. And I assume you've asked her for more details."

"Yes. As gently as possible. I'm treading a thin line between wanting to know more and not wanting to scare her off. I keep thinking maybe she's just, you know, been burned in the past or something. And maybe it takes time to get through the barriers she's set up. The other night, I asked her last name. Figured that was harmless enough."

"Yeah."

"She gave me a look. And said, 'Smith.' Now, like I said, I don't know a lot about her, but I can almost guarantee that her last name is not Smith."

"Uh huh. Does she get defensive at all when you ask questions?"

"A little. After Friday night when she somehow got out of the bar without anyone seeing her, I...saw her again on Saturday. I asked her, you know, how and why she ditched me. She said she had a lot of experience disappearing. Pretty easy to believe. A girl who looks like that has probably had to escape a fair share of geeks chasing after her."

Berman was just looking at me tight-lipped.

"Yes," I said. "You can say it. Guys like me."

He laughed.

"Anyway," I continued, "later that night I asked her something and she said I was only allowed one inquisition per night. She said it with one of her dazzling smiles, but the message was pretty clear."

"Hmmm." Berman sat thinking.

I purposely didn't tell him about the bar bully and getting knocked out. As of that moment, nobody from the office knew about that episode, and I wanted to keep it that way.

"Sounds like she's hiding something," he said finally. "Whether she's married, engaged to someone in the mob, has an extensive arrest record...it's impossible to say. But there's definitely something she wants to keep under wraps. If your relationship continues, and depending on how serious her deep dark secrets are, you'll either find out about everything in time, like you said, or you might never find out. So you have to come to grips with that, decide how serious you are about her, and ask yourself if you can live with not knowing everything about her past."

I just nodded. "Yeah. That's about what I figured." My mind flashed to the chubby little weirdo who gave me his phone number. But I wanted to keep the possibility of calling him as a last resort. Who knew what his relationship with Lyria was all about? "What I do know is that she's the most amazing woman I've ever been around. In addition to the physical part, we get along great. She's fun to be around. With a wicked sarcastic streak, by the way. I honestly never thought I'd have even a remote chance of being with someone like her."

"Then maybe the best thing to do is just hang in there. Enjoy the ride, so to speak. Maybe you'll eventually break through the ice. Until then, what you can do is reassure her that you won't book it if you find out something bad about her. Let her know that you'll stay with her no matter what."

"Hmm. Yeah. That might be possible. Maybe I'll stack some furniture in front of the door before I say that. You know. Just in case."

Berman laughed.

"Well, I guess we'd better get back. Thanks, Larry. I appreciate your perspective. It's good to hear from someone who isn't charged by the hour for his experience with women."

We both had a laugh thinking about Boof Parsons, and headed back to the cube farm.

Chapter Fourteen

Detective Grace Garvey returned to the precinct after a long day of gathering information about the presently dislocated Mr. Arnold Shaw. It was late, but when she got to her desk, she saw that Parker Gebelein, the other missing persons detective, was still working. She liked Parker in a distant way. He was a good cop, but a little lacking in the sense of humor department. Grace always felt that her way of coping via humor kept her sanity intact.

"How they hangin', Parker?"

Parker looked up from a stack of papers. No smile. "It's been better," he said.

"How's that downtown case going? Your guy was some kind of druggie, right? And his momma thought he was out at Boy Scout meetings every night? What was his name? Darren—"

"Dylan. Dylan Cavey, and as far as I can tell, the guy dropped off the face of the earth. Usually with tweakers, we just have to watch the arrests reports and rehab centers and they eventually show up. But this guy has gone deep. Nearest I can figure, he's off living on someone's stolen credit card so there's no record of him. Maybe in the Bahamas. I bet it's nice this time of year. Anyway, word on the street is he hung with a regular meth-head buddy, guy's name is...uh, let's see.... Lucas Corsi."

"Irish guy?"

Still no smile. "Yeah, so here's the weird thing. Corsi has

disappeared too. I checked his last known residence, and apparently he was shacking up with some broad in Dorchester. Met her in a halfway house. She was panicked 'cause she hadn't heard anything from him. She knew who he was — he didn't have a nine to five every day — but it was unusual for him to be away from his crib this long. But she hadn't heard a peep out of him since last Friday. The same day Dylan went bye bye."

"What do you think happened?"

"Who knows? Maybe they picked the wrong pocket and got iced. Or maybe they're both down in the Bahamas, laughing at us chasing after them. Anyway, they're just a couple of low lifes. You got the money job. Find out anything about the mayor's buddy?"

"Arnold Shaw. Nothing really important, except he still hasn't shown up at home or at work. If he went on a bender it must have been a doozy. Or if he has a girlfriend, he must have picked up some industrial-strength Viagra to have lasted this long."

Gebelein just nodded, no hint of amusement.

"Anyway, you know how it is with these cases. The longer the subject remains missing, the worse the prognosis," said Grace. "According to his coworkers, Arnold had some regular hangouts. I've checked out a couple of them, but nobody remembers Arnold from Saturday night. Still got a couple to look at. Did you check the morgue for your guys?"

"Yep. They're a no-show at the morgue too. Don't get excited, I looked for Arnold while I was there. Nothing. Just a pedestrian clump of stiffs who no one is looking for."

"Oh. Well, thanks for looking. So there are three MPs, all from the same general vicinity and timing. Maybe we got ourselves a serial killer who's just learning his trade. Maybe he got bored with hookers and decided to step it up a notch. You know, add a little challenge to his life."

"Wouldn't be the weirdest thing I've come across in this business. You headed out again?"

"Yeah, gotta pick up my messages. Then I'm heading over to some place up on Beacon Hill. Couple of people from Arnold's company mentioned it as one of his favorite haunts."

"What's the name of the place?"

"Uh, let's see. Yeah. It's called The Hill. Real original."

"Oh yeah. I know the place. Classy. The designer musta got a deal on mahogany."

"Oh yeah? High class babes hangout too?"

She was half busting on Gebelein, but he looked like he was thinking about it.

"Yeah. I guess so."

She smiled. "Hey, thanks Parker. I'll let you know if I need a consult on that."

Parker rolled his eyes and went back to his stack.

"All kidding aside," she said, thinking, especially 'cause it's not doing any good, "keep me up to speed on your druggies if you don't mind."

He looked up again. "You don't really think there's a link, do you?"

"Probably not. But it's like you said, weirder things have happened. See you, Parker."

***

When I got back to my desk, my phone was ringing from an outside line. I didn't even think to check for Shrek, I just rushed around to pick up, hoping I hadn't missed the call.

Okay, and honestly, hoping it was Vicky.

"Hello?"

"Hey bro. Whoa, you sound out of breath. Did I call at a bad time?"

"Oh, hey Carly."

"Don't sound so excited. What, were you expecting it to be

139

your new girlfriend or something?"

"No...."

"Stop! Don't tell me any more."

"What's wrong?"

"Nothing, but I just know you're going to say something that will make me crazy. Something like, 'She doesn't have my work number.' So let's just leave that subject alone."

"Okay."

Carly paused. "She doesn't, does she?"

"Doesn't what?"

"Have your work number. Your new girlfriend doesn't have it, does she?"

"I thought you wanted to leave it alone."

"You're right. You're right. So, are we still on for tomorrow night?"

"Yes, but Lyria's not going to make dinner. She'll meet us for a drink afterward."

Another pause. "I don't suppose there's any chance you know why she's not coming to dinner."

"No."

"Conner—"

"Carly, it's too early in the relationship for me to be pressing her for details. Isn't that what bothers you about Brent? That he wants to know where you are every second? Look, I'm the first to admit that I don't know what I'm doing. But what I have discerned is that Lyria is very private, and I'm trying my best not to scare her off by pushing too hard. When I'm with her, it—"

"If you say it makes it all worthwhile, I'm gonna hurl."

"Okay, then I won't say it."

"Oh boy. You really are hopeless. What am I going to do with you?"

"You're going to meet me at Grotto tomorrow night. Call it seven. We'll have a nice dinner. Just the three of us. You, me, and

Brent. Won't that be lovely?"

Carly laughed. "You're too much, brother. Then we'll get to meet her, right?"

"Yes, she's excited about meeting you. But it's only because she doesn't know you yet."

More laughs. "Okay. See you tomorrow. Don't blow me off or there'll be hell to pay."

I never did hear from Vicky that afternoon. But with Shrek being mysteriously AWOL, we all left the office at a decent hour for a change.

***

"Would you like to go for a walk tonight?" I asked Lyria. She had arrived a few minutes earlier, and I didn't know how she felt about walking some more. I assumed she walked to my place since I saw no evidence of a car or cab when she arrived. I also had to overcome some misgivings about walking with her since I had been held up at gunpoint just a few days prior. But that was a night with thick fog, which I was sure the robbers used to their advantage. And tonight was clear. And I was used to walking at night.

"What a lovely idea," said Lyria. "Just don't let it sap too much of your strength for later."

I could feel myself blush, which made Lyria laugh. "Come on, sweet Conner." I thought she was kidding about tiring me out, but I obviously had no idea what I was in for. My request fell into the category of "Be Careful What You Ask For."

She was wearing a dress as usual, and it just then occurred to me that she never wore any kind of coat or outerwear. It was a cool October evening. "Do you want to borrow one of my windbreakers?" I asked, but she declined and off we went.

Our walk started off normally enough. Our hands were down by our sides, but when they brushed together, we ended up interlocking our fingers. It felt so natural.

"Your hand is warm tonight," I said. "I'm glad. I was worried you might be getting sick last night."

"You're my sweet Conner. Thank you for your concern, but I hardly ever get sick."

"That's great. Does being healthy run in your family?" I figured that was a safe way of trying to break through her privacy wall without scaring her off.

"Something like that," she said. "I really love the architecture around here. It looks new, but still has a rustic feel to it. I'm glad whoever did the renovations in this area decided to maintain the character of the buildings."

My amazement at how similarly we thought about the architecture—and, for that matter, just about everything else we had discussed in the last week—made it okay that she had so swiftly changed the subject. "I feel the same way," I said. "Sometimes I walk after work to relieve the stress after a tough day in the office. I end up just gazing at these buildings and my stress is history." I looked at her and she was fixing me with one of her brilliant smiles.

"You're so lucky to live up here. Must be expensive though, isn't it?" she asked.

It was the question I had dreaded since we met. Like, how can an analyst afford to live on Beacon Hill? She was pretty savvy about the subject of investment banking in general. And I didn't think it would be getting us off to a good start if I tried to pretend to be someone I wasn't. So I thought, Here it is, Conner boy. If Lyria is a gold digger and only wants to be with you because of your address, you're about to find out. I stopped, faced her, and took her other hand.

"Lyria, I want to be honest with you."

"Of course, Conner. What is it?"

"My father bought me my place. He's made a fortune in investment banking. I couldn't even come close to affording my townhouse on what I make. In fact, if I even wanted to pay the condo fee on my own, I'd have to stop eating. And, still being honest, my Dad helped me get my job. He wanted me to follow in his footsteps, so he pulled some strings. BHA is so firmly entrenched in the industry, they normally require three to five years experience. But I skirted all that. Because of him."

I was watching her beautiful face for a reaction. She let out a breath and smiled again, making me weak in the knees. But I managed to keep from falling down.

"Mr. David," she said. "Why on earth would you think that made any difference to me?"

I exhaled too. But mine was a sigh of relief.

"I'm sorry."

"No apologies," she said.

"It's just that this friend of mine in the office. His name is Boof Parsons—"

"Boof?"

"Well, his real name is Edwin, but we all call him Boof." I was praying she didn't ask why, so I continued real fast. "He said that...uh...how should I put this? Well, he said that some women might be attracted to me just because of where I live."

She laughed and we started walking again, still holding hands.

"Conner, I can assure you that where you live makes absolutely no difference to me. Or how you got your job. I like the Conner that I've gotten to know for himself. The rest, as they say, is details."

I exhaled again. "I'm so glad. I...I was worried."

"Conner, I want us to have the kind of relationship where we can ask each other questions openly. How long has this been bothering you?"

"Well, since...since you started coming over. I'm with you, I want us to be open with each other too." I considered asking for some personal background, but thought it might be pushing my luck. "I don't want you to have any questions about me."

"Well, I do have one question," said Lyria. I tensed up.

"Wh...what is that?"

She smiled. "My question is, is this what you call walking?"

"Huh?"

"Come on, sweet Conner. I think it's about time we whipped you into shape." She let go of my hand and started power walking. "Try to keep up, slow poke."

I practically had to run to catch up with her. She was keeping a torrid pace, and I was just hoping I didn't pop a hammy.

We reached the fringe of Beacon Hill in no time, and she was heading into the north end of the Boston Common, a scenic patch of land in the city, with green grass, trees and all, but a park not known for its safety after dark.

"Lyria? Maybe we should stay on the main streets." I couldn't say too much more because it messed up my breathing pattern, and I was determined not to gasp for air.

"Don't be silly. I walk here all the time. I promise, it's perfectly safe."

We were buzzing through the park like there was no tomorrow. The south end of the grounds was heavily wooded, which made me even more leery, but Lyria just plunged on ahead. Before I knew it, we were at the border of the Common at the corner of Boylston Street. She stopped.

"You look pretty gassed," she said. "Do you want to take a break?"

"A break. Yeah. A break would be good."

She laughed and sat down on a park bench. There was nobody else around, and I was still a little nervous, but Lyria was calm as could be. And, she wasn't even breathing hard, while I was fantasizing about a portable oxygen tank.

She let her head fall back and took a deep breath. "Don't you just love the night air?"

"Yeah, sure. But there's a Dunkin' Donuts across the street. Can I buy you a coffee or anything? Or a bear claw? I'm sure there'll be plenty of night air left when we come back out."

She hit me with the megawatt smile yet again. "You don't get off that easily, Mr. David. We're just taking a quick rest, then we're hitting the pavement again."

"Sure, I mean, that's cool. But maybe we don't have to hit it quite so hard. I'm sure the pavement has feelings too, you know."

She threw her head back and laughed. Her laugh sounded like a music box on steroids. "Of course, darling. I guess we don't have to get you completely in shape tonight. We'll go half-pace and head up Arlington Street. Would that be okay? Think you're going to make it?"

"Yeah. Sounds good. That way we'll be closer to home in case you have to carry me for any significant distance."

More musical laughter. "Come on, sweet Conner." She held out her hand and we headed back at a more normal pace. But, when we got close to the townhouse, we had to go uphill—Beacon Hill didn't get its name because of a flat terrain. Once again Lyria never broke speed. We were holding hands, and for a time, it felt like she was dragging me behind her.

Finally we were home, and I, of course, was gasping again.

"Okay, you're right," I said. We're going to need some more practice to get me into shape."

"Not a problem, my dear. Before very long, I'll be struggling to keep up with you."

"I seriously doubt that. Phew, that was a good workout."

"Past tense?" she asked.

I looked at her quizzically. She came close with her arms around my neck. "Our workout has just begun," she purred.

***

We were lying side by side. "Does it seem like my stamina's

getting a little better?" I asked, then cringed. I needed a better filter between my thoughts and what actually came out.

"Definitely," said Lyria. "Especially considering that you had already been taxed physically once tonight."

Then we were quiet for a moment. I thought, No guts, no glory, David.

"Lyria, I've been meaning to mention something."

"Uh oh. Sounds heavy. I'm not sure I can handle this," she said with a smile.

"No, it's nothing bad. It's just that...I know you're a private person. And I respect that. I...I obviously want to know more about you, but I don't want to push your boundaries."

She put her hand up on my face. "My sweet Conner."

"Believe me," I continued, "the last thing I want to do is push you away. I...I care about you very much. Since I met you, I haven't really thought about too much else, and I think you know that my experience — with women — is pretty limited, so if I should shut up, please just tell me."

"I don't ever want you to shut up, Conner. I love hearing what you're thinking."

"Ah. That's great. You know...in addition, I wanted you to know that if there's anything that you don't want to tell me about, that's fine. But even if you did...you know...tell me something bad...about you...not that I think there is anything bad...I mean... you're...you're perfect. But if I did find out something bad about you...it...it wouldn't make any difference. To me, I mean. It wouldn't change the way I feel about you. Seriously. No matter what..."

Lyria was looking into my eyes, and I sensed that she was thinking about what I said. I thought, That's it, Conner. You blew it. The best relationship you've ever had, and you had to screw it up. I was also wishing I had pushed the sofa over in front of the door.

146

After what seemed like an eternity, Lyria smiled. "My Conner. You are the sweetest man. Thank you for sharing your feelings. What you said...."

She hesitated and I tensed up.

"It means more to me than you can imagine," she said.

I let out a breath.

Then we lay still, holding each other on our sides.

"Oh, and there's one more thing," I said, and I quickly flipped over, straddling on top of her with my hands on her shoulders. She looked at me quizzically.

"You're pinned," I said.

She laughed. "I'm pinned?"

"Yes," I said with false bravado. "You may be able to out-walk me, but when it comes to bed wrestling, I'm the master."

I felt a whoosh of air, and before I knew what was happening, Lyria was on top pinning my shoulders down.

She had a huge grin. "As a master, you should know better than to under-estimate the value of a good reversal," she said.

***

The next morning, I had soreness in muscles I didn't know existed. When I got to the office, I decided I would try to lay low, keep working on my current projects, and try to keep movement to a minimum. My Shrekoscope wasn't active, and I thought about trying Vicky again, but it was still early and I didn't want to wake her.

A little while later, I looked up and the guys from my group were all lined up in my doorway. The arrangement was comical, and I thought they must have planned it out. They were ordered by size, starting with Razor, then Berman, Stillwell, and Boof, tallest to shortest. They all had their arms around each other's shoulders, and were wearing what I believed were commonly called "shit-eating grins," although why anyone eating shit would be grinning was always beyond me.

"What's this?" I asked. "You guys all look like cats who ate the pet canary."

"Ah, it's much better than that, my boy," said Berman. "Chauncy, since you made the discovery, we'll give you the honor."

I could count the number of times I had seen Stillwell smile on one hand, but even he was sporting a devious smirk. "Well, my Shrekoscope hadn't been active all morning," he said. Then he started to laugh.

I thought, this has to be good. Chauncy was so serious, I had rarely even heard him use Dobson's nickname, never mind acknowledge the presence of a Shrekoscope.

He continued. "So I looked, and sure enough, Mr. Dobson wasn't in his office. I called a friend of mine in HR, and he said he'd check into it. And about a half an hour later he called back...."

The four guys all started snickering.

"Yeah? What did he tell you?" I asked.

Chauncy said, "Conner, you're about to hear four words I never thought any of us would utter." He paused for effect. Then he said, "Shrek called in sick."

I just sat looking at him. My jaw felt like it was hitting the floor. I heard a click, and realized Boof had taken a picture of me with his phone.

"I got it, you guys. The greatest expression of all time. Saved for posterity," said Boof, and the other three started cracking up, even the normally stoic Razor Rojas and Chauncy Stillwell. I still hadn't found my voice.

But then I sputtered, "Are you sure?" This, of course, caused an intensification of the laughter spasm.

"It's over," yelled Boof. "The reign of terror is over."

"I...I'm shocked," I said. "Hey, I never thought this would happen either, but it doesn't mean the reign of terror is over. Shrek's not gonna suddenly be Little Mary Sunshine when he gets back."

"No, don't you see?" asked Boof. "It'll never be the same. He always had this power over us. Not only was he our boss, he was like this evolved superhuman who had never called in sick. Who hadn't had a sniffle since Moby Dick was a guppy. Now, all he'll have is a title. He knows that we know he's just a mere mortal like us."

"We have to let Vicky know," said Razor. "And tell her she'll never pay for a drink again."

"Huh?" I asked.

"Yeah," said Berman. "Whatever she has, she gave it to Shrek. She made the guy sick, God bless her heart. Oh, and Boof—no sly comments about having close personal contact with the boss, you understand?"

Boof sported a "Who, sweet innocent little me?" expression. Then his face turned serious. "Hey, wait a minute, guys. This may not be such great news after all."

We stopped mid-laugh and looked at Boof.

"What do you mean?" asked Chauncy Stillwell.

"Well, we all know that Shrek always had a hard on to break John Bauer's perfect attendance record, right?"

"Yeah. So?" asked Razor.

"So, Shrek himself just called in sick. And we all know about it. Like I said, he knows that we know he's human. And fallible."

"Ah," said Chauncy.

"What? So what?" I asked.

Boof said, "So, if he wants to appear to be Mr. Perfect again, he's gonna have to stock the shelves with a whole new set of analysts. He won't want any witnesses to his show of weakness. So, he's gonna have to get rid of us. Or have us all killed, one or the other."

"Oh, come on," I said. "The company's not going to let Shrek fire, or execute, six analysts just 'cause we know he can get sick."

I tried to sound convincing, but I could see the other guys were thinking it through.

"Look at it this way," said Boof. "The guy's got to have an in with someone. How else do you explain him getting his job? He's about as bright as a five-watt bulb. Sometimes when you're trying to explain a financial issue to him, he gets this blank expression. It's like trying to teach a two-year old about rocket science. He must have something on a higher-up. And you know he thinks we're about as valuable as a box of pencils out of the supply cabinet. Who's to say he wouldn't be able to just rub out all the witnesses to his imperfection and start over with a whole new crew?"

"Man, you're some kind of killjoy, you know that?" asked Berman.

"You guys do what you want. I'm gonna go start spiffing up the old resume. Just in case."

And with that, Boof was gone, along with all of our good moods.

The team headed back to their cubes. I overheard Chauncy Stillwell ask Larry Berman, "You don't think he'd actually have us killed, do you?"

Chapter Fifteen

I managed to get through the rest of the day, though my mind was swirling in a million different directions. There was Lyria, Boof and the other analysts, Lyria, Shrek, Vicky, Lyria, the security of my job, analyst assassins, Lyria, the fat little schmuck with the phone number. And Lyria.

Lyria, Lyria, Lyria.

As late afternoon came rolling around, it occurred to me. I was supposed to go out with Carly and her asshole boyfriend Brent that night. And Lyria was supposed to meet us for drinks afterward.

Take me now, Lord.

I seriously considered calling Carly and shit canning the whole idea, but I didn't have the strength to listen to the endless stream of crap that would be forthcoming. Besides, I would have to somehow inform Lyria, and I had no way of contacting her.

Honestly, Lord, taking me now would really be okay.

With Shrek out sick, the team packed it in early—well, early for financial analysts working in the investment banking industry, anyway. The guys individually came by my cube to say goodnight. The elation of our boss being out had apparently returned, despite Boof's worry-wart warnings about everyone being let go. Or killed. It was so rare to leave work while it was still light out at this time of year, and we had the added bonus of this happening on a Friday night. So, despite the dour ending to

151

our earlier get-together, everyone's spirits had soared back into the stratosphere.

Even Razor was smiling. "Hey, Conner," he said on his way out. "What are you still doing here? We're in a Shrek-free zone, remember?"

I had to laugh. Razor cracking a joke was a true rarity. "Got any big plans for our newly-expanded weekend?" I asked.

"Nope. Just gonna flick on the tube, wet my whistle, and fall asleep in my favorite easy chair. Not even the Boston traffic on a Friday night could spoil my mood. See you."

Chauncy Stillwell followed a couple of minutes later. He conveyed pretty much the same message as Razor, but in Chauncy-speak. "Conner, I highly recommend that you take advantage of our ability to leave early. Who knows when the next time an occasion like this will come around?"

"Yeah," came a voice from outside my point of view. Then Larry Berman joined his twin in my doorway. I should have known they'd exit together. "Leaving while it's still light out on a Friday? And not having to come in on Saturday or Sunday?" said Berman. "It's like Christmas in October. I could get used to this Shrek getting sick business. I think it should happen more often." Then the twins were laughing in sync.

Of course, finally there was Boof. I figured the only reason he hadn't left yet was he was busy applying for other jobs.

"Hey man," he said as he burst in, all packed and ready to fly. "What say we hit the club early tonight? We can skip the funeral parlor at The Hill and check out The Good Life. Maybe we can get a quick crack at the babes who might want to exercise poor judgment this weekend. Get a head start on getting them juiced up, know what I mean?"

"Can't do it this weekend, Boof."

"Why not? Oh, don't tell me you're going back to The Hill and hope Ms. Gorgeous shows up again. You gotta give it up, man. Usually there's a reason a chick ditches a guy at a bar, and it isn't that she wants to have his babies. Move on, bro. There're other fish in the ocean. Maybe not many that look like she did, but hey, maybe there's a librarian's convention or something in town. We can scope them out during the eyeglass competition. That'd be more your speed."

"Uh, thanks for the vote of confidence. Weren't you the one giving me a pep talk just recently? Saying how you can't explain nature or how a beautiful woman could be interested in me, but to go with it because it is possible?"

"Hey, I was just trying to keep you from sticking your head in the oven. But that broad's like the signing of the Magna freakin' Carta. She's history, dude. So, what say we get started finding a replacement, huh?"

"Sorry, Boof, but I have plans tonight. I'm having dinner with my sister."

"Your sister? Holy shit, it's worse than I thought."

"No no. She's going out with a guy who's kind of a jerk. She wants to give him one last chance, and wants me to be there to keep him from being his usual asshole self."

"So, a threesome with your sister and her jerk-weed boyfriend. Well, I can certainly see how you couldn't pass that up."

"Never mind, smart guy. Anyway, you'll probably do better on your own. Without me weighing you down."

Boof thought for a few seconds. "Yeah, that's probably true. But you do have the fancy address. That could work to our advantage. Like we get a couple of babes and, you know, tell them that we own BHA. They don't have to know we're just a couple of peon analysts. They see that townhouse of yours, they'll be shedding clothes before we get through the door."

I laughed. "Good plan, Boof, but maybe some other time."

"Yeah. Count on it. Maybe next weekend. Anyway, have fun with your sister tonight." Then Boof was gone.

153

With the office emptied out, I figured it was the perfect time to call Vicky again. So, I dialed her number but there was no answer.

"Hey Vicky, it's Conner. Just wanted to check on how you were feeling. I thought you might like to know that our favorite boss to hate, the one and only Darren Shrek Dobson, actually called in sick himself today. Sorry you missed it — the office was a bit of a party. And if it turns out he has what you have, you'll be canonized in these halls forever. Anyway...I hope you're feeling better."

I didn't really know what else to say. Despite our recent conversations, I still knew virtually nothing about Vicky's personal life. For all I knew, she could be recuperating on her billionaire boyfriend's yacht floating around in Boston Harbor.

As I packed up to leave, I found myself in the same good mood that had infected my coworkers. Yes, I was worried about Vicky. And yes, I was semi-dreading the "double date" that night. But I was leaving work in the daylight on a Friday, and that made everything seem okay.

I got out the door and stood for a moment, inhaling the fresh air and basking with the sun on my face. I thought, I bet non-investment bankers don't appreciate this feeling as much as they should. But as I turned to head home, the glint from a pair of glasses hit my eye, and I saw somebody short and stout scurry around a corner out of sight. I immediately knew it was that little weirdo who was built like R2D2. I took off on a run after him. I didn't know who this little shit was, but I wasn't going to put up with him doing surveillance on me.

When I got around the corner, there was no sight of him. I lost it a little bit. "HEY. IF YOU HAVE SOMETHING TO SAY TO ME, SAY IT NOW!"

My voice echoed in the city streets, and I noticed passers by giving me a wide berth. But there was no sign of Mr. Roly Poly, and there were streets going off in all different directions. There was no way to tell where he had gone.

I looked up at the sky. Since everyone on the street was avoiding me anyway, I thought there was no harm in speaking some more.

"You're slipping, Lord," I said. "That good mood lasted almost five minutes. Would have been a new record."

***

I got home and had to get turned around for my "date" rather quickly. As I focused on what I had ahead of me that night, the anticipation grew exponentially.

Translation: I realized I was scared shitless.

This was really the first time I would be out in public with Lyria. The initial two nights in the bar didn't count, from my point of view. The first evening ended with her pulling a Harry Houdini on me and disappearing into thin air. The second night she was in full view when she left, but she was with some man-ape who had just knocked me senseless. Nope. Blotting out both of those memories completely.

But tonight, I would be with Carly. I normally enjoyed time with my sister, but I didn't know what to expect from this guy Brent. Would he behave himself because I was there? Or would he cause a scene anyway and force me to me to act? Clearly not my strong suit. And what if he did something while Lyria was there? Would she expect me to gallantly protect my sister? Would I look like a total tube in front of her when she realized how inept I was physically, if it came to that? Aside from all those worries, even if Brent didn't act up, how would Lyria get along with Carly?

Was there any way, ANY WAY AT ALL, that I could still get out of this??

I continued getting myself ready, trying really hard to convince myself that the occasion didn't have disaster written all over it. I even considered calling someone to talk it through, but then I realized that I would normally call Carly in a situation like this, and I sensed that wasn't an option. Vicky crossed my mind, but I had already called her enough this week. Any more would make me close to being a stalker. My mother? Okay, Conner, have you gone insane? Well, that about did it for the females in my little slice of the universe. I figured I would simply have to tough it out and hope for the best.

I had no idea what to wear. Grotto was a pretty casual place, so I didn't want to overdo it. Then again, I wanted to make a good impression with Lyria. I didn't want her to get to the restaurant and see me wearing classic dweeb. Might make her wonder what on earth she possibly could have been thinking. The problem was, she always looked sensational. I didn't do sensational. Best I could hope for was smashingly above-average. So I settled on a casual pair of slacks and a sweater. When I looked in the full-length mirror behind my closet door, I thought I fell somewhere between a freshman frat boy pledge and a reject from an Abercrombie & Fitch ad. I suddenly panicked. "Why didn't I ever have laser surgery?" I asked my image in the mirror. The thought had never come to me before, but standing there looking like the polyester prep king, I thought my glasses put me over the top into the ultimate-nerd category. And here I was, getting ready to meet one of the most gorgeous creatures on the planet. People would probably think she was having a pity-dinner with her mentally limited little brother.

I sat on my bed with my head in my hands, strongly considering going the no-show route. But Carly was depending on me, and it was too late for emergency laser surgery, so I had to suck it up and get going.

I left the house half expecting to run into Bob the Minion again, but there was no sign of the little twerp. It was a beautiful evening with a cool breeze that rustled the leaves on my tree-lined street. I took my sweet time walking over to the restaurant, focusing again on the beauty of the architecture on Beacon Hill and fighting off the familiar nagging notion that I didn't deserve to live there.

I arrived at Grotto, took a deep breath, and headed on in. At that moment, I was glad that Lyria was just meeting us for drinks later. It would give me a chance to get acclimated to the restaurant and deal with the flood of self-doubt that was dominating my mind. The place was packed with wall-to-wall people waiting for a table. I thought, Wow, all these people have a real social life, how about that? I started wading my way through the throngs toward a pretty girl taking orders for a table. I ignored the impulse to run and hide, and was about to reserve a spot on the list when I heard Carly's voice.

"Conner! Over here!"

She was sitting at a good-sized crowded bar with a glass of white wine. A husky guy in a black leather jacket was standing shoehorned in next to her, holding a brown beer bottle. I figured, well, that must be Brent. He had longish, unruly brown hair and a somewhat handsome, but weatherworn face. And he was big, probably about as tall as me, but twice as wide, with a muscular looking upper body physique and a slight beer belly. His jeans, work boots, and red plaid flannel shirt gave him a man's man look. I approached, thinking, So much for being able to help Carly in a physical confrontation. Brent looked like he could brush me off with one hand, like he was removing an annoying piece of lint from his shiny-looking jacket.

Carly looked great. She was wearing a beige cashmere crew neck sweater and a brown skirt. Her blonde hair looked freshly washed and was flowing over her shoulders.

"We already put in for a table," she said. "We got here early—we knew it would be jammed on a Friday night. But it's still going to be another few minutes. Come have a drink. Brent, this is my brother Conner. Conner, Brent."

"Hello, Brent." I could see he was sizing me up, probably relieved that I presented absolutely no physical threat whatsoever.

"Hyadoin?" he said. We shook—his hand felt rough and he squeezed hard, but I managed not to cry out. I guessed that Brent made a living doing some kind of manual labor. Remarkable how much better a guy's strength develops when his days aren't spent sitting behind a desk.

I ordered a beer. Brent was probably expecting me to ask for a Mai Tai, or some other frou-frou drink like that. There was a bit of an awkward silence.

"So, how was work today?" asked Carly in a semi-desperate attempt to break the ice.

"It was pretty exciting. Our boss called in sick."

"I thought calling in sick wasn't allowed in your department."

"It isn't. But it's because of our boss. Said he'd never called in sick in his life. Now that streak is over, I would imagine some of the starch has been taken out of his shorts."

Brent made a kind of pssshhh sound, and I could only guess from what Carly had told me previously that he always wanted to be the center of attention. Carly gave him a subtle look, but I knew her well enough to know there was some worry in her eyes.

"So, where do you work, Brent?" I asked. Okay, so it wasn't the most brilliant conversation starter ever, but I honestly couldn't think of anything else to ask.

"All over," he said. It was more like a grumble, and I had trouble hearing him over the crowd noise.

Carly jumped in. "Brent works in construction. His company has jobs all over Boston and in some of the suburbs. So, he really does get around." She laughed weakly. This guy definitely had a major 'tude. I wondered what Carly saw in him. Outside of the smoldering good looks and muscles in his teeth, that is.

I had trouble coming up with a follow-up question. There honestly couldn't be two more disparate ways to make a living than construction and doing financial analysis for an investment banking company. And aside from being around the same height, we were apparently polar opposites in just about every other way you could think of. He looked and acted like a modern James Dean on human growth hormones. I was a bookworm decked out in my finest preppy nerd look. When Brent glanced at me, I could tell he found me about as interesting as an earthworm, and about as significant.

"That's great," I said finally. "Working on anything interesting around town?"

His look of disdain made me unconsciously take a small step backwards.

"I'm gonna go check on our table," he said. He waded through the crowd toward the girl with the seating chart.

"What is up with this guy?" I asked Carly.

"I'm sorry. He's been pissed off ever since I picked him up tonight. We had a fight on the way over here. He wanted to know why we were having dinner with my brother. Did I think I needed a chaperone to be with him? That type of nonsense. He always wants my attention strictly focused on him. And heaven forbid I should talk to another guy. I bumped into someone when we came in. Total accident. The guy didn't know I was with Brent, and he looked me over and said something like, 'I was going to say I'm sorry, but that would be a lie.' Brent looked like he wanted to kill the guy. I purposely stayed in his way. I know how he is. He told the guy to 'move on before he was sorry he lost all his teeth.' I got him over to the bar and got him a beer, hoping that would calm him down. Then I went back and put in for our table. Believe it or not, there are times he can be very nice. But this is the last straw. It's over after tonight. Let's just get through dinner. And I can't wait to meet—"

"Lyria."

"Lyria. What a pretty name. She is still coming, isn't she?"

"As far as I know."

Carly gave me a look, but somehow fought off her yearning to bust my chops.

Brent was making his way back through the crowd. I noticed how people were getting out of his way. Whoever thinks size doesn't matter has probably never been a scrawny guy in this life. When I made my way through a horde like that, I might as well be invisible. I got shoved, stepped on, spilled on, and moved out of the way as if I were a misplaced piece of furniture. Brent hardly even had to turn sideways. Then Mr. Personality was back.

"It'll just be another couple of minutes," he said. "I got her to move us up on the list some."

I had the urge to say, "Damn man, I bet you could charm the birds right out of the trees," but the desire to continue living kept me from doing so.

Then the uncomfortable quiet was back. Amazing how you can be amidst throngs of people and still be conscious of every cough. I looked at Carly and could see annoyance building up. I was pretty good at annoying her myself, so it was a look I was very familiar with. I was praying we'd get called for our table before her displeasure boiled over.

"Brent, I think Conner asked you a question earlier."

I thought, Well, that would be a big nope.

"No, it's okay, Carly," I said.

"It is most certainly not okay," she said. There may as well have been icicles hanging on her words. "We're having dinner together, and it's just common courtesy to answer somebody when they ask you a question. Ignoring them is beyond rude."

Brent was staring at my sister, his face getting red. I thought that was probably how a wolf looked at a sheep just before chowing down.

Carly stared right back. I was holding my breath because I

knew that if he went at her I would have to step in. Come on, table. I was wondering if it would take Brent enough time to brush me out of his way that Carly could escape.

"What did you ask?" Brent spoke through clenched teeth, and without breaking off his staring contest.

"Oh...no big deal. I was just wondering if...you know...you had any interesting construction jobs around town. Around Boston," I said. My heart was beating about twice its normal rate.

"No. No interesting jobs," he said.

"Oh. Okay. Cool," I said, looking back toward the hostess.

I thought that might be the end of it, but Carly had other ideas.

"Oh?" she said, the icicles still present. "Aren't you adding an entire floor to an office building on Tremont Street right across from the state house? That borders on Beacon Hill, where Conner lives and works. I bet he would have found that interesting."

Brent's face got even redder and my life started flashing before my eyes.

"David. Party of four," said the hostess.

I released my breath and we started heading for the dining area. Maybe a change of venue and the prospect of food would tone down the tension.

I honestly thought the evening had to get better from there. It certainly couldn't get much worse.

Boy, was I wrong.

***

We were seated at a table that backed up to a wall, with other patrons a few feet away on both sides. At first, the mood did seem a little better once we sat down. Maybe the prospect of getting fed made Brent a little happier. It was worrisome to me, though, that he continued pounding down the beers. He didn't even wait for anyone from the wait staff to come over. When he was getting low, he simply made his way back over and graced the bartenders with his warming presence in person.

"I'm really sorry about this, Conner," said Carly while Mr. Charm School was out of earshot.

"Hey, it's not your fault. I'm sure a lot of girls have lousy taste in men."

She smiled a little. "I should have known better. All the signs were there. You could write an entire article in Cosmopolitan about the things that went wrong with us. And yet I still kept giving him more chances. He'd get all sweet and apologetic for acting like such a clown, and I'd think, well maybe there's hope. Stupid. Just plain stupid."

"Don't be too hard on yourself. Besides, if you get real desperate, I bet Boof Parsons would make himself available."

She just stared me down, then let out a laugh when she realized I was kidding. "No offense, Conner. I know he's a friend of yours, but I'd rather become the love slave on a remote island full of cannibals than get involved with Boof."

I laughed. "You'd probably rather have your wisdom teeth removed through your ear."

Now Carly was laughing too. "I'd rather have a bikini wax with duct tape."

"Whoa, now we're getting personal," I said, and we both continued to laugh.

"Well, isn't this just a cozy little scene?" Brent's massive presence loomed like a giant shadow blocking out the sun. He had picked up two beers, and I initially thought one was for me as a way of apologizing for acting like such a Neanderthal. But Brent kept both close to the vest and looked like he'd eviscerate anyone who tried to take one away. He'd really just gotten two as a safeguard in case it took us a while to be waited on. Carly's laughter and smile evaporated. "Seems like the only time you two find something to laugh about is when I'm not around."

I thought, Yeah, imagine that. His personality didn't exactly evoke gaiety or good moods. It might evoke suicide if you had to spend any measurable time with him.

Of course, I would have let the absurd comment slide, but not my little sis. "Well, you're not exactly being Mr. Congeniality tonight, Brent."

Brent glared at her.

I said, "Carly —"

"No, I'm sorry. We come into Boston to have a nice dinner with my brother, whom you've never met before. We're going to meet his new girlfriend for the first time, and you're acting like some gorilla with a hair across his ass."

Brent sat back and took a swig that emptied about half of bottle number one, his eyes never leaving my sister. "Are you finished?" he asked in a soft tone that sent shivers down my spine.

"No, as a matter of fact...I'll bet it isn't a hair across your ass. I'll bet it's more like barbed wire."

That's it, I thought. I'm going to have to peel him off her and my life will be over. But a tall, thin, good-looking young man in a restaurant uniform appeared at our table.

Maybe my stars were aligned after all.

"Good evening sirs, miss. My name is Hans and I'll be waiting on you tonight. May I start by refreshing or supplementing your drinks?"

"Bring me two more of these," said Brent, holding up one of his bottles. "I have a feeling I'm gonna need them."

Carly ordered another glass of wine and I asked for another beer, even though I'd only taken a sip out of my first one. I had a feeling I was going to be needing it too.

Hans walked through the specials, all of which instantly blurred in my mind. "May I bring you an appetizer?" he asked. "The calamari is usually a crowd favorite."

"No. No appetizer," growled Brent.

Hans started walking away, probably as anxious to get away from Brent as I was, when Carly, my svelte sister, whom I had never known to order an appetizer because she didn't want to spoil her appetite, blurted out, "Yes." Hans came back as Brent stared in disbelief. "The calamari sounds wonderful. Guess you'll only need to bring two appetizer plates."

***

Brent thumped his menu open so hard he almost tore the pages out of the fancy binder. He stood up suddenly, making me jump a little. "I'm gonna hit the can," he grumbled.

"Jesus, Carly," I said. "This is bad enough. Do you have to keep antagonizing him?"

"Hey, I'm not going to let him get away with acting like that. He's just a big loser. What are you worried about?"

"Right now I'm worried about staying alive long enough for the entrees to come."

"If he keeps on drinking like this, he'll be too pickled to start anything," she said, but I wasn't convinced.

Brent lumbered on back, and he had picked up two more beers on his way. Then Hans brought him two more, along with our drinks. If he kept this pace up, we'd have enough for a pretty impressive beer bottle pyramid in no time. Hans looked at Brent's collection of bottles doubtfully, and I had a spark of hope that maybe they'd have some bouncers who'd give him the boot. Or at least cut him off. I even considered the possibility that since we were in an Italian restaurant, maybe the owners would save themselves the trouble and just have him rubbed out. I knew the Mafia wasn't what it once was, but there must still be a hit man around somewhere who was bored and looking for some action.

But after a few minutes of stone silence at the table, Hans came back to take our orders, and there was no sign of Vito Corleone. Putting the kibosh on any notion of chivalry, Brent busted in and ordered before Carly. He wanted spaghetti and

164

meatballs. No flies on this guy. "And bring me two more beers," he said, causing my sister to roll her eyes and me to think back to whether my medical insurance covered emergency room visits. Carly and I both wanted veal Parmesan.

"Oh my," said Brent. "Aren't we being fancy tonight?"

I was like, fancy? Veal Parmesan? But Brent tilted his head back and laughed at his own "joke." His face was getting flushed and he was smiling to himself a bit more. I figured even a big guy like him had to eventually succumb to the amount of alcohol he was taking on. Carly was now completely ignoring him.

The calamari came, and Hans actually did bring three plates. Carly and I had a couple of pieces, then Brent, who had made it clear he didn't care for an appetizer, took the plate and dumped about half the calamari onto his little snack dish.

Carly put her head in her hands, and I thought she might be crying. Brent looked at her. "Oh, hey baby, I'm sorry." He put his arm around her chair and Carly shifted forward as if whatever was wrong with this guy, it might be communicable. "No, seriously honey," said Brent, with the beginnings of a slur. "I'll be a complete gentleman from now on. I promise. Did I tell you how hot you look tonight? You look smoking fucking hot tonight. Oh, sorry." He laughed, clapping his hands. "I didn't mean to get rude with your brother sitting here. Cooper, I'm really sorry, meant no disrespect."

"Conner," I said.

"What?"

"My name. It's Conner."

"Oh yeah. Sorry again." More laughter.

Carly said, "Brent, will you please try to behave? Let's just try to have a nice dinner, okay? Can we do that?"

Brent took a slug. "You bet. Best behavior. Wouldn't want to act up in a classy joint like this. This is nice." He looked around the restaurant as if we'd just arrived. "Nice place. Don't you think so, Cooper? Bet the food is fucking awesome here."

Carly took a deep breath. "Brent, why don't you tell Conner about that construction project on Tremont while we're waiting for our food?"

I could see that Carly was trying to keep him occupied so that he didn't start break dancing on the table or something. Brent looked around for Conner, then his cloudy eyes settled on me.

"Oh. Yeah, sure. Most fucked up building you can imagine. We got into it and we was all surprised the whole thing didn't just fall down. I'll tell you, not only were the construction codes total shit when this one was built, we was convinced they didn't have any codes. So, we get the demo done—most fun part of any job by the way—and based on the condition of the building underneath, my bosses, who asshole to asshole couldn't produce a beer fart in a wind storm, decide they'd better bring in one of these chickenshit structural engineers. They was afraid the frame wouldn't hold the additional floor. Can you imagine that, Cooper?"

I thought surely the question was rhetorical, but Brent was actually pausing his narrative, giving me a chance to answer. I didn't really know what to say. I was envisioning an entire floor crashing down on people innocently working at their desks. But before I had to come up with a response, Hans once again rode to the rescue and dinner was served.

***

The meal portion of our evening started out pretty calmly. Brent was really getting into his spaghetti and beer, and didn't seem to mind Carly and I speaking quietly to each other.

"What time do you think Lyria will get here?" she asked.

"I um...I'm not sure."

"Conner, there is a Lyria, isn't there? I mean if you made your new girlfriend up, it's...it's okay. I'm your sister, you can tell me."

"I didn't make her up. Why do you think I made her up?"

"It's just hard to believe you've been seeing her for what, a week now? And you don't even have her phone number? You don't know where she lives. You know nothing about her. Look, I know living alone can do a number on your psyche. You're holed up all day, working hard, with a bunch of people with no personality to speak of. And in Boof's case, a personality disorder. It's just that...your mind has a chance to wander. If that's what happened —"

"Carly, Lyria is real. I've been with her every night this week. The first couple of nights, okay, I was wondering if I was dreaming too. But I promise, I'm not hallucinating."

"Don't think I didn't notice you eyeing that pretty boy waiter either." Brent blurted out his latest pearl of wisdom to Carly while slurping up a strand of spaghetti.

Carly looked at him in disbelief. "Excuse me?" she asked.

Brent answered, looking down at his food. "Yeah. What's his name? Hans?" I thought, Oh sure, you can get the waiter's name right. "He's good looking in a pretty-boy kinda way. I saw you givin' him the eye." Brent took another huge slug of beer. "It's not that I mind — you know me, I'm pretty easy going. Just don't get any ideas in that pretty little head of yours. You came here with me, you're gonna leave with me."

Carly let out an 'ugh' sound. "I wasn't giving anyone the eye. And you're drunk. I have a good mind to leave here without you and let you find your own way home. Either that or end up in the drunk tank in Boston. I don't really care."

Brent stopped eating and stared at my sister. "You're making a big mistake, little miss."

"Don't call me little miss. The only mistake I made was thinking it was worth giving you another chance."

"You were givin' me another chance?"

"Yes, despite the fact that Cosmo said that with your traits you

167

gave every indication of being an abusive, psycho, control freak. And don't think I haven't noticed you stalking me everywhere I go. I must have been out of my mind agreeing to go out with you again."

Brent leaned over close to Carly. "Wait a minute," he said. "Who the hell is Cosmo?"

Carly's face turned beet red. "That's it," she said, standing up. "That does it."

I had the feeling she was about to storm out. I was wondering if Brent would chase her, and again thought about having to intercede. A picture came to my mind of Brent outside the restaurant keeping Carly pinned underneath one arm, holding me up by the neck with the other hand, and shaking me like one of those rubber chickens.

"Hello, Conner. Sorry I'm late."

The voice sounded like it was coming from the heavens. I looked up and Lyria was standing at the side of the table. Despite the fact that we had indeed spent every night together for the past week, I was still stunned speechless when I looked at her. She was wearing a bright yellow print dress with her brown hair cascading over both shoulders. And her face—her face was almost otherworldly, and I looked at her as if I was seeing her for the first time. Her perfect features had an aura about them. It might have been my imagination, but she seemed to be...I don't know exactly how to describe it. Glowing? Yes, it was like she was glowing. The fact that we were in a crowded public restaurant didn't matter. It somehow seemed like we were the only ones there.

"Holy shit."

I looked at Brent and saw that he was staring slack-jawed at Lyria as well. Carly, who just a moment ago had stood in anger, ready to charge out into the street, sat back down in her chair with a muted thud, looking wondrously at my vision/date. I can't deny that I probably sported a bit of a smirk, as if to say to my sister, "See? I told you she was real."

Lyria was holding a wine stem with a reddish liquid that I took to be wine. I started breathing again and stood up. I gave Lyria a brief embrace, and kissed her lightly on the cheek. "You're not late. In fact, you're just in time. It's really good to see you," I said.

"No way," said Brent, still staring. "No fucking way. She's with you? This is your date, Cooper? This babe? With little Cooper here? It can't possibly be. It can't possibly fucking be."

Lyria leaned close to me. "Who's Cooper?"

I gave her a look. "I am."

"Ah," she said with a smile. "And you must be Carly," she said to my sister, extending her hand. "I've heard so many great things about you."

Carly looked totally dumbfounded. I guessed that she was thinking the same thought that Brent had just so brilliantly espoused. She shook Lyria's hand. "Yes," she gasped. "I mean... yes. I'm Carly. Cooper's sister...I mean Conner...."

Lyria laughed. "Again, I'm sorry I'm late. This must be a very good restaurant considering how crowded it is." She took a sip of her drink and looked at me.

"Oh, sorry," I said. I stood up suddenly, almost knocking the table over, and pulled out Lyria's chair. "Please, have a seat."

"Why, thank you, kind sir," said Lyria, with her music box voice.

"Can't possibly fucking be," said Brent.

***

"Please don't let me interrupt your dinners," said Lyria.

I looked down, and it seemed like the arrival of our veal Parmesan hadn't registered before. "Would you like me to get you something?" I asked. "I can get the waiter back over —"

"No. Thank you, sweet Conner. I've already had dinner. But

you should eat. And you, Carly. Your dinners look wonderful." Carly was just staring, making it the first time in recorded memory that my sister was actually speechless.

"Hey, I'm Brent." Brent wiped his hand on his sleeve and stuck it toward Lyria.

"Oh...yes, sorry," said Carly, as if she had forgotten her date was there. "This is Brent."

Lyria shook his hand briefly. "So nice to meet you, Brent. How is your spaghetti?"

Brent just stared for a moment. "What? Oh, my spaghetti. Yeah. Great. Hey Hans, need two more beers over here."

"So, Lyria," said Carly. "I...I understand you met Conner at The Hill."

"Who's Conner?"

Lyria completely ignored Brent's blurt out. "Yes. Isn't it amazing the way things work out?" asked Lyria. "I had just stopped in there for a quick moment. Turned out to be fortuitous." She didn't say anything about having seen me while we were both walking in the fog separately the night before. And I sure as shootin' wasn't going to bring it up.

"Yeah. Especially for me," I said, and Carly and Lyria laughed.

"For me too," said Lyria. "One doesn't meet someone as sweet as your brother every day."

"You can say that again," said Carly. It was clear she was taking a dig at Brent, but he was too plastered to realize it. Plus, he was still staring agape at Lyria.

Suddenly, Brent leaned forward. "All bullshit aside. What is the scoop here? Does little Cooper have something on you? Do you owe him money or something? That's gotta be it, right? He floated you some cash, and instead of paying him back, you agreed to be seen with him in public." The big man sat back and had a hearty laugh at his own joke.

Carly exhaled a sound of exasperation. "Brent," she said softly. "You're being rude."

Brent looked at her with a reddening face. "I'm being rude?" His voice sounded a couple of dozen octaves louder than Carly's. "Why? 'Cause I'm saying what we're all thinking? How can your little squirt brother land a patch of Grade A prime pussy like that? Huh? Go ahead. You explain it to me."

Carly looked as mad as I'd ever seen her. I glanced at Lyria and she looked as calm as ever, as if nothing had happened.

"I want you to leave," said Carly.

Brent looked stunned. As in, "Who, innocent little me?" "You what?" he asked.

"I said, I want you to leave. Get out. Go home. Better yet, hit a couple of bars on the way home and get hammered some more. And don't follow me around anymore. I don't ever want to see you again."

Brent looked ready to explode.

"Excuse me, sir?"

We all looked up. We hadn't noticed that Hans had come back to our table, along with a big guy in a suit.

"You talkin' to me?" asked Brent.

"Yes, sir," said the big guy. "My name is Antonio Costanzo, I'm the manager of Grotto. Might I have a word with you in private, sir?"

Mr. Costanzo nodded toward an opening that I was pretty sure led to the kitchen.

"No, you might not," said Brent. "Hans, what's up with my beers?"

"Please, sir," said Mr. Costanzo. "I would appreciate it if I might speak with you for a brief moment."

Carly, Lyria, and I were all watching the scene unfold. It reminded me of denizens of a town watching their homes get washed away by a tsunami.

"And I would appreciate it if you would get me the beers that I ordered. And do it now," said Brent.

Costanzo and Hans gave each other a look. "Sir," said Costanzo. "I was trying not to embarrass you in front of your party, but I'm afraid we can't serve you any more alcohol. However, I would be happy to get you some coffee on the house."

Thinking back on what happened next, it all seems like a blur. Brent stood up slowly looking at Carly. His rage was so intense, at first he couldn't find any words. Then he pointed at her. "You're responsible for this, aren't you?" he said quietly. "What did you do, give your pretty-boy boyfriend Hans the high sign? Get him to cut me off?"

Before I knew what I was doing, I stood up. "Hey, wait a minute, Brent." At that particular moment, I was really glad we had the table between us.

"I don't remember asking you anything, pipsqueak," said Brent in the same simmering tone.

Hans stepped forward. "Sir, please calm down." I noticed other members of the staff gathering behind Antonio Costanzo. But before they could get in range to prevent something from happening, Brent swung and leveled poor Hans with a clout to the jaw. There were screams from the other patrons.

Carly yelled, "Brent! Stop it right now!"

She stood up and grabbed Brent's arm as the crowd of employees rushed forward. Before anyone could stop him, Brent swung his other arm and hit Carly on the side of her face with his fist. She cried out briefly and went down in a heap.

I felt a burst of anger that I honestly didn't know I was capable of. I remember yelling "Hey!" and without thinking, I, Conner David, perhaps the most unlikely action hero of all time, turned the table over and ran at the big bruiser construction worker. Italian food went flying in every direction, and I heard Lyria yell, "Conner, no!" Mr. Costanzo and another member of his staff had by this time grabbed Brent's arms and were trying to pin him down. But Brent's strength was magnified by the alcohol. He shook the two men loose, grabbed me under my arm, picked me up, and sent me hurtling through the air in a move that I was sure would have made any professional wrestler proud. The other restaurant customers were all standing up watching the melee. I landed on the floor and skidded into a nicely dressed couple, knocking them off their feet like a bowling ball picking up a spare.

I looked up and a team of Grotto workers were holding onto Raging Brent, and trying to get him out the front door. I looked back toward the space formerly known as our table. Carly was getting up off the floor holding her cheek and trying to regain her senses.

Lyria ran over to me. "Conner, are you all right?"

Clearly still not thinking straight, I said, "Yes, I'm fine. Please go help Carly." Lyria looked concerned, but did what I asked and helped Carly to her feet.

I heard my sister wail, "Oh my God. Conner. Lyria. I'm sorry. I'm so sorry." Then she ran toward the exit.

The Grotto team finally got Brent outside. My only thought was to go after Carly. When I got to the cool outside air, I could see Brent still tussling with the restaurant employees. I heard a siren in the distance, and assumed the police were on their way. Apparently Brent heard it too. He disengaged from the Grotto guys and took off, going south on Bowdoin Street. I could see Carly ahead of me running north. I called to her but she didn't stop.

"Carly, wait! Are you all right?" But she was gaining ground. Damn. Was everybody faster than me? Carly disappeared around a corner, and when I got there, she was nowhere in sight. I had no idea where she had parked, so she really could be anywhere. I ran and looked down a couple of side streets. Nothing. I tried calling her cell. No answer. So I just stood in the middle of the empty downtown street, a mountain of frustration built up inside of me. I yelled out, "CARLY." But the sound just echoed off the surrounding buildings. Then I thought, That's twice I was yelling to nobody in the middle of the city. I'd better stop that, or at some point I am going to get locked away in a padded cell somewhere.

I didn't know what to do next, but then I remembered that I had left Lyria alone in the restaurant. "Oh, good Lord," I said out loud, and I started high-tailing it back to Grotto's. I thought, Sure. The first time we're out as a couple in public, and my family is in the middle of a brawl in a nice, respectable restaurant. How could she not want you now, Conner? If she didn't realize what a catch you were before....

I was running as fast as my non-athletic legs would carry me, but as I came in sight of the restaurant, I skidded to a halt. Antonio Costanzo was out front with a couple of Boston police officers. They were just standing there talking, but I was afraid they'd want me to give a statement or something. That was always what they did on TV, anyway. But, I was worried about Lyria, and I didn't want to get delayed.

So, I crossed the street, then changed roles from action hero to superspy sleuth. I peeled off my sweater and yes, even removed my glasses in an effort to keep from being recognized. Since I could barely see, I also had to keep from getting run down crossing back over, but I managed. Fortunately, there were a bunch of other people milling around the entrance as well, so I approached the doorway trying to look as casual as possible. Sure enough, I walked in without being noticed. There are advantages to looking nondescript, although I had to admit, this was the first time that thought had ever come to me.

I made my way around to where we had been sitting. Members of the staff were cleaning up and picking up displaced furniture. There was no sign of the couple I had bowled over. Guess they'd probably had enough excitement for one night and went home to call their lawyer. Other people were still seated, having their dinner as if nothing had happened. But what I noticed most of all was that there was also no sign of my date.

Lyria was gone.

***

I thought about asking a member of the staff if they had seen her leave, but I wanted to avoid getting involved with the criminal justice system and possibly needing a membership in the witness protection program. So I started slinking back toward the exit.

"Hey. Aren't you the dude that was here earlier?"

I stiffened. Drat, my disguise had failed.

I turned around, trying to look innocent. A guy in a waiter's uniform was regarding me carefully. He didn't look real sure of himself.

"No. No, I just got here. What happened?"

The super sleuth thought he would ask an innocent question to throw the predator off his tail.

The guy just shook his head. "Some big asshole got smashed and started wrecking the place. Not even a full moon tonight. Seemed like a quiet evening before all this broke out." Then he went back to clearing the destruction.

I figured I'd better not push my luck and headed out. The crowd and police were still gathered around Costanzo, and nobody noticed me leaving. I thought, Maybe I should grow a mustache or something. I headed south on Bowdoin, the direction Brent had taken off in. I figured if Lyria had gone north I would have seen her coming back. Although I had to admit, she was an expert in evasion if there ever was one.

As I got farther away from Grotto, the street crowds thinned out. I kept walking. I can't tell you now exactly what it was that drew my attention, whether I heard something or noticed movement out of the corner of my eye. But I passed a dark alley on a side street, and was impelled forward. Sure, Conner, I was thinking. Seems like a real good idea, checking out a dark alley at night in downtown Boston. But for some reason I couldn't understand, I kept moving toward the back of the alley.

What I saw next is not something I will forget anytime soon.

***

As my eyes adjusted to the dark, I could indeed see movement, and heard a noise that I couldn't identify. I kept moving forward slowly, and started to make out a heap on the ground ahead. There seemed to be a regular up and down motion, and almost like a churning sound. Or chugging. My immediate thought was that someone was humping back there. But then I could see a figure on top hunched over. Wearing yellow. What looked like its head was jerking up and down. And there was someone else— another figure who looked to be prone, lying on its back. It was huge, and its legs were spasming. I got closer, but my mind at first refused to draw the inevitable conclusion. The person on top was wearing a familiar print dress. She had one hand pinning the bottom figure down on its left shoulder. The other was holding its head down sideways. Her head was pressed against its neck, bobbing up and down. Now I could see the bottom figure more clearly. The massive body was wearing work boots. And jeans. And a red plaid shirt.

"Lyria," I shouted.

I stood agape as Lyria lifted her head up from Brent's neck. She looked up at me, and I barely recognized her face. A torrent of blood poured down her chin, and she gurgled to swallow the rest. Her eyes were like black marbles, and she had huge canine teeth that I had never seen before. Blood continued to poor out of Brent's neck, and his body was still in a spasm.

"LYRIA, MY GOD, NO!" I wailed as I turned toward the mouth of the alley.

"CONNER," she yelled behind me. Gone was the singsong

voice. This sound was more like a gravelly low growl. "CONNER, WAIT!"

I ran blindly out into the street. It was only by the grace of the good Lord that I didn't get hit by a car as I plunged across Bowdoin Street. I ran north and headed for my home, running as fast as I could manage. I wasn't even conscious of anyone else's presence and, for all I know, I may have knocked some bystanders out of the way. Maybe several people. I kept up the full sprint until I was through my front door. I was gasping for breath, but I ignored the pain in my chest.

I had an immediate need to double lock my door, and I ran frantically, ensuring my back door and every window was locked tight. I knew Lyria somehow got in and out seamlessly, but I thought, she can't get through a locked door or window. Can she?

After I had secured every opening, I ran around and checked them all again. Even when I saw a window was locked, I tried it, pulling up with all my might. I did that a couple of more times before I collapsed on my bedroom floor. My body couldn't sustain the heavy breathing and I blacked out, a sea of stars before my eyes.

When I came to, I tried to convince myself that the whole thing was just a bad dream. But I felt soreness on my side from where I landed after Brent tossed me down like a newspaper delivery boy providing a customer with the latest edition.

When I thought about seeing Lyria, I started hyperventilating again. "Stop, Conner," I said to myself, trying to regulate my air intake so I didn't pass out again. I sat up on the floor and leaned against my bed. I had no idea what I should do. I was afraid to move. I was afraid that if I went back downstairs Lyria would be there. I had seen her. Would she need to come for me next? Should I call the police? Or maybe an exorcist? There was the hyperventilating again. I barely got it under control before returning to Never-never land. No, I thought. I can't call anyone, they would probably think I was just another crank on a Friday night binge. And how does one find an exorcist anyway? Are they listed in the Yellow Pages?

After considering all my options, I decided that sitting right there on the floor in my room was the best alternative. And that is what I did. I sat in that spot all night long, jumping at every noise, shuddering every time the wind blew. I was still there when I suddenly became conscious of two things at the same time. One, it was light out. And two, someone was ringing my front doorbell.

Chapter Sixteen

Vicky Temerlin's days were all dark. Truth be told, she couldn't discern the difference between night and day anymore. Every hour seemed the same. She knew a few things about her current situation. One was that she had never felt worse in her life. She was in constant pain, and barely had enough energy to raise her head. She knew that she was still having the dream. The circumstances never varied. The cloak of darkness, feeling paralyzed, the woman. Gorgeous at first, then hideous. The pain. The burning, searing pain. Trying to scream, but having no voice. She had what she could only think of as visions of who the woman was and where she came from. Vicky knew that she was cold. Even more of a concernty, she knew that she was being restrained, although she wasn't exactly sure how.

Vicky also realized that there were two critical pieces of information she was missing, and she thought that the rest all seemed pretty minor in comparison.

One, Vicky had no idea where she was. And two, she didn't have the first clue how she had gotten there.

***

I stood up and every muscle in my body cramped, a rousing objection to having been stuck in the same position for so long. I crept over to my front bedroom window and peeked through the shades. An unfamiliar car was sitting out front. I made my way slowly down the stairs, got to the atrium, and paid homage in my mind to whoever thought up the idea of peepholes for your door. I looked through and let out a deep breath that I wasn't aware I was holding when I saw that it wasn't Lyria out front. It was a good-looking young blonde-haired woman wearing a windbreaker. I couldn't see her lower body.

She must have heard me come down the stairs, because she knocked loudly. "Mr. David?" she asked.

I thought for a minute, then I said, "Yes?" through the door.

"Mr. David, I'm Detective Grace Garvey of the Boston Police Department. Would it be possible to ask you a few questions?"

I looked back through the peephole and the detective was holding her badge and ID up on the other side for me to see. I thought, Huh, she knew I was looking through the hole. Guess she's done this before.

My mind raced off in a million different directions. My most likely conclusion was that they had arrested Lyria for murder. I consoled myself to having to tell them the whole story of how I met her, but I wondered if this detective would believe me. I didn't believe parts of it myself.

I couldn't think of a better alternative, and I wasn't up to sneaking out the back door and living my life on the lam. So, I opened up.

Grace Garvey looked to be in her late twenties, and I had underestimated her in my instant assessment of her looks. She resembled one of those models playing a cop on TV. "Breaking the law is a bad idea, Mr. Perpetrator. Now, stand aside while I fix my makeup." She had nice features, and her long blonde hair was pulled back in a ponytail. I couldn't tell for sure because of the windbreaker, but I thought she had a body in the "killer" category. She was wearing tight jeans and dark colored sneakers. I realized she was assessing me at the same time, though probably with vastly different results. Finally, she smiled brightly and broke the silence.

"Mr. Conner David? Hey, Conner, by any chance did you happen to be at a nightclub called The Hill last Saturday night?"

Her manner was more like someone you might meet at the bar, very casual and affecting. It put me somewhat at ease, but I had to keep in mind that she wasn't here to socialize.

"The Hill? Last Saturday night? Uh, let me see now...."

"I'm sure a good looking young guy like yourself has a busy social calendar. But if you could try to remember, I'd really appreciate it."

I managed to emit a little laugh that belied the fact that I was figuratively shitting Twinkies. "Sure. Yeah. Um. Yes. I think I did check out The Hill last Saturday."

"May I come in, Mr. David?"

"Oh, yes, of course. Sorry." Well, it didn't take long for me to start falling all over myself now, did it?

Grace scanned the interior of my townhouse. "Nice little crib you have here. Do you live here alone?"

"Yes. I do. I, you know...have visitors sometimes. But I'm the only one who lives here. Yes." I thought, Good Lord. It's a wonder I'm allowed out in public.

I thought I detected a slight smile from Detective Garvey. "Any visitors right now?"

"Uh, no. No. There's nobody else here."

"Okay. Would it be all right if we sat down?" She nodded toward the couch and I couldn't help but think about Lyria.

"Yes. Yes, of course. Would you like anything? Coffee? Or tea? I have all kinds of tea." It was like my brain was throwing up.

"No. No thanks."

Grace moved over to the couch and I noticed that she did so without turning her back on me. She was carrying a valise with a shoulder strap. No doubt to keep her hands free in case she had to draw down.

Okay, Conner. You definitely watch too much TV.

Grace sat on the edge of the couch and I took the adjacent chair. She took the valise off her shoulder and reached inside, pulling out what looked like a photograph. Then she whipped out a pencil and a small notepad and wrote something.

"Conner, I'm investigating the disappearance of one Arnold Shaw."

The name didn't ring a bell, but when she held out the picture, I felt my heart clutch in my chest. It was the bully from the bar. From last Saturday night. The guy built like a side of beef. The picture was a glamour shot. Shaw was wearing what looked to be a really expensive suit and was smiling warmly at the camera. So this wasn't about Brent?

Grace still was acting very casual, but she was looking at me closely as she continued. "Mr. Shaw is a honcho from a downtown insurance company." She leaned close as if about to convey a secret. "His family was a big supporter of the mayor in his last election. So we're anxious to get a resolution on this case."

I had just met Grace Garvey, but I could already tell that she was good at her job. Between her looks and technique—like she was letting me in on a little inside information—she made me feel like I could share my deepest darkest secrets. Even though, at the time, she wasn't aware of what a whopper of a deep dark secret I was a part of.

"Anyway, he's one of these guys who likes to let off a little steam at the end of a long work week. You know the type? He has a few favorite places he likes to go, and one of them is The Hill. By any chance do you recognize this guy?" She held the picture up closer.

"No. Ah. Well, yes maybe. I mean, I go to The Hill quite a bit. With my colleagues from work. After work, of course. Not during, ha ha. I uh...might have seen him there...at some point. But it's hard to remember specifically when...."

Grace reached over and patted my knee. "Hey, Conner. Just try to relax, okay? We're only at the fact-finding stage of the investigation right now. We're nowhere close to hauling in any suspects and breaking out the waterboarding equipment. Not yet anyway."

She smiled, and I couldn't help but smile in return. She had a perfect smile. Bright white straight teeth. No fangs. "Yes. Sure. I'm sorry. I'm not used to talking to the police. I...I'm a financial analyst at Beacon Hill Associates. We're an investment banking company. Not the most exciting job in the world. Our idea of a big moment is when the discount rate changes." Time to shut up, Conner.

She laughed lightly. "Yes, I heard that was where you worked."

"You...heard?"

"Yeah, when I found out The Hill was one of Mr. Shaw's hangouts, I went down and asked if I could speak with whoever was on last Saturday night, y'know? 'Cause that was the last time he was seen. So I finally got ahold of the bartender and the waitress. Cute girl named Amy. Do you know her?"

"Amy? Uh no, I might know her if I saw her."

"Right, of course. But, they both confirmed that Arnold Shaw was in the bar on Saturday night. And Amy remembered you too. She said Mr. Shaw had a run in with one of the guys from BHA. She even remembered your name. She said she remembered it because you have two first names."

I started cursing my parents in my mind.

"But, honestly, I think Amy might have taken a liking to you. Another girl can always tell. Might be something you want to follow up on. Unless you got a steady going on."

I just nodded.

"Do you, Conner?"

"Do I...?"

"Do you have a girlfriend? Someone you see regularly?"

She asked the question with a smile and a wink that succeeded in throwing me off guard.

"Yes. No. I mean...kind of...."

Grace laughed. "We'll get back to that. I looked your name up in the phone book and took a chance on this address since it was so close to The Hill. So you are the Conner David who works at Beacon Hill Associates, and who had a bit of a kerfuffle with Mr. Arnold Shaw on Saturday night at The Hill, right? I mean, there's not another one of those floating around town, is there?"

My head was hanging at this point, and I suddenly knew how the phrase "trapped like a rat" came about.

"No. I mean yes, it was me. But I don't know anything about him disappearing. Honest."

"Of course not, Conner. Remember, we're only fact-finding. Trying to trace Mr. Shaw's last steps before he became a member of the displaced."

"Sure. Sure. I understand."

"Awesome. Can you tell me what happened?"

"Yes. Absolutely. I was at the bar and I had met somebody. She was...a woman. That I had met there. We were just talking. And this guy—Mr. Shaw, I guess—he seemed pretty drunk. He came over and started being...you know...kind of obnoxious with my friend—the woman I was talking to. He's, you know, a pretty big guy. And I think he was interested in the girl...the woman too. But I don't think she wanted to talk to him. He was being really rude. And then he kind of pulled her up, like over toward the dance floor. And I...well...I didn't think she wanted to dance with him, you know? So I went over. Can you imagine? Me going over to him? That's like Mickey Mouse challenging King Kong. Ha ha. Anyway, we had a little bit of an altercation. Wasn't much, really. He shoved me away and I...hit my head on the floor. And he left with the girl. That's the last time I saw him."

The detective nodded. I was hoping that my account was close enough to what she heard from the bar employees, albeit with a slightly more stilted delivery.

"Yeah. I heard that Mr. Shaw is kind of a mean drunk. Were you hurt? Did you seek medical attention?"

"No. No, I was fine. Just a little dazed."

"What did you do next?"

"Well, I kind of...ran out...you know, looking for them. But they were gone. So I just came home."

"What was the woman's name?"

I tried to act cool, but I'm pretty sure I stopped breathing for a moment.

"The woman...I was talking to?"

She nodded.

"Uh, let's see. Like, as I said, I had just met her. It was something like Linda...Lara...something along those lines."

"You don't remember her first name?"

"Well, not exactly. I had probably had a little to drink as well."

"Uh huh. Last name?"

"Sorry. Never got there." I thought, Though not for lack of trying.

"And this was the first time you had seen this woman there?" The detective's friendly manner suddenly evaporated and her eyes bore into mine. I figured I'd better stick as close to the truth as possible. This Detective Grace Garvey was a sharp one.

"Um. No. I had actually met her the night before. I was out with some friends of mine...from work. And I met her there."

"What happened that night?"

"Nothing really. We just danced a couple of times. You know...talked a little...."

"And then?"

"Well, frankly, I went over to talk to my friends, and when I

185

went back to the bar, she had left. Guess I didn't make that great of an impression." I smiled, but Grace's serious expression didn't change.

"And then you just happened to run into her again the following night?"

"Yes. Well, okay, I might have gone back hoping to see her again. But I was really surprised when she was there." I felt like I was starting to sweat.

"So this girl had made an impression on you?"

"Yes. I guess you could say that."

"And yet, you don't know her name."

"I know it sounds strange, but...I'm not exactly used to meeting girls—women—at a bar. My sister tells me nothing good can come from a relationship like that...guess she's right. Her name...I think it was Lisa. Or Linda. But I honestly never found out her last name."

"Do you know where she lives?"

"Uh, no. I have no idea."

Grace sat looking at me for what seemed like an eternity. Then she smiled and shifted closer again. The casual, "I'm your friend" manner was back, and I was impressed with how easily she shifted gears.

"So who's the lucky girl that you're kind of seeing regularly?"

"Oh. Nobody really. We...uh...we work together, so we're trying to stay, you know, kind of quiet about it."

"I get it. Yeah, dating somebody from work gets complicated. What's her name?"

I paused. "Vicky." As soon as I said her name, the possibility of Grace Garvey questioning Vicky about our dating made me want to throw up.

"Vicky...."

"Um, if it's okay, I'd rather not get her involved in this. You know, with me meeting another woman at the bar and all. It could get a little sticky."

The detective laughed amiably again. "Sure, Conner. I get it. We'll just leave Vicky out of this. For now, at least. But I want to be sure. The woman you're kind of seeing isn't the woman from The Hill last Saturday night—right?" She looked me squarely in the eye.

"Right. No. Not the girl from the bar. Not at all."

She nodded. "Have you seen her since Saturday night?"

"Who? Vicky? Or the—"

"No. The girl from the bar."

"Uh. No. No, I haven't."

"Okay. That's too bad, because I would really like to have talked to her. For all we know she might be the last person to have seen Mr. Arnold Shaw before he disappeared." Another intense look. "Heck, he might be shacking up with her. Maybe Mrs. Shaw should stop worrying about her missing husband and start worrying about finding a good divorce lawyer."

I nodded, but didn't say anything. I was conscious of the fact that I was averting my eyes from her piercing look. And I wondered to myself, Could I be any worse of a liar? I was petrified that this sharp, beautiful police detective was seeing right through me.

"Anyway, why don't you tell me what she looks like? The girl from the bar, that is."

"Um, tall for a woman. Little shorter than me. Long brown hair. Beautiful...that is...nice looking face, kind of angular with high cheekbones. Very...I mean, she looked like she was in good shape. Physically, that is."

"Slender build?"

"Yes. Slender, but...."

"Yes, Conner?" Grace Garvey hit me with a devilish grin.

"Just very well put together." I could feel myself blush.

"I see. And what was she wearing?"

187

"I'm pretty sure she was wearing a dress."

"Nice. Classy. What color was it?"

It was white on Friday night and yellow print on Saturday, but I said, "Ah, I really don't remember. Light colored."

"Okay. Anything else? Any distinguishing characteristics? Besides her being very well put together, that is."

I blushed again. "Uh...no...nothing I can think of."

"Okay. Did anybody else meet her?"

"Anybody else?"

"Yes. On Friday night? You said you went to The Hill with some other people from work. Were there any women in your group?"

"No. No, it was all guys."

"Ah. Too bad. I can guarantee you another woman would have remembered exactly what the woman was wearing. And what she looked like. So, did any of the other guys meet this mystery woman?"

I thought for a moment. "Just Razor. He met her very briefly." I was instantly kicking myself for bringing Razor into this.

"Razor?"

"Oh, yeah, sorry. His real name is Fernando Rojas."

"Why do you call him Razor?"

"I think it's 'cause he always looks like he needs a shave."

Grace had a hearty laugh at that one. "You're funny, Conner. Any chance you have Mr. Rojas's number? I might want to check with him to see if he remembers anything else about our Jane Doe."

I gave her Razor's number from my cell phone. "Do you think it will really be necessary to call him? He only met her for a brief moment, and I'm not sure how much help he can really be."

"You'd be surprised, Conner. Most of the time guys have a very vivid memory about meeting an attractive woman. You never know what kind of detail might turn up. He might even remember her name."

Her eyes went into boring mode again.

"Lyria," I said.

"What?"

"Her name. It was Lyria. I'm sorry. I was just trying to...be discreet, I guess. I apologize."

She dropped the intensity a notch and patted me on the knee again. "That's all right, Conner. I appreciate the honesty." She jotted in her book. "While we're in full-disclosure mode, can you remember any details about her? Did you get her last name?"

"No. No, I honestly never got it."

"Okay, Conner. Let me just finish up a few notes here." Grace finished writing. My heart was hammering so badly I was worried that she might be able to hear it.

"Okay. I think we're done. For now. Here's my card. Please call me if you think of anything else that might be helpful. My email address is on there too."

"Sure. I will."

She stood up and looked around again. "This is a great place. Terrific location too. BHA must pay their financial analysts pretty well."

I kicked at the carpet a little. "Well, to be honest, I had a little help from dear old Dad in getting this place. I couldn't come close to affording it on my own."

She laughed. "Nothing wrong with that, Conner. Sounds like something my father would do for me. If he could. Well, hope you get to enjoy the rest of your Saturday. Any big plans?"

My only plan right now was to nosedive into my couch and get my heartbeat back to normal, but I said, "No. No big plans. Just gonna take it easy today."

"Sounds good. Try to get some rest."

Detective Grace Garvey walked toward the front door. "Oh, just one more thing." She had stopped suddenly, and I almost plowed her down.

"Yes? Sure, anything, Detective."

She reached into her valise and pulled out two more pictures. "By any chance, have you ever seen either of these two men?"

I thought the ordeal was over, but when she held up pictures that looked like mug shots of the druggie-robbers Spider and Vape, I just about died right on the spot.

When I caught my breath, I sputtered, "Uh...no...no. I've never seen those guys before."

"Are you sure? You looked like you might have recognized them."

"Uh...no...I mean yes, I'm sure. You just surprised me a little. No, I don't know either of those guys. Should I? I mean...who are they?"

"It's not important. Thanks, Conner. I'll be in touch."

***

Grace Garvey hadn't been working missing persons for long, but she realized that simply talking to someone from the police scared the living crap out of some people. And just because a person being questioned acted nervous certainly didn't mean that they were guilty of anything. But she knew for sure that Conner David knew more than he was telling her. She had clearly caught him in a couple of lies. And she believed it centered around the girl — the woman he had met at The Hill. Grace already got a good description of her from the people at the bar, and from what they told her the woman was stunningly good looking. Grace thought a woman like that could get a guy like Conner David under her "spell" pretty easily. Even if, as Grace believed, Conner was basically a good person. And, she had to admit to herself, kind of cute. In a bookwormy sort of way.

Grace couldn't picture David actually being responsible for Arnold Shaw's disappearance, and certainly not Dylan Cavey or Lucas Corsi's either, although Conner almost shit himself when he saw their pictures. She was glad she got the pics from Gebelein, and didn't honestly know what to make of Conner David's reaction. But did this mystery woman have something to do with Shaw's going bye bye? And if so, did she have Conner David covering for her? All that was easy to picture, but she either needed to come up with some proof or she needed to get Conner to admit it and give her some details.

Grace Garvey thought the latter possibility held more potential for a breakthrough on this case.

Much more potential.

CHAPTER SEVENTEEN

It took a solid hour for my breathing to get back to normal. As soon as Grace Garvey was out the door, I went face first into the couch. What am I doing? How did I get myself into this mess? Why didn't I just tell her the truth about Lyria? I couldn't bring myself to tell Grace that I'd caught Lyria in the act of drinking my sister's boyfriend's blood in a dark alley last night. Even if I did tell her, Grace Garvey probably would have written me off as a complete whack job. I also couldn't admit that I'd slept with Lyria all last week, but still had no way of contacting her. I didn't have a phone number, I hadn't the first clue where she lived. Even I had trouble believing my situation—I couldn't very well expect someone else to believe it. If I did tell Grace the truth, would she have hauled me in for further questioning, or was that another TV-based delusion on my part?

At any rate, I was in deep now no matter how one looked at it. If the truth did somehow come out, and Grace Garvey found out I had lied to her, I was pretty sure her very effective "I'm your friend" act would be replaced by "I'm your jailer." I was sure I'd be criminally charged. Aiding and abetting—was that a real thing, or did they just use it on CSI?

And what about Lyria? Who was she? What was she? Was she responsible for Arnold Shaw disappearing? Before last night, I would have thought the notion was absurd. But now? And what about Spider and Vape? When Grace Garvey had shown me their pictures, I almost had the big one, right there on my atrium carpet. Had they gone away too? I remembered them vanishing in the fog, but I had almost convinced myself that I had imagined that whole scenario. But now I wasn't so sure. Of anything.

The overwhelming stress and the fact that I'd pretty much been up all night combined to take me out. I fell into a deep, dreamless sleep. Later, I thought that was probably what it felt like to be in a coma.

I woke up thinking I probably had big time upholstery wrinkles on my face. I had no concept of time. In fact, it took me a while to realize where I was. I stood with not a small amount of difficulty and walked over to the front door. I peered through the peephole and was surprised to see that it was dark out. I had slept the whole day.

I turned around, and Lyria was standing in the middle of my living room.

I gasped. "How did you get in here?"

She looked drop dead gorgeous again. She was wearing a pink dress, and there was no sign of the river of blood I had seen on her the previous night. She smiled and I looked closely. No fangs.

"Not the nicest greeting I've ever had. But understandable. I thought you deserved an explanation."

"Oh, really? You're going to explain what happened last night? I'll buy tickets to that."

She said, "Conner...," and started approaching slowly.

"Stay back!" She stopped and the look on her face was...I couldn't say for sure, but I thought I detected hurt.

"That's not what you were saying to me last week."

"Last week, I didn't know you were a...a...I don't know what you are."

"I'd really like to have the opportunity to explain."

"And what happens if I don't give you that opportunity?

193

Huh? What happens then, Lyria? What happened to Brent last night? Is that what you're going to do to me?"

"Conner. You have to know that I would never hurt you. If that's what I wanted, I had plenty of opportunities already. I would just ask that you listen to me. And after that, if you want me to leave, I will. And I promise you will never see me again."

The tension in my body eased slightly, but then I thought, What if this is a trap? Fact is, Conner boy, you don't really know who—or what—you're dealing with here. A crazy part of my brain started poring over my possessions. Did I have a cross anywhere? Or garlic?

Lyria said, "Can we at least sit down? I...I would really like to just sit and talk for a bit. Would that be okay?" She floated on over to the sofa and sat at the very end. She was giving me as much space as possible in case I felt brave (stupid?) enough to join her.

I inched my way out of the front doorway toward the living room. But before I sat on the way opposite end of the couch, I blurted out, "What happened to Brent? Is he...?"

"Conner, there's something you need to know."

"Answer me, Lyria. Is Brent dead?"

She hesitated, looking at me with her big beautiful brown eyes. Her face was expressionless. Then she said, "Yes."

I was too stunned to speak. I got up and started backing toward the door again, and strongly considered running through it.

"Conner, I need to tell you—"

When I found my voice, I sputtered, "I don't want you to tell me anything. Get out. Get out, Lyria! Get out...and don't come back here anymore." At first, Lyria stayed seated, continuing to gaze into my eyes. I swung the front door open. "I mean it. GET OUT OF HERE!"

She stood up slowly. When she spoke, she was very calm. "I

need to tell you something important. Won't you at least listen?"

"There's nothing you can tell me that will make any difference."

"Brent was going to kill Carly."

I stood slack-jawed in the doorway. "How could you know that? Is that what he told you?"

"No, he didn't tell me. Not in the traditional sense, anyway."

"Then how did you know?"

"I saw it."

"You saw it? Oh, what? You're a mind reader too? In addition to being a.... I don't know what—"

"It's hard to explain unless you hear me out. Allow me tell you what is happening. Brent felt that if he couldn't have your sister, then nobody could have her. He had been stalking her and he knew where he would find her. He thought she was going to her friend Beth's house last night. He had a rage about him. And they weren't just idle thoughts, Conner. He was genuinely planning to do it. Last night."

Beth? Lyria knew about Beth? Carly's best friend? How could she have known that? Carly hung out with Beth, usually at Beth's house, whenever she wanted to escape from the family. Or, apparently in this case, an abusive boyfriend. He'd read about these nutcase guys wanting to possess women. And hurting them, or killing them when they were rejected. I had only been with Brent for a short while last night, but he definitely seemed like the type who would do something like that. He was violent. And volatile. And drunk off his ass.

I was standing stationary, assimilating all this information.

"Won't you please close the door and come sit down?" asked Lyria. "I know this is all a shock, but I'll do everything I can to make this more real for you. More understandable. And my promise to leave you alone afterward still stands. If you decide that's what you want." She sat back down.

After another few moments, I closed the door and looked over at Lyria. She suddenly looked so normal. Her off-the-scale beauty was still there, but there was a.... I didn't know at first how to pinpoint it, but then I realized...it was a vulnerability that I had never seen evidence of before. My heart ached. She didn't look like the being I had seen last night hunched over Brent. She looked like the girl...the woman I had been intimate with just last week. I realized that I had developed feelings for this woman-creature in our short time together. I was astonished that I was actually feeling bad about the way I had treated her.

My fear was gone. I walked over and sat down, close to the middle of the couch. Lyria smiled slightly and shifted over a bit. She wasn't on top of me, but she wasn't pushing up against the arm of the sofa either.

"Thank you, my sweet Conner. Is this okay?"

She reached her hand out and without thinking, I put mine out as well. She felt soft and warm. I remember thinking, Well, there have been a lot of firsts for good old Conner David in the last couple of weeks. This is another one. Holding hands with a confessed murderer on my sofa.

I said, "So, you were going to make this all clear for me?"

She smiled. "I have a story to tell you. And, just be forewarned, it may stretch the boundaries of what you understood to be reality. But I would ask that you keep in mind that most lore, most legends, have at least some basis in truth."

I said, "I'd believe just about anything right now."

She laughed. "Good. Sit back and relax. This is my story."

Chapter Eighteen

"I was born in Romania. You look surprised. Did you think I was from New Jersey? At any rate, in order for you to fully understand who I have become, I must take you back to the early 1700s. No, I am not that old, but this is where my tale must begin.

The northern region of my country was known as Transylvania. It was not a discreet city as many now imagine. Transylvania was known as Ardeal in Romania, and the area had a rich history. Ardeal means 'Stone Mountain,' and refers to the territory's terrain and abundant natural resources. In ancient times Ardeal was home to a plethora of gold mines, which, as I'm sure you can imagine, attracted much attention. The Roman Empire went to war to control the mines, and met little opposition to their overwhelming strength. The Romans exploited the mines and built access roads and forts to protect them. After they felt they had gotten sufficient use of the territory, the Empire withdrew, setting up centuries of conflict and rule by various tribes, including the Carpi, Visigoths, Huns, Gepids, Avars, and Slavs. By the Middle Ages, there was an eclectic mix of nationalities within the population of Transylvania, including Turks, Germans, and Hungarians, among others. There was, of course, mixed breeding between the ethnic groups, and eventually, a population which considered itself Romanian above all the other nationalistic identifications. In the early 1700s, Transylvania was ruled by Hungary, and Romanians were relegated to second-class citizen status. It might interest you to know that it wasn't until 1920 that borders were redrawn and all of the Transylvanian territory officially became part of Romania, much to the chagrin of our neighbors from Hungary.

In 1711, there was a teenage boy named Aurel living near the population center of Alba Lulia. The word aurel means 'golden,' and he was so named because of his unique yellow hair. His coloring led his mother Daciana to believe that they descended from the Romans. Like much of the Transylvania region, the city of Alba Lulia was ruled by the Hungarians—in this case, a particularly ruthless man named Zoltan. Daciana was fair, and she scratched out a meager subsistence sewing garments out of textiles, while Aurel's father worked merciless hours in the mines. Daciana would sell her wares in the marketplace, making barely enough to feed herself and her child. Aurel's father was Nicu, and he was paid irregularly if at all by Zoltan, so the family more often than not found themselves depending on Daciana's trade.

The Romanians in Alba Lulia lived in what could be appropriately described as ghettos in today's parlance, while the Hungarians lived the high life, so to speak, reaping the rewards of the resource-rich land. Largely unbeknownst to Aurel, his mother was also a member of a mysterious group of thirteen local women who met at various intervals outside of the incorporated boundaries of Alba Lulia. Daciana would slink out of their apartment as quietly as possible so as not to rouse her son, in order to attend the get-togethers. The women were practitioners of the dark arts. There was much hysteria about witchcraft in that era, even in the United States. In Europe and in Romania, however, the authorities did not bother with such formalities as trials. Suspected witches would be summarily tortured until they confessed, and then executed. As such, secrecy was of the utmost importance for Daciana and the others. The focus of the women was to summon ill will upon their Hungarian tormentors. They were led by Lenuta, a seer who knew how to conjure and command spirits in order to achieve their goals. Most of the coven's sessions were spent with relatively simple incantations, but Lenuta had some more serious spells available to her.

One of Zoltan's guards was Laszlo, and he was known to seek Romanian women to satisfy his lusty needs. He had taken a daughter of a member of the coven, and she had been raped and brutalized. The group had assembled, and Lenuta had summoned the spirits that would see to Laszlo's ill fate. Sure enough, whether coincidental or not, the guard was found with his throat cut a short time later. Daciana was relatively certain that the girl's father had been responsible. Nevertheless, the killing gave the women renewed faith in Lenuta's ability.

What Daciana didn't know was that Aurel was, in fact, aware that she was leaving him alone to attend her meetings. When he heard her leave, Aurel himself would sneak out. He was meeting Amalia, a Hungarian daughter of the ruling class. Their love was beyond forbidden. Should they be discovered, Aurel would have been castrated and beheaded, and Amalia would have been stoned to death. Regardless, Aurel found Amalia irresistible, and the threat of certain death somehow gave their clandestine relationship life.

One morning, Daciana felt extra excitement heading to the market. She had been working on a dozen high quality cloaks that she felt would bring more than her usual compensation. She had spent extra time sewing each garment, and waited until she had enough quantity to satisfy the expected large number of potential customers. She would debut her goods that day.

Daciana occupied what we would call a 'booth' at the local marketplace, alongside other women, some of whom were also members of the coven. She proudly displayed her work and immediately attracted the attention of passersby. Soon enough, there was a crowd around her booth and business was brisk. But, seemingly without explanation, the shoppers began to disperse, and Daciana and the other merchants were suddenly alone. The reason became apparent as Zoltan and his guards rode through the marketplace. Whether by quirk of fate or by design, the ruler stopped in front of Daciana's small shop. He took a liking to her cloaks and ordered his guards to procure the pieces that had not already been sold. Daciana pleaded with the men as they helped themselves to her wares. Her pleas were falling on deaf ears, so she ran toward Zoltan's steed and begged the leader, telling him her garments were all she had to feed her family.

Zoltan struck the woman down with his staff. Another merchant came forward to lend Daciana assistance, and Zoltan ordered that they both be flogged. The women's screams ignited the leader's lustful urges, and he commanded his men to bring them back to his encampment. Zoltan and the guards took turns raping and beating the two women until they were near death, then flung them out into the street as if they were bundles of trash. The women were returned to their homes, where they recovered from their injuries. When Aurel saw his mother, he was filled with rage and vowed to seek revenge on Zoltan. His mother kept the boy at home, however, until his passion had cooled. When she and the other victim were able, the coven was set to reconvene. Daciana told Aurel, who had been doting on her every need, that she must go out on the night of the meeting.

"Are you meeting with your group of witches?" asked Aurel. Daciana was stunned. "Yes, Mother, I know of your meetings. And if I know, you can be sure others from the town will know. Zoltan will surely be watching. And you know what happens to witches, correct? They will not give you the option of imprisonment. You will be beaten until you confess, and then burned at the stake."

"My dear boy," said Daciana. "I have underestimated you.

But this group...it is our only chance for salvation with these barbarians who rule our land. The men of our city are all forced to work the mines. What else can a group of women do to contest such brutal beings with their armaments? Our leader is Lenuta. She will know what to do. She will wield enough power to mute the superiority of these animals."

The argument would continue, but in the end, Daciana had no choice but to attend the meeting. She knew that Lenuta would have to conjure more evil force than ever before, and the possibility frightened her. But if she was hesitant at all, she would think back to being beaten and raped, and her hesitancy would vanish.

Aurel, meanwhile, was not willing to let his mother assume such risk on her own. Unbeknownst to Daciana, he took his sword, snuck out, and followed his mother from a distance. When Daciana arrived at the meeting place, the other women were already there, and Aurel was watching from the woods nearby. The boy noticed a young girl tied to two stakes in the middle of the women's circle. She lay prone, her arms spread wide, each hand tied to a stake. Judging from her clean clothes, he thought she was Hungarian. She had a cloth wrapped around her mouth and she struggled against her bonds. There was a fire burning nearby, providing light in the pitch-black woods.

"It is time to begin," said Lenuta. The other women seemed perplexed by the presence of the Hungarian girl, but one witch, an older woman, was simply looking down, as if she knew what was about to happen. Lenuta was holding a straight stick that appeared to be made of hazel, and which had a strange inscription Aurel could not read from a distance.

"We must all shed our garbs. Our prayers to the supreme one must be made with purity of mind and soul, while we are disassociated from our worldly bonds." The women, some a bit more hesitant than others, disrobed, then resumed their places in the circle around their Hungarian captive.

Lenuta continued. "Know ye now, my fellow worshippers, that if any one of you should falter in your beliefs and desires, our prayers will not be answered. We must merge our power, for the spirit we summon is not a weakling who is recently deceased, but the most powerful energy in the world, the center of our subject of worship—the almighty Lucifer and his demons of choice. To gather his attention requires the sacrifice of a virgin, so that the almighty will find evidence of our love and commitment. We must all drink her blood to ensure that our devotion is complete. During the sacrifice, I will call to the almighty Lucifer, to pray that he show his power, that he should bring a forceful death to the heathen Zoltan and his band of pig followers. I call upon you all. If anyone cannot bring themselves to carry out their duties, the time to leave is now. Once I start beckoning to our king, I will be in a trance where my spirit will be merged with his."

From his perch in the woods, Aurel prayed that his mother would get up and leave. Surely she could not be a part of this unholy alliance. The Hungarian girl, upon hearing the intentions of the coven, redoubled her struggle against her ties, but it was to no avail. Her eyes were wide with unbridled terror. And Daciana stayed in place, her bare back facing Aurel as the head witch started her incantation.

The older woman raised her wand above her head. Her eyes were closed and her head was back, her face wearing an expression of rapture that almost looked orgasmic to Aurel. She moaned and spoke words in a language that Aurel could not understand. Then she stood, her arms spread wide, as if to receive an embrace. She held the wand in her right hand and her body rocked back and forth. After a few moments, she began to speak in a different voice that sounded like that of a man.

"I invoke and conjure thee, O spirit Lucifer, do forthwith appear and show thyself onto me. Lucifer, and your princes

Asmodeus and Astaroth, we will show our willingness to suffer and be purified in order to learn. We pray that you will provide the strength to bring vengeance upon the ruler Zoltan and his followers. We ask that you bring your wrath down upon them, that they be smitten from this earth, as they are unworthy to serve you."

At that moment, Aurel was stunned as the fire went out and the ground shook slightly. He had to emerge from his hiding space to continue to see the proceedings in the dark. His mother and the other witches had their heads back and wore the same orgiastic expression that Lenuta had shown earlier. He thought he heard them moaning, and when his eyes adjusted, he saw that each of them had released one hand and were reaching down between their legs.

Lenuta's manly voice went on. "In return for the foregoing promises, I swear and vow to deliver into your power this virgin girl. And we shall all drink of her blood to prove our unanimity and commitment. We step forward with you in a new alliance, and submit ourselves to you both in body and soul, forever into eternity."

The ground shook again. The women moaned even louder as Lenuta stepped toward the Hungarian girl. She had stopped struggling, and watched helplessly as Lenuta brought the shard end of her staff down to her neck and sliced it clean across. The old woman swooped down with uncommon agility, her mouth covering the fountain of blood. The women screamed, a piercing sound of explosive pleasure. They all rushed forward and took turns drinking the girl's blood. One would chug down, then another would seamlessly take her place. Very little blood was spilled, but when they had each had a share, the girl's body had been drained and her head lay back, the eyes open but now sightless.

The ground continued to shudder as the women resumed

their positions in a circle. Aurel was focused on his mother. She had blood dripping down her chin as she returned to her spot, and the boy was stunned to see her wipe as much as she could onto her finger and lap up the remains with her tongue.

Lenuta's regular voice was back. "Our sacrifice and our commitment are true. Lucifer, come presently, come visibly. Manifest that which I desire. Do come without tarrying. Come fulfill my desires."

The ground shaking got worse and suddenly there was an aura in a circle above the women. It descended as if to envelop them. Aurel rushed forward to pull his mother away, but it was too late.

Lenuta raised her arms and yelled in the man's voice, "Persist onto the end, according to mine intentions...."

The aura came down upon the coven, knocking Lenuta off her feet. Aurel was caught next to his mother, and the force incapacitated him. The women and the boy convulsed without control. Aurel could see only blackness, and his body was wracked with a burning pain which penetrated down to his soul. He could feel himself shaking, but he could not control the endless spasms. He felt the life, as he knew it, leave his body, to be replaced with the essence of the aura, a new life-force. He was still Aurel, but he was something new as well. He was pondering the change when he lost consciousness, and was thankful to be relieved of the pain.

***

It was still dark, but on the verge of dawn when Aurel came to. His naked mother lay prone at his side. "Mother. Mother wake up." He shook his mother to consciousness as the other women started to rouse as well.

"Aurel? Aurel, where are we?"

"We are here, Mother. In the woods. With your coven. But something has happened to us. We are...we are...changed."

Above all else, Aurel felt a driving hunger. But somehow, he was not hungry for food.

As Daciana put her clothes on, Lenuta arose. She stood and looked down at her own body, as if seeing it for the first time. She looked toward the sky. "Come," she shouted. "Come, we must seek shelter. At once!"

One of the young witches named Anca stood, examined herself, and crouched. Then she jumped skyward and continued going up. She went as high as the treetops, and when she came back to earth, she hardly made a noise. It was as if a feather had dropped. She threw her head back and laughed. Aurel saw her elongated canine teeth and felt his own.

"Anca, no. No, you musn't," hissed Lenuta. "We must get to cover. Now."

"But look, Mother Lenuta," said Anca. "Our prayers have been answered. Look what I can do." She ran toward a tree and continued running up the side, seemingly defying gravity. Aurel, Daciana, and the others were looking on in wonder. "Look how high I can go!"

Anca scurried to the top of the tree and propelled herself up into the sky. She went so high that she was suddenly hit by a ray of the rising sun. Anca screamed, her body convulsed, and she burst into flames. Her smoldering remains fell back to the earth. The witch emitted another blood curdling scream as the flames intensified and then went out. There was nothing left but a charred blotch on the ground where she landed.

"That will happen to all of us," shrieked Lenuta. "There is no time. We must bury ourselves in the soil. We will reemerge at nightfall."

Aurel looked at his mother. The other witches wasted no time. They burrowed themselves in the ground and then reached up and covered their own bodies with dirt. Aurel and Daciana started digging their own self-made graves.

"I...I feel so strong," said Daciana. "Surely I could not have dug so far so fast before." She looked at Aurel and a small smile crossed her face.

Aurel had been digging too. They lay in their graves and covered themselves with the remaining earth. Once settled, Aurel felt a sense of complete rest, and rather than describing what happened next as falling asleep, Aurel sensed that his consciousness simply discontinued.

***

Aurel opened his eyes, but they were covered with dirt. His immediate thought was that the dirt must have kept him from taking in air, but he decided that he had stopped breathing during his brief hibernation. He dug himself to the surface and saw that it was indeed nighttime. The others were arising from their graves as well, and all felt the same thing.

An overwhelming hunger.

Aurel looked at his mother. She stood erect over the hole where she had slept. She was feeling her new body and she smiled, this time a grin that lit up her entire countenance.

"Mother...," said Aurel, but before he could continue, Lenuta called out.

"Let us go to Alba Lulia," she said.

They all hit the town seemingly in the blink of an eye. Aurel wasn't even sure how they had traversed the distance so fast, but he had no time to ponder the question. He was consumed by an odor so strong it enveloped him, and he could think of nothing else. He looked at Daciana. She had her head back and was inhaling deeply.

"Aurel...do you smell it?" she gasped. "It is the most wonderful scent I have ever experienced."

The other witches were doing the same thing.

"To the palace!" yelled Lenuta.

They headed in the direction of Zoltan's abode, but Daciana

stopped suddenly. Aurel noticed a lone passerby some distance down the road leading into town, dragging a burlap bag behind him. Before Aurel could react, he saw Daciana move so fast she was a mere blur. He followed, but by the time he arrived, Daciana held the man on the ground, her mouth on his neck. Aurel could see that she had ripped open the man's throat and was drinking his blood in huge gulps. She jerked up with every slurp, pulling the man's prone body up in a spasm each time.

"Mother," yelled Aurel. "Mother, stop."

Daciana looked up at him with an expression of ecstasy, the blood dripping down her chin.

"Drink, Aurel," she said. "It is what we were hungering for. It is what we were smelling. It was the humans around us, the humans in this town."

Aurel thought of fleeing, but the aroma overwhelmed him, and he shot forward and found himself drinking what was left of the man's blood. When there was no more, he let the man's body slump to the ground. Aurel was gasping for breath, a feeling of bliss and of wonderment filling him.

"His name was Doru," said Aurel. "He was a simple farmer returning home with the wares he was unable to sell today."

"Yes, I know," said Daciana, but his mother wore a sinful grin, with her tongue lapped at the blood staining her teeth and fangs.

"Mother, don't you see? We have killed him. And we saw his life as we...fed. He has a wife. And children. Mother," he yelled, grabbing Daciana's shoulders. "What is this? What have we become?"

It was as if Daciana didn't hear a word that was said. "I'm still hungry," she said with the same malevolent grin. "Come," she said, taking her son's hand. "The others are heading for Zoltan. We must not be late, there may be nothing left for us."

Aurel shook free of his mother's grip, but she headed toward the palace, disappearing from his sight. Aurel wandered the streets, lagging behind. He had no concept of time, but he found himself at the gateway leading to Zoltan's palace. Two guards lay dead at the entrance, their throats ripped open. Aurel rushed forward, but when he entered the doorway to the ornate house, he found himself in an orgy of bloodletting. The witches had seized members of the household staff and some guards, now helpless to stop their advance. The only sound Aurel could hear was the women chugging their victims' blood.

His mother tossed aside the body of a maid. "I am done with this one," she said. "Now on to the one I really want."

The others didn't even notice her ascending the stairs. To Aurel, it was more like she floated up to the second floor. He heard his mother say, "So, we meet again," and heard a man scream.

He found himself on the second floor without being conscious of climbing the stairs. A guard outside a set of chamber doors lay dead with his head twisted at an unnatural angle. Another guard had his sword out in front of him with his shield, backing away from Daciana.

"Look here, Aurel," said his mother. "These two took part in beating and raping me, along with the pig Zoltan. Remarkable how things have changed, is it not?"

"Stay back," yelled the guard. "You are a witch. You are the devil!"

Daciana laughed. "Very logical in his thinking, don't you agree, my son?"

The guard lunged forward, Daciana making no attempt to dodge the attack. "Mother!" yelled Aurel as the guard's sword plunged into Daciana's chest. Blood spurted out as she looked down at the wound, more with curiosity than any sense of being injured. The bleeding stopped as her chest instantly healed itself.

Daciana looked at Aurel and emitted a blood-curdling

laugh. "Look, my son. Do you see? These pigs cannot hurt us." The guard was looking on in shock, but when he turned to flee, Daciana grabbed him, pulled his helmet off, and held his neck up toward Aurel. "Come, my son. Feed. Would you not avenge yourself on your mother's attacker?"

Aurel tried to stay in place, but he could smell the blood and he moved forward almost involuntarily. Before he knew what he was doing, he had bitten into the man's neck and the blood washed down Aurel's throat. The blood. The wonderful blood. Aurel was overcome by a feeling of joy that he had never before experienced. As the man neared death, Aurel saw his life. As a boy, born to aristocracy. As a young man, a bully, but who was appointed to the coveted position of a guard for Zoltan. Then he saw him on top of his mother, others around him, including Zoltan himself, laughing. His mother's face beaten. Aurel felt rage build up. He had consumed all the man's blood, and he saw himself grab the guard's shoulder and hair as he tore the man's head off and tossed it down the stairs. The torso hit the floor with a thud.

He heard Daciana laugh. "That was a nice touch, my son. I fear I have not given you enough credit for your creative ability." More laughter as Aurel came to his senses. Daciana walked over to the doors. "Shall we?" she asked.

The doors were locked, but his mother pulled them from their attachment to the wall with little effort and tossed them aside. They entered the lavish chambers, but were disappointed to see that Zoltan was not there. The wind was whipping through an open window frame.

"The pig must have fled," said Daciana. "Come, my son. He could not have gotten far."

But Lenuta appeared behind them. "We must return. The sun is about to rise," she said.

Daciana looked disappointed, and it seemed that she would

chase after Zoltan regardless.

Aurel took her arm. "Come, Mother. It will do us no good to go after him. Do you wish him to see you die in flames?"

Daciana hesitated, but gave way. The flock headed back to their burial grounds from the previous night. Aurel could see the sunlight start to appear on the treetops, and hastily covered himself with dirt just prior to the blackness.

They were so frantic to reach their graves, they didn't see, or smell, the hunter, scouring the local woods for prey.

***

The next night the coven returned to Alba Lulia, intent on avenging themselves on the Hungarian population, who they saw as intruders and repressors. They were also determined to be sure that the monster Zoltan was not in hiding among the masses.

Aurel reluctantly went along, the hunger for blood overriding any remaining feelings of morality. The witches were indiscriminate in selecting their victims. Entire families would be wiped out, children and all. Aurel searched for evildoers, mostly former guards or followers of Zoltan. He would see their lives as he fed, and sensed many intentions to "cleanse" the area of those of Romanian heritage. At that point, he knew he had chosen the correct one to feed on. The air in the village was filled with screams and slamming doors in futile attempts to keep the demons from pillaging households. Aurel watched Daciana take part in the assault. He was shocked to realize that his mother was perhaps the most vicious killer of all, with an insatiable appetite for blood. She genuinely seemed to enjoy inflicting suffering and snuffing out lives.

It was getting toward daylight and Aurel had lost track of his mother. He went in search of her, certain he would have to interrupt her reign of ecstasy and force her to go back to the burial grounds. He headed down a side street from the center of the village. He heard a desperate scream and what sounded like a young girl pleading for her life. The voice had a ring of familiarity, and when he headed for it, he saw that Daciana had a girl by the hair. She was holding her victim off the ground in front of her face, mocking the girl's pleas.

"Oh, please," said his mother. "'I have money, you can have anything...please don't kill me.' You, my dear, will be the most delicious treat of the night. So young...and pretty...and tasty, I'm sure."

Aurel realized to his horror that his mother was holding Amalia.

"Mother NO," he shouted. He rushed forward, grabbed Amalia from his mother's grip, and shoved Daciana away, sending her hurtling into the side of a building. Daciana was stunned, but stood and looked at Aurel with a rage the boy had never seen before, baring her teeth and fangs.

"You dare. You dare take the side of one of these...mortals. I am your mother. Now put the girl down and go find your own treat. This one is MINE." She came toward Aurel, who kept his body between Daciana and Amalia.

"Mother, it is almost dawn, you must go back. I will tend to this one."

Daciana looked toward the sky, then back at Aurel. She hissed, "We will have further words on this...betrayal." His mother then disappeared.

Amalia clutched onto Aurel with all her remaining strength. "Aurel, my God. Thank God. You...you saved me. I.... Do you mean to say that creature...that monster...is your mother?"

"Yes, my darling Amalia. Please, there is no time to explain. Not tonight. I will take you back to your home. Stay there. Stay inside until it is light out. I will come back at darkness tomorrow night, and I will do my best to help you understand."

With daylight drawing closer, Aurel picked Amalia up and

dashed to her home so fast the girl nearly passed out from the lack of oxygen. The window to her bedroom was up a story, but the boy discovered that he could scale the wall. He lay his love down on her bed. She looked up at him with questions in her eyes, but before she could say anything else, Aurel was through the window and headed back to his self-made grave.

***

When Aurel raised his head above the dirt the following night, he could see that Daciana was just starting to stir. He hurried away before she could say or do anything to him. He got to town in a flash and headed directly to Amalia's house. The townspeople had boarded up their doors and windows, and hung crosses on the front of their homes, none of which could serve as a deterrent. Some residents had considered leaving town, but honestly had nowhere else to go. Besides, for all they knew, these creatures of the night were everywhere. Was this the end of the world as they knew it?

Amalia was awake and alert when Aurel appeared in her room. They looked at each other, hesitated, and then rushed into an embrace.

"I was so...."

"It seemed like this day...."

They spoke at the same time and stopped. They laughed.

Aurel said, "I'm sorry. Go ahead."

"I started to say that I thought this day would last forever. I'm usually not in a rush to see time pass so, but today...today was different."

"All I could think about was getting back to you."

"Those people...those monsters...will they come back tonight?"

Aurel looked her in the eye. "Yes. They are avenging what they see as years of mistreatment. They are after Zoltan. They seized his manor two nights ago, but he fled. They are still searching for him. I should say...we...we are still searching for him."

"We? Do you mean...?"

"Yes, my darling Amalia. I am a creature of the night as well."

Amalia moved away from him. "Do you...mean to do harm to me?"

"No, of course not, my darling. I admit that I feel hunger in your presence. But I will control it. I would rather die myself than do harm to you."

"Hunger?"

Aurel nodded. "This being I have become. That we have become—myself, my mother, and the rest of the coven—we... are no longer human. We subsist on human blood. We appear to have great strength and speed, much more than mere mortals. And, it is my belief that we cannot be hurt or killed. My mother... she was stabbed in the chest, and a few seconds later, it was as if the wound had never existed. The only way we can be harmed is with...daylight."

Amalia felt tears flow down her cheek. "Oh, Aurel." She rushed forward, taking him in her arms. "How? How did this happen?"

They sat on the end of Amalia's bed and Aurel related the story. How the potent witch Lenuta had summoned Lucifer, and how the spirit had responded. And how Aurel himself accidently got caught up in the evil aura that had changed him forever.

"You must believe me," he continued. "I never intended to be a part of this. I could never have imagined myself being able to harm someone. Kill someone. Certainly not an innocent stranger. But the hunger for blood, it is strong...I must learn to control it. But I don't know for how long."

Amalia reached up and took his chin. "I believe you will be able to do this. Last night you saved me. I still believe in you. I still...love you. As I always have."

They kissed, and before long they were making love. Aurel had admitted to himself that he was worried about being capable of loving as a non-human. But it seemed that he needn't have worried at all.

***

"AMALIA!" Her father's voice thundered from the hallway.

She broke away from Aurel and rushed to the door. Aurel thought, my God, it is almost dawn. How is that possible?

Amalia threw a blanket over her naked body and intercepted her father in the corridor. She had slammed the door shut. Aurel could hear them talking, but couldn't make out what was being said. She came back in the room looking frantic as Aurel heard her father stomping out of the house.

Amalia said, "The townsmen. They have discovered your... hiding place."

"What? How is this possible?"

"There was a hunter, in the woods nearby. He saw the members of the coven burying themselves."

"My God. I must get back. My mother...."

"No! Aurel, you must not go. It is Zoltan. He and his remaining horde, they consulted an old mystic. They know of you. Or your...kind. They call you the strigoi. And they know about daylight. They will expose you—all of you. You must stay. We will conceal you...somehow."

"No! I must try to warn them."

Aurel hurtled out the window and headed back to the burial ground as fast as his supernatural speed would allow. But he was too late.

He stopped near the edge of the woods. The onset of daylight had already begun. Zoltan and his men were digging in the burial ground. Aurel knew that he had to get buried or he would die. He plunged deep into the woods and felt weak. He was barely able to get himself under sufficient dirt to block out the rays of the sun. Everything went black.

***

Aurel awoke and rose from his quickly fashioned grave. He was disoriented when he looked around, not knowing where he was. His memory came rushing back. His mother...the others... Zoltan.

He bolted back to the original plot, but what he saw made him fall to his knees. The graves of the coven members were piles of dirt. There was a burned splotch of land around each pile. His mother and the other witches were gone.

There was a crudely made sign at the end of the field. It said, "I Zoltan, supreme ruler of Alba Lulia and Transylvania, have dispatched the evil strigoi so that they may take their rightful place in Hell."

Aurel felt his blood boil and he sped toward the town. He felt weak, and remembered that he hadn't fed the previous night. That was the misfortune of the guards in front of Zoltan's manor as he ripped into their bodies with a ferocity he had never felt before. He drained them both and tore down the front doors. Servants inside scrambled away from this blond-haired creature in a rage with blood covering his entire front. Aurel felt a spear pierce his back, looked down, and saw the front edge protruding from his stomach. He pulled it through, turned, and saw the guard looking on in disbelief. He ignored the underling and raced up the stairs toward Zoltan's chamber. Two guards came at him, but he sent them both hurtling down the stairs as if they were annoying insects.

As he entered the chamber, the ruler was again trying to make an escape out the window. Aurel caught him this time with his superior speed. He held Zoltan up by his neck, a look of pure terror in the evil ruler's eyes.

"You are the evil strigoi," Zoltan stammered. "I cast thee out!"

215

"I am Aurel, son of Daciana. You may not know the name, but you have raped her and you have killed her. How many others have suffered at your unclean hands?" He pulled Zoltan closer. "Is it hundreds? Thousands? We will never know. One thing we can be sure of, however. There will be no more."

The last things the despot would see were the fangs. Aurel plunged them into Zoltan's neck. The ruler spasmed backwards, went stiff, and then went limp. Aurel tossed his body aside as he heard troops rushing up the stairs. He flew out the window and disappeared into the vast countryside."

Chapter Nineteen

To say I was transfixed would have been the understatement of the century. Under normal circumstances, I would have said that my dear Lyria was a prime candidate for an exclusive suite in the local insane asylum—and one of those jackets with no sleeves. But, lacking any alternative explanation for every nutzo thing that had gone on lately, I actually found myself believing her story. And it was like she said—most mythology does have at least a basis in fact.

"Do you need a break?" she asked.

"What? A break? What are you breaking?"

She laughed. "No. I mean do you want a rest? Or do you want me to go on?"

"You mean there's more?"

She flashed another megawatt smile. "My sweet Conner. That's the beginning of the story. Now, you need to hear my story."

"Oh, by all means. If it's anything like the first part, I'm sure it's a real doozie. But I gotta tell you, Lyria. This is a bit much. Remember, I'm just a measly financial analyst. Before all this happened, my biggest worry was whether my acne was going to clear up by the time I reached thirty."

"Yeah? And how's that working out for you so far?"

I smiled in spite of myself. In spite of everything. She still had...I could only describe it as a power over me.

"Nice to see that smile again. I was beginning to think it was a lost art," she said.

"Well, there hasn't been a whole lot to smile about lately."

"Not even last week?" She hit me with a mischievous look.

I laughed. "Point taken. All kidding aside, I do want to hear your story. When you come right down to it, knowing more about you is really all I've been thinking about lately."

"Your chance is here, my dear boy. My story starts some two-hundred plus years ahead, to the year 1920.

***

It was the year I was born. I know, you're thinking I look pretty good for an old broad, right?

My hometown is the city of Iasi in northern Romania. My upbringing can only be described as idyllic. My family lived on a farm, with acres of hillside property. Our entire existence revolved around caring for our land and our animals. The air. It is hard to imagine now how pure it was, and we certainly didn't appreciate it at the time. Nor the inherent beauty of the green rolling hills around us. It was all we knew. We thought that was how everybody must have lived. Our family was close. I had a brother — Petru — and my mother was Mihaela. Her name meant, 'who is like God.' But I was closest with my father, Iorghu — the "earth worker, farmer." We worked long hours tending to the farm. My father always wanted me to be alongside him, and it was what I wanted too. We toiled, and talked, and became inseparable. My father always wanted to protect me from the ills of the world. Petru and I knew nothing of the geopolitical instability that befell our nation. We would never have guessed that our father was a leader in an underground movement that acted as an insurgency against a sadistic dictatorial leader.

One morning, Papa and I were tending to a field of crops that made up what would be one gigantic backyard by today's standards. The work was mundane and repetitive, and many

218

times we would find ourselves reaping, collecting, and weeding without really thinking about what we were doing.

"My God Lyria, look at this!"

I rushed over, intrigued by the urgency in my father's voice. He held an ear of corn in his hands and had pulled the husk back. "What is it, Papa?"

He looked down in wonder. "This is not merely corn. It is a unicorn!" But when I focused on the ear, he tackled me and tickled my ribs until I had to beg him to stop. I had tears of laughter running down my cheeks. Then we were back to the routine, our brief break in the regimen over.

Prior to 1940, my twentieth year, Romania was ruled by King Carol II. He was a benevolent leader, but his reign was marred by civil war and external factions looking to seize and conquer Romanian lands, still known for their rich natural resources. The fascist Iron Guard led violent social revolution against the political and economic establishment, and warred with the king's Romanian police. My father supported the king's forces, but they were powerless to stem the rise of the Iron Guard, and in 1940, King Carol II was forced to abdicate his throne. He was replaced by the butcher, General Ion Antonescu. Antonescu immediately affiliated himself with the Nazi Axis alliance. His Iron Guard grew and transformed itself into a vicious group of ultra-national, anti-Semitic, anti-Communist, anti-Capitalist military men who led Antonescu's persecution of anyone opposing his rule.

At night, after Petru and I were sleeping, my father, Iorghu, would lead insurgent attacks on known Iron Guard members and their facilities. But the war between the Axis and Russia was heating up, and Antonescu had chosen to side with the Nazis. Petru was conscripted to serve, and was dragged away by Iron Guard soldiers, my mother clutching at his trousers in a state of hysteria. One of the soldiers rammed the butt of his rifle into her side, and she went to the ground in a heap. We would never see or hear from Petru again.

My mother and I cried ourselves to sleep for many nights after Petru's kidnapping. We stayed in the same bed, as we were both unable to let the other out of our sight.

One night our father woke us up, in a frantic state. "We must leave here. Immediately!" he said.

We didn't know what was happening, but we rushed out to our front room. Father was throwing some necessities into a sack, and I noticed he was doing everything with his left arm. I approached him and saw blood streaming from a wound in his right shoulder.

"Papa...you are hurt."

"Never mind that. Get dressed. You too, Mihaela. Do it quickly."

We threw on some simple clothing, but a moment later, the door was smashed open. Iron Guard soldiers rushed inside and immediately pinned my father to the ground. They came at me, but my mother stepped in front. A soldier threw her aside.

"Look here," he said, grinning to his other troops. "We may be able to use this one."

"NO!" My mother shrieked, and rushed at the soldier. I heard a single gunshot and my mother fell to the floor.

"MOTHER!" I yelled, and my father howled in anguish.

"This is Iorghu," said one of the men, pointing to my father. "He is to be taken alive. We will get much valuable information about his traitorous compatriots. We will bring along the pretty one here. She will serve us well also. All in all, a fruitful excursion." This brought about laughter from the other soldiers, and my father and I were tied up, blindfolded, and dragged out into the night.

***

We were thrown together into a barren prison cell, which already housed other people. They all looked malnourished and tired, and they regarded us with little interest through their sunken eyes. My father and I huddled in a corner. I tended to his arm as best I could.

"Your hair," he said. "We must cut it short." I looked at him with questions in my eyes, but he said out loud, "Does anyone have anything sharp that we may use?"

There was some general shifting among the other inmates, but nobody came forward.

My father said, "Please. It is of the utmost importance."

Finally, one of the human skeletons walked over. He had scraggly, unkempt hair, and looked as if he hadn't eaten in a very long time. He handed my father what looked like a small homemade knife.

"I am very grateful," said Iorghu. He tested its sharpness.

"I'm sure it will do what you want," said the inmate. "I have been sharpening it for some time."

My father nodded and indicated that I should move closer to him.

"Papa, why—?"

He interrupted my question. "It is for the best, my child. My loved one." He sheared off my locks as close to my skull as possible without cutting my skin. He looked around again. "Your hat," he said to another prisoner. "I beg of you. May I have it?" The man didn't move. "Please. Whatever ration of food we are given, you may have mine."

It was all he could bargain with. But, from the looks of these other inmates, our captors certainly were not feeding them well, if at all.

Regardless, the man tossed his hat in our direction.

"Bless you, my brother," said my father. "Lyria, you must put this on. Keep it pulled down as low as possible."

To say the hat looked unappealing to wear is a vast understatement. But I saw the look in my father's eyes, and I

221

complied. I knew now what he was doing. He was hoping to pass me off as a male to keep the guards from having their way with me. I was wearing clothing that could easily have been unisex, simple pants, and a farmer's worktop. My father looked me over.

"It will have to do," he said. "Your natural beauty is impossible to hide completely, but we will have to keep hope."

My mother's death sank in at that moment, and I cried. "Father. Who are these men? Why have they brought us here?"

"There is much you do not know, my dear. And much I have not been able to tell you. These men...they will be coming for me shortly. You must not be seen with me. You must fit in with another group. Look as nondescript as possible. My hope is that whoever comes will be different from the men who brought us here. And they will not know about you. Go now, my dear. Move to the other side of the cell."

I continued crying and refused to move at first, but upon further urging, and seeing the look of desperation in my father's eyes, I walked over and sat in the middle of a group of men. To my recollection, there were no other girls or women in the cell, and when I first sat down, the ragged-looking men around me looked me over with a—how should I describe it? —a hunger.

My father yelled from across the room, "None of you shall be untoward to her. If I hear different, you will feel my wrath. I have many associates. Take care of her. See that she is not harmed in any way."

For what seemed like an eternity, nothing happened. I sat among these men, their smell permeating my nostrils and eyes. I would glance over at my father, who was sitting expectantly, his eyes shifting between the door to the cell and me. When our eyes met, he conveyed a sense of deep love and, above all else, regret that I was caught up in whatever trouble he had brought upon his family and his associates, whoever they may have been.

It seemed that I sat for an eternity, sobbing among these

rotting souls. Not one of the men laid a hand on me — indeed, I got a sense that they became protective of my identity. Whether that was truly in response to my father's warning or just an affront against our captors, I'm not sure to this day.

Without warning, soldiers in drab grey uniforms stormed into the cell. They ignored everyone on my side of the room and made a direct beeline toward my father.

"This is Iorghu," one of them proclaimed. "Mighty leader of the underground rebels — or rats, more appropriately." The other soldiers laughed. "You others, see how mighty he looks now." With that he delivered a kick to my father's side. I emitted a cry and moved to intercept my father's attacker, but the other men stopped me.

"I was told that your lovely daughter was brought in as well. We will make good use of her. Where is she? Have you hidden her among these other traitors?" The soldiers looked in my direction. I kept my hat pulled down and stayed still, trying to blend in with the others who had crowded in front of me.

"Ah, so clever," said the soldier. "What did you do? Cut her hair? Try to make her look like one of these skeletons? No wonder you are a leader of your underground rats, your group of traitors." He looked to his other men. "Go through those skeletons," he said, nodding toward my compatriots. "It shouldn't be very difficult to find Iorghu's lovely little one. We will all be rewarded for our efforts."

The other soldiers came in our direction, but just then my father broke toward the open door of the cell. The soldiers swarmed on him, but he fought with all his remaining strength, wounded shoulder and all. It took all of the men to contain him and drag him out, and they had forgotten about searching for me, which I'm sure was my father's intention. The struggle continued in the hallway, but as they hauled my father away, the apparent leader yelled into the cell.

"You have a temporary reprieve, pretty one, wherever you are. We shall be back for you later."

***

The other captives and I sat for what seemed like hours. I felt hunger and thirst, but it was nothing compared to my worry about my father. What were they doing to him? Were they torturing him, trying to make him identify other members of the "underground traitors?" It became clear to me that my father was some sort of leader of the resistance against Antonescu.

The soldiers dragged my papa back in a heap and threw him to the ground as if he were trash. I peeked up from under my cap and through the others, who were still gathered around me. Papa's face was battered and bloody, and he lay still for the longest time. I cried, thinking they had killed him. When it was dark and there were no signs of the soldiers, I crept over to him. The other men were snoring, asleep.

"Papa," I whispered.

He looked up through his swollen eyes. "No." His voice was more like a gasp. "Go back, child. You must not be seen with me."

I said, "I don't care. Here." I sat up against the wall and held his head in my lap. He resisted at first, but had no strength and was soon asleep.

We were both awoken by a different group of soldiers some time later. They held their rifles out in front of them and told us all to move. I helped my father to his feet, and we were all taken outside. We were grouped with other captives and led on a march. There were enough of us that nobody took notice of individuals—we were more like a parade of walking dead.

We eventually came to a set of railroad tracks, where we were told to stop. The soldiers tossed bread into the crowd and enjoyed themselves watching everyone scramble for the crumbs. I grabbed a handful and put it to my father's mouth. "No child,

224

you take it. You must eat." But he was injured and needed the nutrition more, and I got him to take some in.

A train came along, and we could see that there were many others stacked into wooden freight cars with doorways and gaps between the slats. We were crowded on board, crammed into a mass of humanity in these death trains. Conner, to say the conditions on these freight carts were miserable does not do the description justice. There was barely enough air to breathe, and the smell of human decay and excrement was overwhelming. A general moan floated throughout the enclosure, and soon the train was moving. I managed to find a small space on the floor where my father and I sat wedged between other people. Papa was in and out of consciousness as we endured the seemingly endless journey.

I could not honestly say if it was hours or days before the train pulled to a stop. I would later find out that we were being taken to a concentration camp in Transnistria, which is in northern Romania. The grounds are now ruled by the country Modova, but at that time, it housed prisoners who were hostile to Antonescu's regime and enemies of Nazi Germany. Although we had been loaded onto the death train in large groups, they took us off individually, under the close watch of a group of Germans in the dark uniforms of what I would later discover were part of the dreaded Schtuzstaffel Totenkopfverbande, or SSTV, the members of the Nazi's elite troops responsible for concentration and extermination camps.

Most of the prisoners were pushed forward out of the way after they were checked out. The emptying of the railcar took hours. I held my father up as we made our way forward. We finally made it to the exit and gasped for air. Our relief was short-lived, however. I saw the SSTV man who looked to be in charge. His black uniform was spotless and neatly creased. But what I remember most were his eyes. He had a leering evil gaze about him as he searched every passenger individually. I held my father tightly and tried to get by the man quickly.

My body stiffened as I heard the man yell, "Halt!" The line stopped. I glanced up in horror as I realized this devil was coming toward my father and I. "Ah, vas is das?" he said, and his terrifying visage broke into a grin that made my body shudder. Soldiers grabbed my father away from me. He cried out in protest, but a Nazi rammed his rifle into his chest and my father crumbled to the ground. The leader was directly in front of me. I was too afraid to meet his eyes, but the name badge on his chest said, "Wurfel."

He pushed the hat off my head, took my chin, and lifted my face up, brushing at my shortened hair. I looked into his eyes and nearly fainted to the ground. Wurfel said something in German to the other soldiers and they all laughed. He grabbed at my chest. I tried to turn away, but the other soldiers held me by my arms. Wurfel squeezed my breasts, a look of glee about him. My father wailed and lunged at the SSTV man, only to be beaten down by his underlings. I screamed as one of the soldiers pointed his rifle at my father and looked ready to execute him, but Wurfel ordered him to stop. The man put his foot on my father's chest, pinning him down. Wurfel ripped down my pants and I stood completely exposed. He looked down at me and his hands roamed down all across my lower body, the ever-present lascivious grin plastered on his face. My father grunted in protest, but another soldier delivered a kick to his ribs.

Wurfel apparently finished his manual tour of my body and called out some orders in German. The men holding my arms pulled up my pants and started moving me away from the crowd of refugees. Wurfel said something else, and some other men picked up my father and the two of us were taken to a small white building separated from the main camp. We were thrown into a cube of a room with two small cots covered in straw. The room had pale grey walls and no windows. A single bulb provided the only light. The guards slammed the door shut as I went to my father and got him situated on one of the cots.

"Papa? Papa, what is happening? Why have they taken us here?"

My father had an overwhelming look of sadness as he looked at me. "My child," he gasped, holding his side. "These men, who have taken us. They...are evil. It is my deepest regret that you have become caught up in this, and I hope in time you will find it in your heart to forgive me. These men...they will do unspeakable things to you."

I started to cry and my body was shaking.

My father continued. "Please, my child. I have no right to ask anything of you, but I must request that you do one thing as you go through this ordeal."

"What?" I sobbed. "What is that, Papa?"

"Survive."

"Survive?"

"Yes, my dearest child. No matter what happens, be strong. Survive. For despite whatever horrors await you...await us...if I know that in the end you will still be alive, still have a life to live, my soul will be able to rest in peace. That at least one member of my family shall have lived through this...ordeal. My life will have had meaning. That all will not be dark."

With that, my father passed out, and I sat on the floor next to his cot awaiting my fate.

***

I had fallen asleep on the floor, but was awakened by the door to our room being opened. I looked up, and Wurfel and another man were there. I stood immediately. My father remained asleep, his breathing raspy but regular. The new man was taller than Wurfel, and looked to be his superior. He wore the same dark uniform. Wurfel spoke in German. The taller man walked toward me and I reflexively stepped back.

"No, my child," he said in Romanian. "I mean you no harm. I'm sure you and...." He looked down at Papa. "Your father?" I just stood still without answering. "Ah," he said with a smile. "Yes, I thought as much. I'm sure you were expecting to be treated very badly. But we have high hopes for you. I'm sure you will be pleased. Here, let me have a close look at you." I inhaled sharply and moved away. "Please," said the man. He took me by the shoulders and looked me over from head to toe. He put his hand under my chin and lifted my face up to the light. "Very beautiful," he said. He stepped back and looked at Wurfel. "Ja," he said, and Wurfel smiled. "Thank you, my child. We will move you to more pleasant surroundings. We shall have some food and water brought in for you and your father. And we will tend to his injuries. After you have recovered from your recent trip, you will have a much more pleasant excursion."

I found my voice enough to sputter out a question. "Wh... where will we be taken?"

The tall man smiled. "Bucharest. I'm sure you will find the accommodations much more acceptable." With that, the two men left.

***

Whoever this man was, he was telling the truth. We were moved to what could only be described as a suite. It seemed like we were staying in the officer's quarters of the concentration camp. We were given clean clothes—nothing fancy, mind you, just dungarees and work shirts, but they felt luxurious. Papa and I each had our own rooms and bathrooms, and within an hour, servants brought us a sumptuous meal. I must admit, I felt guilty because of all the emaciated prisoners we had seen on the death train, but my hunger overcame such feelings. My father must have felt the same way.

"What about the others?" he asked one of the servants. "Will they be fed like this as well?"

The servant either didn't understand or just ignored him. They left without saying a word.

"Come, Papa," I said. "You must eat and regain your strength. You will not be able to do your associates any good if you starve to death. Or die from your injuries."

Papa started eating reluctantly, but finished everything put in front of him. A short time later, a man came in and tended to my father's injuries. Papa tried questioning the man about why we were being treated so well, but he was met with the same stony silence as with the servants earlier on.

We stayed in our luxury accommodations in Transnistria for another day, but the second night we were told we would be taken to Bucharest shortly. I had no idea what day it was at that point, but our captors were prompt coming in the next morning to get us.

We were put on a very different train this time. We sat in our own cushioned seats. The compartments were lined with velour and were perfectly clean. We could see the concentration camp out the window as we pulled away, and the feeling of guilt came about once again. The tall Nazi without a name sat next to us, along with the ever-leering officer called Wurfel. In addition, there were armed guards near us the entire trip, and we got the sense of being valuable cargo being transported to market.

When we arrived in Bucharest, a car pulled up to the train station, more Nazi guards jumping out as soon as the vehicle came to a stop. We were rushed into the back seat, a guard on each side of us closest to the door. I suppose this was to keep us from jumping out of the car. The tall officer, Wurfel, and a nondescript driver crammed into the front seat, and without anybody uttering a word, we were on our way. My father tried in vain to find out more about what was going on.

"Where are you taking us?" he asked the tall officer in

Romanian. "I am a Romanian citizen, and I demand to know what is happening."

Wurfel and the tall officer exchanged slightly bemused looks, but said nothing. I guessed at the time that being a Romanian had no bearing on these men, even though we were in Romania. The butcher Antonescu had made a deal with the devil, so to speak, and the Axis, including the Nazis, now had free reign in his country.

We drove to what seemed like the outskirts of the city. Our destination was a plain looking one-story white building behind heavy barbed wire fencing. We drove up to a small shack near a gate, and as we approached, two Nazi soldiers jumped out and aimed automatic weapons at our car.

"Halt!" one of them yelled, and our driver stopped. More heavily armed soldiers appeared and rushed toward the vehicle. Several of them stood in front of the car, while one came over to the driver's side, pointing his machine gun at the window. The driver opened up, but said nothing. The soldier stuck the barrel of his gun into the car, but stopped when he saw the tall officer. The tall man said something in German. The soldier said, "Ja," and barked some orders to the crew blocking our way.

All this time, I was clutching my father's arm so tight, I may have drawn blood. But he didn't complain, he just kept patting my hand as if to say, "Everything will be all right."

The team parted ways, allowing the car to proceed. We had to stop again at the gate entrance while another soldier checked us out. The tall man called out some orders and we proceeded to the building. We were ordered out of the automobile, and then the one thing happened that I feared the most. My father and I were separated. Two guards held my arms firmly as they dragged my father away.

I screamed, "Papa, no. Please don't take him away from me. PLEASE...!"

He protested as well, but the soldiers probably didn't understand him, or, for that matter, care what he was saying. He fell to his knees, but the men simply picked him up and carried him to a plain metal door entrance to the building. Then my father was gone. As I look back on my life, Conner, I can honestly say that that moment was the time when I felt most alone.

The tall man came over to me. "Do not worry yourself, my dear," he said in Romanian. He put his hand on the side of my face. "So beautiful. You must not spoil your face with worry lines. Your father will be well taken care of. You have my word."

"Wh...when will I be able to see him again? Please...."

"In time, my dear. In time."

I was taken inside the building. The smell was antiseptic, like a hospital. The hallways were a plain grey color with absolutely no decoration. We came to a doorway with no markings.

"This will be your home for some time," said the tall man. "You will be treated well. You, my dear, are very important. As long as you do as you are told, there will be no trouble for you. And your father will be tended to."

Then the man's visage changed completely, from the friendly stranger and something of a protector and mentor, to a look of anger that sent chills down my body. He grabbed my chin and squeezed it hard as I whimpered in pain. He pulled me up close to his now bright red face. His next words were hissed out rather than spoken.

"If you do not do as you are told, or make any attempt to escape, your father will be put to death in as slow and painful a way as we can devise. Is that clear, my dear?"

I was too frightened to speak, so I just nodded. The guards opened the door, released my arms, and left me alone, slamming the door closed behind them.

***

The room was well furnished with a bed and a chair and it

had a bathroom, but no windows. It was very comfortable, but I was worried about my father and about what these people had planned for me.

The next day, servants brought me a sizable meal along with an armed guard. I ate the entire meal—I was determined to keep up my strength. Plus, in all honesty, I still felt hunger from the previous few days. Shortly after, a woman entered my room along with the same armed guard. I jumped as the door swung open. The woman had a stern look about her. Rail thin, with a narrow, almost sunken face, she was dressed in a plain skirt that went down to her ankles and a conservative top. Her hair was pulled back tightly in a bun. She had a German air about her, but much to my surprise, she spoke Romanian.

"I am Ula," she said as she looked me over closely. "Ah, I see they have chosen well. I will be your matron, responsible for teaching you. You are beautiful, but there is much you must learn."

"Learn? Please...may I see my father? I am very concerned about—"

"Take off your clothes."

I stood speechless and glanced over at the guard. "My clothes? I don't understand—"

"The clothes. NOW!"

The guard raised his rifle and aimed it at me. I stared at him, terrified. But I could see the hint of a smile on his face.

I saw no alternative but to comply. I was completely naked, my clothing in a heap at my feet. My arms were held tightly over the front of my body, my legs clamped firmly together. I chanced another look at the guard. He still had his rifle raised, but his eyes were running up and down my frame. I whimpered in fear.

Ula walked over. "Now relax, my child. Let me see." She pulled my arms to my side, leaned over, and inspected every inch of my body. Then she walked around behind me and did the same close inspection. She would utter an occasional, "Uh huh. Uh huh." When she finished her observations, she stood back out in front of me. "Yes, very nice. You will be perfect."

My arms went back up in front of me as I stammered, "Perfect? Perfect for what? Please, may I get dressed?"

"Of course, my child. Of course."

I didn't even bother with my foundations. I hurriedly covered myself with my shirt and pulled my pants up quickly. The guard was still leering, but he had lowered his weapon.

"You have much to offer," said Ula. "But we must sharpen your looks. Who gave you this haircut?"

"My...my father. He—"

"Ah, unfortunate. But we will have time for it to grow in. I will show you how to...present yourself. We will exercise daily. When our lessons are finished, you will no longer look like a farm girl, but a woman of class. And elegance. You will learn how to carry yourself. How to speak. Do you speak Russian?"

"Russian? No...I don't."

"Ah, well. We will teach you enough to get by."

"Please... Madam—"

"You will address me as Mother Ula."

I had trouble bringing myself to address her in this manner. Especially having just seen my real mother brutally murdered.

"Of course...M...Mother Ula. Please, may I be taken to see my father?"

"As long as you cooperate, and work hard in your training, your father will be well attended to." Ula and the guard walked to the door. She suddenly turned around and grabbed my shirt, pulling me forward. Her face was now bright red. "But understand something, my dear. I will be evaluated based on the success of this project. And, if it should fail, for any reason whatsoever...you will never see your father alive again."

Ula released her hold, but her vehemence and threat caused

my legs to collapse under me. She looked down as the guard opened the door.

"Get plenty of rest. Our training begins tomorrow."

***

My "training" routine was nothing if not rigorous. Every morning, Ula would put me through a laborious exercise regimen, although, to give the woman credit, she did everything alongside me. The guard was ever-present. She would allow me to shower and recover for about thirty minutes, then we would dive into our Russian lessons.

I showed a good proclivity for the new language, and one day, when Ula seemed pleased with my progress, I got up the nerve to ask her a question.

"Mother Ula?"

"Yes, child?"

"May I ask...what exactly is it that I am training for?"

Ula looked at me straight in the eye. I sensed that she was about to give me an explanation, that she wanted to, but in the end, all she said was, "That will become clear to you in time, my dear."

The other part of my education fell into a category that I will call "presenting myself." I was taught how to walk, how to behave, how to use proper etiquette. Of course, having grown up on a farm, many of these concepts were completely new to me.

Mother Ula was harsh in her corrections.

"NO, Lyria," she barked when I sat down at a table. She carried a switch and whacked me on the thigh. "You wait for the gentleman to pull your chair out, sit sideways with your legs together, then gently swing them under the table. Together! You are a lady, not a pig farmer."

The meals they fed me were sumptuous. I asked several times if my father was being given the same rations, but never got a reply.

Ula taught me about how to use makeup, and, as my hair grew longer, how to fashion it "for maximum effect."

Aside from the worry about my father, I must admit I came to enjoy the teaching. Mother Ula was pleased, and said I was making great progress. But then, after a seemingly very long period, there was another aspect of my training that would not be so pleasant.

***

Ula sat me down at our training table. Her mien was more dour than it had been before.

"I must ask you a question, my dear, and it may come as a shock to you," she said.

I stiffened. Despite falling into a positive groove with my teachings, I had expected all along that there was something sinister in these people's intentions. "Yes? What is that, Mother Ula?"

"Have you ever...been with a man?"

"Been with a man? Do you mean like working on the farm, with my father and my brother?"

Although my response pretty much answered her question, she persisted. "No dear. I mean have you ever been with a man... sexually?"

I admit that, even though I was over twenty, my knowledge of such matters was extremely limited. My real mother was not open about sharing, and my father would certainly never speak of such a thing. I had never attended school, so I had few female friends outside of the farm.

I remember blushing. "No, Mother. Never. If I understand your question correctly, that is."

Ula was staring me down. "Do you even know of such a subject?" she asked. "Did you not ever discuss such matters... with your mother?"

I was ashamed and sad, thinking about my mother. "No,

Mother Ula," I said.

She sighed, sounding exasperated. So in addition to our other lessons, I was taught about the more adult subject. Which would have been acceptable, but my captor's intention was for me to have real experience as well.

***

One night, as I readied for bed, the door to my room swung open and Ula appeared along with two men—the usual armed guard and another dressed in civilian clothes. The civilian was wearing a mask.

I was frozen with fear and immediately pulled up my blanket in front of me. "Mother Ula. Wh...what...?" I sputtered.

The guard aimed his rifle at me. Mother Ula said, "You will do as you're instructed. Everything will be all right." Her voice sounded stern, but she looked down at the floor as she spoke. The masked man looked me over and said something to the guard in German, and they both laughed. When he approached, I screamed, but the guard came over and they held me by my arms.

I won't go through the details, Conner, but suffice it to say that I was tied down and raped by the man in civilian clothes. I begged and pleaded with Mother Ula and my captors, but it did no good. When the act was finished, I was untied and the three simply walked out. I lay crying and in pain all night.

The next morning, Ula appeared ready for our exercise, acting as if nothing ever happened. I was still curled up in my bed.

"Come now, Lyria," she said. "Our lessons will continue as before."

"I...I cannot," I cried. "Why...why did that happen to me last night? Why...did you allow that to happen?"

Ula sat on the side of the bed. "It is part of your preparation, child," she said as gently as she was able. "Part of making you into a mature and capable woman."

"But why, Mother Ula? Why must I go through this? What am I being prepared for?"

She took my hand. "You will know soon enough, my dear. You will be part of greatness. Of a superior race taking its rightful place as leaders of the world. And you will play an important role in the ascendancy. But you must be properly coached. You must be...developed. Now come. Get out of bed. I will come back shortly and our lessons will continue as before."

And continue they did. Exercise, Russian, self-presentation, and, as it turned out, sexual experience. Yes, rape. By the same masked man. Every day.

Seemingly months went by. My hair was long, as it is now. Nobody ever answered my inquiries about my father. Then one day, the routine was no more. And everything changed.

***

I was left alone for an entire day. Ula didn't appear in the morning. Servants brought my meals, but they were the only people who came in. Until that evening.

Ula barged in, again causing me to jump. She held an exquisite-looking white dress that looked as if it was made of satin.

"Put this on, child," she ordered.

"Mother Ula? What is this? What is happening?"

Ula shouted, "PUT IT ON. NOW."

I was frightened into silence by her tone. Gone was my mentor. She was now simply another captor, one who had allowed me to be raped repeatedly. I had no choice but to do as I was told, and I did so in silence.

Once the dress was on, another matron came in and worked on making me up. When I looked in the mirror, honestly, I barely recognized myself.

"There, that will do," said Ula walking over. "You look beautiful."

237

I said nothing. Was I to be raped again? By someone else this time?

"Now just sit and wait," said Ula. "I will be back shortly." She left.

I sat on the edge of my bed, shaking with terror. It seemed like an eternity went by.

The door opened and I involuntarily emitted a small scream that sounded more like a whimper, but it was all I could muster. Ula came in with the guard. But they were joined by the tall German officer who had my father and me transported.

"Stand up, Lyria," ordered Ula. The guard readied his weapon. I stood and the tall man walked toward me. "Please," I whimpered. "Please no more—"

"My dear," said the tall man. "I will do you no harm. You have my word as an officer. I merely wish to look at you. See who you have become. Ah, yes." He looked me over as if he were a bovine buyer assessing a prized head of cattle. He took my hand and turned me around. "Very nice. Frau Ula, you have performed well. Above expectations." He walked toward the door. "The next phase of our plan may now take place. See that there is no delay."

***

Ula had me change into a plain-looking pair of pants and a buttoned shirt. I pleaded with her to tell me what was going to happen. But when I was finished changing, she motioned for me to join her sitting on the bed.

"I will not lie to you, child. I hope we have established a bond over the course of our time together. The near future will be difficult for you. But, I would ask that you keep the ultimate objective in mind and persevere. You will be a leader in establishing the superior race. The greatness that awaits all of us. There will be many...what I will call heroes in our effort. And you will be one of them. I shall not see you again child. But I leave you with my blessing. And...my prayers."

With that, my 'mother' Ula walked out. I was left by myself, worrying about my fate. I had heard tales of the Nazis doing medical experimentation on some prisoners, and I wondered if that was what they were going to do to me. But then, I thought, why the lessons in manners and grace? Why the focus on my appearance? Why the rapes by the masked man? I had no answers, but I was making myself sick thinking about it. I wished beyond all wishes that my father were there to comfort me. Somehow, even when my family's outlook was bleak—whether it was a flood, a drought, a crop disease, whatever the cause—my father would find a way to make everything all right. He was the rock around which our family was built. But, as of that moment, at least, I didn't even know if he was still alive.

A group of uniformed men came in, pushing what looked like a medical transport cart. They made me lie down and, despite my pleas and questions, silently secured my hands and feet, strapping me to the cold metal cart. They wheeled me out into the hallway.

"Please," I begged. "Where are you taking me? What are you going to do with me?"

"Be silent," one of the men ordered in Romanian.

They continued pushing me through a maze of corridors, until we finally came to a door that looked like it led to a vault. Wild thoughts were running rampant through my mind. More rape? A scientific experiment of some kind? Whatever my fate, being bound so tightly to this moving table did not bode well.

There were multiple armed guards standing near the doorway, and one of them moved to a latch. They spoke in German, words I could not understand. Then the door was opened. All the men had raised their weapons, as I did all I could to keep from passing out from the fear. Two of the men pushed me into a room with plain concrete walls. There were no windows in the walls, but there was what looked like thick glass overhead, allowing daylight into the room. I looked around. At first, I saw nothing else there, but when I looked off to my left, much to my horror, there was a stand, and on the stand was a thickly wooded structure. My mind refused to identify it, but down deep, I knew what the structure was, and all the nightmare ideas running through me no longer seemed sufficient.

The structure on the stand was a sarcophagus. More commonly known these days as a coffin.

I screamed, and I was barely cognizant of the men leaving the room before I completely blacked out.

***

When I came to it was dark in the room, and it took some time to remember where I was. The horror of my situation returned, as I realized I was still strapped to the metal cart.

I cried out, "Hello? Please, can anyone hear me?"

There was no answer, but a realization came to me, which made matters even worse.

I sensed that there was someone else in the room.

"Hello?" I uttered with more of a sense of urgency. "Is there someone else here?"

My question was met with silence, but as my eyes adjusted to the dark, I looked frantically at my surroundings. I scanned as far as my vision would take me, but I couldn't see anything or anyone. But something bothered me, and at first, I was not able to pinpoint what it was. I looked around again, my vision improving. I suddenly realized that something was indeed terribly wrong. My breath caught in my chest as I stared to my left. At first, I thought I was imagining things, that my trauma had gotten the better of my senses. I started gasping for air as the comprehension dawned on me that I was not concocting false images. What I saw was real.

The lid to the coffin was open.

***

I cannot honestly say how long I screamed. It could have been just a few seconds or thirty minutes—I really don't know. I only stopped when a being appeared at my side. I felt as if I would pass out again, or perhaps die on the spot, as I was sure my heart had stopped beating.

"Do not be afraid, my child."

The being was a young man. He had a handsome, narrow face, and long, somewhat scraggly blond hair, and was wearing a burlap tunic over his upper body. That was all I could see. He was looking down upon me with what I could only guess was a combination of affection and sorrow. I immediately thought that this was my next rapist. Ah, if it had only turned out to be that simple.

"Who...who are you? What do you want?" I sputtered.

"My name is Aurel," said the man. "The rest of your questions will be answered in time. But first, I must ask your forgiveness for what I am about to do."

I was frozen with fear, unable to speak at first. Then I finally managed an utterance.

"Please. I beg of you. Please do not hurt me. I...I was captured... with my father...I mean no harm to anyone. I—that is to say, my family—we are farmers. I had no knowledge of what my father was doing. I still know very few details."

He put a hand on my cheek. It was very cold, and I inhaled sharply.

"Rest easy, my child," he said. His voice was barely above a whisper. "I do this because I must. I was left with no alternative. Our captors will reveal me to the daylight that I have not seen for hundreds of years. But I have a plan. You will have a new beginning. And if all goes according to my plan, you will be able to save your father and avenge your capture."

I was speechless at first.

241

"You...you said hundreds of years. I don't understand. You... are a captive as well?"

"This will all become clear, my child. Now, look up, through the window that serves as a roof to our cell. Close your eyes, my child. That is it. Rest, relax. Be easy...."

I did as I was told, but continued to plead. "Please...please sir...."

My words were interrupted by pain, which seemed to emanate from my neck and course through my entire being. I tried to cry out, but I couldn't make a sound. The pain became a sense of...euphoria, of seeing the world as if I had just opened my eyes for the first time. And there was Aurel. Everything was Aurel. I didn't understand how, but it seemed as if Aurel and I were the same being. That we shared each other's thoughts. He 'spoke' to me, without saying a word. He was attached to me, and suddenly I understood.

He had been captured by the German army. Somehow, his resting place had been found, and he was dragged out under cover, but during daylight when he was unable to defend himself. He was taken to this cell. This had been months ago, and the soldiers weakened him by not allowing him to "feed." I recognized that he was feeding on me, right at that moment, and that was the reason we had this mental connection.

You must understand my story, he said in his thoughts. And his origin, the story I related earlier, all became clear.

Will you kill me? I asked. Will you take all my blood, as you did with Zoltan? Is this what our captors want?

No, my child. I'm afraid it is more...shall we say, complicated than that.

He then communicated his understanding of the situation, and his intentions.

The Germans had found a mystic, one familiar with ancient rites and legends. He told them that I would be able to make another of my kind. They brought subjects in, all female. Without our captors' knowledge, I drank only part of the females' blood — I did not want to share my fate with another. As I replaced their blood with my own cursed fluid, their bodies reacted. The subjects all died. One must be strong, Lyria — not everyone can be changed. Their intent was to find one with great physical beauty and strengthen her, in hopes of a successful conversion. And, I was told that if I am unsuccessful with you, they will remove me from the coffin during daylight and I will be no more.

But why? Why would they want...another?

I could sense a hesitation before conveying his answer.

They intend to use you as a weapon.

A weapon?

Yes, their battle with the Russians is intensifying. They would have you attend parties and functions where senior Russian officers will be present. Someone with your looks would have no trouble attracting their attention. Then, once you were alone with an important officer, you would...kill him.

My thoughts, all of which Aurel could see, ran rampant. I was stunned by this revelation. After some time, I finally got a coherent thought together.

I will refuse. I will do no such thing. What will they do? Expose me to daylight? Then all their effort will be for naught.

They still have your father.

My...my father? He sent his thought and it all became clear. If I did not carry out their plan, my father would be put to a painful and tortured death.

**

I lay silent in my thoughts as Aurel continued to feed.

I told you I had a plan, he thought.

Yes? What is it?

It is not without risk.

Please, Aurel. I have no concept of a fate worse than what

you are describing. What is your plan?

Again, a sense of hesitation.

This conversion...it can be done a number of ways. The basic idea is that my cursed blood replaces some of your own. What they do not know is that I can make you stronger. The more of your blood I replace, the stronger you will become. However....

Yes, what? Please?

I could give you strength beyond their comprehension, but I must drain you completely and then fill your body with my own blood. You may not survive. Such a drastic measure, it could kill you. These men, they only know of me in a weakened state. But, if the conversion is successful, you will be strong beyond their limited understanding of our kind of beings. I do not know if you could thwart their plan to use you as an assassin, to save your father, but you would be more capable. I...I don't even have a good grasp of what you would be capable of. It would give you an advantage that I did not have.

If I die, that means the Nazis will kill you as well? Because the conversion has failed?

Yes, my child. It would be the end of our kind. My concern is not for myself, however. I have lived long enough. But you. You...are so young....

There was silence between our thoughts.

Yes, I said finally. This is what I want. I am willing to take the risk.

You are brave. I sense great strength in you. These men have chosen you for the way you look, but they have no knowledge of how you think. I feel that they are in for something of a surprise.

All this time, Aurel had been drinking my blood—feeding on me. And we were communicating silently between ourselves. He continued, This will take some time. I believe that, at some point, your thoughts will go blank. I will stay with you...in the sarcophagus. When you awaken, you will see the world differently. You will move faster...be stronger than the mortals. To my understanding, only the daylight can end our lives. If we are wounded, or have caused an injury that would be fatal to a regular person, our cursed blood heals the wound instantly. We do not age. We are looked upon as demons, but we can use our difference for good as well. You must feed, but there are many with evil in their souls. The world is better without them. You will be able to see these beings, and focus your needs on their kind. This is how I have passed my existence, how I have managed not to break down, how I have managed to...survive. Bless you, my child. I will be here to help guide your actions.

Much as Aurel had surmised, a short time thereafter, everything went dark.

***

I awoke in complete nothingness, surrounded by the smell of cedar wood. I sensed that Aurel had been next to me, but he was not there now. I pushed the lid of the coffin up. It was nighttime again, as there was little light coming through the glass ceiling. But I could see perfectly, as if daylight were flooding the room. Aurel was nowhere to be found. I was confused, but when I scanned the floor of the cell, I could see an area that looked as if there had been a fire, and I knew what had happened. The men, our captors, had come in during the day and taken Aurel out of the coffin. They had no further use for him now that the conversion had been completed. My blood boiled with anger as I thought about Aurel, my captivity, and the fate of my father. They wished to use my father to control me, to make me do their evil bidding. However, they had made a mistake in their tactics. Several mistakes, actually. I could somehow sense that my father was nearby — they had not taken him away. And they didn't have an understanding of my ability, my power.

I leapt out of the coffin and stood crouched at the ready. Were these men going to enter the cell? They would have to eventually, but I was not going to wait. I would use the element of surprise.

I thought back to Aurel's story, how he had come to be. It came back to me how Anca, the witch, had jumped high into the sky as if she was flying, before immolating from the touch of the sun. Looking skyward, I understood how I would escape. I picked up the coffin — it had probably taken several men to bring it in. Holding it in front of me, using it as a projectile, I squatted and jumped up toward the glass. The coffin smashed into the thick window and it shattered with the impact. Soaring upward into the night air, I dropped the sarcophagus and it splintered on the floor of the cell. Now I was waiting on the roof of the building where I had been held.

Sure enough, three soldiers, roused by the noise of my escape, charged into the room, their rifles at the ready. They looked around the empty cell, then up, and realized what had happened, but it was too late to do them any good, as I swooped down with speed that the mortal eye could not follow, and soon all three men were on the floor, incapacitated. Looking down at them, I was overcome with a driving hunger of a type I had never before experienced. At that point, I realized that I had elongated canines, fangs if you will. One of the unconscious men stirred, but I sank my razor-sharp teeth into his neck. The blood flowed freely, and he shuddered as I drank. The taste...Conner, I must be honest...it was beyond any euphoria I had ever experienced before. The man's life played before me, but I was engulfed in the drinking of the blood. Before I realized it, I had drained his body completely, and I dropped the corpse to the floor. One of the other men had come to and he looked at me with stark terror. He raised his rifle and fired. I felt a thud in my right shoulder, but no pain. There was a hole in my shoulder, but it quickly closed up. The man felt light as a feather when I lifted him and held his neck close, then I sensed others nearby. Looking up, I saw the tall officer standing in the doorway. There were two men at his side with their rifles aimed at me. The man I was holding dropped to the floor and scurried away.

The officer was smiling. "Put those guns down, men. Can't you see that they will do no good?" he said to the soldiers. "My dear, you have awakened. Our journey is complete. Now we must begin our mission. I trust you understand how you will help ensure that the superior race will prevail?"

I stepped forward. The guards backed away, but the tall officer stood his ground.

"You also understand, my dear, that as long as you do our bidding, your father will be treated well. He is comfortable, being fed regularly, and safe. That will continue as long as you are cooperating. If, however, that should change...well...let us just say that he will meet a rather unpleasant fate."

"Where is he?" I asked, baring my fangs.

The tall officer just laughed. "Another time, my dear. Shall we go and discuss our plans for your mission?"

I walked slowly forward and concentrated, using my knowledge of how the complex was laid out. I could see him—I could see my father. And an understanding came over me. The men in the room were staring at me agape as a rage built up in my expression.

"You bastard," I said softly. "You've killed him already."

For the first time, the veneer of this tall, ever-smug officer cracked. I saw fear in his eyes. "No," he said. "Your father is well. After your mission, he will be...released."

I bolted forward and seized the officer. The guards fled and we were left alone in the room. There was raw terror on the officer's face. I bit into his throat and drank. He groaned, then I pulled back.

"Major Bitterlich, is it? Well, Major, don't think that you will endure the fate of your soldier in the cell. I know from personal experience that to die this way is too pleasant, virtually no pain.

Indeed, even providing a certain sense of euphoria at times. You may have felt that just this moment, no? You, however, will feel much pain. Much as my father felt. Much as...Aurel felt. And perhaps significantly more."

Conner, again, I will spare you the details, but suffice it to say that Major Bitterlich suffered greatly. I was able to find my father's body. While I still had darkness, I carried him and sped back to our farm in Iasi. I laid him to rest, burying him near the fields where we had spent so much time together. I prayed at his grave, then headed back to where our home had stood. It had been burned to the ground. One of our barn structures still stood, and I buried myself in the ground inside and waited to arise the next night."

CHAPTER TWENTY

I was still holding Lyria's hand as she finished her story. She was sitting with her head down, an expression of sadness on her beautiful face. Without thinking about what on earth I was doing, I moved forward and embraced her. I can't really explain why, it just felt right. Of course, after hearing about her origin, it also would have felt right to, say, call in a SWAT team, but when she returned the hug, those thoughts all dissipated.

Ah, the male libido, willing to literally risk life and limb just to get in a good squeeze. No wonder men die younger than women.

"That's...quite a story," I said.

"Yes."

"So, this...cursed blood that Aurel passed on. Does that mean that you're...possessed?"

Lyria sported a sad smile. "I've had a lot of time to think about questions like that. And even I don't have all the answers. But what I have figured out is that there are many forms of energy in our world, and some of them are strong enough to live through others. These life forces, if you will, can be both good and bad. Aurel and his band of witches were strong enough to summon the evil energy, and it took possession of their souls. This cursed existence lives on through me, and I am the last of its kind. But I have tried to continue in Aurel's spirit. He only fed on those with inbred malevolence in their souls, and I have as well. Trust me when I tell you that there is no shortage of candidates."

"Like Brent?"

Lyria hesitated. "Yes. Like Brent. I was...only going to weaken him. I've learned over the years to stop before...."

"Before it's too late?"

She smiled. "Yes. Exactly. But when I saw the rage he felt toward Carly, I...didn't stop. I couldn't just let him kill your sister."

"But, what if they find the body? Couldn't they find your DNA...or something?"

"They won't find a body, Conner."

We just sat looking at each other. "Lyria...."

"Yes? Conner, please tell me what you're thinking. I know this all comes as a shock. And, I meant what I said earlier. If it's too much...if you want me to go away, I will. I promise, you'll never see or hear from me again." There was such sadness in her eyes.

"What...what do you want with me?"

She smiled. "Despite being...different, I still have feelings. I have the capacity to love. In many ways I can function just like a 'normal' girl."

"Yes, I've noticed."

We were so close together. Before I knew what was happening, we were kissing. And kissing some more. I couldn't bring myself to tell her to leave. Things actually started getting heavy.

"Um, before we get too far in the process," she said. "It's getting late. I might need a rain check 'til tomorrow."

I sat back and tried to catch my breath. "Sorry. Looks like I got carried away."

"No apologies," she said with a smile. "Think about... everything. I'll come back this evening. If you want me to."

"Yes...I want you to come back."

She turned on the megawatt smile. "Until later then." We

kissed again and she got up and walked out the front door. I looked out the window, but she was gone.

I laid back on the couch. Needless to say, my head was swirling once again. Lyria. Everything was Lyria. Hard to believe that a very short time ago I was blending into society, a non-descript financial analyst living out my days in Boston with way more questions than answers about my future. Well, Conner boy, I thought, you were clamoring for a relationship. Man, did you ever get one.

Then Lyria became a part of my life. And everything, and I do mean everything, changed. What to make of this woman, this mysterious woman who was now dominating my every thought? Her story was beyond belief, yet I didn't have anything close to an alternative explanation for what had happened since I met her. She seemed to love me, and I had to face the fact that I might also be in love with her. Lyria had said it herself — most lore has a basis in reality, and my reality was now based in lore.

Lyria. A part of me dreaded her, but another, bigger part, dreaded the thought of living without her even more. There were so many contradictions churning up my feelings about her.

She was the woman of my dreams.

She was a monster.

Her beauty took my breath away.

But how many people had she killed?

She almost assuredly had saved my sister's life.

And, perhaps mine as well.

She was gorgeous.

She was deadly.

But, none of that stuff really mattered. Like it or not, I was entwined in this reality. Our reality. Lyria said she would go away if I wanted her to, but it wasn't that simple. I wasn't capable of spending every waking moment thinking about someone, and then just erasing her from my existence. It was like she was...a part of me. I had to face up to what she was, no more denial.

When you boil it all down, Lyria was now, unquestionably, my girlfriend, the vampire.

Chapter Twenty One

"Ah, working on a Sunday, eh?" said Don Halberton, interrupting Grace Garvey's thoughts as she sat at her desk in the precinct. "Or was it that you just couldn't wait until Monday to be in my presence once more?"

Grace looked up at her boss and rolled her eyes. "You got it... what's your name again?"

Halberton laughed. "You're doing a good job pretending that I'm not occupying all your waking thoughts. So, any news on our lost boy?"

"Seems Mr. Shaw had quite the social life. Unfortunately, very little, if any of it, involved Mrs. Shaw."

"He's a player, huh?"

"Oh yeah. At first, folks in his office didn't want to say anything. Y'know? Trash the boss? Too bad, 'cause that's a really fun pastime."

Halberton ignored the barb and nodded for her to go on.

"Anyway, I knew it was just a matter of time before they opened up to me. Especially the guys." She winked.

"I'm acknowledging your unique talents, G.G., but are we ever going to get to what you found out?"

"Yeah, sorry. Pretty much just what you said. The guy's a player. And a skirt-chaser. Not above using his position to get favorable treatment from the women at his company. One gentleman told me about an office party where he had cornered a good-looking young secretary. Seemed to the people watching like he was making her uncomfortable and she was trying to gracefully get away from him, but he was using his bulk to keep her in position. The other guys were joking that when she emerged from the corner, she would be a vice president."

"Hmmm. That's trouble."

"Right. That's what I thought. A guy like that is going to make some enemies among jealous husbands and boyfriends. And from what I learned by canvassing some of his favorite evening haunts, he was almost constantly on the make after work as well. He figured that with his size, he didn't have to worry too much about confrontations. Most people were scared off just by looking at him."

"Geez."

"But fear not, big boss. Don't forget who you have on this case."

"I'm not likely to forget that anytime soon."

"Right, I would never allow it. So, the last night Casanova was seen, he was at The Hill. You know the place?"

Halberton shook his head.

"Classy joint over on Cambridge Street. Probably why you haven't been there. But it seems our boy got into a tiff over a woman that night."

"Really."

"Yeah, well, fact of the matter is, it wasn't much of a tiff. The other guy involved was the tall, skinny, bookworm type. Works as a financial analyst at Beacon Hill Associates. Apparently, Mr. Shaw muscled in on his girl, or at least the girl he was with, and when Mr. Bookworm objected, Shaw swatted him away. Then he, Shaw, left with the babe in question. He hasn't been seen or heard from since. From the description I got, the girl was a real knockout."

"So, maybe he's still shacked up with her."

"Doubtful. Like I said, this guy's no stranger to extracurricular activity. But none of his associates could ever remember him blowing off work before. All the guy ever does is work, drink, and screw around. But he takes the job very seriously. I'll tell you, Mrs. Shaw must either be very patient or simply satisfied with a posh lifestyle."

"I know I don't even need to ask this, but did you find the other guy? Mr. Bookworm?"

Grace pursed her lips in a sarcastic grin and looked at Halberton out of the corner of her eye.

"Let me rephrase the question," said Don. "How did your conversation go with Mr. Bookworm?"

Grace laughed. "Very interesting. His name is Conner David. Lives on Beacon Hill, but he admitted that his old man paid for his place. He himself is about as unlikely a murder suspect as you could ever come across. He looks like a good breeze would knock him on his butt. And I can't picture him using any kind of weapon. But he got a bit squirrely when I brought up the girl from that night. First he claimed that he didn't remember her name, but I knew that was a lie. Later he said her name was Lyria. Didn't know her last name. He said he hadn't seen said babe since the night he ran into Mr. Shaw. But, I'm relatively sure he was lying then too. He said he was just trying to be discreet. Possible, but also possible he knows this Lyria more than he's letting on."

"That is interesting. Anything else?"

"Yeah. Just for kicks I showed him pictures of Dylan Cavey and Lucas Corsi—you know, Gebelein's low-life MPs? The kid nearly bought it on the spot. He got his composure back and denied knowing them, but his first reaction was classic."

"Wow. Are you going to...? Wait...I should ask, when are you going to talk to this guy again?"

Grace smiled. "I thought I'd bring him in here for the

next session. I'm willing to bet he's never seen the inside of an interrogation room before. And, I've got another hook."

"Of course you do. What is it?"

"He told me he had actually met Lyria the night before in the same place, The Hill. He was there with some work friends. I asked him if anyone else had met her, and he said one of his friends did. Guy by the name of Fernando Rojas — his friends call him Razor. Then he immediately looked like he regretted telling me that. Probably didn't want any of this getting back to his place of work. So I thought I would see how much he wanted to avoid getting Razor involved."

"You are scary. Glad I'm not your enemy."

"Ah, never assume."

"Very funny. When will you be talking to him?"

"I have some records checks going on for Mr. Conner David. Not that I expect they'll come up with anything. But I was thinking tomorrow."

"Excellent. Maybe we can go Starsky and Hutch on him."

"Stansky and who?"

"Not Stansky. Starsky. Please tell me you're not too young to remember Starsky and Hutch? The TV show?"

"Sorry, boss."

Halberton looked at the ceiling. "I should have known. Anyway, these guys were great at doing the good cop — bad cop routine. Think we need to use that on Mr. David?"

"Well, just in case that suddenly seems like a good idea, why don't you stay unshaven tomorrow, wear your best hobo chic outfit, mess up your hair really bad, and come to work with a hangover?"

"It was just a suggestion."

"Why don't we see how much I can get out of him first? But I promise, if I'm not getting anywhere, you can come in and act like a caveman. Maybe bring one of those big dumb-looking clubs with you. Then you can work out all your frustrations. Deal?"

Grace could see that Halberton was suppressing a smile. "Deal." Her boss walked away. "Good work, G.G.," he called out over his shoulder.

***

I woke up around noon, still lying on the couch. Sleeping on the sofa again, huh? I thought, Well, if nothing else this is saving me from having to wash my sheets so often.

I staggered toward the kitchen, but my phone rang, delaying my quest for caffeine. It was Carly. I clicked on immediately.

"Carly? Are you okay?"

"Yes, big brother," she said, and it sounded like she was sobbing. "I was more concerned about you."

"Me? No, I'm fine." I had to stop myself from saying, "Don't worry about me. I've got my girlfriend, the vampire, to look out for me."

Carly said, "Conner, I'm so sorry about last night. I...don't know why I'm attracted to such losers. It's my problem, but last night, I brought it on everyone else. Is everything okay with Lyria?"

I hesitated for a moment. "Oh sure," I said, sounding way more confident than I felt. "Lyria's fine. We're all fine on this end."

"Are you sure? I detected a hint of uncertainty there."

I had to be more careful. I forgot how well Carly knew me. "No, we're really good. We were...just worried about you. You didn't...hear from Brent again, did you?"

"No. I stayed at Beth's last night. Her father's the overly protective type, and when he saw me—you know—all bruised up, he got really mad and said he hoped Brent showed up there. I think he got his gun out and carried it with him. Stayed up all night downstairs."

"Where are you now?"

"I'm heading home. I called Mom and forewarned her about what had happened. I figured there was no way to hide my face until the bruises went away. She said she would let Dad know, as gently as possible. So, if you hear a loud noise coming from out west, you'll know it's Dad blowing his top. I'm sure I'll get the inquisition once I get home. I...just wanted to tell you how sorry I was." She started crying again. "I never thought Brent would act like that."

"I know. You always try to see the best in people. But when you've exhausted all the other possibilities, you just have to conclude that Brent was just a big dumb jerk who liked to hurt people when he got sauced." I cringed a little inside for referring to him in the past tense. Hopefully Carly thought I meant it in terms of her relationship.

"You're right. He is a big dumb jerk. I kept thinking there must be some positive qualities buried there somewhere. But, from now on, I'm going to stop kidding myself. Your girlfriend must think I'm a total loser too."

"Don't be too hard on yourself, Carl. Lyria's been around enough to know how it is. He was an abuser, and you're lucky to be rid of him." Achh, there I go again.

"Yeah. Okay, well, I'm pulling in the driveway. Oh boy, Mom's running out to the car. Looks like she's been crying. It's gonna be a long day."

"Good luck," I said, and then we hung up.

Not two minutes later, my phone rang again. It wasn't anyone in my contacts, and my mind started racing through the possibilities. One person I knew it wasn't was Lyria. For some reason, that thought struck me as funny, and I started laughing uncontrollably. It took effort, but I got myself under control in time to pick up the call.

"Hello?"

"Hi there, Conner. Detective Grace Garvey. Sounds like I

caught you in a good mood."

A mood which instantly vanished at the sound of her voice. "Yes. Oh...hi there...Detective. Um...what can I do for you?"

"Did I catch you at a bad time? Or a really good time?"

"No, it's fine."

"Good. Hey listen, Conner, I thought it might be a good idea to make sure we're on the same page on this Arnold Shaw case."

My heart froze in my chest, but I tried to sound casual. "Arnold Shaw...Arnold Shaw...oh, you mean the big guy from the bar? Is he still missing?"

"Yeah, 'fraid so. And the more we're finding out, the more it seems as if your lady friend from The Hill that night was the last one to see him before he went bye bye."

"Really? Well, like I told you, I don't know too much about her—"

"Oh, I know, I know," she interrupted. "We just want to be sure we have our facts straight before we go out looking for this mystery woman. The sequence of events that night and all. Hey, would it be possible for you to come in here? To the station? I've got a lot of following up to do, and it sure would save me some time. Like, maybe tomorrow?"

"Tomorrow? Uh, tomorrow's Monday. I have to work."

"No big problem. How about after work? You know the address?"

She had subtly, but very effectively, let me know that this might have been a request, but it was a strongly worded request. "Uh, yeah, sure. I guess that would be all right."

"Awesome. I appreciate it. I'm sure a young guy like you has a busy social life—one lined up every night. So I'm grateful for the...cooperation."

This Grace Garvey had a way of making it seem like she could see right through me, which gave me even more of a queasy feeling in my stomach than I already had. "Okay, so...tomorrow evening?"

"I'll be here. Thanks, Conner."

***

I thought all day about what I was going to talk to Lyria about that evening. I paced around the townhouse endlessly, willing the hours to go by faster. I finally went upstairs, laid face-down on my bed, and pulled my pillows up over my ears and head. I felt like Myrtle the Turtle hiding in her shell. I wondered again how my life had gotten so royally screwed up in such a short time. It was bad enough that my significant other was among the undead, but now the police wanted to talk to me about a guy who might be one of the permanently dead.

Granted, Lyria might have been protecting me. Arnold Shaw had looked like the kind of guy who could kill me with his bare hands without even trying. I remembered her going with him that night and, knowing what I knew now, figured she was truly trying to get him away from me before he could do any further damage. Just like she had said. And the druggie-robbers Spider and Vape? It looked like she had taken care of them too. But they were in the act of robbing me, and who knows? They might have done away with me if they had had the chance. Not that I had anything valuable on me at the time — unless you consider about twenty-three dollars and a half-eaten pack of 5 Gum valuable. But I got a good look at their faces, and they didn't know that I would have been too big of a chicken to be part of prosecuting them. They might not have wanted to take the chance.

So, okay, my girlfriend was protecting me. But talking to the police, in a police station yet, was definitely out of my comfort zone. I had never stepped foot in a police station before. Heck, I'd never even had to stay after school. Suppose they put me in one of those rooms with no windows and tried to sweat the truth out of me?

Again, maybe I watched too much TV.

Besides, what was I supposed to tell them anyway? I started framing the conversation in my head.

"Well, you see, my girlfriend is a vampire, and she thought those guys were going to hurt me, so they're now charter members of that big 'I Hate Conner David' fan club in the sky. But don't worry, she got a couple of good meals out of it, and she was nice and warm while we were rolling around in the hay all last week."

They'd probably have me put away to avoid having me come in contact with any sane human beings.

No, the truth was definitely out of the question. And what scared me most was that I was a lousy liar. And Grace Garvey was sharp as a tack, and would see right through me. I might even be lined up as a suspect. I could picture Grace now.

"So, Mr. David. By any chance, did you off Mr. Arnold 'cause he slapped the make on your girl? I mean, let's face it, there's a pretty big looks discrepancy between you and your girlfriend. Seems like a jealous rage in the making."

And what about work tomorrow? Was I just supposed to go in and try to act normal with the interview looming in the evening?

All these thoughts and more were running through my mind, and every scenario played out badly for me. I knew I'd see Lyria that night, and I would vent to her. But unless she came up with something brilliant, I had to face up to a very vivid fact.

No matter how I looked at it, I was royally screwed.

***

"Hey handsome."

My subconscious built the voice into a dream I was having. Lyria and I were living in a castle surrounded by an alligator-ridden moat. There were villagers dressed in Nazi uniforms pelting the walls of the castle with spears and rocks from the grounds outside the water. The alligators were snapping at the invaders, forcing them to keep their distance. The Nazi village

261

people were yelling, "Monsters! Death to the monsters!" They had those old torches wrapped with twine, and I wondered why those things never just burned out in the movies. I was running from window to window in a frenzy, worried that the invaders would find a way into the castle and we would be toast. I turned around and Lyria came into the room. She was wearing a little teddy, the kind that keeps teenage boys awake at night. She looked insanely gorgeous, and didn't seem at all worried about the mob outside wanting to burn us at the stake. She floated on over toward me. "Hey handsome," she said, just about stopping my heart cold.

I slowly came to and realized that Lyria was there in my room, and had actually voiced those words. She was sitting next to me on the bed and she wasn't wearing a teddy, but she still looked drop dead gorgeous. It occurred to me that if I was going to hang with a vampire, I might want to think of another description for her.

She leaned over and kissed my cheek, her long soft hair sending my thoughts all a kilter by brushing against my face.

"Dreaming of anything interesting?" she purred.

I smiled. "Oh, nothing really. Just you and me in a castle with a bunch of Nazis wanting to hang us. But not to worry. Our pet alligators were keeping them away from us."

She smiled and moved closer. "Interesting. What were we doing?"

"Not sure, but I think we were about to have sex."

She laughed. "That's my boy. Always focus on what's really important. Even in the face of a violent death." She kissed me. Then again. She sat up, reached back, and unzipped her dress, letting it fall all the way to her waist. "I know there are no Nazis around," she said. "But I think your dream self had absolutely the right idea."

***

262

Afterward, we were in bed holding each other. I got up on one elbow facing Lyria. She had her arms around my waist and I started stroking her face. "That was amazing...as always," I said.

She smiled. "You see?" she said. "My theory of improvement with practice is coming true."

I said, "Now that I know all of your secrets —"

"Um," she interrupted, "You know some of my secrets."

I looked at her.

She said, "I think it's healthy for a couple to have a little mystery between them. Don't you?"

I laughed. "Not many couples have our kind of mystery."

"Okay. You have a point there."

"So, can I ask you a question?"

"There's no harm in asking."

"How do you get in here?"

"What do you mean?" She asked with a sly grin that told me she knew exactly what I meant. But I explained anyway.

"Into the townhouse. Last night I was pretty freaked out, so I went around like five times making sure all the doors and windows were locked up tight. And you somehow got in. And again tonight. How do you do that?"

"Let's just say I've learned some tricks along the way. You have to remember how old I am. I look pretty good for my age, don't I? Anyway, over the years, I've found out that there are... things that I can do. There's really no way to explain them in normal, everyday terms. But most locked doors and closed windows are nothing more than a minor inconvenience."

"Any other of these...things...that you'd care to let me in on?"

"No. You'll probably learn about most of them in due time."

I couldn't help but smile. Well, I thought, she definitely has a hold on me, that's for sure. But I had to bring up a more serious subject.

"Lyria," I said.

263

"Oh boy. We're going to get serious now, aren't we?"

"Yes. The police were here asking about you."

If Lyria was at all concerned about this revelation, she didn't show it. "Tell me more," she said calmly.

"Well, a detective—a woman—from the Boston Police showed up here. She was asking about a guy named Arnold Shaw. I guess he's that guy built like Godzilla from last Saturday night at The Hill. Seems he's a mucky muck from some big insurance company in Boston, and he's buddy buddy with the mayor, or at least his wife is. He hasn't been seen since that night, and they traced him back to me. And you."

Again, virtually no overt reaction. "Okay," was all she said.

"Lyria...I don't really want to ask, but did he...did you...?"

"Conner, the man was nobody you should be worried about. He's hurt a lot of people. He even beat someone to death. Got away with it scot-free. And when I saw him hurt you...."

I let her statement hang in the air for a moment. Then I said, "She was also asking about those two robbers. The ones I asked you about, that first night I saw you."

She reached up and stroked my face. "You don't have anything to worry about. Trust me."

"Well, this detective, she's really sharp. And scary. She wants me to come to police headquarters tomorrow after work. I'm a little nervous. I've never been a very good liar. She asks a lot of questions about you. I've been evasive, but I feel like she sees right through me. I'm afraid I'll stumble and give you away."

"Just relax. What is this detective's name?"

"Garvey. Grace Garvey. She works out of missing persons. She wants me to come to the headquarters on Sudbury Street. I just hope they don't break out the rubber hose or something."

"They'd better not. Besides, waterboarding is much more effective."

I laughed. "Doesn't anything ever bother you?"

"Again, old lady wisdom. You should take advantage of it. People too often worry about things they can't change, or aren't worth worrying about." She leaned forward and kissed me deeply. To put it gracefully, it got things stirring again. She reached down for me. "Now, this is something a lady would do well to be worried about."

***

Detective Grace Garvey was getting an early start in the morning, as usual. She liked the change of seasons, but didn't like it still being dark so late in the morning this time of year. Working a heavy caseload, she often left for work in the dark in the morning and got home in the dark at night. "I feel like a vampire," she said to herself. But the Arnold Shaw case was soaking up a lot of her time lately, and she still had other cases that needed her attention. She was using the early hours and post peak lulls to catch up on her other investigations, making phone calls, and keeping her files up to date.

Grace had been a police officer long enough to have developed a cop's "sixth sense." Passed off by some as an ongoing state of paranoia, most veterans avowed that they could "feel" when something was amiss. The phenomenon sometimes took place when interviewing suspects, but not always. Don Halberton had told Grace that he could sense when there was someone in a house when he walked up to the front door. Others swore they got bad feelings right before some disaster or other, which was inherent in police work, took place.

Grace was getting that oogey feeling as she was walking from her parked car to the station house on Sudbury Street. It was a calm, cool morning, and she couldn't hear anything unusual. Just the normal street sounds of a city waking up. She turned quickly around, looking behind her, but there was nobody there. "Get a grip on yourself, Grace," she muttered.

She thought, Okay, maybe some of it is paranoia. But she

quickened her pace just the same, and found herself seeking the reassuring touch of the handle of her Glock 9 mm pistol, which was holstered on her hip.

After a few more steps, the feeling was overwhelming, to the point where she actually pulled out her gun. She swirled around again, this time aiming her weapon behind her, but there was still nobody there. Grace's first thought was that she was glad there was no one else to witness this spectacle. She started reholstering her gun and turned back toward the building when she felt a crushing pressure on her hand.

"I'll just take care of that," said a woman's voice, and Grace lost the feeling of her gun.

Her breath caught in her chest as she looked into the eyes of a she-monster, a combination of a stunningly beautiful face and the eyes of a demon. And suddenly the teeth. The creature grabbed her other shoulder, immobilizing her. Grace mounted a scream, but it stayed in her airway as she helplessly watched the woman come closer. The last thing she remembered was feeling a tearing sensation in her throat as her whole world turned to darkness.

***

Vicky Temerlin knew that waiting was just part of her reality now. She existed in a world of darkness, and her only stimulus was when she came in to "feed." In a strange way, Vicky had begun to feel an affinity toward her captor. She had a distant memory of a phenomena called The Stockholm Syndrome, where kidnap victims start identifying with their abductor. She had never paid much attention, but now she understood it a little better.

She had somehow communicated with Vicky while she was, to put it in her terms, "feeding." Vicky had come to recognize why she was there. Seems her name was Lyria. Vicky had a basic understanding of how Lyria came to be, although many of the details were not shared. And it was apparent that the basis for

Vicky's capture was erroneous. Lyria had seen Vicky kissing Conner David on the cheek and misunderstood. Vicky couldn't honestly convey that she had never felt any attraction toward Conner. He kind of stood out among her other coworkers. Between the ultra-nerdy twins, Razor Rojas's dark-strong-silent persona, and the overt lecherousness of Boof Parsons, about the only chance for a normal adult conversation rested on the shoulders of Conner David.

But Vicky truly never had any romantic intentions that evening after work. Conner had just shared a potentially embarrassing episode with her, ironically about Lyria ditching him at The Hill. And Vicky was just showing the affection of a friend and coworker. Lyria understood that now, but she couldn't let Vicky go. Not as yet, anyway.

Vicky came to grasp how Lyria tended to satisfy her nutritional requirements. She normally focused on "evil-doers," as she put it. Those animals walking the earth that humanity would truly be better off without. Murderers and rapists were her usual targets, and this had something to do with the way she was "created." But if Lyria went for any material length of time without feeding, her skin would turn unnaturally cold. This would present a problem, especially now that she was "involved" with Conner. So Lyria made it a practice to keep a steady supply nearby — a human blood bank, if you will. Someone she could feed on just enough for her to present herself as normal, without doing any long-term harm. And right now, that someone was none other than herself. Ms. Vicky Temerlin.

Once the confusion over Vicky's intentions toward Conner David was cleared up, Lyria promised her that her life would return to normal at some point. And now, the wait was on. Waiting for Lyria to find a suitable substitute. Vicky felt a little guilty wishing this existence on someone else, but to her way of thinking, she had paid her dues. And she so wanted her life back.

More than anything, she wanted her life back.

Vicky had no concept of time of day. Lyria would just periodically appear, bring Vicky sustenance, and feed herself. Vicky wouldn't agree that she had "gotten used" to the whole process, but it didn't freak her out like it did at first. During Lyria's feeding, there was a strange mental connection between the two, and Vicky understood more about Lyria every time.

She dozed off for an indeterminate period, and she woke up startled, knowing Lyria was there.

"Good news for you, pretty miss." It was one of the few times that Lyria had actually spoken out loud. "Your big day is here."

Vicky started to speak, but her vocal cords were dysfunctional from lack of activity.

"How's that again?" asked Lyria, and Vicky thought she detected a smile in her voice.

"Did...did you find someone else?"

"Just close your eyes for a moment. When you wake up, you'll be back home, and you won't remember any of this."

Vicky did as she was told—she had come to learn it was futile to resist. She felt the familiar pain and pleasure, and saw Lyria bringing her out of the room. She was barely conscious of being back in her apartment, and it was a happy place again. She heard Lyria's voice off in the distance.

"Looks like you might need just a touch of special replenishment," said Lyria. She closed in on her again. This feeling was different, as if a surge of warmth was spreading throughout her body. Then she felt Lyria rubbing wet fingers on her neck. "There, those punctures are closing up nicely. Now sleep, pretty miss. When you wake up, you'll feel better than you ever have."

With that, Lyria leaned down, kissed her forehead, and Vicky's world went dark.

Chapter Twenty Two

To say that my mind was preoccupied that Monday morning in the office would be like saying that Boof Parsons thought about sex every once in a while—a vast understatement. Lyria had, at least for the time being, occupied a significant, and seemingly fixed, portion of my consciousness, basically since the day I encountered her out on the street.

So what's the big deal? I wondered silently to myself. I had met the woman of my dreams and she was into me. And she was several levels higher on the looks scale than I ever realistically could have hoped for. Okay, so there was a downside as well. She was a vampire. And I didn't even believe in vampires. Well, I hadn't before I met Lyria, anyway. Her story made me believe that it could actually be true. But I admit, there was a part of me that was wondering once more whether I was just going to wake up at some point and discover that the whole thing was a dream. That she was a dream.

Now I had a police interrogation that evening staring me in the face. I had come to fear this Grace Garvey way more than my girlfriend the vampire. Despite everything that had happened, my feelings for Lyria were strong, and getting stronger every day. She hadn't asked for what happened to her. I just couldn't face the possibility that something I said would expose her to trouble. But being deceptive with a sharp cookie like Detective Garvey was for street-wise, experienced criminals, not for a skinny nerd financial analyst. Before a couple of weeks prior, the biggest danger I faced was cutting my toenails too short. Now I was going to be grilled about my potential role in the disappearance of an important local businessman. I actually took to slapping myself in the face to see if I would come to and set everything back to normal, but it didn't do any good.

Before I knew it, the still all-boy gang was sitting downstairs for lunch. I wasn't in much of a mood for conversation, and was secretly hoping we could get through our break and the rest of the day without incident.

Razor, Boof, and I arrived first, and were joined shortly thereafter by the twins. They came over to the table muttering to each other, and giggling like a couple of schoolboys who had just looked up a girl's skirt. They continued their little private bantering after they sat down, which was fine by me as long as I didn't have to engage.

"You two seem like you're having fun," said Razor. "Want to let us all in on it?"

I hit Razor with a look that could kill, but he just adopted a slightly bemused smile.

"Well," replied Chauncy Stillwell, trying unsuccessfully to stifle his giggles. "You know Perkins from underwriting? He paid Larry and I a little visit. Seems he wasn't satisfied with our analysis of the Restyle Inc. takeover that we finished last week. Right, Larry?"

"Right," Berman teeheeheed his response.

"The funny part of it was, we nailed it right on the head." Chauncy had to stop his narrative periodically to address a giggling fit. "We had the static determination of financial ratios, cost-volume profit, asset turnover, you name it."

Berman broke in. "Tell them, Chauncy. Tell them what Perkins asked about." The two put their heads together, bent over at the waist in a fit of chortling. I looked at the other guys.

Razor seemed to be enjoying the whole scene, but Boof had his elbows on the table and was holding his head in his hands.

Chauncy said, "Perkins said he thought our population mean and variance were off. Hee hee hee. But he was describing a normal distribution of the data instead of the log-normal distribution." The twins were looking at each other, laughing hysterically. "I told him that we had covered both the deterministic and stochastic equations, and the ratios all tied out. Hee hee hee. Then I was like, any questions?"

"Hey, I have a question," said Boof. "Did your mother have any kids that lived?"

The twins stopped their laughter in unison and straightened up. They looked like a pair of meerkats after a juicy-looking bug just ran by.

"What...what do you mean by that?" asked Stillwell.

"It means we don't have to wonder how you've managed to stay single all these years, Stillwell. But Berman, how'd you actually get a human female to agree to marry you? What are you, holding one of her family members hostage or something?"

"I..I don't think that's entirely called for, Boof," said Berman.

"Oh yeah? Tell me, is that how you get your old lady all hot and ready for action at night? Talk her up with a little regression model banter right before you hit the sheets?"

The twins were completely befuddled on how to respond. I was trying to spare their feelings by not laughing out loud. And Razor's bemused expression hadn't changed.

"Hey guys."

The female voice made us all turn in unison. Now we were a pack of meerkats. And we were all shocked to see Vicky Temerlin standing with a lunch tray and a big smile.

"Sounds like I'm missing a good conversation. Sorry I'm late today, but I'm also famished." Vicky plopped down and started eating while we stared in stunned silence. Vicky's face spread in a saucy-looking smile. "So, did I hear right? We're talking about using regression models?"

At that, we all started laughing. Even the twins. There was a hubbub of welcome backs and inquiries on how Vicky was feeling.

"Honestly," she said. "I've never felt better. I was really down and out for a while there, but now it feels like my batteries are completely recharged. I don't know how you guys survived without me for a whole week. So, bring me up to speed on what I missed."

Vicky's ebullient mood quickly spread to the rest of us, as a stream of chatter filled the air — some about business, some about personal subjects and weekend activities. I skipped the part about learning that my girlfriend was the type of person I thought only existed in the movies.

As we were meandering back to the office, Boof lagged behind to catch a private word with Vicky.

"Hey, Vicky, I just wanted to apologize for getting you upset a couple of weeks ago. And I promise, I'm gonna clean up my act around you from now on."

Vicky said, "Oh, don't worry about it. I clearly wasn't myself. Let's just forget the whole thing, okay, Edwin?"

Boof stopped short.

Vicky burst out laughing. "I'm just busting you, Boof. Ahah. You should see the look on your face."

***

Lunch was so much fun, it made me temporarily forget about the interview that evening and all the other issues I was dealing with. There was a general air of frivolity in our little cube farm. You could just sense a higher level of activity and interaction now that Vicky was back.

About mid-afternoon, my phone rang with an outside call. I couldn't really explain why, but a sudden surge of dread replaced my uplifted mood. Well, Conner, I said to myself, you can't not ever answer the phone again, right?

I considered that for another second, then I picked up and was relieved to hear Carly's voice on the other end. I asked how she was feeling.

"Okay, I guess. Mom and Dad insisted on dragging me to the doctor, even though I told them I was all right."

"How did Dad react when you got home?"

"Oh, he freaked, of course. Called in every favor he had with the local police departments to have them find Brent and arrest him for battery. I honestly don't think he was intending to have him prosecuted. He just wanted him brought in so he could go beat the shit out of him himself. But so far, no sign of him. Hopefully, the asshole got out of Dodge while the gettin' was good."

"Yeah," I said with a weak voice.

"How are you doing? And how is Lyria?"

"She's...she's good."

"You dog you," she said, sounding like my sister again. "It appears everyone, myself included, underestimated you. Scoring a babe like that? Amazing."

"Yeah, well, there's something to be said about having that nerd factor going for you. Some girls just find it...irresistible."

Carly laughed, and it sounded so good.

"Listen, I couldn't have made much of a worse impression on her. And I really don't want my brother's girlfriend thinking I'm a total loser, or that I have a thing for lunkheads who want to slap me around."

"She doesn't think anything of the kind. She's just glad you're all right."

"No, but I want a chance to make it up to her. Plus...."

"Oh boy. What?"

"Well...I told Mom and Dad about her, and now, of course,

they're dying to meet her."

"Oh geez." I knew what was coming next.

"And Caden too. Think of it as scientific curiosity. We all want to see for ourselves what has to go wrong in a beautiful woman's mind that she wants to hook up with our Poindexter brother. You know, was there a problem with her upbringing? Was she dropped on her head as a baby? Does her father wear pantyhose? That type of thing."

I laughed. "So, what are you planning? You gonna strap her to a chair under a hot spotlight for questioning by the panel? Play really loud music until she breaks?"

"No. I mean, we may do that at some point, but for now, we want to have her over for dinner. At Mom and Dad's. Maybe sometime soon? Maybe some night this week?"

"Ah, I don't know, Carly...."

"Conner, listen to me. Your chances of having a girl like this to show off to the family are likely to be few and far between."

"Your faith in me is inspiring."

"I know, huh? Anyway, I figure you'd better get this one in front of the group before she comes to her senses and the opportunity is lost."

"Oh, is that what you figure?"

"Yes. Now, I know you don't want me to explain how I'm always right again, do you?"

"No, I'll spare myself that little pleasure. But I don't know about dinner."

I had to figure a way of getting out of a meal situation other than asking my mother to arrange for a human sacrifice for my girlfriend.

"Why, what's wrong with dinner? It will be good for you to have something that isn't made by Swanson to be cooked in the microwave."

"Very funny. It's just that I haven't been seeing Lyria that long. And I...I like her, but submitting her to the scrutiny of a dinner at Mom and Dad's is not a real great way of showing it."

"Hmmm...."

"You know I'm right about that."

"I hate when that happens. Good thing it's such a rarity."

I snorted a laugh. "Tell you what I'll do. I'll ask Lyria if she would mind us stopping over Mom and Dad's to meet them. Some evening. Real brief. Just 'Hi. How you doing? Yes I'm real. Nice to meet you. Good night.' That type of thing. That way, everybody has their curiosity satisfied and I don't have to worry about my girlfriend leaving the country afterward. How does that sound?"

"Well, I guess that would be okay. What night do you want to come over?"

"Let me talk to Lyria and I'll let you know."

"You know I'm going to hound you until you make this happen, right?"

"I told you, I'll ask her about it."

"I know, but I also know you. You'll try to put this off until you figure everyone has forgotten about it. Listen to me, Conner. I'm. Not. Going. To. Forget. Got it?"

"I got it. I'll let you know."

"Okay. I'll call you tomorrow to see where you're at."

"Good deal. Carly?"

"Yeah?"

"It's good to have you back."

There was a brief pause. Then she said, "Thanks. For everything."

We said our goodbyes and hung up.

***

I got out of work around five that evening, and decided to walk right over to the Sudbury Street police station. My reasoning was that if I went home and stewed over this meeting, it would

275

probably be worse than getting it done as soon as possible.

I was literally shaking as I walked through the precinct doors. Talk about intimidating, especially because of the reason for my visit. It's not like I was going to donate a dozen donuts to the cause. I was going to be questioned in a criminal matter by a sharp-looking detective, who somehow managed to get me excited and terrified all at the same time.

Whoever designed the building had apparently flunked Feng Shui 101. The hallways were painted plain gray, were completely devoid of any decor or pictures, and had a faint smell of bleach. I walked up to the front desk, which was being manned by a gruff older cop in uniform who was staring me down something fierce. Even though I hadn't done anything, his glower made me feel guilty. I had a completely irrational urge to throw myself face-first onto the floor and beg for mercy.

"Can I help you?" he asked. His voice sounded gravelly, and I guessed that he was a long-time smoker.

"Uh, yes, um...I'm, uh, supposed to meet with Detective Grace Garvey."

Officer Gruff just let my statement hang in the air momentarily while his eyes continued boring holes in my psyche.

"Your name?"

I actually had to pause and think for a moment.

"David. Conner David."

"What's this in regards to, Mr. David?"

"Uh...well...."

My voice caught in my throat. How was I supposed to describe my circumstances? "Well, you see, this big oaf was picking on me in a bar and my girlfriend the vampire may have taken him out." That's what I thought, and I had to fight off a sudden impulse to start laughing hysterically.

But what I said was, "Uh, Detective Garvey called me and wanted to meet after I got out of work." I instantly cringed at how incredibly lame that sounded.

I was avoiding Officer Gruff's eyes, but I was pretty sure he was still staring. I stood there in silence for what seemed like an eternity. Officer Gruff cleared his throat, causing me to nearly jump out of my skin. "Just have a seat over there," he said finally. He indicated a row of plastic chairs along the wall.

The chairs were blue at one time, but had apparently been worn down by all the criminals who had used them over the years. There was a set of four, and they were all attached to each other and bolted to the floor. I sat on an end chair, and thought it was so uncomfortable the police could use it to break a suspect without even asking him a question.

Thankfully, there was only a modest level of activity in the lobby, although I noticed that every uniformed cop who walked by gave me the once over, probably wondering what I was going to be charged with. Officer Gruff was now ignoring me, and it occurred to me that he hadn't called back to let Grace know that I was there. But about the last thing I wanted to do was go ask him about it, so I just sat with my mouth shut.

After a while, my butt was starting to go numb from the hard plastic chair. I stood up to get some feeling back, but Officer Gruff honed the laser beams on me, so I quickly sat back down. I sat and sat and sat, my mind running through every potential outcome of my impending interview. The possibilities ranged from getting thrown in the slam to hooking up with Grace Garvey on the sly. I even considered how amazing it would be for Grace to be my daytime girlfriend while I continued seeing Lyria at night. My emotions ran the gamut while I waited. I wanted to laugh out loud — I wanted to cry like a baby.

"Mr. David?"

I jumped again. I looked up and Officer Gruff was waving me back to the desk. I propelled myself out of the chair and came close to a total face plant.

"Yes...yes...sir?"

"Detective Garvey isn't here. Not sure when she'll be back."

"Oh. So...what? Should I...where should I...should I wait? Do you want me to come back?" I thought, You are one smooth dude, Conner.

"Just go on home, Mr. David. I'm sure the detective will be in touch to reschedule your meeting. She has your phone number, right?"

"What? My phone number?"

"Yes. You know, the number someone would call if they wanted to talk to you?"

"Oh...yes...my phone number. Yes, she has it. She has my phone number. She can call it if she wants to talk to me. Yes."

I wondered if Officer Gruff knew why I was being questioned. The way I was acting, he probably thought I was being hauled in for somehow making a spectacle of myself in public. I imagined him asking me, "What did you do, Mr. David? Pee yourself in the company of others?"

"Okay, just be available for when the detective calls you back. I'll let her know you were here."

"Okay," I said, backing toward the door. "Thank you. Thank you, sir."

I swung around and nearly plowed down another cop who was innocently passing by. "Whoa, careful there, buddy," said my near victim.

"Oh, excuse me. I'm sorry...terribly sorry...."

I looked back at Officer Gruff and thought I detected the hint of a smile.

"Have a good evening, Mr. David," he said.

***

"Can I ask you a question?"

I was holding Lyria after our first bout of the night.

"Let me save you the trouble," she said. "Yes, you're getting

278

better. I knew it was just a matter of repetition."

"No. That's not what I was going to ask...but, good to know anyway."

"Right."

"And, let me add that if you're lying about that...I want to thank you from the bottom of my heart."

She laughed. "So what were you going to ask me?"

"If this is too sensitive a subject, you don't have to answer."

"Don't worry. I won't."

"Seriously, it's no big deal —"

"Out with it, Conner."

"Right. Well, I was just wondering. Where do you...sleep?"

"Most nights, right here."

"Come on, Lyria. Get serious. The last thing we do when you're over here is sleep."

"Fair point."

"No, I mean, during the day. Where do you go? Are you sure you're safe? What if somebody found you?"

She reached over and stroked my cheek. Her hand felt warm. "My sweet Conner," she said. "If I didn't know any better, I'd think you were worried about me."

I raised up on one elbow. "Of course I'm worried. I'm...."

"What?"

"Nothing. Never mind."

"No. Tell me what you were going to say."

"I was just about to give you yet another example of my lack of experience and, for that matter, maturity."

"Oh, this I have to hear."

"Well, again, I'm far from an expert, but I have very strong feelings for you."

"Why, Mr. David. Are you trying to say you love me?"

"Well, actually, I was trying in my best awkward, geeky way not to say it."

"But why? Why would you withhold such an important expression of your feelings?"

"Because I didn't know if it was too soon? Not soon enough? Remember, Lyria — awkward, geeky, inexperienced, lack of maturity working here."

She had a hearty laugh at that one. She said, "I don't think a feeling like that emerges on some kind of schedule. You either feel it or you don't."

"Right, but since this is my most intimate relationship since... ever, I just wasn't sure."

"Well, let me see if I can make it easier on you. Mr. Conner David, I love you."

I just stared at her in stunned silence. "You do?" I asked when I rediscovered my voice.

"Yes sir, I do. You're the sweetest, most caring man I've ever met. And I've met some doozies in my time, let me tell you."

I laughed. "Yeah, I bet." I laid back down and put my hands behind my head. "Son of a gun."

"What?" she asked.

"No, it's just that I never thought I'd get a girl like you to... love me. Or even like me, for that matter. Most girls who look like you, honestly, wouldn't give me the time of day."

"That's their loss and my gain."

"Yeah. I guess so." I was sporting a huge grin.

"Ah. Ahem."

"Huh?"

"Aren't you forgetting something?" she asked.

"Uhhh. Not that I know of...."

She looked at me like I was the hopeless case that I considered myself. "I just told you that I loved you. Mightn't there be something you want to say in return?"

"Oh, yeah." I raised back up on my elbow. "Uh, Lyria...."

"Yes Conner?"

"I...love you."

She smiled. "There. Was that so difficult?"

"I just always pictured the girl laughing hysterically when I said that."

"Well, I'm not laughing." She leaned up and kissed me deeply. I slumped back down to my pillow.

"Wait a minute," I said, rising back up.

"What's wrong?"

"You got me all sidetracked here. I was asking about your resting place. Was this whole business a way of getting out of answering my question?"

"Conner, I expressed my true feelings for you. My resting place is completely safe, I promise."

"Can I...see it?"

"I don't think so. Not yet, anyway."

"Why not?"

"I just don't think you're ready for it yet."

"Not ready for it? After what we just said to each other? After what I've been through the last couple of weeks?"

She reached down and squeezed. "It hasn't been all bad, has it?"

"Oh God. No, most of it has been amazing. But I finally meet the girl of my dreams and find out she's...."

"Go ahead. You can say it."

"A vampire. Do you call yourself that?"

"I don't call myself anything. But I realize that while most lore has its basis in reality, there are labels...names that get applied. Some of the legends are true, some are complete nonsense. That name is actually a product of the movies more than anything else. But I'm here. And I'm real. And I'm...really glad you're with me."

We were just staring at each other. I stroked her hair. "And I'm really glad you're here," I said. "I know we just met a short time ago, but right now, I can't honestly imagine my life without you."

"My sweet Conner."

After a pause and some serious goo-goo eyes, I said, "So what is it about your resting place that you don't think I can handle?"

"Oh boy. Are you still stuck on that?"

"No, I'm just wondering."

"Conner, I sleep in a coffin."

"You...a coffin? Really?"

"I know, talk about playing to stereotype, right? But the truth is, it keeps all the daylight out. And I never found another way to do that since that first night with Aurel. The place I keep it is safe. But I...don't necessarily want you seeing it. Not yet anyway. I would just ask that you respect my judgment on this. We'll get there...in time."

I looked into her eyes again. "Of course. I understand."

"Good." She cozied her remarkable body over close to my rather ordinary one. "Now, where were we before we got sidetracked?"

"Oh, just one more thing."

She gave me a look. "What?"

"I got you a present." I handed her a small box. When she opened it, she smiled.

CHAPTER TWENTY THREE

When I got to work the next day, I sensed a certain tension in the air. I couldn't put my finger on a reason, but it was as if a giant vacuum cleaner had sucked all the oxygen out of the building.

Boof meandered by my cube, his eyes looking upward toward the far wall the whole time.

"Hey dude," he said in a semi-whisper.

"Boof, what's going on? How come it feels...different in here today?"

"Don't you know?" I shook my head. "Shrek is back. He came in early looking like death warmed over, schlepped into his office, and closed the door. He hasn't even poked his head out since, but we're all just waiting for the explosion that's sure to come."

"Explosion? What for?"

"You know how this guy is. He'll probably accuse us all of screwing off while he was out. You know, taking extra time for lunch, leaving early, that sort of thing."

"You know what worries me about that?" I asked.

"What?"

"We actually did all those things."

"Well...yeah, that's true, but I'm pretty sure we got all our work done on time. Did you miss any deadlines?"

"No. Heck no, but it's like you said, Shrek doesn't have to be logical about delivering his beatings."

"Also true. Well, I'd better get back to my cubbyhole. No offense, buddy, but if I'm gonna get in trouble for kibitzing with someone, I'd want it to be Vicky."

"Uh, you agreed to start treating Vicky with respect. Remember?"

"Ahhh. That was when I feared for my life when Vicky went off on me. She was all out of sorts that day. Whatever I said doesn't count anymore."

"Oh, I see."

"And I'm not sure how much I'll be able to stop by to see you for a while either. Now that the boss is back, no offense, but you're somewhat radioactive, know what I mean?"

"Uh huh. The depth of your friendship is touching."

"Well, I'm assuming Shrek still has a hair across his ass for you. And I don't want any guilt by association."

"I don't blame you, Boof. See you at lunch? Or do you want me to sit a couple of tables over just in case?"

He thought about that for a minute. "No," he said finally. "Lunch should be okay. Shrek hardly ever comes downstairs. Besides, if I have to sit with just Razor and the twins, I'd seriously have to consider suicide."

With that, Boof ducked his head and went back to his cube. I had to resist the urge to yell out, "Hey, why are you ducking? You're too short to be seen over the cube walls anyway." Maybe the previous week, when the office was Shrek-free, but this week it was too risky.

So, my nemesis was back. It made me realize how relaxed the atmosphere had been while he was gone. Boof was right—I found myself anticipating Dobson's initial outburst, and it stood to reason that I would be the target. I had submitted some project results to the higher-ups in his absence, but I did leave a couple of reports for him too. So, he had ammunition if he wanted to catch up on some Conner-abuse and come tell me what pieces of shit they were.

But lunchtime came around without an outburst. We all gathered in the hallway and agreed to grab something and bring it back to our offices to show what good doobees we were, and to at least present the (false) possibility that this is how we ran while he was gone.

That afternoon, I felt like my run of luck had expired. Shrek sent an email to the group, asking us all to gather in his office at three. My immediate thought was, oh boy, not only is he going to tell me how useless I am, he's going to do it in front of all my coworkers.

The remaining time before the meeting absolutely crawled by. I did my best to keep busy, but it was difficult to concentrate. I also had a nagging thought in the back of my mind that I should be worried about something else. But it didn't crystalize until just before I had to head into Shrek's den of torture. Then I realized, I was also waiting to hear from Grace Garvey about when our interview was going to be rescheduled. When I pried myself out of my chair to head into Shrek's office, I felt like a condemned man walking into the gas chamber.

I was the first one there, and a little later I understood why. Shrek was sitting at his desk trying to work his way through a mountain of paperwork that had accumulated while he was out. He looked more pale and drawn than normal, and I theorized that whatever had been wrong with him must have been bad to cause such a hard case to actually miss work.

"Hello, Conner. Have a seat."

Conner?? I had to think, but I was pretty sure that was the first time he had ever called me by my first name. Usually, it was simply "David," but had also trended recently toward such endearing nicknames as "numbnuts," "dinkweed," or even "douchebag."

I was so surprised I just plopped down in a chair in front of his desk without responding. Out of the corner of my eye, I saw somebody peeking through the frosted glass in Shrek's office door, and swore I heard a voice saying, "Okay. We're ready."

The rest of the team shuffled in, and it became clear why they had waited for me to come in first. They all wanted to be sure they weren't situated anywhere near me. The twins, Boof, and Vicky sat at Shrek's conference table, while Razor pulled the other chair away from the front of Shrek's desk to about as far from me as possible without falling out the window on the other side of the room.

At first I was a little peeved about my friends, but I came to the realization that I probably would have done the same thing were the situation reversed.

Everybody was silent as we waited for Shrek to start the meeting. He dropped the paper he was reading and cleared his throat, causing me to jump a little in my seat.

"Uh, thank you all for making yourselves available on such short notice."

Wait. Did he actually just thank us? I realized that I had stopped breathing.

Shrek continued. "I wanted to apologize for missing time last week. And I wanted to express my appreciation for maintaining our deadlines while I was out. Upper management had nothing but good things to say about the work that was submitted."

I didn't dare risk a glance at my associates, but I could sense that not only wasn't anybody saying anything, nobody was even moving. We were all frozen in shock.

"Conner," said Shrek. I thought, Here it comes. He was just setting me up. I imagined him saying, "The rest of you were all great, but as for you, you little schmuck...."

But what he actually said was, "I reviewed your initial data pull on Corcoran LLC. Very interesting. And very thoroughly researched. I'll get to everybody's work in time. I have quite a bit to wade through, as you can see." At that point Shrek did another thing none of us had experienced before. He sported a little smile. "That's all. Back to business as usual. Thanks again."

We all walked out, looking like zombies seeking out their next meal. We got to the hallway outside our cubes and stood staring at each other.

"What...what do you make of that?" I asked. Berman and Stillwell looked at each other and shrugged. Even the normally stoic Razor Rojas looked slack jawed and ashen. Vicky was looking back and forth for an explanation.

"We must have passed through a time warp into an alternate universe," said Boof. "Either that, or some sort of pod creature has taken over Shrek's body."

Stillwell looked like he was considering that possibility. Then he said, "Or, maybe Mr. Dobson came to see things in a new light with this illness. It must have been pretty bad to keep him out for a week. Perhaps he just learned that you have to appreciate life and those around you more. That life is too short to act like an ogre all the time."

We were all thinking about that, and nobody said anything for a while. Then Razor, the quiet one, blurted out, "I like the pod story better."

***

"I want another chance at walking," I said to Lyria that evening. "You took me by surprise last time, but I think I'm ready for you now."

"I was wondering when you were going to ask for a rematch," she said. "Lead the way, Mr. David."

We headed out of the Beacon Hill area down toward Boston Common again. I hesitated to enter the wooded area in the dark, but I remembered her telling me that we were perfectly safe the last time we walked, and didn't want to come off as a complete wienie. Besides, knowing now what I didn't know

287

then, I understood why we were safe. I still hoped we wouldn't get robbed or mugged, but this time it was because I was fearing for the safety of the criminals.

Lyria was walking at a reasonable pace, which I really appreciated. I related the day's events and how Mr. Darren Dobson, aka Shrek, had turned in his ogre credentials, at least for a day. Lyria was, as usual, a great listener, taking in all the details with an occasional "uh huh" spliced in. As I told the story, a couple of revelations occurred to me. The first was that if Dobson retained his kinder, gentler approach to managing, we were going to have to assign him a new nickname. He was about as far from an ogre as one could get that afternoon. The other revelation was more of a question, and without thinking, I blurted it out to my girlfriend.

"Lyria?"

"Uh huh?"

"You didn't have anything to do with Shrek changing his ways...did you?"

"Oops, be careful. Look out for the pothole," she said.

"Thanks. So...did you?"

"Do you really want to talk about this now? While we're having such a nice walk?"

I stopped cold in my tracks. "You did. How did you...how did you...?"

We were in the middle of the Common. It was dark and the trees were swaying under a gentle evening breeze. Fortunately, there was nobody else on the winding walkway in case the conversation swerved into vampire territory, which it seemed to be doing at that very moment.

Lyria took both of my hands. "Conner, I know we have a unique relationship. I'm aware of that. But I want you to know that I'll always do my best to be honest with you. I know you must have a lot of questions in your mind, and I appreciate your not letting us get bogged down, even when you have doubts. We've definitely grown closer as a result. I promise, I'll tell you more as we progress. But right now, I still think there are some aspects of my life that you may not be ready for. Do you understand what I'm trying to say?"

Looking into her gorgeous face, with her body that close, it was difficult to get riled up. Her big brown eyes had an imploring look about them, like she really wanted me to understand.

"I do," I said. "I understand. And yes, I do have a lot of questions. And I'm willing to wait on most of them. But I really need to know about Dobson. About what happened with him."

We were close, still holding hands, looking deeply into each other's eyes.

"Please," I added.

She hesitated. "Okay," she said finally. "That's only fair."

She kept hold of one hand and led me over to a nearby bench, where we sat down. I had been a bit cool when we first headed out, but between the walk and the turn of the conversation, I wasn't feeling any temperature impact at all.

"I didn't like the fact that Mr. Dobson was singling you out for the harshest criticism. It wasn't fair. I thought he needed...an attitude adjustment."

"No argument there. But, what did you...how did you adjust his attitude?"

"I visited him. A couple of times. I've described how I can make a mental connection. How I see people's past and so forth."

"You mean...while you are...."

"Yes, Conner. While I'm...feeding, if you will. It weakens a person. Makes them more susceptible to suggestion. I made such a suggestion to Mr. Dobson. That he needed to stop mistreating people. You especially. Frankly, he needed it. He's an abuser from way back. I believe his wife will notice a difference as well."

I just sat quietly. My head was spinning with the implications

289

of her revelation. "Wow," was all I could muster at the time.

She moved closer. "Conner, what I did, I did for you. I couldn't stand the thought of you being hurt."

"I know, but...."

"But what? Please tell me what you're thinking."

"I...I honestly don't know what to think, Lyria. Part of me is appreciative, of course. But, in business, one of the realities you face is that you're always going to run across people you might not get along with. People I may not like, and who might not necessarily like me. Shrek was always one of those guys. For some reason, he took an immediate dislike to me."

"He resents the fact that your family's well off and that your father helped you get your job. And that your father was a higher up in the company."

I nodded. "Yeah, that's what I figured. But you can't give everybody I have a conflict with an attitude adjustment. It...alters their whole personality. Is something like this permanent?"

She shrugged her shoulders. "Sometimes."

I took her hands. "Please, promise me you won't do anything like that again. I have to work out these issues myself."

For the first time since I had known her, Lyria actually looked sad. "All right. I promise. And I'm sorry. Are you angry?"

I had to smile. This gorgeous creature was worried about me being mad. Who'd a thunk it?

I drew her close in an embrace. "I could never be angry with you. Not for very long, anyway. Something like this is like a...like a growing pain in our relationship. It's just a different kind of growing pain than anyone else would experience."

She laughed a little. And we stayed in a clench on the bench, holding each other, not saying anything.

"My sister wants to have us over to my mother's house," I said after a few moments.

She looked up at me. "Really?"

"Yes. She was originally talking about dinner, but I made some excuses and got it down to just a meet and greet. My mom and dad heard I was going out with a beautiful woman, and they had to see it for themselves."

She laughed. "When is this taking place?"

"They wanted to do it this weekend, but I didn't make any promises. I didn't even actually agree to go at all, in case, you... didn't want to."

"Conner. I would be happy to meet the rest of your family."

"So, it's okay to confirm? For, say, Friday night?"

"Absolutely."

"Okay," I said, smiling. "I think they were wondering if I'd ever bring a girl home to them."

"Meeting the parents is pretty serious," she said. "If I didn't know any better, I'd think we had something pretty genuine going on here." Her head snapped to attention. "Stand up, Conner."

"What?"

"Stand up. And stay close to me."

I did as I was told. "Wh...what's going on?"

A gang of rough-looking teenagers emerged from the darkness of the woods. I counted five of them at first, and it was pretty clear they weren't collecting for the Boy Scouts. They were dressed in ragtag clothes, but were wearing denim vests that had what I assumed was a gang insignia on the back. They quickly formed a circle around us. I felt my chest clench, but my first instinct was to get in front of Lyria. I looked at her and she looked calm. She moved beside me and put her hand around my waist.

"Yo, mama," said one of the gang. He couldn't have been much older than eighteen, but was wearing a do-rag that made him look older. And dangerous. "Damn, we hit the gold mine wit dis one, boys. Whatchy'all doin wit dis skinny little dude, mama? He ain't enough man fo you."

The circle was closing in. "Hold onto me," said Lyria. I put my arms around her. She crushed me to her like a vise grip. Then my vision was a blur and I couldn't breathe. I sensed movement, but it was like we were in a time warp, Lyria and me. Suddenly we were at the south side of the park. The Dunkin' Donuts was across the street. The gang of thugs was nowhere in sight.

"What just happened?" I asked.

Lyria's expression was like she just finished folding the laundry. She shrugged, "Oh, I move pretty fast when I have to. Comes with the territory. So, shall we finish our walk?"

***

Missing Persons Detective Parker Gebelein was starting to feel overwhelmed. He had a backlog of old cases, as evidenced by the stack of folders on his desk. He had exactly zero clues on his latest MPs, the two tweakers Dylan Cavey and Lucas Corsi. The only inkling on that front so far was what Grace had told him she had found out in the much higher profile disappearance of Arnold Shaw. Grace had told Parker that she had shown Dylan and Lucas's pictures to a lead in that case, one Conner David, according to his notes. She said David had a reaction, but she had also said the kid was an accounting nerd and the nervous type, so she didn't know how much weight to assign to his reaction. Just the same, Parker made note of it, especially because he didn't have anything else.

Then, he was hit with yet another MP. One Brent Worley, a construction worker in his early twenties. According to his family, he hadn't been seen since this past weekend. Parker had gone out to his parents' house and written up the fundamental information—personal characteristics, last known location, regular business, and personal associates, etc. He learned that Mr. Worley was known to tip a few after work, and his mother admitted that he was no stranger to bar scraps. She said her son did tend to get combative when he had had a few. That sounded similar to what Grace had found out about Mr. Arnold Shaw.

But those two likely travelled in different circles. He meant to talk to Grace about it, but he hadn't seen her all week. Parker figured she must be into some heavy pavement pounding for the Shaw case, since there was a ton of political pressure to get that one solved. Their boss, Don Halberton, had been at a counter-terrorism seminar in Florida all week, but he was due back today.

Just then Don walked in. Weird how that happens, Parker thought. Don was carrying a briefcase and had a stack of documents under his arm. He lifted his chin to acknowledge Parker, then headed to his office to unload his piles. Parker knew he would always be second fiddle as far as Don Halberton was concerned. Don had taken on the role of mentor with Grace Garvey. He'd rescued her from the barbarians in South Boston, and taken her under his wing here in missing persons. And Parker had to admit that Grace had a knack for this work. She had a glowing personality, and being honest with himself, he knew she had an advantage because she was an attractive woman. Whenever they brought a male suspect in for questioning, they let Grace do the honors. And Parker and Don would lay odds on how long it would take her to break the guy. Usually, whoever had the least amount of time would win.

But Parker Gebelein was well respected in the department as well. He had gained a reputation as a dogged worker, and while he would never win any personality awards, he would successfully crack his share of cases.

"Parker, how's it going?" asked Don Halberton.

"Ah, not so good. Total whiff so far on the two druggies. Plus, I got another case in today." He gave Don the lowdown on Brent Worley. Predictably, the boss didn't seem that interested.

"Any idea how Grace is doing on Arnold Shaw?"

"No. Honestly, I haven't seen her all week."

"Yeah, I expected her to call me with updates while I was away, but I didn't get any." Don looked concerned. "I'll give her a call in a bit."

"Yeah," said Parker. "Last I heard, she was set to talk to that kid, the financial analyst, or whatever. She had some suspicions about him. Or maybe it was his girlfriend."

"Right. What was the kid's name again?"

Parker checked his notes. "David. One Conner David."

"Right. Let me try her cell." Don called Grace, but didn't get an answer. "Huh, that's weird. Unless she's in the middle of shaking somebody down."

They both laughed a little, but there was tension in the air.

"Wait a minute," said Parker. "David. Last name David. Why is that sending off flares all of a sudden?"

Don Halberton didn't answer. He knew when it was best to let his detectives sift through the usually massive amounts of information in their brains.

Parker sat thinking, wracking his brain. He shuffled though his current notes, but didn't find anything right away.

"Well, let me know if you remember," said Don, walking back to his office. "And when Garvey gets in, send her in for a beating for not staying in touch."

"Will do, boss."

Parker knew there was something nagging at the back of his mind, and it annoyed him to no end when he couldn't figure out why. The name David was at the center of it, whatever it was.

He thumbed through his old files but found nothing. Then he thought, Well, just for giggles, let me look through my current folders.

Dylan Cavey. Nothing.

Lucas Corsi. Also nothing.

Was it even worth looking at his new folder? This Brent Worley? Heck, might as well.

He scanned through the pages of notes and suddenly stopped cold. He pulled the paper closer and reread it. He did everything but pinch himself to be sure he wasn't imagining things. Nope, it was real.

"Holy shit!" he yelled out.

CHAPTER TWENTY FOUR

The next day at work was what I would call blissful. It seemed that between Vicky's endlessly positive mood and Shrek's new outlook on life, everybody was in good spirits. We all put in a solid day on our current projects. I heard a lot of laughter — with Shrek in his office. That was unheard of before. People casually stopped by my cube and we chatted about business and personal matters. And I did the same with others.

That afternoon, I was waiting for the other shoe to drop. It seemed like whenever everything felt hunky dory in the recent past, something bad would happen to pour cold water all over my good mood. Then I thought, hey, don't be such a gloomy Gus. Maybe this is a real turnaround. Have an upbeat outlook. Perhaps this is the start of a positive trend for good old Conner David.

Indeed, the rest of the week was a joy as well. I worked in my new Shangri-La during the day, and saw my beautiful girlfriend at night. I noticed I didn't think of her as my beautiful girlfriend, the vampire. When we were together, there was fun, laughter, chiding each other, and, of course sex. Lots of sex. No bloodsucking. She didn't up and morph into a bat or anything. I figured that had to be part of the movie-based lore that was bullshit. No, she was just my beautiful girlfriend. And I loved her. I loved spending time with her.

Before I knew it, it was late Friday afternoon, everyone was finishing up at work, getting ready for the weekend, and life was good.

Then I remembered. Oh boy. We're supposed to go to Mom and Dad's tonight. If there was ever the potential for big time buzz-kill, that was it.

***

I was upstairs in my condo wondering what I should wear when Lyria walked in. It didn't even freak me out anymore that she just somehow appeared, even though my doors and windows were locked.

"Hello handsome," she said in her best seductive voice. "So, are you ready for the parental unveiling?"

"Is that me unveiling you to them, or me unveiling them to you?"

"Well, it's a little of both, I guess."

We came into each other's arms and kissed deeply.

"Speaking of unveiling," she said, and started lowering my zipper.

"Hey, come on," I said. "We're meeting my parents tonight, remember?"

"Oh, I think there's plenty of time. Besides, wouldn't it be better if we arrived in a good mood? Show them how being in a relationship brings out a glowing aura in our countenances?"

I sighed. "Guess I can't argue with that logic."

***

A while later, I called for Uber to drive us out to the house. We were sitting in the back seat holding hands, just like a real couple. Who'd a thunk it.

Lyria noticed I was being unusually quiet. "Whatcha thinking about there, sport?"

"Me? Oh nothing. Just that it's the first time I've introduced a woman I was serious with to my parents. My father is just to the left of Attila the Hun, and my mother is convinced I'd never have a committed relationship. And then there's—"

I had to be careful of what I said in earshot of the Uber driver. I wasn't sure he even spoke English, but if we started talking about vampirism and he took a quick detour to the nearest insane asylum, I'd know he understood more than he let on.

I continued, "Then there's Carly. And my brother Caden will be there with his wife and three-year old son. Yep, you're being paraded out in front of the entire clan. Maybe we should forget the whole thing and turn around."

"Don't be silly. Everything will go fine, you'll see." As usual, Lyria looked completely unaffected by the proceedings.

"When's the last time you worried about anything?" I asked her.

She had a hint of a smile. "Well, right now, I'm a little worried that you'll completely implode before we get to your parents' house." She moved over close to me. "Seriously, don't worry. In case you haven't noticed, I have the ability to make a good first impression."

My stomach was tied up in knots, but that did make me smile. "Yes. I have noticed. I'm sorry. I guess it's really my father. I always felt that no matter what I did, I wasn't measuring up to his expectations. And for some reason, when you have a parent like that, you can't help but go out of your way to please them."

"How could he not be pleased with having such a wonderful young man as a son?"

"Oh, trust me. He always finds a way. When I look back, I realize that everything I've done in my life, I've done for him. Do you know, I originally wanted to study oceanography in college? Of course, when I told him that, the look on his face was like I had told him that I'd discovered that I liked dressing up in women's clothing."

Lyria laughed a little.

"And that I was planning to join the circus and run off with the bearded lady."

She laughed again. "I'm sure it wasn't that bad."

"It was, I swear. From then on whenever anything about the ocean was mentioned in the news, or just in the course of general conversation, he would say something like, 'And what does a future oceanographer think about that, Conner?' When he said oceanographer, he looked like he was tasting liver and onions for the first time."

More laughter. "So, what made an oceanographer become a financial analyst?"

"Dear old Dad. He made a fortune in investment banking, and wanted me to follow in his footsteps. I had a better aptitude for numbers than Caden, so I was a natural. Except my father overlooked one little detail."

"What was that?"

"He failed to realize that his success came in an era that was largely unregulated. And he succeeded by being predatory. Going for blood in these business transactions. I...I just don't have that in me."

"In other words, you're too nice?"

"Yeah. I guess that's another way of putting it. You do have to be a bit of an asshole—a bastard, to get ahead in my field. I could see the trait in my dad, but from a distance, you know? I never dealt with him on a business level. But now, I see the people who have gotten ahead in my own company. And, let's just say, there ain't a choirboy among them."

Lyria squeezed my hand a little tighter. "Well, I think you turned out just fine. Maybe you should do something else. Go back to school for oceanography."

I hesitated. "I could, but it would mean a lifestyle change for me."

"What do you mean?"

"Well, Dad has made it clear, without coming out and saying

it, that my continuing to live in my posh townhouse on Beacon Hill is dependent upon me staying in investment banking. And succeeding in investment banking. In other words, if I'm still an analyst in five years, I could end up rooming with Boof Parsons in Winthrop."

"That doesn't sound so bad as long as you're doing something you love. Besides, the pressure would be off. You wouldn't need to fight off convulsions every time you visit your parents."

"Yeah. I have to admit, that would be nice. And different."

"Let's just give it some thought. Maybe there's a workable solution we can come up with."

I looked at her. "We?" She just smiled. I said, "You've got that twinkle in your eyes. I'm starting to recognize that twinkle."

"And tell me, Mr. David. Has anything bad ever happened after seeing that twinkle?"

We moved closer together. "Not so far," I said.

Just then, we pulled into my parents' driveway.

"Damned bad timing," I said.

***

The David "mansion" loomed large in the background. The façade would have intimidated an A-list celebrity—a mixture of stucco and brick siding, spires reaching up to the sky, a huge, perfectly manicured yard surrounding the walk. All that was missing was a moat and a drawbridge leading to the entrance.

My mother opened the door before we were halfway up the walk. I muttered under my breath, "Let's forget the whole thing," and made to reverse direction, but Lyria held fast to my hand and we proceeded toward the door.

As we approached, my mother's eyes grew in shock at seeing this stunning woman with her son. I think she envisioned me with someone who could win a "Janet Reno look-alike contest." Plain-looking, bespectacled. Wouldn't be out of place in a librarian convention. And yet, here I was bringing Lyria home to her.

300

And, of course, Lyria looked incredible, even by her standards. She was wearing a shorty, tight white dress that accentuated her body perfectly. Her long brown hair was flowing around her shoulders. Mom looked elegant as well. She was wearing a pearl colored pantsuit that probably cost more than the wardrobes of all the BHA financial analysts combined. Mom had hardly gained an ounce since high school, and had allowed a mere tint of gray into her updraft hairdo. She had probably spent the day in the salon. I was far from an expert in women, but it had been my experience that women always wanted to look good for men. But they wanted to look picture-perfect for other women.

Lyria let go of my hand and rushed forward, her hand extended toward my mother. I had a crazy vision of her lunging for Mom's throat, and ran up closely behind just in case. But instead, my girlfriend was the picture of grace, saying, "Mrs. David. I'm Lyria. What a pleasure it is to meet you."

They grasped hands briefly before coming together in an embrace.

"Please, call me Carol," said Mom. "And the pleasure is all mine. Hello, Conner." My mother greeted me but couldn't take her eyes off Lyria. It occurred to me that maybe I should feel offended at her shocked reaction to Lyria's looks.

"Hi, Mom. I'm over here," I said.

"Oh, yes, of course. Hello, dear." Mom peeled herself away from my girlfriend and gave me a brief peck on the cheek. I already understood that I was like a secondary accessory for this evening. This was all about Lyria.

"Please come in," said Mom. "Everyone is anxious to see you, Conner."

She said this looking at Lyria. I almost said, "Right, well, I'll just wait out front, while you all dissect my girlfriend with your eyes." But I muttered a "Yeah, sure" under my breath instead.

We made our way down the opulent hallway, which was

lined with expensive artwork, into the even-more opulent living room. The place was spic-and-span clean. The back wall had a gas-powered fireplace with a gigantic mirror above that made the room look twice its size. My siblings and I always knew that the living room was only for special occasions. There was no TV, just a pair of facing couches and chairs. It had the air of a luxury hotel reserved for state visits by royalty. I didn't exactly know why, but I felt a sense of embarrassment at my surroundings. Then I pinpointed the reason in my mind. If Lyria wasn't already convinced that I was just a spoiled little rich kid whose Daddy bought him a primo bit of real estate downtown, walking through this mansion ought to remove all remaining doubt. Then I figured there wasn't much I could do about the formative stages of her feelings for me, and I let it go.

My mother was holding Lyria's arm as they walked about ten paces ahead of me. She was either being the gracious host or keeping Lyria from coming to her senses and fleeing the scene. They were speaking in a low voice, and all I could hear was Lyria saying what a beautiful house it was. They stopped when they got to the entrance to the living room. I was far enough away that I didn't run into their backs, not that they would have noticed if I did.

"Everyone," said Mom. "This is Lyria." She sounded like she was introducing the queen to her plebes. Carly was the first to walk over. Mom didn't want to lose her status as the emcee. "I believe you've already met Carly," she said.

"Of course," said Lyria, flashing her megawatt smile. "Carly, how nice to see you again."

"You too," said my sister. Then she moved close and adopted a conspiratorial tone. "I'm so, so sorry about the whole scene at the restaurant. That was just...such a terrible night."

Lyria took her arm. "Don't be silly," she said. I half expected her to say something like, "And don't you worry about that knucklehead Brent. He won't be bothering you or anyone else anymore." But she gave Carly a brief embrace. "None of that was your fault," she said softly. "Conner and I are just glad you're okay."

Carly said, "Thank you. Oh, hey Conner." I smiled in response, and my sister knew me well enough to have known exactly what I was thinking. As in, "Get me out of here!"

Next, my older brother Caden paraded forth, holding his squirming three-year old in one arm and his wife Lisa's hand with the other. He started to introduce himself, but Mom the emcee broke in just in time.

"And this is Conner's brother Caden, his wife Lisa, and the little one is Jason. Our only grandchild...so far." Mom nudged Lyria's arm and started laughing. Caden, Carly, and Lisa laughed too. I wanted to crawl under the luxurious Persian rug. Lyria took the whole thing in stride and pretended to enjoy the repartee.

"Hello, Lyria," said Caden. I could see that his eyes were the size of grapefruits looking at my girlfriend. And, I'll be honest, it was the first time I felt a bit of pride in seeing how men reacted to her.

"Caden, how nice it is to meet you," said Lyria, shaking my brother's hand. "And you as well, Jason." Even little Jason, who was something of a malcontented child, seemed awed. My brother had drawn consternation in naming the child, but he said he wanted to break the cutesy run of Cs — Charles, Carol, Caden, Conner, Carly. Might as well add Ralph to the list. No, I know it doesn't start with a C, but the whole exercise made me want to ralph.

Jason had temporarily stopped his fussing and looked agape. "Hello, Lisa." Lyria continued making the rounds. "Your baby is beautiful."

"Thank you," said Lisa. "I've never actually seen him behave for so long before. You must have a magical effect on him." More laughter. More stifling wisecrack vampire remarks on my part.

Lisa was exceptionally attractive with a pretty face, long blonde hair, and an athletic figure. But she looked at Lyria with a kind of wariness that said she understood that as long as my girlfriend was around, she was firmly ensconced in the Miss Runner Up position.

Caden was looking at me, and I knew the kind of comment that was coming. "Whatcha say, bro?" he asked.

I just said, "Hey, Caden."

Then my brother leaned close to Lyria. "Blink twice if you're here against your will."

Oh, everyone got a good howl out of that one. I was nodding in the background. Pretty much what I expected.

I looked around the living room, and there was no sign of my father, which surprised me not even one tiny little iota. Dad would let the pedestrian meet-and-greet play itself out, then make his grand papal entrance, ensuring that he was the sole center of attention.

"Well, shall we all sit down?" asked Mom the emcee.

The troop meandered over to the sitting area and everyone parked their keisters, leaving room for Lyria and I at the end of the couch nearest the fireplace. Jason had gotten through his meeting-Lyria shock, and started wiggling away from Caden and making a beeline for a mountainous pile of toys off to the left of where we were sitting.

As we settled into our spots, I muttered to Lyria, "Am I worthy of sitting next to you, ma'am?" She just glanced at me, looking bemused.

"So Lyria," said my hostess mother. "Would you like a glass of wine?"

I stiffened and immediately thought of Bela Lugosi. "I do not drink...wine."

But Lyria was completely nonplussed. "Why that would be

lovely. Thank you."

My mother stood up. "Would you like red or white?"

Lyria said, "Oh, a red would be fine."

I muttered, "That figures," which earned me a subtle elbow to the ribs.

"So, we never got through our necessary small talk at the restaurant," said Carly. "How, um...how did you guys meet?"

The question was clearly aimed at Lyria. I think everyone just wanted to hear her speak.

"We met out walking one evening," she said. Jason let out a loud wail and Lisa went to tend to him, leaving just us siblings. "Then we had a chance encounter at a club and we just started talking. Your brother is quite the charmer when he wants to be."

Carly and Caden exchanged glances, but were somehow able to stifle what I was sure was a torrential flood of smartass retorts. "We thought the only way he'd get laid was if he crawled up a chicken's ass and waited," and so on.

"And we've been together ever since." Lyria took my hand, just like a real girlfriend. Amazing.

Mom came swirling around the bend holding out a glass of red wine. "Conner, if you want anything, you know where everything is," she said, cementing my second-class citizen status in this little get-together.

"Thank you, Mrs. David...er, Carol," said Lyria.

Big, big smile from the matron of the family. Lyria held the wine stem in her free hand, but, of course, didn't take a sip. Jason was screaming in the background.

"So, do you work in Boston?" asked Caden.

More uncomfortable squirming on my part. But Lyria didn't miss a beat. "I'm living off my investments. Although growth has been a little tough of late. I'm hoping Conner can help with that," she said with her best megawatt smile.

"Geez," said Caden. "I hope you have a backup plan."

Everyone, including Lyria, had a good chuckle at that.

"Either that or a good bankruptcy attorney."

More laughter.

"You know he really wanted to be an oceanographer, right?" asked Caden.

I was trying to remind myself why I agreed to do this.

Just then, we all heard a big "Harrrummmph" from the back of the room. The laughter stopped and everyone's head turned toward the source in perfect coordination, as if we had rehearsed the move for a month.

My father stepped forward into the room. He was truly an imposing figure, and I often wondered how much that had helped him in his career. It was easy to envision him getting his way through physical intimidation, in addition to an incisive mind and a burning desire to get his way.

Dad was tall—it was about the only attribute I seemed to have inherited. He had blocky, broad shoulders, and an athletic physique that had survived the addition of a few post-retirement pounds. Caden had acquired my father's build. I had either gotten my skinny, nerdy-glasses look from my mom, or else she had gotten too friendly with an undernourished, nearsighted mailman while Dad was out conquering the world.

His highness was wearing a smoking jacket over a casual shirt and tie, black slacks, and loafers. He looked like he was headed out to a soiree on Hugh Hefner's yacht after suffering through this nonsense about meeting his kid's girlfriend.

I didn't realize it, but we had all stood up. It was like the judge had entered the courtroom.

Mom said, "Oh, hello, dear. We were just getting to know Conner's new...friend. This is Lyria."

Lyria floated over, her hand extended. She seemed completely calm. "Mr. David, what a pleasure it is to meet you. I've heard so many good things about you."

Even my father, who had all the excitability of a block of granite, showed a reaction. The changes were restrained, but clearly visible to those of us who knew him so well. His eyes seemed to widen and his jaw dropped ever so slightly. And he actually smiled. I thought I could have counted the times I'd seen my father smile on one hand. And it was usually when he was relating how he had succeeded in laying a company to waste at a huge profit.

"The pleasure is all mine," he said. "And please, call me Charles."

I heard Caden gasp and Carly said, "Oh my God," under her breath. It was difficult to keep from laughing out loud.

Just then, Jason wailed and a block of Legos went whizzing by our heads.

"I'm so sorry," said Lisa, who ran over to get the toy.

My mother ignored the interruption. "Won't you come sit down, dear? Would you like a glass of wine?"

"Uh, no. No, thank you. I have some business to attend to in my office."

"Well, it was very nice to have finally met you, Charles," said Lyria, the picture of grace. I was pretty sure that none of the kids had ever heard anyone but mother call Dad by his first name.

"Very nice to meet you, too. Conner, may I have a brief word with you?"

I felt a spike of fear, but I said, "Oh, uh, sure Dad, sure."

Lyria took her place back on the couch as I made my way to the office. Caden called out, "Don't worry bro. We won't tell Lyria too many embarrassing stories about your childhood while you're gone." Everyone laughed again, and I promised myself to take some time to plot my revenge on my brother after we got through this ordeal.

***

Dad closed the door behind me and indicated that I should

sit in one of the chairs in front of his desk. His office had dark paneled walls and two huge bookshelves behind Dad's chair. There were no family pictures or any other evidence that he had tried to personalize the room in any way. Any sound instantly was eaten up, and I wondered whether it was just bad acoustics or whether Dad had somehow soundproofed the walls.

He took his place in his desk chair, his arms on the rests like a king taking his throne.

"So, how is business?" he asked, getting right to the point.

I had to stifle the urge to say something like, "Oh, I'm fine. Thank you for asking." But I played it straight and said, "Good. The team is very busy right now."

"Uh huh. And how are your prospects looking?"

"My prospects? You mean the deals I'm working on?"

"No. I mean your prospects for advancement."

"Advancement? Dad, I've been there for less than a year. Every analyst in my department has seniority over me. So, I guess to answer your question, my prospects don't look much better than the day I started."

"And what are you doing to rise above the crowd?"

This time I couldn't help myself. "Well, I'm taller than everyone else, so I pretty much rise above the crowd every time I walk into a room."

My father, never a connoisseur of sarcasm, or humor for that matter, just looked down at his hands and let my remark hang in the air. I waited him out.

Finally he broke the silence. "Your new...friend...is very attractive. I can't help but think of the time it must have taken to...court her. I'm just wondering if that wasn't time better spent going the extra mile at work. Personally, I never worried about someone having seniority over me. I always knew that the quality of my work would make me stand out. But to do so takes devotion. Do you feel like you're devoting yourself sufficiently to your work? That is the reason I helped get your position, you know. And your living arrangement."

I just sat staring at my old man, counting to ten before I replied. So that's what's put a bee in his bonnet. I couldn't possibly be devoting myself to the job if I spent the time scaring up a beautiful babe like Lyria.

"Dad...you know I appreciate your help. And the townhouse. I hope at some point I can repay you. And I promise, I'm giving the job everything I can. But I have to have time to live, don't I? I mean, didn't you spend some time courting Mom?"

My father didn't say anything, but was staring me down. I concentrated on returning his stare despite my heart beating at double its normal rate.

After what seemed like an eternity, he let out a deep breath. "How is Darren doing? I understand he's missed some work of late. That's very unlike him."

"Darren?"

"Yes. Darren Dobson. You do know your boss, don't you?"

"Yes, Dad. I know my boss. Do you know him? And how did you know he'd missed work?"

"Oh, I keep my ear to the ground."

I had forgotten that Dad was buddy-buddy with most of the senior management at BHA. And that that was how I got my job.

Dad continued, "And as for Mr. Dobson, he used to work for me."

"He...he did?"

"Yes indeed. I dare say he owes much of his success to my influence."

This was a shock, but it made so much sense. Everyone knew that even though Shrek was a nose-to-the-grindstone kind of guy, he was something of a dimwit when it came to finance. Apparently, my father had even more sway in the business than I had thought. But if he owed my father, then the reason he was always busting my eggys had to be more than resentment for Dad getting me my job.

"You seem surprised," he said.

"Well, yeah, I am. I...I don't know why he missed work, but Dad...let me ask you something."

"Go ahead."

"Mr. Dobson has always been pretty hard on me. And it's not my imagination, everyone in the office has noticed it. Did...you have anything to do with that?"

My father just sat silently, as if thinking of an appropriate way to answer. His hesitation told me everything I needed to know already.

"I can't believe this," I said.

"Conner, the investment banking business is very competitive. You might even call it cutthroat. Most people who aspire to success in this industry would kill to get a position like yours in a company like BHA. I wanted to be sure you understood that despite having an advantage in getting your job, you would have to be tough and go the extra mile to get ahead. Yes, I asked Darren to be especially demanding with you. But I honestly felt you would benefit in the long run. Plus, I wanted to be sure...."

"What?"

"I wanted to be sure your heart was in this job."

"My heart?"

"Yes. I know I pushed you to choose investment banking. That it wasn't your first choice."

I thought about Caden's quip about oceanography.

"But I thought you had a better propensity than your brother. If Darren challenged you and you bailed out, well then okay, the business was not for you. But if you persevered, you would be ready to take the next step, and you would be better prepared for more responsibility in a very tough business."

"So, what? Am I supposed to...thank you?"

310

"No, I just wanted you to understand my motives. I'm telling you this now because you've had a taste of the business. And despite what you might think of Darren Dobson, he speaks rather highly of you. He says your work shows promise. But there will be a lot of hard work ahead. And I just hope you're not too distracted...."

Back to Lyria again.

"Don't worry, Dad. If anything, I've been able to focus better since I've been seeing Lyria." Okay, that was a bit of a stretch, but all to keep my father appeased.

Dad was looking at me deeply, as if he could sense this. But thankfully, he didn't push the issue any farther. He stood up, which let me know that my audience was over.

"I'll let you get back to your company," he said.

I didn't argue. I had a lot to digest from this conversation. As I walked out of the soundproofing, something seemed different, and I immediately realized that I didn't hear Jason wailing away. When I walked into the sitting room, Mom, Carly, Caden, and Lisa were talking quietly among themselves. Lyria's spot on the couch was empty. I stopped short and gasped. "Where's Lyria?"

Mom smiled. "Oh, she volunteered to take Jason into the playroom. She must have that magic touch. We haven't heard a peep out of him since."

***

I tried to look casual even though I thought I might upchuck on the spot. I was able to spit out something stupid like, "Oh, heh heh. Isn't that nice...?" as I walked quickly toward the playroom.

My mother shouted out behind me, "Being good with children is such an important trait. Don't you agree, Conner?"

I said, "Sure, Mom. Sure." Gag me.

I truly didn't know what to expect as I threw the door to the playroom open. And I honestly didn't know why Lyria being alone with my nephew had jolted me so. Did I really think she would...?

My fears were allayed as I stood in the doorway. Jason was laughing a hearty child's laugh. Lyria was sitting in a chair tossing something up. Whatever it was twirled some, and Jason moved on typically unsteady feet underneath to try and catch it. He missed and the thing bounced off the carpet. My nephew laughed some more, retrieved the object, and brought it back to Lyria for another round.

Lyria looked up at me, hesitated for a moment, then said, "Oh, hello Conner. We were just playing catch."

"Catch?"

"Well, to be honest, we haven't actually caught any, but we're having fun anyway."

"Again Loora. Again," cried Jason, waiting expectantly in front of her.

"Okay. Ready? Here you go."

Flip. Miss. Laugh. Repeat.

I took a few steps forward into the room, but I still couldn't make out what they were playing with. It was shaped like a finger, which made for great twirling motion while it was up in the air.

Lacking anything brilliant to say and having my heartbeat just now drop back to normal, I stammered, "That's nice. I bet my mother and sister-in-law appreciate your taking some time with him. What is that, anyway?"

Lyria flipped it up again and Jason retrieved. I came up close, and much to my dismay, I realized that not only did the thing look like a finger, IT WAS A FINGER!

"Is that? Lyria, good God. Is that...real?"

Lyria looked at me, but I couldn't read her expression. She didn't say anything at first, then she flipped it up again. "I've played this game with a lot of kids. It never fails to amuse."

"But whose...where did you...?"

"It's my finger, Conner."

"Yours? You mean you—"

She held up her right hand, and sure enough, no index finger.

I felt woozy, so I sat on the floor right where I'd been standing. "Oh good Lord," I muttered.

"You play, Uncle Conna," said Jason.

"Uh, no thanks, buddy. Hey, how about you show me a couple of your new cars out in the other room?"

"Okay. Can we do one more, Loora?"

Lyria looked at me.

"Sure. Why not?" I held my chin up on my hand as Lyria and Jason played another round of finger-catch.

"Okay," said Lyria. "Come give us a hug." Jason lurched into her arms. "Thank you, honey. Now, why don't you go show Uncle Conner those cars?"

"Okay, Loora. Come on, Uncle Conna."

I held Jason's hand as we made our way back to the living room. I glanced back at Lyria, but she was looking down, not meeting my eyes.

Jason and I sat on the living room floor near his pile of toys, and he picked out his new cars from among the mass. Lyria came out of the playroom a few seconds later and walked back toward the couch. I couldn't help but glance at her hand on the way by. All five fingers were in place. I felt a little woozy again.

After a few minutes, Lisa came over and rescued me. "Thank you guys so much," she said. "I don't get a break very often." Then she gave Caden a smarmy look that told me that in addition to thanking Lyria and me, she was taking a dig at her husband.

I sat back down next to Lyria. We chit chatted with the family a little more, but it seemed like my girlfriend was a bit more subdued.

"You about ready to get going?" I asked her.

She glanced at me. "Sure."

"Okay, I'll see if I can get an Uber." I took my phone out of my pocket.

"Not necessary," said Mom. "I have a driver standing by."

"A driver? You mean Dad's limo?"

"Of course. You think after meeting such a beautiful young lady, I'm going to let you drive off with one of those criminals that drive those Uber-cars?"

I had to laugh.

***

We made our way to the front door and said our goodbyes—sans Dad, of course. There were kisses and hugs everywhere, along with open invitations to return anytime. I couldn't remember seeing Mom look so pleased.

The limo pulled up and we got in the back seat. There was a huge partition that looked like it might even be bulletproof separating the driver and us. "Pretty different from the drive down, huh? A little more privacy?" I said.

"Yes," said Lyria. She was as subdued as I've ever seen her. The partition was closed and the driver took off.

"Lyria...I'm sorry."

"Sorry for what?"

"My reaction. When I realized you were...playing with your finger. It...came as a bit of a shock, that's all."

"Conner, I'm afraid I've made a mistake," she said.

"A mistake? Hey, don't worry about it. Nobody saw the whole finger thing. And Jason probably forgot about it ten seconds after we left the room."

"No, I'm not talking about my finger. I'm talking about... getting you involved in all this."

"Getting me involved? In all what? You mean...us?"

"Yes. Us. I know your reaction when you saw me playing with your nephew was a shock. But it says a lot just the same. You have a beautiful home and a lovely family. You don't deserve to

314

be...with me. You should find yourself a real girl. A normal girl. A girl you can have a future with. You deserve to be able to...be happy. To have a family of your own. To have all the things that I can't give to you."

"Lyria," I said and I reached for her hand, but she pulled it away, all fingers intact. I spoke softly. "Look, I'll admit this has been an adjustment for me. In a lot of ways. It has changed my basic understanding of reality. I mean, I never thought I could be with anyone who.... But I know what you did, you did for the right reasons. Brent...he was going to hurt my sister. Lyria, I never realized I could feel the way I feel when I'm with you. No, it hasn't been perfect, but what in this world is? I wouldn't give up what we've had together for anything."

"Do you remember those thugs coming up to us in the Common?"

"Remember? Yeah, I don't think I'll forget that anytime soon."

"Well, do you know what would have happened if you weren't there?"

"Uh, let's see...you would have booked out of there a lot faster without me slowing you down?"

"No, Conner. If you weren't there with me, I would have killed them all."

My eyeballs involuntarily doubled in size as that phrase reverberated in my ears.

"In fact—look at me, Conner." Lyria took my hands and brought her face in close to mine. When she opened her mouth, she had fangs. And her pupils were completely dilated, making her eyes look black. I think I stopped breathing. "The truth is, Conner—the truth is, I wanted to kill them all."

"My God, Lyria...."

"This is what you need to understand, Conner. Since I... changed, I've needed to feed. I've focused on evildoers. People the world would truly be better without. Those thugs, they were perfect. They live on the misery of others. Beatings, robbery, rape. What do you think would have happened to us if we were just a normal couple out for an evening stroll? Those men were scum. But are you prepared to be with me knowing that? Knowing that I live by feeding off of others?"

I sat without saying anything for what seemed like an eternity. "But you didn't kill them."

She just looked at me.

"All I'm saying is, maybe we can work together. Maybe we can...."

"If you think you can change my nature, you're naïve, Conner. I didn't ask for what happened to me, but it happened. And I will continue to feed. And kill."

More silence.

Then I said, "You don't kill everyone you feed off of."

Lyria hesitated. "No," she said.

"Then, how about this?" She looked at me as if she knew what I was about to say. "Just hear me out. When you need to feed, you can feed on me."

"Aghh."

"No, seriously, my blood cells would regenerate," I said. "We could try it. And still be together."

"You don't know what you're saying."

"I know that I love you. I know I do, because I've never felt this way before. Nothing even close."

Her look softened. She actually smiled. The fangs were gone. "My sweet Conner. You know my feelings for you. But I can't ask you to live this way."

"You're not asking. I'm volunteering."

She thought for a minute. "Will your father's driver take us anywhere we want?"

"What? Yes, of course. Why?"

"Do you remember you asked to see where I sleep?"

"Yes."

"Then let's go. I think you need to see it. And there's something else you need to know about me. And about us."

***

She had me give the driver an address in an industrial area south of downtown. She told me we would still have to walk some from where he dropped us off. She didn't want the driver knowing her exact location.

When we stopped, the driver ran around and opened Lyria's door. I got out on my own. He came around to me, looking at me like I was nuts.

"Sir, are you sure this is where you want to be dropped off?"

I couldn't blame him for asking. The street was dark and deserted, and we were surrounded by multi-story industrial buildings, most of which looked empty. Under different circumstances, I would have worried for our safety. But once again, I found myself worrying about anyone who might attack us instead.

"Yes...uh...thank you," I stammered. He hesitated to get back in the limo and drive off. I was sure it wouldn't do much for his career path if Dad found out he left us here and we ended up getting fished out of Boston Harbor. "We'll be fine. Really."

He looked anything but convinced, but lacking alternatives, he eventually did leave.

"We have to walk another couple of blocks," said Lyria.

I moved closer to her. "Are we speed walking? Like we did in the park?" It was a weak effort to lighten the mood a bit, but her expression didn't change.

"No," she said. "I think it will do you some good to see my neighborhood."

We walked a couple of blocks further south. If anything, the surroundings got more bleak. The streets were dark and deserted.

The wind was whistling between the buildings. It looked like a post A-bomb apocalyptic vision. As a fledgling businessperson, I couldn't help but think of all this valuable real estate sitting idle. But if you were looking to live someplace anonymously, this area certainly fit the bill.

We finally stopped in front of a four-story building that looked like it might have been a warehouse at some point, but now just looked like one of the many nondescript cement-gray structures that surrounded us.

"Home sweet home," said Lyria.

I thought she was kidding. "Here? You live here? There's... not even a doorway."

"It's around back. Come on."

She took my hand and led me down an alley to the back of the building. There was absolutely no light, and if I wasn't holding Lyria's hand, I would have been completely freaked out. As it was, I was only partially freaked out.

She pushed her way through a metal door that scraped the ground as it opened. The first level was empty, with a concrete floor and metal posts spread out at various points, hopefully holding up the rest of the structure. I tried to convince myself that I didn't hear things scurrying around as we walked in. Lyria slammed the door shut behind us, a noise I wasn't expecting, and that made me jump and, I'm ashamed to say, cry out a bit. I thought, Well, if that doesn't convince my girlfriend that I'm not right for her, probably nothing will. But she had the good grace to pretend she didn't notice.

"Come on," she said. "We have some stairs to climb. Judging from our walks, you can definitely use the exercise." At least she hadn't completely lost her desire to bust my chops.

We trudged up the stairs to the fourth floor, where we entered an empty hallway with one door. Lyria went to the door and entered a code on a keyboard I hadn't noticed before. She pushed the door open and we entered another hallway. She closed the door behind me. I didn't jump or cry out this time. Progress. This corridor was dimly lit with gray walls and what looked like the entrance to a vault at the end to our left, and a thick curtain on the adjacent wall. I assumed there was a window facing out to the front of the building. There was another entryway to our right. Whatever that room was, there was a light on, a rarity for this evening's travels. But our sights were set on the vault door, and Lyria took my hand as we walked toward it. As my eyes adjusted, I sensed something was amiss with this door. It was a thick steel vault door, the type usually seen holding the loot in a bank. I couldn't pinpoint what was off. Suddenly, something else put my senses on alert. I was hoping I was just creeped out by my surroundings, but I didn't think so. I looked at Lyria—she was completely calm, as usual. But I was frantically looking around, trying to understand what was making me so jumpy.

Then, I knew. There was movement coming from the other room, the one with the light on. And a startling realization came to me.

There was someone else there.

***

"Lyria, is there—?"

I stopped as an ancient-looking man shuffled out of the lit room.

"Good evening, miss..." he said.

He stopped in surprise as he saw me, and we both looked at each other like we were discovering a new species for the first time. I couldn't even estimate his age, somewhere between eighty and 110. He had a wrinkled face, a bald head, and glasses, and was wearing a heavy sweater, simple jeans, and work boots.

"Conner, this is Radu," said Lyria.

"Uh...hello," was all I could manage. Radu didn't say anything or offer his hand, just continued staring. I couldn't really read his

319

expression, but it definitely fell short of a warm, "Hey, nice to meet you."

"Radu, we'll be inside for a few minutes," said Lyria, apparently meaning the vault.

"Yes, miss," said Radu in a scratchy voice, and he turned and shuffled back to his room, but not before tossing me a deadly glance over his shoulder.

"Come on, Conner." Lyria took my hand and led me into the vault. As I passed the door, I realized what was off. The only lock mechanism and handle were on the inside of the door. The outside was just smooth plain steel.

The interior was pitch black. Lyria flicked on an overhead light bulb, then pulled the huge door closed. She pulled the handle up and punched some keys. "Now we're locked in from the inside," she said.

I looked around the plain box of a room. A single light bulb and a small vent in the ceiling. And a coffin. It was elaborately designed and looked solid and heavy, and sat on a stand about four feet off the floor. Lyria lifted the lid. The interior was dark red, with a cushioned velvety look.

"You wanted to see where I sleep. This is where I sleep."

I stood slack jawed, staring at the coffin.

"I didn't mean to shock you, Conner. I just thought you needed a bit of a...what's the expression these days?"

"A reality check."

"Ah, yes. A reality check."

I looked at her. Her expression was hard to read, but I thought it was sadness more than anything else.

"Lyria...who...what is Radu to you?"

"Really? That's your only question?"

"Far from it. It's just the main one right now."

"He's my caretaker."

"Your caretaker?"

"Yes. He takes care of my business needs. And, he guards the entrance during the day. While I'm sleeping."

I was feeling overwhelmed, and I slumped up against the coffin.

"Have you seen enough?"

Without waiting for an answer, Lyria punched another code into the door, lifted the handle, and swung it open effortlessly. I wondered to myself if I could even budge the massive gateway to her living space. She took my hand and led me out. She didn't say a word to Radu.

When we were back outside in front of the building, she stopped and held me close. "I'll take you home," she said.

"Lyria, wait. Okay, so it's not Ozzie and Harriet." She didn't understand my reference. "Uh, the ideal lifestyle. You sleep in a coffin. In a vault with a backward door in a deserted building. Got it. Okay, high on the weirdness factor. Believe it or not, I think I can deal with all that. But what I'm really wondering about is Radu. Is that really all he is? Your caretaker? Your guardian?"

She finally smiled a little. "Why, Mr. Conner David. Are you jealous?"

"Should I be?"

"Conner, Radu has been with me since shortly after I was... made. We're...the same age."

"That doesn't answer my question, Lyria."

Her smile evaporated. She looked at me closely. "I didn't mean for you to compete with Radu, Conner. I wanted you to replace him."

"Replace him??"

"Yes, Conner. If you want the truth. Do you know how you've been talking about the reason we were together? Why I was attracted to someone like you?"

I nodded, sensing that I wasn't going to like what followed.

"When I first saw you, you struck me as being...alone.

Someone with few strings attached. Soon, Radu will be gone. And I need somebody else. You...seemed like a good candidate."

I was stunned to silence. Then I was surprised to feel a new emotion building up. Anger. "A good candidate, huh? It's a nice way of saying that I looked like kind of a loser that no one would miss. Is that it? So, all that talk about love. That was all a crock? All part of the plan?"

"I meant every word I said, Conner. It is because my feelings for you are real that we can't continue on like this. I was wrong. You have a beautiful family and a lot of people who care about you. Without me, you will have a bright future. You deserve a chance to realize that future."

With that, she pulled me in close and the world became a blur again, like it had in the park. I sensed movement, but I felt like we were in a vacuum. No air available.

We stopped, I gasped for breath, and I realized we were out in front of my townhouse. When I got my wits about me again, I looked at Lyria. Her look was as sad as I had ever seen it. She came over and we embraced. She pulled me close and kissed me.

"Goodbye, Conner," she said.

"Lyria, WAIT!"

But it was too late. She was already gone.

Chapter Twenty Five

I woke up on Saturday morning feeling hung over, which was especially strange since I hadn't had anything to drink the night before. The string of events with Lyria and my family the previous evening seemed surreal. Not to mention seeing Lyria's abode. And meeting her boy toy.

But I wondered if that was all just water under the bridge. I wondered above all else whether I would ever see Lyria again. I was sitting in my kitchen sipping coffee and pondering the meaning of life when there was a violent banging on my door. I quickly shook back to an alert state, thinking, Oh God. What now?

I looked out, then cracked open the front door and an angry-looking man shoved a badge in my face.

"Conner David?" the man yelled.

"Y...yes?"

"I'm Detective Don Halberton of the Boston Police. This is Detective Parker Gebelein." He indicated another pissed-looking guy to his left.

I opened the door the rest of the way. "What...what can I do for...?"

Halberton shoved a bunch of paper into my hands. "We have a search warrant for your premises. Would you stand aside, please?"

"Wait a minute...what is this all about?"

Before I could get an answer, a bunch of uniformed cops shoved me out of the way and stormed into my townhouse.

"Is there someplace we can talk, Mr. David?" asked Halberton.

I was watching the group of cops start to systematically tear my place apart.

"MR. DAVID?"

"Uh...yeah, sure. Let's go in the kitchen." I didn't think this was exactly a social gathering, so the cushiony seats in the living room were out. Besides, from the looks of things, there wasn't going to be much of a living room left when these guys got through with it.

"Lead the way," said Halberton, apparently not wanting to let me out of his sight.

Halberton, Gebelein, and I sat in the kitchen with the sound of the search brigade rummaging in the background. The thought of my home getting destroyed made me mad, but in the back of my mind, I knew that whatever this was, it had something to do with Lyria.

Even though my insides felt like they were turning to jelly, I didn't want to show the intense fear that I was feeling, so I summoned up the courage for a bit of bravado.

"Would it be too much trouble to ask what this is all about? Why these men are tearing my house apart?" Hey, maybe dating a vampire had toughened me up some.

Halberton barked, "We'll ask the questions here, Mr. David."

I said, "Yes, sir."

So much for toughening up.

"You were scheduled to meet with Detective Grace Garvey on Monday, is that correct, Mr. David?"

"Yes. I went to the station, but Grace — er, Detective Garvey — didn't show."

"Mr. David, Detective Garvey is missing."

"Missing?"

"That's correct. Nobody has seen her since last weekend. You wouldn't know anything about that, would you, Mr. David?"

I remember telling myself, Don't throw up. It will make you look really guilty.

"Me?" I looked at the two men incredulously. This was nothing like my talk with Grace, with her casual, flirty questioning style. These guys meant business. Halberton looked like he wanted to skip the niceties and head right to the torture chamber. Gebelein hadn't said anything, but he was staring at me intently. This wasn't about some insurance executive who might have made a booze run to the Bahamas with his secretary. Now the missing person was one of their own.

"What makes you think I would know anything about it??"

Gebelein broke his silence. "We've been investigating a number of missing persons over the past few weeks. And they all have a common link back to you."

"B...back to me? How is that possible? I'm...I'm a financial analyst."

Halberton said, "Detective Garvey spoke to you about Arnold Shaw. He was last seen leaving The Hill with a female acquaintance of yours. We just got a missing person report on a Brent Worley. Low and behold, Detective Gebelein noticed that Mr. Worley had been dating one Carly David. That's your sister, isn't it?"

I sat staring into the two angry faces. I gave myself a lot of credit for not fainting outright onto the floor.

"Mr. David?"

"Uh, yes. Carly is my sister."

"Right. And then you were supposed to meet with Detective Garvey on Monday and nobody has seen her since."

He let the last statement hang in the air like a lead balloon.

"Then there were these two guys," said Gebelein, holding up pictures of the two druggie-robbers Spider and Vape.

I fought off the bile rising in my throat and said, "Look, Detective Garvey asked me about them. I don't know anything about those guys."

More cold hard stares.

"And Brent is an asshole. He made a scene in a restaurant and hit my sister. Then he ran off. We were at Grotto. You can ask over there. A lot of people saw him. He was probably afraid Carly was going to press charges."

"Who were you with when you met up with Arnold Shaw?" asked Halberton, holding up a picture of Godzilla Arnold.

I swallowed hard and said, "I told Grace this as well. I met a woman at the bar. The Hill. This guy...I guess this guy Shaw. He muscled in, shoved me away, and went off with her. Maybe they ran off together, who knows?"

"And who were you with the night of the disturbance at Grotto?"

"I...had a date. It was supposed to be a double date, but before my date got there, Brent was already smashed. He nearly started a brawl. He hit my sister. You should be out looking for him instead of harassing me."

"What was your date's name?"

I hesitated. I remembered telling Grace that I had been with a "Lyria" the night at The Hill with Arnold Shaw. They probably had that in their records somewhere.

"Look, I don't want to get her involved with the police. I barely knew her. She had nothing to do with Brent disappearing. The guy made a major scene, smacked my sister, and even caused some damage in the restaurant. He probably went to Mexico. Or Canada."

Halberton looked at me. "Her name, Mr. David?"

"Liz. Liz Jones."

Gebelein wrote that down, but I sensed that they knew I was making that name up.

"And what's Ms. Jones's phone number?" asked Gebelein.

"I don't have it."

Four eyes bored a hole in my psych.

"I asked for her number, but she didn't want to give it to me."

"You realize you can be charged with a felony if you withhold information, right, Mr. David?" asked Halberton in a monotone voice.

"I'm not withholding anything. Lots of girls don't want to give me their phone number. And you can't seriously think I had anything to do with Detective Garvey disappearing, do you? I'm a financial analyst."

It was the second time I had said that, as if that precluded me from being involved in a violent crime.

After staring me down for a while longer. Halberton got up. "Just sit tight. I'm going to check on their progress."

Gebelein continued to glower. I sat there silently. To say the atmosphere was awkward would have been a huge understatement.

"You dating anybody now, Mr. David?"

His voice made me jump.

It seemed like an innocent enough question, but my mind was swirling with the possibilities. They were bound to talk to my sister. And maybe even my mother. And Caden. Maybe even Lisa. They were going to find out about last night's meet and greet with Lyria. What if I told them and they found Grace's notes about Lyria at The Hill with Arnold Shaw. And they would ask Carly about the night at Grotto. She'd tell them I was with Lyria, not waiting on Liz Jones. Oh crap.

"Uh, nobody serious."

"How about any casual relationships?"

Halberton came back in. Just in time, I thought.

"Nothing so far," he said.

"I don't know what you expected to find." A handful of dead

bodies, perhaps?

The guys continued to press me for details for what seemed like an eternity. When it was over, I was really proud of myself on two fronts. One, I didn't disclose any information on Lyria, and two, I managed to keep from defecating during the interview.

Halberton looked dissatisfied, but he and Gebelein eventually nodded to each other, which I was sure was top secret police code for, "Let's drop this dweeb."

The men made their way to the front door. "We'll be in touch, Mr. David," said Halberton. I suppressed the urge to follow up with a wisecrack like, "Ooh, I can hardly wait." The crew all left without another word. The townhouse was in shambles, furniture overturned, drawers emptied. This search process definitely didn't have the Good Housekeeping seal of approval.

I wandered around, mindlessly cleaning up the mess and trying to keep from completely freaking out. But I knew that any success on that front was only temporary.

***

Detective Don Halberton sat in his car outside Conner David's residence. He had sent the rest of his team away. Halberton knew that they had only touched the surface in their questioning of David, but he didn't want to push too hard and make him lawyer-up. After not finding anything in the home, Halberton knew that they didn't have anywhere near enough evidence to charge Conner David with anything. But his cop's instinct had been raging inside of him ever since they had talked to the young financial analyst. Halberton couldn't pinpoint why, but he would bet his pension that the kid knew more than he was telling.

Don couldn't picture the kid himself being responsible for Grace and the other missing persons — he looked like he couldn't hurt a fly. But whatever this feeling was, it was somehow associated with this mystery woman. The one who had been with him the night of Arnold Shaw's disappearance. Was it the same woman who was supposed to show up at Grotto as David's date at the dinner with Brent Worley? It was clear David had made the name Liz Jones up on the spot. Who was this woman? Where was she when Grace went missing? Halberton's instinct told him it would be better to catch David in the act of meeting up with this girl. So, rather than pushing too hard in the interview, having to read him his Mirandas, and taking the chance of a lawyer entering the picture, Don was going to watch Mr. Conner David. If he was in cahoots with this woman, she was bound to show up eventually. Or Conner would go somewhere to meet her. And Don Halberton would be there when that moment occurred. Even if it meant a 24/7 surveillance. Grace was depending on him. And he wasn't going to let her down.

***

I found myself in my now-familiar position of lying face down on my couch with the two pillows over the sides of my head. Before, I had only been in pre-panic button mode. Now, I had danced up and down on the panic button and was actually picturing my future in a prison cell, being the girlfriend of some guy named Bruno.

Oh my God. Grace Garvey was missing. A police detective. And she went missing the day after I had told Lyria that I was going to be interviewed downtown.

There wasn't really any question in my mind that my woebegone girlfriend was responsible. Had she killed her? Like Brent? In order to protect me? She had told me she would do so to keep me safe. But this was a police woman. And it appeared I was their only suspect.

What was I going to do? Tell the police about Lyria? Somehow, I couldn't bring myself to do that. Every heinous act she had committed, she had done for me. She saved me from becoming yet another victim of drug violence by Spider and Vape. She kept King Kong Shaw from peeling me like an oversized banana. She probably kept Brent from hurting or killing my sister. She kept that gang of thugs in the park from making me their bitch. And now, she had apparently saved me from being questioned by the razor-sharp Grace Garvey.

I still had feelings for Lyria, but this was over my head. My story, the one I had told the detectives, was weak. It was going to fall apart fast, as soon as they did some more checking. So, whatever I decided to do, I had to do it fast. For now, I decided to wait. To see if Lyria showed up that night. But somehow, I didn't think she would, so I'd better start devising plan B. Now.

***

I spent the night awake on the couch. I jumped at every creak and each time the wind blew. But, much as I suspected, Lyria never showed.

I had run through a million options in my mind. They ranged from swallowing a bottle of pills to donning a fake mustache and wig and trying to leave the country. But the thought of being discovered and tackled at the airport with my faux hair flying everywhere, and the whole scene being immortalized on YouTube, was too depressing for words.

There was another option lingering in the back of my mind. At first, every time it found its way through to my consciousness, it was summarily rejected as ludicrous. But as morning dawned with my alternatives scant, I started actually considering it. I held a small slip of paper in my hands, and anyone looking on would have thought it was radioactive. Whenever I brought it up close for a look, I stuffed it back in my pocket in disgust, like, "What was I thinking?"

But before I knew it, late morning had arrived, along with a healthy dose of desperation. I looked at the shriveled piece of paper one last time.

A phone number.

Without thinking, I whipped out my cell and dialed the

number. The accented voice on the other end said, "Mr. David?" As if he had been expecting my call, and only my call, all along.

"You have me at a disadvantage," I said. "I don't even know your name."

A short sniffle-chuckle. "Yes. My name is Mikolaj Babka. When can we meet?"

CHAPTER TWENTY SIX

It seemed like I had barely hung up the phone and Mikolaj was at my front door. I thought, What, was this guy camping out in an alley nearby?

Even though I had seen him before, I had to keep from laughing out loud when I opened the door. Mikolaj really did look like a minion. He was short, round, and bald. He had a fringe of gray hair on each side of his head, glasses with telescope-thick lenses, and buck teeth that would have made Bugs Bunny proud. I suppose I had seen odder-looking creatures in my time, but I really couldn't remember any off the top of my head. With my tall, scarecrow-thin build, if we were to stand next to each other, we would have passed as a comedy team that generated laughs just by the contrast in our appearance.

"Uh, hello...Mr. Babka, is it?" I said.

"Please, Mr. David. Call me Mikolaj. Or Mik, for short. I know you Americans are fond of nicknames."

"Mik, sure, very good. Uh...come in. And please call me Conner."

"Thank you, Conner."

Mik started to take off his coat, and I wondered if the outerwear was contributing to the look of his stature. I took his coat and laid it over a table in the hallway. Nope, I thought. He was wearing a plain, short sleeve casual shirt that hung down over his pants, and he still looked like a Volkswagen Beetle.

"Why don't we go sit down?"

I led the way to the living room. Mik kind of shuffled when he walked, and I estimated that his legs must have been like six inches long. He sat at the end of my couch and I planted myself in the adjacent easy chair. We were taking measure of each other before anyone began to speak. I noticed what looked like some kind of markings on the back of Mik's left hand, but I couldn't make out any details.

"You sounded like you were expecting me to call," I said finally.

"Yes indeed, Conner. I trust you know more about Lyria than when you first...became involved with her?"

"Yes, I know quite a bit about her. I'm interested in how much you know."

He smiled. At least I thought it was a smile. With his buckteeth, it was hard to tell. Might have been gas.

"I know about Lyria, Conner," he said.

"You know what about Lyria?"

"I know she is, how do you Americans put it? A creature of the night."

I just stared at this strange little man. "And how did you come to know that?" I asked.

"I have been following her for some time. First in Europe. Then in the United States. I have looked to help people who come in contact with Lyria. I've found that, eventually, most come to realize that they need help. That they ultimately come across a situation they do not know how to handle."

He was looking at me expectantly. The little bugger had me pegged. He must have understood that I wouldn't have called him looking for a new BFF.

"Where are you from?" I asked.

"I am from Poland, Conner. But please. May I assume that you need some assistance, or guidance in your dealings with Lyria? If that is the case, the likelihood is strong that it is a matter of some urgency. Might you describe your current circumstances?"

It was his polite way of saying, "Hey, enough about me. Tell me your favorite vampire story."

"Okay."

I gave Mik a synopsis of my "current circumstances," as he said. I started out with a Cliff Notes version of how Lyria and I had met and what had happened since. He listened intently, and I realized that I didn't remember him blinking. Focus, Conner. Focus.

When I got to the part about her describing her origin, he actually moved forward on the couch. I kept talking, but I was also making what I hoped was a discreet effort to see what was on the back of his hand. When I got to the end of Lyria's story, Mik muttered an, "Ah." I couldn't tell if this meant that what I was saying agreed with his understanding, or if I had left out something important.

He didn't say anything, which I guess was my signal to proceed. I told him about the Boston Police getting involved. How Detective Grace Garvey had questioned me about the disappearance of Arnold Shaw and Spider and Vape. I was careful not to say anything that might have incriminated Lyria. After all, I didn't know who this little troll really was. For all I knew, he could have been wearing a wire loaned to him by the esteemed Mr. Don Halberton.

So, I kept it to the facts. I was supposed to meet with Detective Garvey at the police station, but lo and behold, Grace herself was now among the missing. I finished my monolog by describing my meet and greet with Halberton, Gebelein, and their storm troopers, and how they had committed savagery on my home furnishings.

Mik sat pondering my story. He was looking down, lost in thought, which afforded me my first clear view of his hand. The markings looked like a tattoo that had been inked a long time ago. I was seeing them upside down, but it looked like he had the initials SSTV just below his knuckles and, unless my eyes were deceiving me, a skull and crossbones in the middle of his hand.

He looked up suddenly, and I jerked my eyes away from his mitt.

"The chances are strong that Detective Garvey is alive," he said.

I was still a bit leery, so I just said, "I'm listening."

"Lyria often keeps a captive as a steady blood supply."

Speaking of blood supplies, mine had run cold from hearing such a frank statement.

Mik continued, "This is particularly true of people who are not evildoers, if you will." Now he was starting to resonate. Lyria herself had told me how she focused her feeding on evildoers. "As you may know, she is often able to connect with a person's mind while she...feeds." I nodded. "She is very powerful. She can even alter a person's thought process in some cases. Make them think differently. Forget they have been held captive, and so on. If she is able to do so, the person could be released at some point. But in an instance where the victim is too strong for their mind to be affected —"

"You mean, she keeps someone captive and...."

"Feeds on them, yes. My experience has been that Lyria is very selective about who she feeds on. And certainly whom she kills. However, in times when there is nobody sufficiently evil in spirit, she still needs blood. A live human is like an ongoing supply for her. It sounds to me like she saw an opportunity to eliminate your tormentor and find a blood supply all at the same time."

"Good God."

"Yes, indeed."

"What...what can we do?" I asked. "Is there any way we

could find Detective Garvey? Would we be able to free her?"

"Let me ask you this," said Mik. "As you became close with Lyria, were you able to find out where she sleeps?"

I hesitated. I felt like Lyria had shown me her lair in the utmost confidence that I wouldn't disclose it to anyone.

Mik noticed my hesitance. "Please, Conner. Mr. David. If we are to save this policewoman, time is of the essence. She may indeed just be a blood supply, but we do not know about her physical condition. She could well die in captivity. Then the situation would be even more dire. Your situation would be more dire."

He was right, of course. But I was still not ready to commit.

"What if she did tell me where she sleeps? What are your intentions?"

"I believe we will be able to scare Lyria off. If she realizes that we know where she is and that we could attend to her while she sleeps, we may be able to get her to move on. And release Detective Garvey in the process."

I thought about that for a minute. I said, "She...has a caretaker."

Mik nodded. "You mean Radu?"

Okay, at that point I knew this guy was for real. "Yes. Radu. Doesn't he...protect her?"

"Radu is a very old man, Conner. It will be relatively easy to immobilize him."

"Immobilize him. We're not talking about killing anyone, right?"

"Certainly not. There has been enough killing. But any such effort must be very carefully timed."

I thought some more. Again, my alternatives were pretty limited. "Okay," I said. "Tell me your plan."

***

After Mik left, I sat thinking for a long time. My feelings

were torn between betraying Lyria and wanting to be sure Grace Garvey was returned to the fold. If anything happened to her, it would, for all intents and purposes, be my fault. I couldn't bear the thought of her dying because of me. I had to trust that this guy, this Mikolaj Babka, was on the level. That his intention was just to scare Lyria off and free Detective Garvey. He had outlined his plan. It was dependent on me taking him to Lyria. I hadn't told him where she was. He wanted to put the plan in place on Monday night, after he had a chance to organize on his side. We would go to her abode just before dawn.

I couldn't stop thinking of Lyria. And Grace. My wig and disguise, get-out-of-town idea was looking better by the minute.

Sunday night rolled around, and I had no expectation of Lyria showing up. This time I was thankful. I was pretty sure I wouldn't be able to successfully keep this whole Mikolaj plot away from her. I wasn't very good at being deceitful, and I was a lousy liar. One time in college, I had tried to buy beer with a phony ID. I acted so nervous that the guy in the store ripped up the ID and threw me out.

Even though I had to go to work the next day, I knew I wouldn't be able to sleep. I started puttering around on my computer, reminding me of how I spent most of my nights before Lyria came into my life.

A thought came to me and, just for giggles, I brought up Google. I was thinking about Mik's faded tattoos. Something was sending up flares in the back of my mind, and I wondered if I could find anything about what they meant.

I started thinking back. What were the letters? SSTA?

All that came back was Salem State University in northern Massachusetts. Mikolaj didn't seem like the visiting professor type, so I must have gotten the letters wrong.

Oh yeah. They were SSTV. I was sure of it. Big time flares as it came to me.

When I typed those in, the top link was for Slow Scan Television. Mik, a cable technician? No, that didn't seem right either.

When I looked at the next link down my heart froze in my chest.

I clicked and read the entire article, my heartbeat elevating with practically every word. And my memory of where I had heard those initials before came roaring to the surface.

"Oh my God. What have I done?" I said out loud.

I sat stunned, thinking, thinking....

I ran back to the living room, picked up my phone, and began dialing despite my trembling fingers.

***

"Very interesting," said Don Halberton, sitting alone in his car. He had no idea who the little gremlin was who had visited Conner David. He would like to have followed him, but remained steadfast in staying on David. He was still hopeful the mystery woman would show up here and his problems would be solved. He was going to stay here until something like that happened. If it didn't, and David just went to work in the morning, Gebelein was going to relieve Don and sit on David's office. Halberton would catch some Zs and be back on the suspect the next night.

***

Monday mornings were always kind of depressing, but this one set a new standard. I had to pretend to focus on my job while it felt like my world was crashing down around me.

Before I knew it, I was with the analysis team sitting at the lunch table downstairs, Razor being a noticeable absence. Boof and the twins were having a discussion/argument over why Shrek's personality had changed so drastically.

"I think he just saw the error of his ways," said Stillwell, Berman nodding beside him. "Maybe his wife convinced him that he could get better results from his staff by being nice to

338

them, rather than treating them like slaves."

Boof thought about that for a few seconds. Then he said, "Nah. But I do think the wife had something to do with the change."

The males all sat looking at Boof, not really wanting to ask for details. Vicky showed renewed interest in her lunch plate.

"Could be she got tired of his antics and cut him off," said Boof without anyone asking. "Maybe he got a bad case of DSB and it changed his personality."

We were all looking at him quizzically. Except for Vicky, who was now face down, inches away from her plate, shoveling food in at an accelerated pace.

"DSB?" said Stillwell. "What's DSB?"

"Come on now, Stillwell. All guys know what DSB is. Especially you." Not getting any response, Boof went on. "You know...DSB...Deadly Sperm Backup."

The guys all just snorted a little. Vicky ate faster.

"Hey, you guys laugh, but if it goes on too long, it can cause brain damage. A little personality change is a pretty mild symptom when you come right down to it."

Now even the men were eating faster.

Not deterred, Boof continued to expand on his theory. "Yeah. It all follows. The wife gets tired of Shrek acting like Tarzan, King of the Jungle, and figures she holds the key. Women all come to that realization sooner or later. They say, 'Hey, behave like I want you to behave, or else the store is closed, get it?' Shrek probably thought he wasn't gonna be bullied, he could hold out as long as he wanted. Probably the DSB took over before he even knew what was happening."

It was hard to tell who looked more uncomfortable, Vicky or the twins.

"I mean, personally, I never let it get to that point," said Boof. "If it went on too long for me, it was like, fist city, you know? Heh heh."

"Okay," said Vicky suddenly, getting up with her tray. "That's enough sex education for me." She high tailed it out of there like the building was on fire.

"Good Lord, Boof," said Berman.

"What? Hey Vicky's been in a really good mood lately. I figured she understood, you know? Heck, she's probably even caused a few cases of DSB in her time."

While Boof and the twins continued to iron out their differences, Razor came to the table. He set down his tray, and when he was sure the others wouldn't notice, he looked at me and nodded.

***

That Monday night, I went to bed at the normal time and tried to get some sleep, but, not surprisingly, I was awake all night. At around 3 a.m., I started to get ready. I never remembered being so nervous and scared. I wasn't exactly the action hero type. About the most dangerous situation I had ever faced before was a panty raid in college. And, okay, to be perfectly honest, that never made it past the planning stage. When it came time to put our scheme into action, we all chickened out. We were afraid we'd get in trouble. Ah, if my academic compadres could see me now.

I thought I had everything I needed when there was a knock on my door. I peeked out and saw Mikolaj and some big guy. I let them in.

"This is Waclaw," said Mik. "He will assist us tonight." The big man just nodded silently.

Waclaw looked like he could bench press a Chevy. He had a mean looking, ruddered face and totally bald head. He was dressed all in black. I didn't ask what Mik saw Waclaw's role as being.

"The timing of our arrival is very important," said Mik. "We must get there right before dawn."

I had checked and dawn was supposed to be shortly before 7

a.m., so the team had some time to kill. "Well," I said, "go ahead and have a seat."

Mik and Waclaw sat in the living room. I eventually landed in the kitchen. I passed time by monkeying around on social media and sweating bullets.

We decided to leave a little early, as we were going to park a ways from our final destination and walk, all to avoid detection. The team piled into a non-descript black sedan, with Waclaw driving. I didn't ask any questions about whose car it was or where they had gotten it. In my brief acquaintance with the esteemed Mr. Waclaw, he hadn't so much as uttered a sound.

I gave directions to Waclaw, who followed them silently. I thought about my mother asking, "If so and so jumped off a bridge, would you do it too?" I was pretty sure Waclaw would have driven right into the drink if that's what I told him to do. We had a pretty good view of Boston Harbor, but rather than have an impromptu scuba lesson without equipment, we parked a couple of blocks away from Lyria's lair.

"We must wait a few minutes more," said Mikolaj. "We must arrive right before dawn."

"Check," I said.

I felt a little ridiculous sitting out there on the largely abandoned industrial street. Again, I thought about my mother. So, not only was I a tall skinny financial analyst who couldn't be much more ill-suited for this kind of activity, but when the going got tough, it appeared I might start crying out for my mom to make everything okay. Anyway, this time I thought about her drilling into my head, "Don't do anything if you'd be embarrassed about it showing up in the next day's newspaper." I wasn't sure exactly how I'd feel if it came out that I was stalking the streets of Boston in an effort to scare off my vampire girlfriend. Embarrassment probably wouldn't cover it.

After waiting for what seemed like an eternity, Mik checked

his watch and said it was time to go. My adrenaline spiked through the roof and my heartbeat became irregular. I calmed myself by realizing that having a coronary right here on the street actually wouldn't be the worst outcome I could think of for this foray.

The Three Musketeers made our way to Lyria's building with as much stealth as possible, which is to say, not much. We went through the gross alleyway and creaked open the back door. I started worrying about Radu, but there was no sign of him as we started up the stairs. I could still hear things scurrying around on the dark first floor. I was so tense that if anyone so much as tapped me on the shoulder, they would have ended up carting off what was left of me on a stretcher.

We got to the top floor and the door was closed. Mik put his hand on my arm, signaling me to let Waclaw take the lead. I thought that was a heck of a good idea until I saw the big man pull some sort of weapon out of his coat pocket.

"You said we weren't going to hurt him," I whispered to Mikolaj.

Mik winced, apparently upset that I had broken the silence.

"It is a Taser. Will immobilize him, not hurt him seriously."

"Are you sure? The guy must be close to a hundred years old."

"It is necessary, Conner." He nodded at Waclaw.

I looked at our bodyguard. He had turned slightly away from the door during our brief discussion, to the point where I was now looking at the business end of the Taser. It occurred to me that, now that I had shown these guys where Lyria lived, they didn't really need me anymore. There was little doubt in my mind that if I continued to object, Waclaw would have used the weapon on me.

So, rather than take an unscheduled trip to electric shock heaven, I put a lid on my concerns for Radu.

Waclaw put some sort of high-tech doohickey against the combination lock and the door popped open. I thought Lyria seriously should have consulted a security specialist before building her nest. The big man opened the door slowly, peering into the opening. He got it open enough for the three of us to squeeze through. The hallway was empty. The light in Radu's room was on, but there was no sign of the old man. We crept silently forward. We probably looked like we were in an outtake for a Three Stooges remake. We heard a noise and stopped in our tracks. Then we all understood what we were hearing. It was snoring.

With renewed confidence, we walked up to Radu's room. Sure enough, the old geezer was sawing the wood on what looked like a sleeper sofa, his head back on his pillow, the maw gaping open. Some bodyguard. Waclaw looked to Mik for guidance. The little man looked around.

He signaled a wrapping motion to Waclaw, then pointed to a doorway in the back of the room that might have been an entrance to the loo. Waclaw nodded and moved forward toward Radu. I had a feeling the poor guy's REM sleep might be short lived. He was probably dreaming about retiring to some island in the Caribbean.

Waclaw pocketed the Taser and whipped out a roll of duct tape. This guy was like Batman. He had all the accessories he needed—all that was missing was a cool-looking utility belt. Waclaw quickly taped Radu's mouth, and before the old guy knew what was happening, turned him roughly onto his stomach and taped his hands behind his back and his feet together. The process was so swift and efficient, it would have won a steer-roping gold medal at most rodeos. Radu's eyes were now as wide as saucers, but his protests were completely muffled. Waclaw tossed him over his shoulder like he was a sack of potatoes, carried him into the bathroom, and shut the door. Problem solved. I thought

Lyria should get a refund on the bodyguard portion of Radu's job description.

The three of us moved to the center of the hallway outside the open vault door.

"What now?" I asked.

Mikolaj gave me a pitiable look. "Now, we wait for Lyria to show." I noted that Waclaw stationed himself over by the window. The big man pulled the heavy shade away from the window and peeked out front. I also noticed he kept his hand on the shade as he looked back inside.

I stood there looking at Mik, who was avoiding my eyes. Ah, the magic was gone in our relationship. I could hear myself breathing and found I was counting my breaths. What can I say? Once a finance guy, always a finance guy.

The little minion waddled over closer to Waclaw and the window, and faced toward the hallway entrance.

Nobody heard either the outside door downstairs, which had a creak that could wake the dead, or the hallway door being opened. But we all stood transfixed as we watched a figure emerge from the shadows at the end of the corridor. I would say there was a change in the air, although that might have been my imagination. Or the vacuum effect of everybody sucking in their breath at the same time.

What wasn't my imagination was my erstwhile girlfriend appearing before us. Even though we knew it would happen, the three of us stared as if in shock. Lyria had come home.

***

She stopped about ten feet away. If our presence shocked or frightened her, you would never have known it. Her expression was one of someone attending a meeting of the local sewing circle. Or getting ready to wash a sink full of dirty dishes.

As always, her appearance was stunning. She was wearing a tan colored dress that brought out her coloring wonderfully. Oh,

I thought. Now I'm a fashion expert too?

"Hello, Lyria," I said. My heart was beating a mile a minute.

"Conner," she said with a sad smile. "You had such a nice upbringing. I thought your mother would have taught you to hang out with a better class of people."

I said, "Lyria, we just want to talk about Detective Garvey."

She shook her head and looked at Mik and Waclaw. "You really shouldn't have come here, Mikolaj. But I have to say, I'm impressed with how well you've used Conner. Then again, he's very book smart, but, is it fair to say, not very worldly?"

I looked at Mik. "What does she mean...used?"

The odd-looking little man ignored me. "Before we proceed," said Mik, "I wanted you to see who brought your reign to an end. I wanted to be sure you understood it was for the Reich. For the sacrificed members of the Deaths Head Battalions who may now rest easy that they have been avenged."

"Wait...what?" I asked.

Mik looked at me with what I interpreted as utter scorn. Although with his buck teeth and thick glasses, it was pretty hard to say for sure.

I said, "We were just going to see if Detective Garvey was still...alive. We were going to scare Lyria off by showing her that we know where she lives."

"Shut up, you fool," spouted Mikolaj. "And you!" He pointed at Lyria. "Come no farther or you will be bathed in sunlight."

Waclaw tightened his grip on the window shade.

Without thinking, I yelled, "No! You can't!"

I charged at Waclaw, a move the big man clearly wasn't expecting. I ripped his hand away from the shade, and before he came to his senses, I grabbed the Taser out of his pocket and pulled the trigger. Waclaw spasmed and still had a look of disbelief that I had done what I had done as he dropped to the floor with a thud. When I looked up, Lyria was moving forward.

"Stop!" yelled Mikolaj, and before I knew what was happening, my former new bud had his arm around my neck and was holding a gun to my head. The little bugger was a lot stronger than he looked. "You come any closer and your boyfriend will join my compatriots in the hereafter."

Lyria stopped. The situation was a complete standoff.

"Nobody move."

The voice was familiar, yet still a surprise to everyone in the room. We turned our heads in perfect sync as Detective Don Halberton came into view, his gun raised at the ready.

***

Even though I was as taken aback as anyone, I took advantage of Halberton's appearance by jamming my elbow into Mik's belly with all the effort I could muster. I was pretty sure I saw that being done in the movies at some point. Mik expulsed the air in his lungs, dropped his gun, and plopped to his knees with a look of pain and disbelief. I didn't have time to get insulted by these guys looking so flabbergasted when they realized I had done something physical.

Lyria had turned slowly toward Halberton, who had his gun pointed directly at her.

"I'm Detective Halberton of the Boston Police. You're under arrest," said the detective. "Get down on the floor. NOW."

Lyria took a step forward. "Oh, I don't think so," she said. "Do you have any idea how much this outfit cost? Tsk, the price of fashion these days."

She moved a step closer. Halberton didn't budge. "I'm serious," he said. "You come any closer and I'll fire."

"You guys are going to have to work on your dialog," she said calmly. "Doesn't sound any different than it did…oh, fifty, sixty years ago."

She kept moving forward. "Stop! I mean it!"

Lyria kept advancing.

The sound of the gun shot virtually shook the hallway. I let out a brief wail as my hands involuntarily went to my ears.

Halberton still had his gun out in front of him, but he looked agape at his suspect. Lyria was still standing right in front of him. He had fired directly into her chest. Lyria heaved a couple of times and coughed. Then she did something I will certainly never forget as long as I live. She turned her head and spit out the bullet with a gob of blood. The projectile went bouncing down the hallway before coming to rest.

"Mmmm," said Lyria. "Tickles the ribs."

She swatted Halberton's gun away from him with one hand, and grabbed the detective by the throat and picked him clear up off the ground with the other. Halberton let out a gasp of air and gurgled a choking sound. His expression went beyond shock and fear. It reminded me of the videos I had seen of an antelope's face while it was being eaten alive by a lion in the Serengeti. He tried to pry Lyria's hands off his neck, but it was a lost cause.

"Thank you for visiting, Detective," said Lyria. "I was getting a little hungry."

Lyria brought Halberton closer, angling in toward his neck.

"LYRIA, DON'T!" I yelled.

"Shut up, Conner."

I ran over to the window and grabbed the shade. "Lyria!"

Lyria looked over her shoulder at me and dropped Don Halberton to the floor in a heap.

She walked toward me. I could see her fangs.

"Conner? Conner...no...don't...."

Our eyes met. "I'm sorry, Lyria."

"No apologies," she said.

I pulled the shade so hard it came off the window completely. There was a loud pop and a brilliant flash of light, and Lyria emitted an unearthly scream. I had closed my eyes, but the other men were temporarily blinded. When their vision returned, all they saw was a singed spot on the floor where Lyria had stood. Halberton and Mikolaj stared at me in awe. What had just happened wasn't really clear to anyone, but it definitely stretched everybody's understanding of the human condition.

What was eminently clear, however, was that Lyria was gone.

EPILOGUE

It's quite remarkable how a little thing like a bout with a vampire can change the way one acts, can indeed alter the fundamental tenets around which one has built their life and career.

Detective Don Halberton, about the most straitlaced, by-the-book guy you'd ever meet, didn't pursue any charges against me. First and foremost, he didn't have a shred of evidence. But I'm sure his primary concern was potentially having to explain how he had encountered the person responsible for the disappearances he was investigating, and she was—well, how should I put this—a member of the non-living? He was probably worried that if he tried to explain that the whole missing persons schlemiel was because of a rogue vampire, his next assignment would be rubber room patrol at the local loony bin.

In addition, from Don's perspective, I had saved him from becoming the main course in a vampire smorgasbord. That had to count for something.

Besides, my understanding was that Detective Grace Garvey reported to work the next day, all fit and pink, her usual spunky self, perhaps with even a little extra dose of Tabasco sauce.

I really have no idea how Don ended up clarifying the situation in his police reports. Maybe they left the Arnold Shaw and other cases open, with the knowledge that justice had, in fact, been served. Anyway, whatever he did might have been good practice for Don in case he decided to be a fiction writer when his police career was over.

As for Mikolaj and Waclaw, they shook off the shock of the confrontation, recovered sufficiently from their Revenge of the Nerd injuries, and left the building with nary a word. Guess they had no further interest in Lyria's present and future lackeys. Hopefully, they flew back to Europe and crawled back under whatever rock it was that they originally came out from, never to be seen or heard from again.

Halberton and I unbound poor old Radu and arranged to have him shipped back to Romania to live out however few days he had left on this earth, vampire-free. I was sure the old geezer had a lot of catching up to do.

***

I went to work that day, despite having had no sleep the night before. I felt a little like Indiana Jones, but, being honest with myself, my going to work had more to do with remnants of the "Thou Shalt Report for Duty No Matter What" reign of the former tyrant Darren "Shrek" Dobson than any real daring do on my part. I actually had a fairly productive day. It's a wonder what getting the police and foreign terrorists off one's tail will do for a person's concentration levels.

I even took advantage of Shrek's new outlook on life to do a little socializing with the members of my team. I wasn't worried about Mr. Dobson doing a dance on my face if I got caught.

My first stop was Razor Rojas. I had to thank him for his assistance. He looked relieved to see me.

"I was worried about you," he said. It was the closest I'd ever seen Razor to admitting to human emotion. "That was about the strangest call I've ever gotten. And those things can be dangerous."

I went to see Larry Berman and, of course, Chauncy Stillwell was in his office. Stillwell was sitting across Berman's desk, but the two were leaning over a stack of papers whispering to each other.

"You two still plotting to take over the world?" I asked.

They both looked up. "Oh, hey Conner," they said at the same time, then laughed at each other.

Berman said, "We were just reviewing Chauncy's use of binomial theorem in dissecting the chance distribution of outcomes in stock swaps factoring in market dynamics."

"Ah, still wild and crazy guys, huh?"

Stillwell ignored that and said, "We finally realized the components had to be nonnegative integers to be arranged to form Pascal's Triangle. Do you want to check to see if the slope looks reasonable to you?"

"Oh, hey, that's tempting, guys, but I never get involved in family matters."

I was about to book while my wits were still intact when Berman blurted out, "So Conner, I've been meaning to ask how that matter we discussed is working out."

"Matter?"

Berman gave me a conspiratorial look. "Yeah, you know, that matter...."

I had forgotten that I asked Larry's advice about Lyria not being forthcoming about her personal information.

"Oh, yeah. That matter has been worked out. Thanks again, Larry, you were very helpful."

Stillwell looked miffed that he wasn't in on the discussion subject, so I moved on before an outright brawl broke out. I heard Stillwell say, "You never tell me anything any more."

"How's it going, Vicky?"

Vicky Temerlin looked up from her desk with a bright smile and fresh, alert eyes.

"Oh, couldn't be better, Conner. You?"

"Good, thanks. It's great to see you in such a great mood

lately."

"Yeah, it is kinda weird, isn't it?" She had a healthy laugh. "I don't know whether my time out of the office just gave me a boost or what, but I've had boundless energy lately. I'm churning out projects like there's no tomorrow. Do you know, I actually turned my status report in to Mr. Dobson before it was even due?"

"That's great, Vick, but don't overdo it. You'll make the rest of us look like pikers."

Another healthy laugh. "Okay, I'll try to be more subtle."

On to Boof, who had all the subtlety of a wrecking ball.

As soon as I walked in, he started in on me. "Conner, DSB alert, man. We're gonna have to get some action pretty soon. This flying solo crap ain't cutting it. Just 'cause a guy hits a club by himself, women look at him like there's a reason he's got no friends, y'know? Like he probably keeps his buddies chopped up in pieces in a freezer somewhere. Or his pals all found other friends while he was in prison. All kinds of misconceptions flying around out there. So, what do you say? You up for it?"

"Geez, you must be desperate. Whenever we hit the clubs together you would tell me I was cramping your style. That you needed to be seen with a different body type. Like Razor."

"Nah. I never said that."

"I think your exact words were, 'The babes see us together, they figured we just escaped from Nerd Haven, USA.' That sound more familiar?"

"Well, yeah...okay. But, on the other hand, you do present a certain wholesome influence. Plus, you look like you could barely lift an axe, never mind hack somebody up with one."

I told Boof I'd think about it and went back to work.

***

The afternoon flew by and I headed home. I was dog-tired, but anticipation kept my motor running. I didn't even consider going for a walk — I was in real danger of falling asleep mid-step. Instead, I took my familiar place on the couch. I sat up in an effort to keep from dozing off, but that was an epic fail.

When I woke up, the condo was dark, but there was a difference in the air. I checked the clock. It was 2 a.m. I went to the kitchen and made some tea. I was sitting at my table where I had been drilled by the police a short time ago. I kept the lights off. It just felt better that way.

I didn't even jump when I felt hands on my shoulders. A threat? Couldn't be, as the hands started kneading the tension out of my back muscles.

"Hello handsome," said Lyria. "I assume the coast is clear?"

***

The night of my meeting with Mikolaj, I looked online to see if I could find out anything about the symbols on his hand. It was more or less idle curiosity at the time, although it was nagging at me that I had encountered those initials before. I came across various interpretations of the initials SSTV, but none of them seemed to fit. Then, I saw a link that almost stopped my heart cold.

The SSTV was part of the Nazi party's Schutzstaffel, or "Protective Squad," commonly known as the SS. The organization was originally formed as Hitler's personal bodyguards, but grew in size and stature to the point where it was almost a state within a state. To say they were the most feared members of the Nazi regime was putting it mildly. They were brutal sadistic killers focused on racial purity, and known for mass executions of political opponents. The "TV" part referred to the Totenkopfvebande, a division of the Waffen SS, which, among other pleasantries, was responsible for administration of concentration camps and slave labor. Their insignia was a Death's Head skull and bones. They were reported to be the most cold hearted faction of the SS, with no compassion for the suffering of prisoners. It all came back to me from Lyria's story. They were also the team that ran a secret scientific research institute in Bucharest, where they did unspeakable tests on prisoner subjects. There was supposedly still a faction of the SSTV around today. They were probably buddies with the other Nazi wannabe nutcases infecting our society.

Sounded like my boy Mikolaj. It became abundantly clear to me that he had no intention of just scaring Lyria off. Whether out of some sense of revenge, or in order to cover up what might have been the SSTV's most twisted accomplishment, clearly, they wanted to put an end to Lyria's long reign on Earth.

After I got my pulse down to normal, I quickly devised a plan.

***

A week or so earlier, I had given Lyria a small present. She had opened the box not knowing what to expect.

"A phone?" she had said.

"Not just any old telephone," I said. "It's a prepaid, disposable phone. Almost completely untraceable. I've become a lot more street since we started seeing each other."

She laughed. "And what, pray tell, am I supposed to do with this?"

"Just keep it with you. When you can. I wanted a way to get in touch with you other than hanging around my house waiting for it to get dark."

She was looking at me with an expression that said, "Get serious, willya?"

"I know what you're thinking. I promise, promise, promise I'll only use it in emergencies. Life or death emergencies. No calling just to find out what you're wearing to bed."

After a little more back and forth, she agreed to keep the phone. And when I found out about Mikolaj, I felt strongly that the situation qualified as life or death.

I dialed the number and Lyria answered immediately. "Hello,

Conner."

The weary sound of her voice told me she thought I was calling for a different reason. It was right after she had given me the veritable dust-off, and she probably assumed I was going to beg her to change her mind.

Did I seem like the begging type?

I quickly described the situation to her to keep her from hanging up.

"I know this man, Mikolaj," she said finally after a long pause. "He was pursuing me all over Europe."

"I assume he didn't want to reminisce about old times in Bucharest."

She laughed a little.

To make a long story short, she acknowledged that Mik was looking for revenge. She admitted that after she was "made," she went on a rampage through the "Research Center" looking for whoever had killed her father and the man who had raped her when she was still human. Her anger was additionally fueled by the SS plan to use her as a supernatural hooker to entice and eliminate some Russian military leaders. Several senior members of the SSTV were summarily dispatched.

"I didn't want to tell you about that part, Conner. I was enraged and out of control. At any rate, Mikolaj has spent the better part of his adult life pursuing what he calls justice for his forbearers."

"Lyria," I said. "I'm so sorry. I actually called this guy. I was going to lead him right to you."

"It's not your fault, Conner." She did, however, admit that she had Detective Grace Garvey and was using her as a "blood bank," just as Mik had described. "I did it to protect you, Conner. I hope you believe me."

We devised a plan that night to finally get Mr. Mikolaj Babka off her case. I felt that it was a good plan, but there was one critical element missing. And I knew exactly who to call.

***

"Hey, Razor. It's Conner."

"Conner?" Razor's voice sounded fuzzy. "What time is it?"

"Too late for me to be calling. But it's an emergency, I promise."

I described what I was looking for, and there was a long pause on the other end.

"Let me get this straight," Razor said finally. "You want me to get you a stun grenade. Right?"

***

The night of the confrontation, everyone was transfixed on me getting ready to pull the shade down, exposing Lyria to sunlight. I pulled it down and the grenade went off in Lyria's hand, causing a blinding light. Lyria screamed, then used her supernatural speed to exit the premises without anyone seeing. Normally a person would have been badly burned by a stun grenade going off in their hand, but Lyria...well, you know. I thought of using the grenade immediately when I realized we had to fake Lyria's death. I have no idea how I knew about such things. Must have seen one on Hawaii Five O at some point.

Everybody present thought the result was vampire fricassee. Just like we planned. Lyria had set up another "sleeping spot" nearby.

We actually didn't expect Don Halberton to be there, but it ended up working out for the best. I guess he had followed me. And I wasn't quite "street" enough to pick up a police tail. Definitely still a work in progress.

***

At any rate, for all intents and purposes, all that was left of Lyria was a burned spot on the hallway floor. Halberton thought Lyria was dead, and all his mysterious disappearances had somehow been explained away. My former new bud Mikolaj

356

thought Lyria was dead, and all the bills left over from an age-old war had been paid.

Funny thing, I ended up essentially taking Radu's place after all. I'm now handling all Lyria's "human" business matters. Lyria says it's just a temporary situation, but we'll see.

We had to find her a new place to reside, but with the high vacancy rates around Boston, that wasn't a huge problem. As far as going out in public, we decided to lay low for a while, just to play it safe. No power walks, forays to The Hill, or supersonic speeding through the Common. For the time being, I've begged off additional entreaties from my family, all of whom were anxious to see Lyria again. It was almost as if they still didn't believe she was with me, even though they had seen it with their own eyes. The more conspiratorial among the group (Mom) probably thought I had hired an actress for the night just to get them all off my back. Not a terrible plan, really. However, I assured everyone that all was well between Lyria and me.

But, honestly, I wondered whether that was really true.

"Talked to Mom today," I mentioned to Lyria one night, sitting on the couch.

"Oh, how is your mother doing?" she asked, her eyes lighting up. "She's such a sweet lady."

"She's doing good. I promised her that everything was still going strong between us."

"Uh huh."

"So Lyria...."

"Yes, Conner?"

"Did I lie to my mother?"

"You? I doubt it. You don't come off as a very convincing liar."

"You know what I mean. About us. Not too long ago, it seemed like you were about done with me. You only wanted me as a stand-in for good old Radu. Remember? Nobody would miss

357

me and all? Is everything really okay between us?"

She hit me with that smile, and I felt the tremors all the way to my toes.

"Conner. I told you that night that my feelings for you are real. I just didn't know if...this path in life was right for you. I still don't, to be completely honest," she said. "Why don't we just take it a little slow going forward? Go day-to-day. Would that be all right?"

What she was saying was correct, of course. Life with Lyria would be nothing like a normal relationship. For every splendid moment there would also be periods of darkness. She was not like any other woman I had ever met. She was not, for that matter, like any other woman on Earth. I knew what she was, and she was not going to change. I had to decide whether it was worth it to take the good with the bad. The good was very good. And the bad? We're talking the stuff of nightmares. Of the worst horror movies, because this one was real.

She noticed my hesitation.

"Conner?"

"I...I'll have to give it some thought."

She nodded. "I think you should."

We were silent for a moment. Then she slid over close and put her hand on my thigh. "After all," she said. "We have plenty of time. We'll be cooped up inside here for a while. We can do a lot of introspection. But we'll have to find a way to stay active as well. Can you think of any way I can help...uh...keep the juices flowing, so to speak?"

I looked at her with the usual amount of wonder in my eyes. I smiled. I really couldn't help myself. "I'm sure we'll think of something," I said. I took her in my arms and we were off. Going slowly.

We were, after all, taking it day-to-day.

Acknowledgements

I'd like to thank Karen Fuller and Maxine Bringenberg at World Castle Publications for all their help in getting my novel published.

I'd also like to thank Donna Northam and Nancy Leibundgut for helping to get the manuscript in shape. And everyone who read a beta version of the book, especially Carol Ciesynski, Jeanelle Taylor, and Don Marsolini.

Hey, it's Robert.

My Girlfriend, the Vampire is about a somewhat nerdy financial analyst in Boston who stumbles across the woman of his dreams. No biggie, right? Come to find out, however, that she has one drawback, but it's a doozy. She drinks blood.

I have to say, I felt uniquely qualified to tell this story. Ok, no, I've never drank blood. But I did spend 30+ years in corporate finance. And, although I don't consider myself nerdy (and opinion that may or may not be shared by others), I have a good feel for the corporate environment where my protagonist makes his living. Plus, I'm a lifelong fan of vampire stories. (Now, let's not examine what THAT says about my personality...)

My career culminated in the position of VP, Finance for a Fortune 500 company. This is my first novel, but I'm sure there will be more, as I reside in New Hampshire where we tend to get snowed in for extended periods of time.

I have degrees from Northeastern and Boston College (pick up on the Boston roots?) I live with my wife Donna. We have two adult children and two grandkids. Other than writing, my hobbies include tending to my house and garden and, now, hoping that you like my book!

Thanks for reading.